THE HOLD

THE HOLD

A RETRO GEN X HAPPILY EVER AFTER

THE CATCH & HOLD SERIES
BOOK TWO

JENNA MALABY*

*FORMERLY WRITING AS JENNA MILES

For A, my compass rose.

"When I say I love you more, I don't mean I love you more than you love me. I mean I love you more than the bad days ahead of us. I love you more than any fight we will ever have. I love you more than any distance that might separate us. I love you more than any obstacle that could try to come between us. I love you most."

*And for Robert, my Happily Ever After, who came into my life **after** I created the character of the same name! Thank you for your unwavering love, support, and encouragement of my writing; and thank you for marrying me on our very own Sunday, December 9th.*

I used to be shy.
You made me sing.

I used to refuse things at table.
Now I shout for more wine.

In somber dignity, I used to sit
on my mat and pray.

Now children run through
and make faces at me.

— RUMI

CONTENTS

PREFACE AND CONTENT ADVISORIES

The Hold is technically a sequel to *The Catch,* but you can easily enjoy it as a stand-alone book without reading *The Catch.*

I wrote *The Catch* in 2012 and published it in 2015. I, myself, have changed a lot since then, and I hope I've also grown as a writer.

One way I've changed since 2012 is that I'm less inhibited writing about sexuality. The sex scenes in *The Hold* are a notch or two "spicier" than the ones in The Catch. If you're worried, see my Content Advisories below for more details.

I'm not the only thing that has changed since 2012 – the world has, too! For example, it wasn't until 2013 that the Diagnostic and Statistical Manual of Mental Disorders, Fifth Edition (DSM-5) did away with the diagnosis of Asperger's Syndrome, folding it under the general umbrella of Autism Spectrum Disorder. Another example: same-sex couples in California (and throughout the U.S.) could legally wed from 2015 onward.

However, since *The Hold* begins in 2012, characters still refer to Asperger's Syndrome; same-sex couples can't *legally* wed in California (boo, Proposition 8!) – and Instagram is still relatively new!

These are just a few examples of things you might read in *The Hold* that seem out-of-date by today's standards.

CONTENT ADVISORIES

I've also included another content advisory with a *major, massive plot spoiler* on my website at www.jennamilesauthor.com/about-3#the-hold-spoiler-advisory If there is any particular romance trope that you absolutely refuse to read, it might be worth checking there first.

This content is either shown on page, and/or comprise plot points in *The Hold*:

- Mental health diagnoses and challenges (depression, anxiety, PTSD), including in children.

- Challenges and discrimination related to neurodivergence (autism, ADHD), including in children.
- Sexual harassment.
- Challenges related to coming out as transgender and undergoing gender-affirming surgery.
- Crohn's Disease
- HIV/AIDS
- Divorce
- Co-parenting challenges
- Challenges in blended families
- Relationship difficulties
- Sexuality in adolescents
- Aging parents / elders
- Pre-term childbirth
- Open door / on-page sex scenes between consenting adults. Sex acts and body parts are described relatively explicitly and/or using swear words. Bodily fluids and their movement are referenced, but relatively less explicitly.

This content is NOT shown on page in *The Hold*, but it is discussed as having happened in the past, and/or the present-day ramifications are shown on page:

- Abuse (physical, emotional, verbal, financial – including of children)
- Substance abuse
- Addiction
- Parental abandonment
- Spousal abandonment
- Suicide attempt by a child
- Self-harm by a child
- Challenging family dynamics (codependency, enabling)
- Unplanned pregnancy.
- Pregnancy complications (hyperemesis gravidarum)
- Abortion

THE HOLD

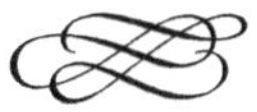

*A*t midnight, when her mother straggled home smelling of fermented grape juice, Julia sat hunched over the sewing machine. Her mother heard the whir of the machine's motor and stumbled into the in-law unit, seeking its source.

"What on Earth are you doing?" she demanded, gaping at the sewing patterns and bright bolts of fabric littering the den's floor.

Julia removed the needle from between her teeth and held up the nearly-finished garment. "Do you like it?"

Squinting, her mother pushed her glasses further up the bridge of her nose until her bangs skimmed the top of the tortoiseshell frames. "What is it?"

Julia blinked. "You can't tell? It's a skirt."

"Really?" Her mother hiccuped, then put a fist to her lips to stifle a burp. "Is that for Paige?"

"No!" Suddenly sheepish, Julia added, "You don't think it's too young for me, do you?"

Her mother stepped forward for a closer inspection. Swaying, she tucked a lock of her gray bob behind her ear. "Well, you always could pull off the younger styles."

"Oh, gee, thanks." Flushing, Julia snickered as she scrutinized the skirt anew.

Her mother eyed the grin spanning Julia's face. "Are you okay?"

Julia lowered the skirt. "Mom, I'm so far beyond okay, I'm ecstatic."

"Really? Then why are you sewing a skirt the size of a postage stamp in the middle of the night?"

Julia laughed. "Why are you staggering home drunk from a bridge game in the middle of the night?"

"Because I was having fun. Diane brought a nice bottle of wine from Sonoma – some varietal I'd never heard of called Cinsaut. It's especially good paired with bridge. I might have had a little *too* much fun, because Diane had to drive me home."

"Well..." Julia held up her hands in a shrug. "I'm just having fun, too."

Her mother stared unfocused for another second, then shrugged right back. "Well, okay then. Maybe we should *both* go to bed."

Julia barked out another laugh. She had never seen her mother drunk. She went to sit on the sofa and patted the seat beside her. "Come sit."

Her mother complied after a moment's hesitation, but flinched when Julia snatched her hand.

"Julia! You're drunker than I am, aren't you?"

"Yes, Mom, I'm drunk with happiness. And there's something I need to tell you."

"Apparently."

"I've seen William."

Her mother's eyes widened a little – surprised, but not shocked. "Okay?"

"He came over here, both yesterday and today. To this house. He knows what I did for his family. And now he also knows about Robert."

Julia had never explicitly discussed the facts of her son's paternity with her mother. It had always been an unspoken secret between them and the rest of her immediate family. Breathlessly, her mother said, "You told him?"

"I didn't have to. He took one look at Robert, and he knew."

One corner of her mother's mouth lifted in a knowing smirk. "So now what?"

"I have no idea. But William is coming over for dinner tomorrow night. And probably most nights from now on, for that matter."

Her mother sighed. "Okay."

"Are you sure?"

Her mother squeezed Julia's hand. "I have to admit, a big part of me is relieved that he knows. I've always felt bad about the role I played in all that."

Julia frowned. "What do you mean?"

"You know... encouraging you to go back to Kevin after he abandoned you and Paige. Sharing my doubts about William."

Julia took her mother's hand in both of hers. "Mom, it was my decision, and no one else's. Leave the blame and the past where they both belong."

Her mother suddenly looked sober. "How are you going to explain to Paige and Robert why he's coming over so much?"

"Paige already knows." When her mother gasped, Julia added, "It seems Kevin's mother told her a couple of years ago."

"That Robert isn't Kevin's?" Her mother shook her head in dismay. "That woman."

"And like everyone else, Paige needed only one look at William to figure out the truth."

"Okay... but what about Robert?"

"Eventually, we'll have to tell him, too. But not right away."

Her mother's lips pressed into a straight line. "How on earth do you explain something like that to a five-year-old?"

"I don't know, but I see a lot of family therapy in our future."

After another moment's contemplation, her mother ventured, "I suppose this means you and William are... you know."

"Yes. We're going to try this again."

Her mother nodded. "I'll pray for you."

"Um, well... I'll take all the help I can get."

Her mother gave a dry chuckle, and then there didn't seem to be anything more to say. But as she got up to leave, she stopped in her tracks and turned around again.

"What do you think we should serve William for dinner tonight?"

Julia shrugged. "Just make whatever you were already planning."

Again, her mother nodded. "I'll let your father know."

Julia offered a grateful smile. "Thank you."

After her mother left the den and trudged upstairs, Julia inspected the skirt again. She couldn't help but laugh at herself. It *was* a bit youthful. And very, very tiny.

She had often fantasized about the last two nights' turn of events. She had even dreamed about it, only to wake to the bitter reality that she was alone – utterly alone, even before Kevin moved to Santa Barbara. Trapped in San Jose, an hour's drive from her family. With William still out there somewhere, oblivious to his own son's existence.

And it might have stayed that way, had William's mother not clued him in to what Julia did for their whole family – fighting to restore his dying father's health insurance, and saving William's whale watching business in the process.

And even then, she and William might never have re-declared their love, had it not been for Paige.

Paige, of all people. Her force-of-nature thirteen-year-old, who lately never had a kind word for Julia. Until, just tonight, she said, "Mom, do you know what *carpe diem* means?"

Somehow, Julia had found the courage to take her daughter's advice. And then she and William spent a blissful hour or two, catching up on each other's lives in the six years since their last, ill-fated attempt to rekindle their relationship – the attempt that resulted in Robert.

The first thing William had wanted was to see pictures of Robert as a baby. Julia cast him a sheepish look and warned, "Kevin is in a lot of them."

"Of course," William said, his voice a near-whisper.

She retrieved the photo albums and brought them to the living room sofa. Sitting beside him again, she thumbed through them, beginning with the photos of just herself.

"This was when I was in the hospital, not long before he was born," she explained.

"You were in labor?"

She shook her head. "I was in the hospital for a few months because of the HG."

His eyes whipped to hers in obvious alarm. "HG?"

"Hyperemesis gravidarum – severe morning sickness. I was vomiting twenty or thirty times a day through my whole pregnancy. I had to be monitored around the clock and receive IV fluid and nutrition. And the drugs they gave me to try to stop the vomiting made me so dopey, it was impossible to function."

He reached for her hand. Turned a pained look on her with those same intense blue eyes as ever. "My God; I'm sorry. That sounds like an absolute nightmare."

"It was." She gave a shaky laugh. "But you see? Here was the end result."

She turned the page to reveal the photos of a newborn Robert. Kevin was there in many of them, cradling Robert in his arms. Julia studied William's reaction from her peripheral vision, but he barely flinched, and his expression remained composed.

She turned the page again, revealing photos of an eight-year-old Paige meeting Robert for the first time. Of Robert coming home, his face already losing some of its puffy redness. Of the grandparents meeting Robert – including Kevin's parents, who looked like they had just bitten into a lemon. With the timing, they knew Robert was conceived before Kevin returned from his self-imposed exile in Brazil. Just like everyone else knew – except, unfortunately, William.

Julia's pulse slammed in her throat, and her face burned. But again, William remained unfazed. So she kept turning the pages, one by one, to reveal more of Robert's milestones.

His first smiles. Batting at the toys on his play gym. His first solid food and first tooth. First holidays and first steps. The whole time, his face and his beautiful, enormous blue eyes growing more and more like William's.

Then came the first birthday pictures, with Robert smashing his cake into his face. After that: Robert toddling around the zoo, unassisted. His first day of preschool. His tee-ball photo.

And all the while, Kevin's appearances in the photos grew increasingly, glaringly irregular.

"After Robert was born," Julia explained quietly, "Kevin went back to Santa Barbara to finish his PhD in Marine Biology. He got his pilot's license so he'd be able to fly himself back and forth. But after the first few months, he mostly just stayed down there. And then, last summer, he got a chance to do some field studies in the Galapagos, but it was going to take at least a year, and the kids and I couldn't come. By then, there was no point keeping up the pretense, anyway."

William's gaze was sympathetic as he stroked her hand. Her pulse quickened at the simple touch, and her cheeks blazed.

"What about you?" she prompted, her voice thin with nerves.

"Me?"

She wasn't going to come right out and demand to know about his romantic relationships. "What have you been up to all this time? Besides getting the business up and running."

"The business was the main thing, yeah. But I also finished my degree."

Her jaw dropped, and at the same time, she couldn't stifle her smile. "Really? That's fantastic!"

"It was just a business degree online. I finished this past December."

"That's impressive, Will! Congrats!"

William gazed at her, searching her face. His eyes softened, and the color rose to his cheeks. Julia's heart leaped at the sight. He was still so overwhelmingly beautiful, even after all this time. Even with his uncustomary beard and close-cropped hair, which had darkened over the years to a shade more brown than blond.

Julia felt the heat rising in her own cheeks, and her mouth twisted into an irrepressible smile. In response, William drew her in for a long, lingering kiss. Her pulse skyrocketed, hammering in her chest; and when they finally broke away, they spent a while studying each other's faces.

She murmured, "Every Sunday night, my sister comes over, and we all eat dinner together. Can you join us?"

His eyes grew wary. "Are you sure your parents would be okay with that?"

"Of course. I'll let them know what's going on. I know they'd love to see you."

He considered a moment. "As long as it's really okay with them, I should be able to."

Julia beamed at him. "Come over around five."

"What can I bring?"

"Yourself."

But he shook his head. "I can't show up empty-handed."

"Then bring a bottle of wine."

That seemed to placate him; and after that, they kissed their good-byes in the tunnel entrance out front. Julia glanced up and down the street, looking for his old motorcycle. Failing that, she searched for any unfamiliar vehicle that might have been his.

"How are you getting home?" she finally wondered.

"Oh." He gave a sheepish laugh. "The old Yamaha V-Max finally bit the dust. This is my conveyance now." He gestured to a bicycle locked around a telephone pole.

She couldn't help coughing out a laugh. "You're going to ride all the way to the Mission on that thing?"

"Well, a combination of riding and transit, yeah."

"Up and down all those hills? On a bicycle?"

"Okay, so it has an electric assist," he confessed good-naturedly.

She laughed out loud now, watching as he strapped the bicycle helmet on. They waved their farewells, and she shook her head in amusement as he pedaled down the street.

That's when Julia – her stomach giddy with butterflies and her mind alight with inspiration – had settled down at the machine to sew a too-skimpy skirt. Not long afterward, her father had come home from work, his tread on the staircase heavy with weariness. Finally, her mother had returned from her bridge game to hear the news and go to bed.

Now, Julia sat motionless on the sofa in the den. But though her body was drained, her brain would not quit running its treadmill.

She cracked open the downstairs bedroom door, just enough to confirm that Robert slept soundly, then meandered upstairs. After checking on Paige, she resumed her seat on the living room sofa, where – just an hour or two ago, against all odds – she and William had re-declared their love.

She ran her hand over the spot where he sat, imagining she could

still see him there. She touched the mermaid pendant around her neck –
the promise he had given her when they were still teenagers. The empty
necklace box still sat on the coffee table, where she had placed it after
returning his Saint Peter chain to him – the same chain that had kept
him safe all those years ago in Alaska. The chain that had snapped from
his neck the night she told him she was going back to Kevin.

Now the doubts came tumbling in, one after another. How would
they find time to get reacquainted when they lived apart and she had the
kids full-time?

How would they ever explain to Robert that Kevin – the man he
had known all his life as Daddy – was not his biological father? How
would they deal with the inevitable fallout?

And besides, what were the legal implications? Who would get
custody of Robert, and when? Who would pay child support?

She reached into her sweater pocket and found the watermelon
tourmaline her Uncle Rob had given her nineteen years ago, when she
told him about William. She turned the polished cross-section over and
over in her hand.

What had Uncle Rob told her then? "If it's meant to be, the details
will work themselves out."

"Rob," she murmured out loud to the empty living room. "I wish
you were here to tell me what to do, and make me laugh at myself."

Her eccentric uncle always had a ready pearl of wisdom in the
toughest moments of her youth. Even if those pearls had been some
New Age-y thing he was into, like Wicca, or crystal healing.

"You make your own magic," he said when he gave her the watermelon tourmaline. "This will help."

Only after he died did she fully appreciate what both he and the
crystal meant.

The next morning over breakfast, Julia's father turned his grim gray eyes on her, and Julia knew that her mother had told him everything.

"I guess we'll grill tonight," he grunted, stabbing into his home-style potatoes.

Julia couldn't help smirking to herself. "Mom's nursing a hangover?"

He muttered something containing the words *at her age*, which Julia took as confirmation.

After breakfast, Julia brought her kids downstairs and sat them both down in the den. She explained that William would be coming over again that night, and that they would be seeing a lot more of him from now on.

Paige smirked. "Does this mean what I think it means?"

"What does it mean?" asked Robert.

"William is Mom's boyfriend."

"Paige," Julia said sharply.

The eyes Robert fixed on Julia were wide and blue. "Does that mean you're going to kiss him?"

"Please, God, not in front of us," Paige entreated.

"Guys." Julia held up her hands to stop them. "I just wanted to let you know you'll be seeing more of William."

"Are you gonna get married?" asked Robert.

Julia affectionately mussed his already-rumpled blond hair. "Slow down, Tadpole; William and I need to spend a lot of time together before we even *start* thinking about that."

Robert, who occasionally was five-going-on-forty, followed that up with, "So how long have you two known each other?"

Paige smacked him lightly on the arm. "Hello? I told you – he took Mom and me whale-watching six years ago."

"Paige, *please* – let me answer the questions," Julia insisted.

"Okay; Jesus!"

Julia ignored the band of irritation tightening around her throat. "Actually, William and I have known each other for nineteen years. But still, for now, he's just coming over for dinner. That's all."

Paige shrugged, suddenly bored, while Robert said, "Can I go outside now?"

Julia rubbed her eyelid, feeling like she, or at least somebody, should be saying something more. "Okay."

"So, you seized the day, after all," Paige observed after Robert left.

Julia's pulse fluttered as she recalled the previous night's events. "Yes."

"Props." Paige offered an awkward fist bump, which Julia accepted with an equally awkward laugh. "I didn't know you had known William for so long. That's, like, more than half your life, isn't it?"

Julia's mouth twisted into a wry smile. "Thanks for pointing that out."

Paige, calculating, lifted her eyes to the ceiling. "Nineteen years... so that means you were..."

"Seventeen. We were both seventeen when we met."

Paige whistled. "That's only four years older than I am."

Julia coughed out a shaky laugh. "It's kind of scary when you put it like that."

After a moment's hesitation, Paige asked, "Was he your boyfriend then, too?"

"Yes, but we drifted apart when I went away to college."

Paige sat thoughtfully for a moment, then got up to leave; but Julia put a hand on her shoulder.

"Paige, just a reminder – don't tell Robert about William being his father. Or anyone else, for that matter. That's a bit of news that William and I need to ease everybody into, especially Robert. If he finds out from you, it could be very traumatic."

"I know, Mom. I won't tell," Paige said airily, getting up again to leave. But still, Julia held her shoulder.

"Promise," Julia insisted.

"Jesus, Mom, I promise!" Paige wrenched herself free, and Julia watched her go, still uneasy.

But it was time to start preparing for the day and the inevitable anxiety it would bring. After her parents left for Mass, she took Robert to his tee-ball game. Then she burned her nervous energy by practicing the latest Bollywood steps she had learned in dance class and tending the saltwater aquarium with Paige. Later, she and the kids harvested vegetables from her mother's garden and began prepping them for dinner.

Julia's sister Alison arrived late that afternoon with her usual booty of pink-and-white-pinstriped pastry boxes. And as usual, Paige and Robert clamored around their aunt, competing for her attention and demanding to know if she had made eclairs or cream puffs this time.

Julia looked on fondly as her cheerful sister dodged their grasping hands and questions. Alison had dyed her pixie cut pink, and she wore a silver hoop in her right nostril. She had always been slender like Julia, but with more curves like their mother. Lately, by Alison's own admission, she had been sampling more of her own product, and the evidence on her chest, hips, and thighs made her even more of a bombshell.

"All right, you two," Alison finally shouted, shooing Paige and Robert from the kitchen with a sweep of her hands. "Get ye hence! I want to talk to your mom."

The second they retreated downstairs, Alison pounced. "So?"

Julia didn't need to say anything – the pure elation on her face told the whole story. Alison grinned and gave Julia's arm a supportive squeeze.

"I guess I should thank you for going against orders and spilling everything that happened all those years ago," Julia said wryly.

Alison blanched. "What are you–"

Julia silenced her with a good-natured shove to the arm. "William said you filled him in on how debilitated I was with the HG. That, and the pressure I was under from Mom and Paige to reconcile with Kevin."

Alison winced and dropped the ruse. "Sorry."

"For what?" laughed Julia. "If it weren't for you, things probably wouldn't have turned out the way they did."

While she spoke, the patio door slid open again. Julia had just enough time to finish her sentence before Robert bounded upstairs, pleading for Alison's help with his mud pies in the garden – since, after all, Alison was the family baker. Alison shot Julia a sidelong wink, then Julia found herself alone in the kitchen.

She glanced at the clock on the wall – four-thirty. Anxious butterflies swirled in her belly. Actually, it felt more like a swarm of rabid killer bees in there. Her father came home, bearing a load of prawns from Cardone's, the fish processing plant William's family owned and operated. It was right across the pier from Dunphy's, her father's restaurant. But before her father could intercept her, Julia rushed to the bedroom to change and get ready.

She didn't want to seem like she was trying too hard. And she certainly didn't need her kids to notice some dramatic departure from her usual look and comment on it in front of William.

But she wouldn't mind making him do a double-take.

So she pulled on a pair of black leggings and a slouchy, dusty-mauve sweater she had knit herself. The sweater had a wide neckline, and if she *accidentally* moved just right, it would expose one of her shoulders.

She styled her hair in loose waves and topped it all off with her favorite pale green cloche hat. But she omitted her usual scarf in favor of William's mermaid necklace.

The doorbell rang only ten minutes later, and she worked off her resurgent nerves by running downstairs. Just before she flung open the door, her sweater's neckline shifted, halfway exposing one shoulder.

Accidentally, of course.

William, on the other side of the door, looked relieved to find her, and only her, greeting him.

"What's this?" she asked. He carried two guitar cases, one sized adult-sized, the other for a child.

"This," he said, lifting the smaller one, "is something I found while scrounging around my parents' attic."

She took it and opened the door wide, inviting him in. Still incredulous that he was there at all, she found herself beaming. His smile was shyer, but at least Julia's wardrobe selections had the intended effect: a flush bloomed over William's cheekbones, and his wide, intensely blue eyes traveled the length of her before he forced them back to her face.

Julia's heartbeat galloped fast enough to win the Kentucky Derby. "Who first?"

"Let's get your dad over with."

Still smiling, Julia gave his hand a reassuring squeeze, then led him upstairs to the living room, where Paige watched TV. She looked up when they entered and droned, "Hey, William."

"Hey," he replied, depositing his guitar case in the corner by the fireplace.

Paige's eyes perked up. "You brought a guitar?"

"A couple, actually." He gestured to the smaller case Julia carried.

"Who's that for?"

"Your mom tells me Robert likes music, so I found this old thing my brother and I used to play. I cleaned it up and put new strings on it. I thought I could give lessons, if anyone's interested."

"I bet Robert would love that," Julia said, depositing the child-sized guitar case alongside William's.

William slung the backpack from his shoulders, unzipped it, and unwrapped two bottles of wine from dish towels.

"I didn't know what was on the menu," he explained, "so I brought a Zinfandel and a Sauvignon Blanc."

"Perfect." Accepting them, Julia tilted her chin toward the kitchen, where her father worked. The muscle ticking in William's jaw was the only clue to his state of mind, but he followed her silently.

Her father was deveining prawns and threading them onto skewers, along with the vegetables Julia and the kids prepped earlier. Hearing them, he turned and cast his signature severe look over the rim of his glasses – the look Julia called his resting bitch face.

"William." Julia's father stepped forward, as if to shake hands. Then, remembering himself, he wriggled his prawn-gut-coated fingers by way of apology.

William nodded in greeting. "Paul."

Julia couldn't help grinning at the spectacle. Her father cleared his throat and tried again.

"How's your mother?"

"Hanging in there. Still grieving, of course. How's the restaurant?"

Her father waved his hand dismissively. "Same old bullshit."

Another awkward silence ensued before her father shrugged and gestured vaguely to the kabobs. "Well…"

Still grinning, Julia set the Zinfandel on the kitchen table and stowed the Sauvignon Blanc in the wine fridge. Her father turned his back again and resumed deveining prawns. Without another word, Julia steered William from the kitchen and back downstairs to the den.

"I think that went well, don't you?" she teased.

Clearly flustered, he huffed a single, silent laugh, but said nothing.

"Everyone else is out back," she said, sliding open the patio door.

Hearing them, Robert ran right up, standing on tiptoes to thrust a tomato seedling as close as possible to William's face. "Do you like tomatoes?"

William's face lit up as he squatted to inspect Robert's offering. "Are you kidding? Tomatoes are my favorite!"

"Come help me and Grandma!"

"Absolutely, bud. Just give me a minute to say hi to everyone, and I'm there."

Beaming, Robert ran back to the garden, and William stood again. At that moment, Alison sprang from her seat at the patio table, rushing to suffocate William in one of her signature bear hugs.

"Oh my God, I still can't believe you have a beard!"

William shot Julia a deer-in-the-headlights look as he positioned his arms in a stiff circle around her sister and patted her back. Then, to make things even weirder, Alison seized William's hands and stepped back, sizing him up.

"And your hair is so short now! It suits you, I guess, but those curls were the bomb. Why would you want to go and hack them all off?"

"Um–"

Even as Julia flushed in mortification, she couldn't help snickering a bit. "Let the man breathe, Al."

Alison laughed and waved her hand dismissively, as if Julia were the one being ridiculous. While Alison pulled William to the patio table, Julia's mother, in the garden, heaved herself to her feet. Removing her gloves, she came to greet William, who shook her hand.

"William. How nice to see you," her mother said genially.

"Nice to see you again, too, Karen."

After the usual pleasantries, William's eyes wandered to where Robert was digging a hole in a raised bed. "You're planting tomatoes?"

"Oh, yes!" confirmed Julia's mother. "The garden is my gym these days. The doctor says it's good for my heart."

"You can get tomatoes to grow out here in the Sunset? Without a greenhouse?"

She chuckled a bit. "It's not easy, but after all these years I've got a few tricks up my sleeve."

"My grandmother did, too, but I still have no idea how she did it. I can barely get them to grow in the Mission."

Her face lit up. "Oh! You keep a garden?"

"Just some potted San Marzanos, descended from the ones my nonna used to grow. Mom managed to keep them alive all these years in her greenhouse. She shared a few seedlings with me when I moved to the Mission."

Julia's mother stood agape. "Well, I never would have pictured that!"

"Farmer William," Alison chimed in from the patio table.

William's face reddened, and Julia shot her sister a withering look. Alison clapped a hand over her mouth, but her eyes were still laughing.

"Well, come here; let me show you," said Julia's mother, beckoning William into the garden, where Robert patted the dirt around a newly-planted seedling. William followed her readily.

Julia sat beside her sister at the table. "Lay off, okay?" she whispered. "I'm sure he's nervous enough without all your fawning and ribbing."

"Sorry," Alison whispered, "but I couldn't help myself. Would you ever have pictured him turning into some hipster farmer?"

"Hipster? Why? Just because of the beard?"

"That, and the plaid flannel shirt."

"He's always worn plaid flannel shirts, ever since the grungy nineties."

Alison's eyes followed Julia's to the garden. Ironically, William was just peeling off his button-down gray flannel, revealing the black T-shirt underneath.

"Oh! What is *that*?" whispered Alison, leaning forward in her chair for a better look.

Julia had spotted it, too – tiny, barely-visible flashes of red, black, and green on William's left bicep, peeking from beneath the hem of his short sleeve. If there was anything more to see, it was hidden under the sleeve.

"I have no idea," Julia admitted. She had not seen his bare arms since reconnecting with him. "He didn't have that one six years ago."

"There's one on his right arm, too," Alison pointed out, and Julia strained to see. She was right – more flashes of color peeked from beneath the hem of his right sleeve. Between the distance and his movements, she couldn't make out anything of that one, either.

"*God*, tattoos are so fucking hot," Alison blurted.

"Hey!" Grinning, Julia swatted her arm.

"Oh, don't worry, Julie. William doesn't have nearly enough for my taste." Her eyes got a bit glassy. "Now Mike, on the other hand..."

As always, Julia grimaced at the idea of William's lecherous brother and Alison.

"Wow, Julie. William looks *great*," Alison practically growled, with a note of surprise.

Julia snorted. "What did you expect?"

"I don't know, but I didn't expect him to look so... *fit*. What else has he been doing to keep in shape? Besides gardening, I mean."

Julia only meant to glance at William, but her attention snagged. He did indeed look more fit than before, though he was still far from bulky or ripped. Just lean, and nicely toned.

"I'm not sure," Julia admitted. "I know he's been riding a bike since his motorcycle died."

Alison guffawed, presumably at the idea of William riding a bicycle. Julia couldn't entirely blame her – it was an adjustment for her, too.

"Well, fun for you." Alison winked. "I guarantee you, he's got a bangin' body under those clothes."

"Jesus, leave it to you to think only of that."

"Don't try to convince me it hasn't been on your mind."

"Of course it has, but I need to make sure we're on the same page about a lot of things first."

Alison looked skeptical, but thankfully she dropped the subject. They watched as their mother and William exchanged gardening advice and taught Robert how to lay mulch around the newly transplanted seedlings.

After a minute, Alison asked in a low voice, "Do you know anything about Mike?"

Resigned to Alison's inevitable curiosity, Julia sighed. "No; Will hasn't said anything about him yet."

"The last time I hooked up with him was, like, four years ago. I'd love to catch up."

"I bet you would."

"The only thing I heard is that William moved out of the apartment they used to share."

Julia hummed. "Will did give me his address the other day, and I could see it was different from the old one."

"Mike also said William dropped out of the band."

That genuinely surprised Julia. "Really?"

Alison nodded. "I kind of got the impression Mike felt hurt, even though he wouldn't actually say so. Do you mind if I ask William about Mike?"

Julia shrugged. "I guess not. Just please, for the love of all that's holy, don't be weird about it."

"There's nothing holy about what I have in mind for Mike," Alison retorted, grinning.

Julia groaned, but at that moment, their father emerged to light the grill, and Julia's eyes snapped to William.

After politely excusing himself from Julia's mother and Robert, William offered Julia's father his assistance. Her father took him up on it, and as William passed the table, his smile reassured Julia that he was feeling more at ease.

Once the men vanished back inside, Julia's mother sidled up to the patio table with a sly smile. She bent down to whisper to Julia, actually blushing.

"He's such a lovely man," she declared a little too breathlessly. "Like a young, more rugged Henry Fonda."

"*Mother!*" Alison gasped, clutching at imaginary pearls in feigned shock. "You dirty old lady, you!"

Julia couldn't help bursting out with laughter. In protest, her mother pinched Alison on the arm and twisted, hard – but she was grinning.

Alison scraped her chair back. "That's it – I'm opening the wine," she announced, snickering as she rubbed her sore arm. "Did you hear that, Mother? You're driving me to drink!"

Back inside the house, while Julia and the kids laid the place settings, her mother retrieved wine glasses from the china hutch. Alison poured the Sauvignon Blanc, and they eavesdropped on the snippets of conversation floating out from the kitchen, where William and Julia's father worked.

Her father groused, as usual, about how you can't get good help these days and how nobody wants to work anymore; screeds that William wisely did not argue with. Meanwhile, William filled him in on his whale watching business, and on everything happening at Cardone's. Sprinkled among those snippets came imperious orders that her father barked at William, and tactful, oblique suggestions for improvement that William offered in exchange.

Just like old times, thought Julia.

The three women carried their glasses back out to the patio table, while Paige carried stacks of dishes. Robert carefully toted the ancient orange Tupperware bowl of fruit salad.

Soon enough, the men emerged with platters of raw kabobs, and they all settled in to watch the spectacle. William tended the grill, with Julia's father practically breathing down his neck. Thankfully, it didn't seem to ruffle William any more than it ever had. When the kabobs were done grilling, he pulled them out two at a time.

It turned into a dance of sorts – William grilling and Julia's father plating, then William contributing a sourdough roll, then her father adding a scoop of fruit salad. Plate after plate. When they reached the end of the line, by unspoken agreement, they worked together to garnish and add the finishing touches. They stepped back to inspect their work, then peered at each other a moment. Grinning, they exchanged a high-five.

"The bromance between those two has always been kind of adorable," Alison observed to Julia after whistling her approval.

Everybody carried their own plate inside, and after waiting for Julia's father to finish saying grace, they tucked in.

"I have to eat like this now because of my heart," Julia's mother explained apologetically as she passed the salt shaker to William. "But that doesn't mean the rest of you have to suffer."

He accepted it, but he said, "It actually doesn't need much because of all the other flavors."

Pinning his sober gaze on William, Julia's father dropped a bombshell. "Would you ever consider coming back to Dunphy's? I'd be willing to train you to be my sous chef."

Without thinking, William shot Julia a look of alarm. "That's really flattering," he finally stammered, "but at this point, with my whale watching business..."

Julia's father waved a hand. "I didn't think you would. It's just so damn hard these days to find anyone halfway competent. I don't suppose you have any suggestions?"

"For sous?" William considered a moment. "It's been so long since I've been in the business."

Julia caught Alison's eye, and they traded smirks. They both knew as well as William did that with its outdated decor, its vintage-eighties menu, and its rapidly-graying patronage, Dunphy's stood no chance of attracting any self-respecting sous chef. And its geriatric chef de cuisine – crotchety and irascible even by chef standards – didn't help anything.

This whole time, Robert had either been wolfing down his dinner or chattering with Paige. Thankfully, at that moment, he piped up with, "William, are you still gonna show us the whales?"

"Yes, on Tuesday," William replied, his eyes softly gleaming. And with that, the conversation shifted to the logistics of their upcoming whale watching excursion.

Between dinner and dessert, they migrated to the living room, where William tuned the child-sized guitar. He taught Robert a few basic chords, demonstrating on his own guitar before helping Robert with his finger placement. Paige watched attentively, and eventually William handed his guitar to her.

"It's too big, but give it a try, anyway."

Eventually tiring of their lesson, Paige and Robert settled at the coffee table for a game of checkers, while Julia, William, and Alison drifted to the patio with their drinks. It was much chillier now, and William wore his flannel again. Julia lit the fire pit, and they dragged their chairs to it for warmth.

"I haven't seen Mike in forever," Alison said finally to William. "How is he?"

"Not sure," replied William, his tone flat, "but if I had to guess, I'd say not well. I'm pretty sure he's using again."

"Oh no!" gasped Alison, blanching.

"Last time I saw him, he was losing weight. Then he started isolating again. He wouldn't answer my calls or texts, or even come to the door. The usual. It's not his first relapse."

"No..." Devastation warped Alison's features. "Really?"

"After his third relapse, I realized I couldn't help him. And being around all that stuff was no good for me, either." William sipped his San Pellegrino, and only then did Julia realize he had never partaken of the wine.

Alison stared, silently inviting him to elaborate, but he didn't seem inclined to. After a moment, she asked, "Will you text me his cell? The last time I reached out, it wasn't his number anymore."

Frowning, William shifted in his chair. "I can, but just be careful. He's an addict, with all the lying and manipulation that entails."

Julia caught herself gaping. She had never heard him speak so harshly of anyone, let alone Mike. She saw the tiny furrow between his brows, and she knew from experience what that meant: clearly, there was some painful history there.

Alison looked equally taken aback, but thankfully said nothing more. After William shared Mike's number, she murmured, "I guess I'll go get dessert ready." With that, she retreated indoors, leaving Julia and William alone.

Julia said the first thing that came to mind. "Thanks for including Paige in the guitar lessons."

He waved a hand, as though it were no big deal.

"I have to admit," Julia continued, "I was surprised at how well she took to the guitar. She's never shown any interest in music before."

William hummed politely, but still said nothing. The furrow between his brows persisted as he sipped his water.

Gently, Julia tried, "What about you? Do you still perform?"

"In public?" He shook his head. "But me and Niall are still good friends. You know – the drummer from Mike's band?"

"Yes, I remember," she said quietly. Her cousin Holly had hooked up with Niall a few times, just before she suddenly moved to Boston.

An awkward silence followed, in which they both swigged their drinks. Finally, Julia ventured, "Was Mike the reason you dropped out?"

"Partially, yeah; but I only ever did one or two shows a month, anyway. And then I just got too busy with work and getting my degree. But I still write and record songs sometimes."

"I'd love to hear them. Unless they're top secret."

He finally smiled. "I'll hook you up with a backstage pass."

Julia's pulse careened out of control and William's smile evaporated as they simultaneously registered the double entendre. William hid his beet-red face behind his glass of San Pellegrino.

They spent a while watching the flames leap hypnotically in the fire pit. Finally, after an excruciating silence, Julia ventured, "I told Alison I didn't mind her asking about Mike. If I told her wrong, I'm sorry."

He shifted his weight and crossed his ankle over his knee. "Remember how I told you that my motorcycle finally died?"

She nodded.

"Well, that wasn't the whole story. The truth is, Mike stripped it and used the money for drugs."

"Oh, no," Julia breathed.

"I didn't press charges, but that's when I decided enough was enough, and moved out."

"That's awful," she murmured. "And so sad."

He shrugged. "At least one positive thing came from it: I didn't have anything to sell or trade in. I didn't want to involve the police or my insurance, so I started biking and walking everywhere out of necessity. The exercise made me feel so good that I just kept doing it, long after I could afford to buy something. It keeps me on the straight and narrow."

Tentatively, Julia ventured, "You also said being around Mike's shenanigans was bad for you."

Slowly, he nodded, his forehead creasing with apprehension. "The honest truth is, Julie... I was an alcoholic. Still am, depending on your perspective – a recovered alcoholic, or recovering, or whatever."

"You mean while you were living with Mike?"

"No – or maybe yes. Again, it just depends on your definition of an alcoholic." At her bewildered look, he explained, "I never let on how bad things got after you and I broke up the first time – back in '95, I mean. Not because I was deliberately trying to deceive you, but I was still in denial, myself."

Gently, she prodded, "How bad did it get?"

His face fell, and he looked away. "As bad as it gets. You already know how self-destructive I was."

She scooted her chair closer to his and reached for his hand. Stroked it until he was able to meet her eyes again. Then, he drew a deep breath.

"I went through full-blown withdrawal."

Her stomach bottomed out, but she continued petting his hand. He searched her face, but she wasn't sure how to respond yet.

"I never want to find myself going down that path again," he continued quietly. "Which is why I couldn't be anywhere near Mike."

She squeezed his hand. "I'm happy for you. And proud."

But his mouth twisted into a rueful smile, and he shook his head.

"Will, you're one of the strongest and bravest people I know." When he still balked, she added, "Shame is just a form of fear, you know. But you've stared it down, and you've still made a life full of purpose – full of people who love you halfway to death." Looking down at their hands clasped together, she was tempted to add *like me, for instance.* But her nerves swallowed the words – ironic, given what she had just said.

He caressed her hand with his thumb, and she lifted her eyes. With a poignant look, he tucked a lock of hair behind her ear and traced the line of her jaw with his fingertip.

"I've been trying to stay healthy," he said softly. "It keeps me sane – the exercise, and eating better. Growing a few vegetables on my patio, and taking care of other living things, like Diego."

Julia drew back. "Diego?"

His eyes flew open wide. "Didn't I tell you about Diego?"

"You definitely did not tell me about Diego."

He smacked his forehead. "Diego is a dog, but he's not really *my* dog." At Julia's perplexed look, he explained, "I live in the ground-floor apartment of a house that belongs to a friend of mine. When she moved to Alaska, she offered to let me live there at very low rent in exchange for being the property manager."

"Sounds like a sweet gig. But what does that have to do with Diego?"

"Diego belongs to the family I rent the house to, but by now, he's unofficially my dog, too. They've all become like a second family. In fact, pretty soon, they *will* be family." Julia's eyebrows lifted, and he explained, "One of them is about to marry my sister."

"Oh! Who's the lucky groom?"

He smiled faintly. "You mean who's the lucky bride?"

"I see. Well, I must admit, I always wondered." William laughed, and Julia added, "But I thought... back in 2006, you said Kelly was a single mom."

"She and Vanessa, her first wife – they're not together anymore. Kelly is the one who carried Xavier and Zach, my nephews. And now, Pilar is pregnant with twins."

"Pilar?"

"The lucky bride."

"Oh, wow. That's going to be a full house over there, with your mom."

"No; actually, Mom is moving out."

Julia reeled in shock. *"What?"*

"She's moving to one of those seniors-only condos, here in the city. She's letting Kelly and Pilar stay in the house in exchange for maintenance and property taxes."

"That's very generous," Julia reflected, but she was already thinking ahead to how her mother would react when she found out.

"It is, but if she hadn't, Kelly and Pilar would have left the Bay Area. They can't afford to buy or rent here."

"I'm sure your mom is relieved they won't have to leave."

His eyes softened. "She is."

"But now, let's get back to Diego. What kind of dog is he?"

A trace of a smile played at his lips. "A mutt. Probably part pittie, among other things. Sweetest kid ever."

Melting, Julia pressed a hand to her heart. "I always wanted a dog when I was a kid, but my parents said it wouldn't be fair to the dog. No one was ever home."

"That's why we never had pets, either, except a few stray cats Nonna left food out for. But between the Ochoas and me, someone is always home to spoil Diego."

Talking about Diego put a smile on William's face and carried away his inhibitions. Julia couldn't help grinning. "You really love that dog!"

William laughed. "Yeah, I guess he kind of wormed his way into my heart. If it's okay with you and your parents, I'd love to bring him over to meet you all. He's the gentlest, friendliest boy, and he's great with kids. He won't tear up the house, but we can keep him on the patio, if your parents prefer."

"The kids would love that! I'll check with my parents, but I'm sure it's fine." Suddenly nervous, but more anxious to see him again as soon as possible, she prompted, "How about tomorrow?"

He raked his hand over his hair. "I'd love to, but I'm afraid it would be rude if I came over again so soon. Won't your parents get sick of me?"

"Your conscientiousness does you credit, but I promise they love you, and they always have. In case tonight wasn't enough to convince you."

He bit his lips in a futile effort to suppress a smile. Their hands had stayed clasped together this whole time. Her heart flickering at the blinding beauty of his smile, she stroked his face with her free hand and drew him in for a kiss. He reached for a section of her hair that hung beneath her hat and allowed the length of it to travel slowly through his fingers. Her pulse thundered through her chest, throat, and ears, warming her whole body.

She could have stayed there with him for the rest of her life. But all too soon, he broke the kiss and smiled tenderly, his eyes crinkling at the corners in their distinctive way. And for her part, Julia could not wipe the giddy smile from her face.

"I have a feeling dessert has been served," Julia speculated softly, "but my sister is making everybody leave us alone."

He nodded, and they dragged themselves to their feet. Sure enough, inside, everyone was already digging into their eclairs. For good form, Alison feigned mortification. "Oh, I'm sorry! I forgot all about you two!"

Julia's mother and father exchanged amused glances, and even Paige snorted at the charade. Only Robert remained oblivious, happily cramming his eclair into his mouth, smearing chocolate icing all over his face.

By the time they finished dessert, it was past Robert's bath time. Alison bid her farewells, and Julia bundled Robert downstairs to the tub, where his vintage Fisher Price toy boat awaited. While Julia supervised Robert's bath, the refrains of William and Paige's ongoing guitar lesson drifted through the ceiling vents.

After Julia tucked Robert under his frog-print duvet, William brought his guitar downstairs to play for Robert. It wasn't exactly a lullaby, but the gentle melody stood well in a lullaby's stead. Very soon, Robert's eyelids drooped, and he unleashed an enormous yawn.

"Good night, William," Robert mumbled, already half asleep, as Julia switched off his light.

"Good night," William whispered from the door.

After tiptoeing back to the den, Julia gestured to William's guitar. "I wish you could stay and sing me to sleep with that thing." Immediately, her face flared with heat as she realized how that might be construed. "I didn't mean it that way. I mean, not that I wouldn't..." She groaned in frustration at herself. "I just mean I haven't been able to sleep much over the past two nights. And I guess it shows."

His face also flushed, and he laughed a bit. "I haven't slept much recently, either. And I'd like to do that for you someday, when the time is right."

He had already retrieved his backpack from upstairs, and now he slung it over his shoulders. Julia's heart sank – he was leaving. But of course it must have been exhausting, trying to make a good impression on everyone; and maybe he didn't want to overstay his welcome.

"I already said my goodbyes to your parents and Paige," he offered.

Julia hid her disappointment behind a forced smile. "We'll eat around six tomorrow. When can you and Diego can make it?"

"When do you want us? We can come as early as four, on Mondays."

"Four it is." She gestured to his guitar case and backpack. "How are you getting home on your bicycle with all that stuff?"

"Oh, I'm not going home tonight. I'll stay with Mom and Kelly."

She nodded, and her face burned again as she realized there was only one thing left to do. A slow, guarded smile crept over William's face as he realized the same thing. She rose up on her tiptoes, and at the same time, he dipped his head, briefly touching his lips to hers.

Her sweater slipped from her shoulder again as he broke the kiss. He smiled a moment longer, his eyes surveying her in what she hoped was appreciation. But he only said, "I'll see you tomorrow."

After seeing him out and locking the door behind herself, she stood frozen, her hand still on the doorknob.

Although he had never been cold, his demeanor was guarded. And although he allowed her to touch and kiss him, they had not once said *I love you*, like they did yesterday.

But again, it was no wonder – he had been on his best behavior in front of her parents and kids. Besides, it annoyed her that she was scrutinizing his every action, expression, and tone of voice. Anything could happen in the weeks and months ahead. There were so many hurdles to overcome. She knew she should not invest so much of her heart in the outcome. She knew she still had plenty to fill her life, even without him.

And yet, with every minute and every interaction, her heart grew impossibly more attached. And it terrified her that the outcome might not be what she hoped.

But she couldn't afford to think about that now. She still had to face Paige, and her parents.

Back upstairs, she found Paige on the sofa, still practicing the chords William had taught her. Julia's father read the newspaper in his favorite chair and made no effort to acknowledge Julia's presence. So Julia wandered into the kitchen to help her mother finish the dishes.

"Here, Mom; let me take over," Julia offered, and her mother readily agreed. After removing her aching joints to the kitchen table, where the rest of her Cinsaut awaited, Julia's mother unlocked her cell phone to scroll through Facebook.

Julia casually loaded dishes into the dishwasher. "Will tells me he has a dog named Diego."

Her mother hummed. "Really?"

"He'd like to bring Diego over tomorrow to meet the kids, if that's okay."

Her mother looked up. "Here?"

Julia nodded. "At four o'clock. Only if that's okay with you and Dad. He says Diego's well-behaved, but we can keep him on the patio if you prefer."

Her mother lifted a shoulder, and her eyes returned to her phone. "I don't see why not."

That, at least, was a good sign. "Did you know that Kelly is getting married?"

"Yes, Ann told me. To a woman, apparently." Her mother's tone carried a note of judgment behind it. "But technically they won't be married, you know. Because of Prop 8."

"Yes, Mother, I'm aware," Julia snapped. "But it's still a marriage, even if the State of California refuses to recognize it."

"And Ann tells me Kelly's fiancée is pregnant with twins." Leaning forward, as if imparting something scurrilous, her mother whispered, "Artificial insemination."

Julia frowned, but decided to ignore her mother's cattiness, for now. "Did you know Ann is moving into one of those seniors-only condos?"

"Yes," her mother sighed. "At least she's not moving very far."

"Really? Where is it?"

"That place called Treemont, in the Inner Sunset, just on the other side of 19th. It's close to Golden Gate Park, too, so that's nice. Plus, for her, it's closer to Cardone's."

"I had no idea Ann was moving until William told me."

"I guess I forgot to mention it. Maybe I don't want it to be true. There's no one left in this neighborhood anymore."

"There are plenty of people in this neighborhood, Mom," sighed Julia. "You just don't choose to know them."

"How can I? They all speak Chinese."

Julia's voice inadvertently took on a sharp edge. "Mom, that's not true."

Her mother lapsed into silence and pretended to go back to scrolling her phone. With a pang of remorse, Julia gently suggested, "Why don't you and Dad go visit Ann after she moves in? You can take a look around Treemont while you're there. See what you think."

Her mother's eyes snapped up again, flashing. "Why, so you and William can move in here together?"

Julia put a hand on her hip. "That's not what this is about, Mom."

Her mother waved a hand in exasperation. "I don't want to talk about this." And with that, she heaved herself from the table and retreated to her bedroom with her wineglass.

Brooding, Julia finished loading the dishwasher. As she wiped down the sink and counters, she began to wonder in earnest if it were past time for her parents to sell the house and move. They had complained for years that all their friends were dying or moving away.

Julia's parents were both seventy-five. Her mother's arthritis and heart problems made it challenging to keep the house and garden up to her standards. Granted, her father still seemed spry, but he had never been much help. He claimed the kitchen as his domain, but he viewed the rest of the house as his wife's.

Finally, at nine, Julia ordered Paige to bed. With a luxuriant yawn, her father also turned in for the night. Meanwhile, Julia tried in vain to quell her mind at the sewing machine. And when she finally dragged herself to her old childhood bedroom, which she now shared with Paige, she lay awake most of the night, staring at the ceiling and listening to Paige's soft snores.

Julia had no time to brood the next morning as she shuttled Paige and Robert to school. Then, like every Monday, she serviced the aquariums of the few clients she had managed to nab so far.

She didn't get home until it was almost time for William to come over. By then, her mother had already picked Robert up from preschool, and Paige had ridden the bus home from school. Julia found Paige in the den, feeding the fish and listening to music through her earbuds. She kissed her daughter's cheek, then ascended the stairs to the living room.

In the kitchen, her parents prepped ingredients for the dinner Julia planned to cook. Robert sat on his stool in the living room, practicing the two guitar chords William had taught him, over and over. When he spotted Julia, he dropped the guitar on the rug.

"Mommy!" he shouted, running to throw his arms around her legs.

"Hey, Tadpole!" Julia knelt to wrap him in a hug. "How was your day?"

"Good," he chirped.

"Awesome! But sweetie, remember what William taught you? If you drop your guitar on the floor like that, it might break." Taking him with her, she showed him again how to store the guitar in its case.

"Mommy, when is William getting here?" he wondered as they latched the case shut. "I want him to teach me more."

Julia glanced at the clock on the wall. "Oh my goodness, he'll be here in ten minutes! I have to change clothes."

After kissing Robert, she dashed to her bedroom to strip out of her grubby work clothes. Ten minutes later, she at least looked presentable in a teal-colored sweater dress. And the moment she finished tying her scarf, William's voice floated up to her through the open bedroom window. Outside, he spoke in a higher register than usual, as if addressing a child; but Julia smiled when she heard the jingle of a dog collar.

She flew downstairs to meet them on the front porch. William approached on the sidewalk, with Diego trotting alongside on a leash. Diego turned out to be medium-sized and almost entirely white, with patches of brown on his ears and rump.

Rather than meeting them halfway, Julia let William bring Diego to her, in case he was shy. But the instant Diego noticed her, his button ears pricked, his tail swished, and his tongue unfurled from his mouth.

Instead, it was William who smiled a bit shyly as they came up the walkway. "Julia, meet Diego," he said simply.

Julia held out a hand, and after a test-sniff, Diego rewarded her with face licks. He didn't jump up on her or bark; he just leaned in and let her rub his flank, his tongue lolling happily from his smiling mouth. Panting, he flopped onto his side, and she obliged with a belly rub.

"Look at you!" she cooed at Diego. "Aren't you a sweet, friendly boy?"

"You're already his new favorite human," William observed. "Should I bring him to the back patio?"

"Oh no; bring him inside. The kids will be so excited!"

As they came through the front door, Paige emerged from the in-law unit. The moment she spotted Diego, her face lit up, and she yanked the earbuds from her ears.

"Robert, Grandma, Grandpa! There's a dog!"

To both Diego and William's credit, they only flinched a little at

Paige's impressive lung capacity. William led Diego upstairs, and the next few minutes were pure chaos as the kids and Diego reveled in their mutual delight with each other. The ruckus drew Julia's parents from the kitchen, and after William unleashed Diego, they lured Diego onto the couch and took turns smothering him with love.

"He looks like he has a bit of Jack Russell in him," Julia's father observed with a rare, wide grin.

"That, or maybe beagle," William agreed.

"And he has the chunky neck of a lab," added Julia's mother.

Robert pointed at Diego and ordered him to lie down, but William said, "Oh no, you can't talk to him like that." At the apparent reproach, the entire room fell silent – until William clarified, "Diego speaks Spanish."

Everyone laughed, except Paige. "How does a dog speak Spanish?"

"How does a dog speak English, for that matter?" prompted William.

Paige's brow unfurrowed as it dawned on her. "You mean you speak to him in Spanish?"

"His family does, so I do, too."

"Wait – he's not your dog?"

"No. Well, kind of." William explained Diego's complex family dynamics.

"How do I say 'lay down?'" asked Robert.

"Echado," William replied.

Robert tried, and sure enough, Diego flopped onto his side and exposed his belly, to the delight of both kids. They rewarded him with copious belly rubs.

"How do I say 'sit'?" asked Robert, after Diego jumped back up.

"Oh wait, I know this! ¡Siéntate!" shouted Paige, and Diego complied. With a self-satisfied smile, Paige explained, "I take Spanish."

"Now you can say 'dame la pata,' and he'll shake your hand," William encouraged.

Paige took his suggestion, and a chorus of approval ensued when Diego offered Paige his paw. Then, of course, Robert had to try.

William pulled dog biscuits and toys from his backpack, and Julia suggested they migrate to the back patio. Once installed at the table with her glass of wine, she and William could enjoy a private conversation while still supervising the kids and Diego.

After resolving the kids' spat over who got to play with Diego, Julia caught William's eye and offered a slight smile. He returned it and asked, "How is Paige doing these days?"

She shifted her gaze to the kids. "Better, since you saw her in January. After all that happened – you know, at Cardone's – her psychiatrist added a third med, and that's helped some. That, and the therapeutic school she goes to, thanks to her IEP. Janus Academy."

He gave her a quizzical look. "IEP?"

"Yeah; it's a legal document. It outlines the accommodations the school district has to provide for Paige."

"Oh, right! I forgot – my nephew Xavier has one because of his Asperger's."

Julia's eyes snapped to his. "That's Paige's diagnosis. They finally diagnosed her last year."

"You mean the public school district pays for Paige's tuition at this therapeutic school?"

"If the public school can't provide a 'Free Appropriate Public Education,' they have to pay for the student to go to a school that can."

His eyes went unfocused for a moment. "I wonder if Kelly knows about that. Xavier goes to public school, but I don't think he's doing so well. What does Janus Academy provide for Paige?"

Julia blew out a breath. "Well, first of all, it's a therapeutic school specifically for 2-E kids."

William tipped his head. "2-E?"

"Twice exceptional – kids like Paige who are neurodivergent, while at the same time very bright."

William dragged his hand over his mouth and jaw. "That sounds like Xavier. The kid's a prodigy with computers and electronics. Programming, digital animation... you name it."

Julia nodded. "Besides a curriculum for kids like that, Janus provides on-call, in-the-moment counseling with a school psychologist. Plus, Paige gets intensive social-emotional, speech, and occupational therapy. None of which any public middle school is adequately equipped for."

Before William could respond, the kids and Diego grew bored of tug-of-war. William pulled a well-gnawed tennis ball from his backpack so they could play fetch. Along with the kids, Julia laughed as Diego hurtled across the yard with all his slightly-overfed might, his ears and tongue flopping around with the effort. Diego brought the ball to William, who wound back and hurled it down the deep backyard with an athletic flick of the wrist. It ricocheted off the fence into the grass, and Diego's head swiveled comically in search of it.

Since Julia cooked dinner on Mondays, she excused herself to get started. After a while, William wandered into the kitchen, Diego at his heels, to see what she was making.

"Oh, it's really basic," she laughed, self-conscious about cooking in front of a former professional. "Just some penne with a sauce of ricotta, parmesan, and lemon. And some peas thrown in to make it more filling. The kids love it."

"Can I help?"

"Sure; you can make a salad," she suggested, reaching into the refrigerator to pull out the ingredients.

Diego flopped down in the kitchen doorway to keep an eye on both the kitchen and the living room, where the kids played Candy Land. His tongue lolled from his mouth while he caught his breath. Julia and William worked quietly and companionably to pull the meal together, and over dinner, they confirmed their plans for the next morning: at eight, Julia and the kids would meet William at the pier, head out to the Farallones, and return no later than four in the afternoon.

"You remember I showed you where the slip is, right?" William asked in a low voice over dinner, the look he gave Julia tinged with meaning.

"How could I forget?" murmured Julia. But as she picked up her fork, she caught Paige watching them with interest.

After dinner, William taught the kids more guitar chords, and then it was time for Robert's bath. Like the previous night, William played and sang a lullaby for Robert. By the time Julia tucked Robert in and turned out the light, Paige had already gone to the bedroom to finish her homework.

Julia poked her head in. "Hey, you. Can I come in a sec?"

Paige shrugged and removed her earbuds. She was sitting on her bed with her lap desk, hunched over a spiral notebook with a pencil. Her algebra textbook lay open on the bedspread. As Julia closed the door, Paige laid everything aside.

Julia sat on the edge of the bed. "How's homework?"

Again, Paige shrugged, her expression unreadable. "It's algebra. I fucking hate algebra."

"Paige..." But Julia remembered Clio's advice – *pick your battles.* Instead, she said, "William and I were thinking of taking Diego for a walk. Do you mind hanging out here with Grandma and Grandpa?"

Once more, Paige shrugged, but said nothing.

With a playful smile, Julia mimicked Paige's shrug. "Is that a yes, a no, or an I don't know?"

Paige pulled a loose thread from her fuzzy blanket and wrapped it around her finger. "Mom... when William asked if you remember where the slip is, and you said how can I forget, were you talking about the last time we went whale watching with him?"

Julia reached into her jacket pocket and found the smooth cross-section of watermelon tourmaline that Uncle Rob had given her so many years ago. Over the years, she had worn it down even smoother, using it as a worry stone. "That, and because back then, he and I formed the whale watching business together."

"What do you mean, 'back then?'" Paige sat up straighter. "You mean in 2006?"

Julia nodded. "William and I reconnected at the restaurant after your dad left. He and I always used to meet outside on the pier during our breaks. Not just then, but also when we were teenagers."

"So is that where you first met? At Dunphy's?"

"Not exactly. We met at Cardone's the summer before our senior year. I would walk across the pier to pick up the daily order of fresh fish. Eventually he came to work at Dunphy's." Julia smiled privately to herself, remembering. "Anyway, when your dad..." She didn't want to say *when your dad abandoned us and ran away.* "When your dad went to Brazil six years ago and I needed a job, I worked at Dunphy's for a while. William was still there, as a cook. We just kind of picked up where we left off, meeting on the pier during breaks. And that's when he pointed the boat out and asked if I'd be his business partner."

Looking down, Paige fiddled with the little thread coiled around her finger. "You should have just told me he was your boyfriend back then. I could have handled it."

Gently, Julia reminded her, "You were seven, and you were grieving your dad's absence. Do you really think that would have been the best time?"

Paige started curling the thread into a little ball, then huffed a sigh of resignation. "No, I guess not." She lifted her eyes again. "But I'm older now. I understand these things better. So you don't have to be all on the down-low or whatever with William. I know you and he will want to... you know." She grimaced, and it was everything Julia could do not to burst out laughing.

"Paige, honey, I think there's a happy middle somewhere between zero communication and TMI."

Paige smirked. "I guess."

Julia patted Paige's knee and smiled. "Diego's waiting. Are you okay staying here with Grandma and Grandpa?"

"Yeah, all right."

"Need anything?"

Paige shook her head and stuffed her earbuds back into her ears.

THE SUN WAS SETTING as Julia and William led Diego through the neighborhood. Julia zipped her jacket against the chill. She always marveled at how warm-natured William was; he needed nothing more than his long-sleeved flannel shirt, even here in the foggy microclimate of the Outer Sunset. For her part, she was thankful that she had worn tights and boots with her sweater dress, and her yellow beanie and scarf helped, too.

"What was it Mark Twain didn't really say about summer in San Francisco? 'The coldest winter I ever spent?'" she joked.

"And he wouldn't have been wrong," William replied, smiling. After another minute or two of awkward silence, he suddenly handed over Diego's leash. "Here – would you like to walk him?"

Diego glanced back when she took the leash, but he didn't seem to care who led him. He trotted and waddled along just as cheerfully.

They continued silently toward Santiago Street, until Julia remarked, "This neighborhood has changed so many times, it's dizzying."

He turned to peer at her. "What brought that to mind?"

"Oh…" She gave a joyless laugh. "Just a conversation I had last night with my mom. We were talking about how your mom is moving into that seniors-only complex. She thought I was trying to kick her and Dad out of the house and steal it for myself. Like I would want to live the rest of my life in the house I grew up in."

After a minute, he asked, "What neighborhood are you thinking of moving to?"

"I don't know, honestly. Probably something between my parents and my shop. Maybe the Inner Sunset."

"That would be close to my mom. Your parents should look into that place – Treemont."

"That's what I was telling Mom last night when she accused me of trying to steal their house," Julia said drily. "But they're feeling so isolated here, and the house and yard is really too much for my parents these days. I'm sure it's sentimental, though. That, and fear of the unknown."

"Confronting your own mortality can't be fun."

"True," she murmured, staring down at her boots.

"How long have they lived there?"

"Almost fifty years."

He nodded slowly, thoughtfully. Diego paused to do his business in a patch of grass, and Julia watched in amusement as William promptly swooped in to pick up the mess with a disposable bag.

"Like a boss," Julia remarked. He gave a single short laugh, and she added, "You're quite the dog-dad now."

"Diego keeps my blood pressure under control." They were crossing Santiago, and the street corridor funneled the sounds of the ocean to their ears. "Let's go that way," William suggested, pointing west down Santiago toward the beach.

Luckily, anticipating that possibility, Julia had worn rain boots. After crossing the Great Highway, they climbed the dunes. But of course, May Gray had arrived, and the incoming marine layer spoiled any hopes of admiring the sunset. The wind whipped Julia's hair and threatened to blow the hat from her head. The waves crashed with their usual violence on the sand.

William unleashed Diego and allowed him to chase his tennis ball along the beach. When Diego returned with it, William was staring unfocused at the waves, so Diego rested on his haunches to stare up at him and wait.

"Here." Grinning, Julia squatted to accept the slobbery ball from Diego. After flinging it across the beach a few times in a row, she turned back to William; but he still didn't seem inclined to talk. The chilly wind made their noses run. He sniffed and avoided Julia's gaze, shifting his weight from one foot to the other.

Dread and panic welled in Julia's chest. William had always been taciturn, but Julia, with her unfiltered motormouth, had always supplied the difference and drawn him out. What if the connection they once shared had severed beyond repair?

Diego had long since returned, but he had given up on both Julia and William. Instead, he settled down to gnaw on his slobbery, sand-dredged tennis ball. When he caught Julia looking, his ears pricked. Squatting, she lulled him into complacency with a few vigorous belly rubs before snatching the tennis ball and hurling it across the sand. Diego barked, bounding after it exuberantly. That seemed to finally snap Willliam out of his trance, and when Diego returned, he pitched the ball a few more times.

Still, to Julia's anguish, neither of them could find much to say before it was time to head home. They descended the dunes and crossed the Great Highway. Julia, on William's left, steeled herself with a deep breath, then reached for his hand. But William chose that exact moment to shift Diego's leash into his left hand.

She didn't think he had done it on purpose, but she couldn't be sure. So, with her heart sinking, she shoved her own hands into her jacket pockets.

It was nearly dark by the time they got back, and since they would have an early start the next morning, they judged it best to call it a night. William gathered all of Diego's toys into his backpack, and after saying goodnight to Julia's parents and Paige, he followed Julia back downstairs to the tunnel entrance.

Julia squatted to bid Diego farewell and accept his kisses. It occurred to her then to wonder, "How did you two get all the way here from the Mission?"

"I have a bike trailer he rides in."

Julia rubbed Diego's ears and cooed, "You are one pampered pooch."

"I rode all the way to my mom's house," said William, "and from there we walked."

"No wonder you're in such good shape," she said, flashing him a cheeky smile.

Reddening, he said, "Don't forget, I have an electric assist on that thing."

"Then what *are* you doing?"

"Sorry?"

"To stay in such great fighting shape. I mean, according to my sister, anyway. *I* haven't noticed."

His mouth hung open, as if willing the words to come out. She rose from crouching beside Diego and came to stand in front of him. Peering up into his eyes, she found the nerve to drape her hand over his bicep, over the blue flannel sleeve and his new mystery-tattoo. She murmured, "Alison wasn't wrong, you know."

His tongue darted out, wetting his lips. It was probably subconscious, but desire still somersaulted in Julia's belly. By now, his face was the brightest red she had ever seen it, and as he scanned hers, he wobbled the tiniest bit. Her heart soared with hope, slamming against her ribcage; and she stepped closer, craning her neck. Rising on tiptoes so his mouth hovered just over hers.

To her almost knee-buckling relief, he cupped her face in his hands, and his eyes drifted shut. He captured her top lip in a soft, sucking kiss, then gave her bottom lip the same attention.

Resting his forehead against hers, his breath came quick now, and so did hers. He opened his eyes with an exquisitely conflicted look. A look that encompassed so much: tenderness, perhaps, but also regret, fear, and longing.

All he said was, "See you at the pier at eight."

Julia reluctantly let go and stepped back, her heart once again plummeting. She gestured to Diego. "You two be safe."

William also took a reluctant step backward. Almost sadly, he said, "Good night."

Julia watched William and Diego exit the tunnel entrance down the front walkway. As they turned down the sidewalk, William lifted his hand once, and she did the same before retreating inside for another fitful night's sleep.

<h1 style="text-align:center">TUESDAY, MAY 8, 2012</h1>

Sure enough, *The Albatross* still docked in the same slip where Julia had last seen it. It was the same forty-five-foot sport-fishing catamaran she and William considered buying six years ago, with its two rows of forward-facing seats, a T-Top, and one row of aft-facing seats. After they broke up, William bought it with the money he had saved from his crab fishing years in Alaska.

From the pier, and with Paige and Robert in tow, Julia spied movement at the helm and called out. But her smile faded when a woman disembarked, waving a friendly hello.

"Oh," Julia stammered, glancing again at the boat's hull. Yep, it still said *The Albatross.* "I'm sorry, did I make a mistake? I was looking for William Quinn."

"No, yeah, you have the right boat." The young woman's smile was wide and earnest. She approached, threading three life vests onto her left arm and extending her right hand in greeting. "I'm Izumi. The naturalist on board."

"Oh!" A wave of relief swept over Julia as she shook Izumi's hand.

"You must be Julia." Youthful vocal fry dripped from her voice.

"Oh yes – sorry. Julia Beale."

Izumi was petite, Asian. Delicate features. Lustrous black hair piled atop her head in a stylish messy bun. Young – no more than twenty-five. Doubtless, legions of dick pics stormed the inboxes of Izumi's online dating profiles.

Suddenly aware of her own gaping, Julia straightened and pulled herself together. "I'm sorry; William just didn't mention the naturalist was joining us."

"No worries; I agreed to come at the last minute."

"I called her last night." William's voice made Julia jump. She had been so fixated on Izumi that she hadn't even seen him approach. "It occurred to me you'd all have a better experience with her providing interpretation, since I'm mostly at the helm."

"Makes sense," was all Julia could think to mumble. She was so disoriented by this turn of events – finding a very beautiful, very *young* woman with William – that the speech center of her brain seized up.

Not only that, but at the sight of William, her mouth went dry. She sucked in a huge gulp of air and held it a moment.

They were entering a heat wave, and it was an almost freakishly warm, sunny morning. William wore only a short-sleeved black tee-shirt, gray cargo pants, and black deck boots. The shirt wasn't tight, but it was more fitted than his usual styles, and it clung lightly to his rather well-defined chest. It struck Julia like a thunderbolt that, with his aviator sunglasses, William could absolutely pass for a Hollywood star, or even a model.

When his cheeks flushed under her scrutiny, she finally tore her eyes away. Unfortunately, they then landed on Izumi, whose eyes, face, and whole *being* lit up as she watched William. And not only that, but to Julia's dismay, even Paige was gaping.

A guffaw threatened to erupt from somewhere deep in Julia's belly.

After a moment, Izumi reluctantly turned back to Julia. After a moment to study Julia's face, Izumi's smile faded somewhat. "I have a degree in marine biology from the University of Hawaii," she offered, as if explaining herself.

Julia snapped her jaw shut and forced what she hoped was an easy-breezy smile. Izumi must have thought she was doubting her qualifications. "Of course! I didn't mean...I wasn't doubting... Did Will tell you I have a degree in marine biology from Santa Barbara?"

As soon as it was out of her mouth, Julia cringed inwardly. In a desperate attempt to seem relatable and find common ground, not only did she sound like she was one-upping Izumi – but she had used William's pet name. The one he only permitted the people he loved to use.

Izumi quirked an eyebrow at Julia. "Will?"

Thankfully, William intervened. "I hadn't really had a chance yet to tell Izumi about our passengers."

Izumi's mouth drooped at the corners, and the color drained from her cheeks. Julia inwardly kicked herself. Now Izumi was putting two and two together.

William tilted his sunglasses to the crown of his head. He lobbed a pointed look first at Julia, then at the kids.

"Right." Julia cleared her throat. "Izumi, this is Paige and Robert. My kids."

Izumi, still flustered, tried her best to smile as she greeted Paige. And then, she squatted to meet Robert.

For three or four beats, Izumi simply froze, as if looking upon the face of Medusa. The only sign of life was her rapidly-fading smile. With enormous eyes, she turned her head back to gape first at William, then at Julia.

She knew.

Of *course* she knew. Who wouldn't, seeing William and Robert together? Izumi would have to be blind not to know.

Julia's pulse slammed in her throat, and she scrambled to think of something to say. Anything whatsoever to defuse the tension.

"Wow!" blurted Robert, still shaking Izumi's hand and refusing to let go. "You're really pretty!"

Paige snorted, and without meaning to, Julia barked out a nervous laugh. Robert's compliment snapped Izumi out of her stupor, and she plastered on an even more overwrought smile. "Oh my gosh, you're so sweet!"

Meanwhile, William scratched the back of his neck, looking uncomfortable. Only then did it occur to Julia – maybe William and Izumi had once shared something more than a professional relationship.

William interrupted Julia's brooding when he took one of the life vests from Izumi. "These things are kind of fussy," he explained to Julia and the kids. "The straps are obnoxious, but we'll help."

After gesturing for Izumi to assist Paige and Robert, William hovered over Julia, fastening and tightening the vest's fiddly straps. Julia couldn't tell whether he was oblivious to Izumi's distress, or just ignoring it.

They boarded *The Albatross,* where William drilled them in safety protocols, oriented them to the boat, and ran down the itinerary. Julia barely heard a word, and Izumi seemed hardly less preoccupied, since her eyes constantly pinballed between Robert, Julia, and William. On one of Izumi's passes, Julia smiled as amicably as possible, but Izumi darted her eyes away without returning it.

Julia didn't have much time to dwell on that before yet another stranger rounded the corner from the stern. He was not much older than Izumi. Loose, dark curls swept forward from the crown of his head and jutted stylishly over his forehead.

"This is my deckhand, Stephen," explained William. "He also happens to be my Aunt Rita's grandson. Stephen, this is Julia, Paige, and Robert."

Julia chuckled as she stepped forward to shake Stephen's hand. "How many aunts and uncles do you have, Will?"

"Nine." Smiling faintly, he added, "And thirty-two cousins, at last count."

"Nice to finally meet you," said Stephen, treating Julia to a dazzling smile. He was at least six feet tall, slim, and good-looking. He reminded Julia of an outgoing, more Italian-looking William, at least from the time when William was younger and beardless. "I've heard a lot about you."

Julia's eyebrows lifted, and she glanced reflexively at a sullen Izumi. "You have?"

Before Stephen could reply, Robert made a beeline for the helm's controls, crying out in excitement.

"Hold up, buddy." William's authoritative tone reined Robert in, even while his laugh kept things easy. "That's coming soon, don't worry. But first – pop quiz."

While Paige groaned outwardly, Julia groaned inwardly, since she hadn't listened to a single word of William's safety lesson. Luckily, though, Paige was his first victim.

Of course, the kids nailed every question. Dread welled in the pit of Julia's stomach as William's eyes landed on her. "Julia – what do you do if you feel seasick?"

Julia blew out a puff of air – that, at least, was an easy one. "Glue your eyes to the horizon, or a fixed object, like a land mass or a structure."

"Okay," William conceded, "you guys are obviously really smart. No more softballs."

Robert's face scrunched up in confusion. "We weren't playing softball."

Paige thunked him lightly on the back of his head. "Idiot; it's just an expression."

"*Paige*," Julia bit out. "He's only five."

"A softball can mean an easy question, buddy," explained William, rumpling Robert's blond waves. After William's treatment, they stuck up even more than usual. An unmistakable fondness softened William's eyes as he stared at the spitting image of his own boyhood. "So, Robert – first non-softball. Are you ready?"

"I was *born* ready!" Robert had picked up that cheesy gem from a tee-ball teammate, but at least it defused the tension.

Well, *most* of the tension. Still gaping at Robert, her feet glued to the deck, Izumi remained a study in shock.

To her own surprise, Julia felt compassion for her. Even after six years, she remembered what it felt like when she believed William was dating a coworker. And then again, a few months later, when she learned how many other women William had slept with in the eleven years since their first break up. Including the one who confronted her in the ladies' room at MacGowan's, warning her not to let William get her pregnant.

Oops!

Julia had let her insecurities factor into her decision to break up again with William and go back to Kevin. It was far from the main reason, of course; and under any other circumstances, it would have been no reason at all. But at the time, she honestly believed reconciling with Kevin was the best thing for her hospitalized seven-year-old who had slashed her own wrists – if not for herself or William.

Learning the less-than-savory details of William's past had sowed those initial seeds of doubt. And then, after making her agonizing choice, she had cited those doubts to herself, again and again, trying to shore up her resolve.

Yet despite everything she had learned and experienced in the years since, those same doubts now creeped back in. After all, Izumi looked nothing short of devastated. Maybe this wasn't just some unrequited crush. Maybe Julia and William were flaunting their renewed relationship in the face of one of his exes. And now they were about to spend a whole day trapped on a boat together, with Julia and William's son thrown in for extra kicks.

"Julia."

The sound of her own name, spoken in William's baritone, snatched her from her anxiety death-spiral. "Huh?"

There was a sparkle in William's eye, as if he knew she hadn't been paying attention. "What should you do?"

"What should... sorry, about what?"

William's lips twitched, but he managed to suppress a smirk. "If you fall overboard."

"Um..."

This was not a hardball question, and it wasn't like Julia was a noob at seafaring. She had worked on plenty of ocean-going vessels during her college years, not to mention all the whale watching excursions she had taken with Uncle Rob. And of course, there was William's uncle's boat, where she and William had shared their first kiss; and Kevin's parents' yachts, *plural*, where she had spent many an unpleasant summer.

She knew seamanship like the back of her hand, but to watch her brain seize up at William's basic question, nobody would have known it.

Grinning, Paige made a *tsk* sound and shook her head. "And Mom says *I* never listen."

Lifting an eyebrow, William turned to Paige. "All right then, *you* tell us – what should you do if you fall overboard?"

Of course, Paige nailed the answer, and against Julia's will, her eyes locked on Izumi's for a loaded moment. Julia's lungs stubbornly refused to draw breath, and Izumi turned away with a sour expression.

In her best imitation of Bette Davis, Julia muttered to herself, "Fasten your seatbelts. It's going to be a bumpy ride."

~

THEY HAD DRIVEN under the Golden Gate Bridge, much to Robert's awe, and were steadily cruising toward the Farallon Islands.

William allowed Robert to help with every aspect of running the boat that he safely could. He let Paige help, too, when she condescended to do so. Six years earlier, when Paige and Julia had gone whale watching with William, Paige had combed over every instrument and compartment, demanding to know its name and function. But now she was thirteen, and she had an image to uphold.

Luckily, William turned out to be a cunning teen-whisperer, while deftly convincing Paige it was her idea to help out.

"I can't take the suspense anymore, Will – how come you're better at manipulating my teenager than I am?" Julia sat beside him at the helm, while at the stern, Izumi pointed out dolphins and porpoises to the kids. Meanwhile, Stephen availed himself of every excuse to hover near Izumi.

"Don't forget, I have two nephews," replied William.

"Your nephews are teenagers?"

"Well, Xavier is about to turn thirteen. And does it count that I was a teenager once?"

"So was I, remember?"

"Yeah, but you were one of those goody-two-shoes teenagers."

"You weren't exactly a parent's worst nightmare. Unless you're counting a little weed."

William cleared his throat and gestured vaguely in the direction of his own back.

"Right... and I guess an albatross tattoo. Is it still there?"

"Um – it's a *tattoo*?" He gave a little wince-shrug, inviting her to think it through.

"Well, you could have had it laser-zapped, or covered it with something else."

"I don't believe in erasing or covering tattoos. They're a map of a person's life – where they've been and where they're going."

"That's very deep, but I'm still not letting you dodge the question."

"What question?" But he smirked knowingly.

"The little question of how you conned my angsty teen into communicating in words, instead of grunts."

He pondered a moment. "Maybe, like a lot of angsty teens, she's more open to input from someone who's not an authority figure. At least, more open than she would be otherwise. And I don't have any authority over her."

"For now," blurted Julia, and her face instantly caught fire as she realized what she had alluded to.

His eyes held hers with a knowing gleam. "The point is, don't take it personally."

She couldn't wipe the affectionate smile from her face, and he mirrored it with his most genuine, unguarded one – that seismic, celestial grin, with the power to rupture fault lines and ignite new suns. The grin that carried away her heart nineteen years ago.

He reached out to caress a lock of hair that escaped from her cap. The fond gesture caught her by surprise, trapping her laughter in her throat with a weird little gasp-hiccup hybrid.

How could he make her heart explode just by touching her *hair*, for Christ's sake?

"Mommy, check it out! A whale!"

Robert's summons, shouted from the stern, zapped Julia back to the moment. With a parting wink at William, she got up to join everyone at the stern – just in time to catch Izumi schooling her frown into something more neutral.

"Izumi says it's a humpback," Robert added.

Julia accepted Robert's binoculars. "Yep, that's a humpback, all right."

"Mom," Paige blurted, "back when you and William started this business, were you going to be the naturalist?"

Julia gripped the railing tighter as hot mortification seared her insides. "I'd like to answer that for you, Paige; but can we talk about it at home?"

Luckily, Paige shrugged her assent. Izumi offered no response apart from her intractable frown, and Robert was preoccupied with the whale.

It was an hour into their trip, and Julia was still ruminating over Izumi. By this point in life, Julia felt comfortable in her own skin, even if her brand of attractiveness wasn't necessarily the conventional kind. But after all, here was this objectively gorgeous young woman, with whom William spent several hours a day in a confined space.

And yet, each time William looked around, his eyes zeroed in on Julia and promptly softened. Not only that, but over the course of their trip, a clear and entertaining dynamic took shape. While William stared at Julia every chance he got, Julia and Izumi both stared at William. Meanwhile, Stephen stared at Izumi, and Paige stared at Stephen.

Well, Julia thought. *At least Paige isn't leering at William anymore.*

Julia upbraided herself for succumbing to old insecurities, and after she resolved to knock it off, the rest of the trip was a success. William had a knack for knowing where to find whales, and they also saw sea lions and seabirds on the Farallon Islands. They even spotted a shark, which William said was unusual at this time of year.

Izumi also proved more than competent as a naturalist. Sure, she sounded like a stoned surfer girl, but she was far brighter and more knowledgeable than her vocal quirks would suggest. Not only that, she had a great sense of humor, and by the end, Julia was genuinely starting to like her.

She had to give Izumi credit for how gamely she rallied her spirits, for the kids' sake. She kept them engaged, and by four o'clock, when William drove the boat back into its slip, she and the kids had become fast friends. From Paige, Izumi even earned the rare epithet of "cool."

As they prepared to disembark, Julia caught Izumi's eye and offered a smile. "Thank you so much for everything. We had a great time."

With a stoic expression, Izumi nodded. "You're welcome."

But Julia couldn't help noticing how Izumi followed William with her eyes as he disembarked with Julia and the kids. The momentary distraction kept Julia from spotting who greeted them at the end of the pier, but when she finally did, she pulled up short.

"Alison!"

With an exuberant wave, Alison called out, "Hey, guys! I was just sitting in my apartment with nothing to do, and I suddenly had this powerful urge to spend quality time with my niece and nephew. You wouldn't mind if I took them to dinner, would you, Julie? I'll even hang out and put Tadders to bed," she added, squatting to accept a hug from Robert.

God bless her. Even Paige jumped for joy at the prospect of spending an evening with Aunt Alison. Julia shot her sister a grateful look, then wrapped her in a quick hug. "You're the best sister ever," she whispered.

"Duh," Alison whispered back. "I've been telling you that since you were born."

After Alison left with the kids, William returned Julia's shy smile with a knowing one of his own. "Give me and Stephen a minute to finish wrapping things up. Then, I know a great burrito place, if that sounds good."

Julia beamed, her heart swelling as its pace quickened. "That sounds great."

His cheeks flushed, and as he turned toward the boat, she caught him fighting a smile.

WILLIAM DIRECTED Julia to the Mission, where she found the closest possible parking spot to the hole-in-the-wall taquería he pointed out. As they walked, William said, "We can bring our food back to my place, if you want. It's just a couple of blocks away. We can eat outside, on my patio."

Julia's pulse tripped over itself at the idea of being alone with him – at his apartment, no less – but she nodded. William ordered their food in Spanish, and as they carried it back to his place, a weighty silence hovered between them. He led her around a corner to a block of attached Edwardian houses with bay windows, then turned down a walkway toward a cheerful turquoise house with vermilion trim. A set of steps led to the main entrance, but at the ground level, off to one side, he unlocked a black metal gate with bars. In the shadows beyond lay another door, which in turn led into a converted high basement.

"The patio is out back," he explained sheepishly, "but we'll have to go through my apartment to get there."

The front door dumped them immediately into his living room, separated from the small galley kitchen by a countertop. The tops of Julia's ears burned, but before dropping her eyes to the blond laminate wood, she registered a sofa, tufted gray and tastefully masculine, in a mid-century-modern way. A rug in similarly-muted shades of black, gray, and cream. A small flat-screen TV on a simple, glass-topped entertainment stand. Two chairs flanking an espresso-colored table, with a small potted plant at its center. Large, framed color photos on white walls – landscapes, cityscapes, and the ocean.

William drew aside the vertical blinds on the opposite wall. A sliding glass door led to his postage stamp of concrete beneath the wooden deck of the main house. A set of moveable screens offered a modicum of privacy, and he had strung cafe lights beneath the rafters.

He gestured to his cafe table, then assumed the seat opposite hers. After unwrapping her burrito, Julia cracked open the beer she had brought from the taquería, while William went back inside to retrieve a bottle of San Pellegrino and mix it with *agua de jamaica*.

They ate in what felt like oppressive silence. Julia blurted the first thing that came to mind.

"Where's Diego?"

"Oh... he's probably upstairs, with the Ochoas. I can go get him, if you want."

Julia shrugged, peeling more foil from her burrito. "Maybe after we eat, we can take him for a walk."

William nodded, and they lapsed into another awkward silence. She racked her brain for something to say. Anything to delay the inevitable, terrifying subject on the tip of her tongue.

For Christ's sake, Julia; just get it over with already. She took a deep breath for courage.

Suddenly, they both started talking at once. Laughing nervously, Julia said, "You first."

"No, that's okay. What were you going to say?"

"I... I was just going to say I'm sorry if you felt like you had to invite me back here to eat. I would have been fine eating at the taquería, if you were more comfortable with that."

William blinked, twice. "I was going to say something similar – I'm sorry if you felt like you had to come back here with me. I guess I thought it might be easier to talk here, without a lot of other people around."

Julia laughed at the irony and pushed her burrito aside. She had only been picking at it, anyway. "You were right. There *is* something I've been meaning to say."

He gaped like a deer in the headlights. With one more centering breath, she steeled herself.

"Will... I still mean every word I said, with all my heart, when I told you I'll love you and make you happy for the rest of your life," she began, her voice quavering, her eyes trained down at her hands folded on the table. "But I'll understand if you feel like you rushed into things, and you're having second thoughts. No matter what happens between you and me, I'll always want you to be a part of Robert's life, if that's what you want. But I don't want you to feel beholden to me in any way, just because of him."

When he didn't answer right away, she peered up at him through her lashes. His eyes were still wide as saucers, but as soon as they met hers, they softened. He reached across the table and put his hand on hers.

"I've been stand-offish, haven't I?"

Wincing, Julia stammered in vain for a tactful reply.

"I'm sorry." With his free hand, William raked his fingers through the close-cropped hair on his scalp. "I think I'm a bit over-whelmed."

Her heart sank. She had often been too much for other people, including, sometimes, Kevin. But she had never been too much for William. "I'm–"

"No," he blurted, squeezing her hand. "Not like that. I just..." Finally, he blew out a ragged breath and lifted his eyes to hers. They broadcast so much raw vulnerability as he quietly admitted, "I'm overwhelmed being in your presence again. Dazzled, I guess. Trust me, I'm trying, but you have me tongue-tied."

In that moment, Julia remembered what it meant to swoon. She bit her lips, but she could no more stop the irrepressible smile than she could stop herself from loving him. Seeing it, he succumbed to his own smile of relief.

"I've been pretty tongue-tied, myself – which, as you know, is rare," she admitted with a laugh. "I've been nervous, and I sensed your nervousness; but also... you've been keeping your hands to yourself a bit, and I wasn't sure what that meant."

He clasped her hand between both of his. "I know in the past, I've probably pressured you to move faster than you felt comfortable with. I didn't want to make the same mistake, so I thought it would be better to take things slower this time. But I guess I went too far in the opposite direction and gave you the wrong impression."

Julia went almost limp with relief, and her heart overflowed with longing. "Maybe you're right – maybe we should take our time getting reacquainted. But I'd like to at least be able to do *this*," she added, glancing down at their clasped hands. "And to kiss you. Like, a lot. Like, maybe even make out a little."

He laughed and tugged her hand. She came around the table to stand beside him. He pulled her down into his lap, searching her eyes to make sure that was okay.

It was more than okay. Her pulse raced out of control at just how okay it was. She stroked his hair; touched the side of his face. He pulled her to him for a kiss and pressed her hand to his heart so she could feel its breakneck speed.

Julia's stomach swooped. After a minute, she gently broke the kiss and looked into his eyes. "I'm kind of desperately in love with you, you know."

"I've always been desperately in love with you, Julie," he whispered back.

She closed her eyes and heaved a sigh. Rested her forehead against his, and stroked his face again, over his beard. For a couple of minutes, he simply gazed at her, except for the handful of times when he briefly closed his eyes and touched his lips to hers.

Then he lifted her hand, and they both watched as he gently slid his palm across hers, entwining their fingers. In return, she caressed his thumb with hers, and her pulse accelerated as she met his heavy-lidded gaze.

He cupped the nape of her neck in his warm palm and drew her in. And even though he initiated it, they both gave little sounds of surprise and pleasure at the open-mouthed kiss.

Her heart stormed her ribcage as his tongue found hers, and she drew a sharp breath through her nose. He disentangled their hands – but only to bring both palms to her cheeks. His fingers splayed, connecting with as much of her face as possible.

Her loins were in very real danger of spontaneous combustion.

After a few minutes of languid kisses, his lips traveled along her jawline. When they reached her ear, he murmured, "Are we making out now?"

It was hard to draw breath. "I'm not making out; you're making out."

He gave a soft little chuckle, nuzzling kisses into her neck, where a field of goosebumps bloomed. "See, this is the problem."

"There's a problem?"

His whisper was warm on her ear. "Trying to find some middle ground."

There was a long-dormant fire-breathing dragon in the very pit of her. William's suggestive tone ignited its first rumblings in six years.

Sensing danger, Julia reluctantly said, "I think... maybe... we should finish our burritos?"

He pulled back, his mouth twisting into a wry smile. "I don't think I was doing much eating, in the first place."

"Me neither," laughed Julia.

"But how do you feel about meeting the Ochoas?"

"What, now?" In spite of herself, she was half-sorry he had followed her lead in slamming on the brakes.

"I was thinking we could borrow Diego while we're there and walk down to Dolores Park. But if you're not ready to meet them, I can go up there myself to get Diego."

"Oh, I'm perfectly happy to meet them; it's just that I don't speak Spanish."

"That's okay; everyone speaks English except the grandparents. I only speak Spanish with them for the practice."

"Practice? You don't need practice. You sound like a native speaker to me."

"Well, I may fool some people, but I assure you, I'm not fooling any native speakers."

"Did you just call me a fool?"

"Absolutely."

Julia laughed, and he signaled her to stand up by patting her backside, just as he had always done in the past. She followed him through his apartment, out the front door, and upstairs to the main porch. Inside the house, Diego had already detected their approach and was barking exuberantly.

"Who will I be meeting? Kelly's fiancée?" wondered Julia.

"No; Pilar lives with Kelly and our mom. But you'll meet her parents and grandparents, and Pilar's youngest two siblings still live at home."

He rang the doorbell, and a moment later, Diego barreled through the open door, wagging himself into a U-shape and snuffling all around Julia and William's legs. A pretty, petite woman in her late forties or early fifties with dark skin and Afro-textured hair followed Diego onto the porch. She and William exchanged greetings in Spanish.

Then William said, "Julia, this is Delfina, Kelly's soon-to-be mother-in-law. Delfina, this is Julia. My girlfriend."

Julia's heart stuttered and William's cheeks turned pink as his last two words landed. Delfina's brows lifted in surprise, but she smiled warmly and extended her hand. She beckoned them into the house, so they followed her past a parlor and staircase into the living room. Two men sat on the sofa, watching a soccer match on a Spanish-language channel. One was middle-aged, like Delfina, while the other was elderly.

When Julia and William entered, the men muted the TV and rose to greet them. A volley of rapid-fire Spanish zigzagged across the room as William politely addressed the wizened older gentleman, followed by the stout, mustachioed younger one. Then William gestured to Julia, and her pulse quickened again as she recognized the word *novia* from her college Spanish classes.

William introduced the younger man as Sergio – Delfina's husband, and Pilar's father. The older gentleman was Gustavo – Sergio's father. An elderly lady emerging from the kitchen in her apron was Sergio's mother, Socorro. And the teenage girl and boy who peeked around the corner at the unfamiliar voices were Lucía and Rafael. No thanks to her unusual amount of nerves, Julia feared she wouldn't be able to retain all of their names.

The grandmother Socorro cast her a warm, toothless smile and repeatedly said *welcome* in English. Meanwhile, Delfina implored Julia and William to stay for dinner. William politely thanked her and explained they had already eaten.

"We didn't mean to intrude; I just wanted to introduce Julia and see if we could borrow Diego for an hour or so. We'd love to take him to the park."

"Of course!" exclaimed Delfina and Sergio in unison; and very soon, Julia and William were walking Diego down 19th Street. The sounds of the Mission drifted out to them as they strolled past the neighborhood's open windows and doors – laughter, snippets of Spanish television, children playing, and refrains of reggaeton, cumbia, and rap. Mouth-watering fragrances wafted from Mexican taquerías and Salvadoran pupuserías along the way. They stopped to admire the vibrant murals adorning many of the buildings' façades.

Once 19th Street dead-ended into Dolores Park, they headed straight to the dog park and unleashed Diego to romp.

"The Ochoas seem sweet," Julia remarked after a while.

"They are. Like I said, over the past six years, they've kind of adopted me as an honorary son. Oh, and by the way – as of about twenty minutes ago, I have strict orders from Delfina to bring you to Kelly and Pilar's wedding."

"Oh!" Julia exclaimed, startled. "But, um..."

"And yes," he chuckled, "Mom and Kelly already know all about you and me. They were blown away when I told them about everything you've been through. Long story short, they're not holding any grudges, if that's what you're worried about. Far from it. They can't wait to see you and meet Robert."

Julia's heart soared. "I can't wait for that, either. But... you know we can't tell Robert who they are to him just yet. Not until I've had the chance to talk to Kevin, and our therapist, and the lawyers. We have to come up with a plan for how to break the news to him."

"I know that, and they do, too. But I'll keep reminding them."

"I still can't believe your mom is the one who made all of this happen for us. When I first came to her with the idea of filing a lawsuit against your dad's health insurance, she was still furious with me. Maybe even more than you were."

William cringed. "I'm sorry."

"No, it was understandable, especially given the limited information she had. I'm just amazed that she changed her mind about me, even before she knew everything."

"You know she always loved you."

"Yeah, but that was before... everything." She shook her head, remembering. "I'll never forget what she said: 'He has a good and loyal heart, and I'll be damned if I'm going to let you anywhere near it again.' I pretty well memorized those words, they stung so much." He winced again, and she quickly added, "But you see? If it weren't for her making you come along to the attorney's office, you never would have found out it was me who got the ball rolling on the lawsuit."

"And I think you've probably already guessed – it was no accident that I came along. Or that the info about you just *accidentally* slipped out during the appointment."

Her heart leaped into her throat "Do you know that for sure?"

He smiled and nodded. "She admitted it."

"But... *why?*" she breathed, in awe. "Why would she do that for *me?*"

"I just told you – she's always loved you. Sure, maybe not after we broke up the second time; but she told me what you said to her." When Julia stared blankly, he explained, "She said you told her that you loved me, but you knew you had lost me. That you weren't trying to get anything from me; you were just trying to help my family and save my business. And everything you did after that proved it was all out of self-less love. That's what changed her heart."

To Julia's dismay, her vision blurred, and tears spilled onto her cheeks before she could stop them. He took her hand and kissed it. Clasped it in both of his, and smiled down at her.

"Plus, she really, *really* wants to meet her grandson."

Julia laughed self-consciously and swiped at her tears. "I never used to blubber this much. I don't know when I became so tender-hearted. Can I blame it on having kids?"

He pulled her into him for a lingering kiss, until Diego came sniffing around their ankles, apparently bored with his canine companions. So William reluctantly released Julia, loaded a tennis ball into the dog ball launcher he had brought, and hurled volley after volley into the distance. After a while, Julia took a turn with the contraption.

William shifted his weight and gazed back out at the field, where Diego romped with his playmates again. "Mom wants to know if you and Robert and your whole family would like to come over on Mother's Day."

Julia gaped at him. "Really?"

"That invitation includes your sister, by the way. The Ochoas will be there, too. It starts at six, so I can be there after my Sunday trip."

Julia considered. "My dad will be working all day, as usual; and the rest of us usually have brunch at Dunphy's on Mother's Day. But I don't see why we can't come over in the evening. I'll check with my mom."

He nodded, and they fell silent for a couple of minutes. Then, quietly, she asked, "Will Mike be there?"

William's face darkened. "Kelly texted him an invitation, and after a few days he finally texted back. 'Sorry, I have to work.' That's all it said."

"I'm so sorry," Julia offered.

He shrugged, struggling in vain to look nonchalant. "Par for the course, these days."

"Maybe; but I can tell it still hurts you."

He sighed heavily. "It's probably for the best, anyway. I don't think he'd be very good at keeping the secret about Robert."

"Oh... speaking of which, will you be preparing the Ochoas for that little bombshell?"

"Pilar already knows. As for the rest of them... normally I'd say let's hold off for a while; but considering Robert is my clone, I'm not sure we can hide it."

Julia laughed. "Considering even Izumi figured it out at first glance, I suspect you're right."

William cast her a bemused look. "Izumi?"

She teased him with some playful side-eye. "Don't tell me you didn't notice."

"Notice what?"

"She spent the whole day shooting dirty looks at me." When William still stared blankly, Julia cackled. "You don't have to play coy. Anyone with eyes can tell Izumi's got it bad for you."

William gaped in consternation. "Izumi doesn't..." William's voice trailed off. "She's just my employee."

"Dude, I guarantee you could have scored so hard with her." Julia threaded her arm through his and winked up at him. "But too late now."

"Okay – whoa." He held up his hands for emphasis. "Let's get something clear here. I have not, nor will I ever score with Izumi. Or any other employee, for that matter. Plus," he added with his own wink, "Stephen already claimed dibs."

"She's a woman, not an auction item."

He laughed and planted a kiss on the top of her head, then on the lips. "You're a menace."

"You love it."

"I neither confirm nor deny."

It was her turn to chuckle; but she soon turned reflective. A heavy silence fell between them, broken only when William said, "I'll talk to the Ochoas after you go home tonight. To prepare them for Sunday."

Quietly, Julia said, "I guess we should talk about what to expect in the months ahead. And maybe get on the same page about some things."

William nodded knowingly.

"I'm not sure what you're hoping for," she added.

"What do you mean?"

"Well... for example, what kind of relationship do you want to have with Robert? What kind of support were you thinking of providing, if any?"

"I want to be his dad, with all that entails. Including support of every kind."

Julia and William still walked arm-in-arm, and she gave his arm a squeeze. "I figured, but I didn't just want to assume. And I want that for both of you, too. But I don't know yet how Kevin is going to react, or what he's going to want. He's been less involved in Robert's life over the past couple of years, but I know he still sees himself as Robert's dad, and he wouldn't want to just give that up."

"And I'm one hundred percent cool with that. Really," he added, at the wary look on Julia's face. "I know that's what's best for Robert, and ultimately that's all that matters. But... in the long run, I would like to be his dad, too. In every way I can. I hope we can figure out a way for him to have two dads, and for everyone to be okay with that, especially Robert."

Julia chewed her thumbnail and gazed out at the dog park without really seeing it. "We have to go about this as sensitively as possible. Which is why I think it would be helpful if you came along with me and Kevin to the appointments with our family therapist. Because I can't even begin to imagine how we're going to introduce this to Robert."

"Of course."

Diego came back with the ball, so Julia reloaded it into the launcher and hurtled it across the field. "And what about us?"

William turned to look at her now, his face sphinx-like. "I think I should let you lead the way on that. I feel like there's more at stake for you and the kids. For me, it's just my heart."

Her pulse hammering in her ears, Julia stepped toward him. She wrapped her arms around his waist, and he reciprocated.

"Your heart is my heart," she said softly, scanning his eyes with her own.

His forehead creased with some intense emotion. She pulled his face down to hers for a kiss, opening her mouth just before his lips and tongue met hers. She thought she heard him make a tiny sound low in his chest – barely more than a sigh. Like maybe the tentative way their tongues explored each other turned him on a little. Just as much as it turned *her* on.

The sleeping dragon was definitely making her wake-up noises.

When she finally broke the kiss, she murmured, "There's what my brain knows, and then there's what the rest of me wants."

"Well, as much as I'd like to start with the latter," he said knowingly, "let's start with your brain first."

She laughed. "Okay; so my brain tells me we should go through the whole process first. You know – meeting with the therapist and the lawyer, and looping Kevin and Robert into the news. Letting the kids spend plenty of time around you, and seeing how that works out. My brain knows there's so many things that can go awry in that process."

"All right. So far, my brain agrees with your brain."

She smiled up at him, shifting her arms tighter around his waist. "But the rest of me hears that it's going to take months to settle all those questions. And the rest of me is impatient."

His eyes gleamed. "Let me get this straight. By 'the rest of me,' what exactly are you referring to?"

She laughed again. "Well... my heart of course. And like I said, my heart is champing at the bit. My heart sees you as non-optional and non-negotiable, and to hell with any other consideration."

"Okay, my heart lines up with your heart on that, too. So are there any other parts that make up the rest of you?"

"I neither confirm nor deny."

His grin flashed before fading too quickly. Their arms were still looped around each other's waists. "Julie... please don't get me wrong – there's nothing I'd like better in this whole entire world than to take you back to my place and make love to you like there's no tomorrow. And I do mean absolutely nothing – except to make sure our relationship sticks this time."

Her heart galloped, and with his explicit admission, the sleeping dragon within her opened both eyes and stirred. And yet, at the same time, her stomach sank to hear him express the hesitation she also felt.

"You're right, of course," she admitted, "but that's not what I was hoping you would say."

He threw his head back in laughter, and as always, she watched the transformation it brought to his face with pleasure. Diego came bounding back with the tennis ball, perhaps thinking William's laughter meant playtime. Julia squatted to accept Diego's offering, and to pet him. William joined her shortly afterward.

After a while, he said softly, "I just really don't want to screw this up, Julie."

"Me neither. But also, I had a bit of an epiphany the other day. I realized my need to feel in control often had the opposite effect. Instead of increasing my happiness, it often interfered with it."

"What do you mean?"

"Well... like with you, for example. Not too long after you and I met, I told my Uncle Rob about you."

"You did?" His eyebrows lifted, and she thought he looked pleased.

"I told him I was afraid that falling in love with you would interfere with my plans to become a marine biologist. But he said, 'Don't be afraid of love. And don't compromise. If it's meant to be, the details will work themselves out.' And when I told him I didn't believe in 'meant to be,' he gave me something."

She stood up again, and beckoned William to do the same. After launching Diego's tennis ball, she reached into her jacket pocket and pulled out the polished, circular cross-section of watermelon tourmaline. After unwrapping it from its protective handkerchief, she handed it to William, who turned it over, examining it. It had a pink inner section, surrounded by a circle of white, surrounded in turn by an outer ring of green – just like a slice of watermelon.

"Uncle Rob said, 'You make your own magic. This will help.' I didn't get it at the time, but after Robert was born, I looked it up. Turns out, watermelon tourmaline is supposed to unblock the barriers to your heart. It's supposed to help bring balance. That's when I finally understood: Rob didn't want me to hand over my own power. He just wanted me to open my mind and heart to the unexpected, and make peace with the forces that were beyond my control.

William examined the stone some more, tracing his fingertip over its polished surface. Julia bent to accept the ball Diego had returned, and she hurled it back onto the field.

"It's beautiful," William said, holding the stone out to her.

But Julia shook her head. "I want you to have it now."

William's eyes flew open wide. "I can't take this from you. This is priceless."

She grabbed his hand and closed his fingers around the stone. "That's exactly why I want you to have it. That, and I don't think I'm going to need it. I think it's done its magic for me – at least for now."

WEDNESDAY, MAY 9, 2012

The next day, during her lunch hour, Julia realized with a gasp that, in all the excitement of the week, she had completely forgotten the kids would be Skyping with Kevin that Saturday. No doubt Robert would tell Kevin not only about their Tuesday whale watching trip, but the events of the entire week – almost all of which involved William. And Julia would never ask her kids to hide anything from their father.

"Where is my brain these days?" she groaned to her empty office, banging her forehead on her desk.

It's not like the kids Skyping with Kevin was unusual – it happened every Saturday. But Julia supposed she had been a bit... *distracted*... this past week. With mounting dread, she realized there was no way around it – she would have to tell Kevin about William before Saturday.

She immediately called her cousin Erin.

"Good afternoon; Whelan Family Law. How may I help you?" It was the receptionist, doing the same job Julia once did for Erin six years ago.

"Um... hi. This is Julia Beale. I'm Erin Whelan's cousin, and I'm also a client."

"Yes; hi, Ms. Beale! How can I help you?"

"Um... well, I have an appointment with Erin next Monday, but I have a fairly urgent issue I was hoping to discuss before this Saturday. I was wondering if it might be possible to squeeze in a quick phone call this week?"

The receptionist sucked an unpromising breath through her teeth. "I'm afraid Erin is super booked these days, Ms. Beale, but let me just check his calendar."

Julia's water bottle stalled in mid-air, halfway through its journey to her mouth. "Check... whose calendar?" When the receptionist hesitated, Julia set the water bottle back on her desk. "Sorry – I was talking about my cousin, Erin. Erin Whelan?"

Another beat. "That's who I was talking about, too."

Julia shook her head, as if to clear it. "I'm sorry... I thought you said '*his* calendar' a second ago."

After another few beats, during which Julia grew more and more impatient, the receptionist said breathlessly, "Ms. Beale... you know Erin is transitioning, right?"

Julia nearly had to stop her jaw from hitting the tabletop. "*What?!*"

A gasp reached Julia's ears across the ether. "Oh my God, you didn't know! But haven't you been working with him on your divorce?"

"That was finalized over six months ago."

"And you haven't talked to him since?"

"No," Julia conceded slowly. She thought back to the previous year, when she met her cousin so many times at his office. Other than the one time he briefly mentioned his divorce, he had never once let on to what he was going through. Julia's head was still reeling, and she flattened her palms on her desktop to steady herself. "If he's changed his pronouns, I'm surprised he hasn't changed his name."

The receptionist laughed. "He just spells it the boy way now!" When Julia stammered in confusion, the receptionist clarified, "A-a-r-o-n. I sent an email to all of his clients four months ago."

"I must have overlooked it," Julia murmured, her mind running a hundred directions at once as she listened to the receptionist's fingertips flying over her keyboard.

"Yeah, I'm afraid he doesn't have any openings at all between now and Monday," the receptionist confirmed, "but surely, as his cousin, you have an 'in' with him."

Julia considered her options. She had Aaron's personal cell phone number, but she didn't think it was right to presume upon their family relationship by texting him about her legal issues. Sure, Aaron was always friendly with Julia when they worked together and while Julia was his client. But they had never interacted outside of those situations – not even as family members.

Still, Julia felt nauseous at the prospect of talking to Kevin without first consulting Aaron.

The shop's doorbell sounded, alerting Julia to a customer, so she thanked Aaron's receptionist and hung up.

Emerging from her office, Julia found the gray-haired couple who dropped by every Wednesday to reminisce about Uncle Rob and Tim. Julia proudly displayed her uncles' memorabilia all over the shop. Mitch and José were among the lucky few to have survived the AIDS epidemic that decimated The Castro and claimed her uncles' lives. They always lingered for at least thirty minutes, and they never failed to buy something for their tank – to make it worth her while, they claimed.

"Taking a trip down memory lane with two people who remember my uncles? That's payment enough," Julia said every time; and they all got misty-eyed together.

After they left with their new artificial coral, Julia finished wiping her eyes, then finally ducked back into her office to call Aaron.

Just before it went to voicemail, the decidedly masculine voice on the other end answered, "Aaron Whelan speaking."

"Aaron!" She was so relieved he had picked up that she practically bellowed his name. "It's Julia. Beale. Your cousin."

"Yeah, I know. I have your name in my contacts, you know."

Julia gave a self-conscious laugh. The background noise told Julia he was in a car. "Are you driving? I can call you later."

"I have that newfangled Bluetooth in my car."

"Oh, right. I just... I wasn't sure if it was appropriate to call you about business on your cell; but now that I'm thinking about it, I guess it's not just business. I'm ashamed to admit I only found out about your transition a few minutes ago, from your receptionist."

"I'm sorry," he breathed out, as if mortified.

"No, *I'm* sorry. Your receptionist told me she sent an email to your clients, but I obviously overlooked it."

"I guess I should have called you personally. You're not just any client; you're family, and a friend."

Julia found that both surprising and flattering, since she and Aaron had never been close outside of work and business. But she said, "No worries! We all have busy lives. I haven't been good about keeping in touch, either."

"Well, maybe we should remedy that. I'd love to hang out sometime."

Her heart soaring, Julia beamed into the phone. "That would be fantastic. And congratulations, by the way!"

"Thank you." He seemed to be waiting for her to initiate the business part of the call. "So..."

Julia chuckled anxiously. "Yeah; so. Wait until you hear this."

"Uh-oh."

Julia cleared her throat. "So, um... William and I are back together."

A long pause. "*The* William?"

"The man himself. And now he knows about Robert."

"Oh, shit."

Julia gave another, rueful laugh. "That bad, huh?"

"More like a massive plot twist. So, wait – does Kevin know yet?"

"No."

"Good."

Wincing, Julia pinched the bridge of her nose. "But I think I should probably tell him today or tomorrow."

"Oh, God... why?"

"Because the kids have their weekly Skype call with Kevin on Saturday. And they kind of already know about William, too."

"Jesus, Julia!" he said, half teasing, half dismayed. "You have zero chill where that man is concerned."

Julia still ducked her head, as if Aaron could see her. "Please don't yell," she quipped. "I know it's less than ideal."

"Understatement of the decade. Do you mean to tell me Robert already knows that William is his biological father?"

"God, no! He just knows Will and I are together – dating – whatever." Grimacing again, she added, "*Buuut...*"

"Ah, yes; there's always a *but* with you, isn't there?"

"Paige does already know that William is Robert's biological dad. Apparently, Phoebe told her two years ago, when Paige was only eleven."

"Jesus effing Christ. Why the hell did Phoebe do that?"

After recounting Paige's story, Julia concluded with, "So I think it's important to tell Kevin before Saturday, because I'm not going to ask the kids to keep any secrets, and it's bound to come out during their Skype call. I mean, what are the odds that Robert won't tell him about our whale watching trip with William?"

"Jesus."

"It's a long story, Aaron, but take my word for it – Robert and William knowing each other wasn't one hundred percent in my control. The way William found out about Robert, and the way Robert met William... And then once they met each other–"

"Okay, whatever you say," he blurted with typical lawyerly impatience. Over her six years of working for attorneys, Julia had learned not to let it ruffle her. "So, you need to tell Kevin before Saturday."

"Yeah, but what are the legal implications?"

"Listen, I'm on my way to a meeting in West Portal, and the kids are with Dirk this week. If you can get away, would you like to discuss all this stuff over dinner somewhere?"

Julia perked up at the possibility, then sagged again when she remembered Robert had tee-ball practice every Wednesday. But she felt sure that, under the circumstances, her mother wouldn't mind bringing him. "Ever been to MacGowan's Irish Pub?"

"I've only heard the horror stories."

Julia gave a rueful laugh. "Meet you there at six."

MacGowan's, on Taraval, looked exactly the same, except the patrons were older and grayer. Walking in, Julia found the same wood-paneled bar in the center of the room; the same tired pool tables and dartboards to the left. The same mirrored Guinness and Murphy's signs, and the same raised stage in the back where she first heard William sing the song he wrote for her. The stage was empty at the moment, so U2 blared over the speakers instead.

Then there was the open doorway leading to the back room, for patrons who actually wanted to talk. Julia requested a table for two and took a seat facing the entrance to watch for her cousin. She ordered a pint of cider and tried to distract herself with her phone to quell her nervous fidgeting.

A minute later, there he was in the doorway between the two halves of the pub, scanning for Julia. A wave of nervous adrenaline surged into Julia's veins, but she smiled and waved until Aaron spotted her.

He wore a stiff social smile as he came forward, and Julia sensed he was gauging her reaction to seeing him post-transition for the first time. She rose from her seat and gave him a smile and a hug, as usual.

"Aaron. You look like a million bucks."

"Thanks. That's about what it cost."

After a moment to gauge if he was joking, Julia finally let herself laugh when his eyes sparkled. While he settled into the chair opposite hers, she surveyed him, from his neatly trimmed salt-and-pepper hair and day's-worth of stubble, to his perfectly tailored charcoal suit.

"Has anyone ever told you you're a dead-ringer for Daniel Day-Lewis?"

He gave a full-throated laugh. "Um... definitely not?"

"Work that," she said, winking. "How are the kids?"

"They're good. Rina's about to graduate from Davis, and Tula's about to graduate from high school."

Julia's jaw dropped. "You're kidding. Already?"

Aaron leaned back in his chair and crossed his ankle over his knee. "Believe it when they say it goes by fast."

Not for the first time, Julia reeled at the reminder that Paige would be an adult in less than five years. "I believe it. Where are they headed after graduation?"

"Rina has a job waiting for her with Dirk. And Tula's going to Cal, of course." Grinning, Aaron added, "Don't tell Holly."

The friendly rivalry between Aaron, a Berkeley grad, and their mutual cousin Holly, a Stanford alumnus, was legendary. Like the rivalry between Cal and Stanford, themselves. "And Theo? How old is he now?"

"Fifteen. All the changes have been hard on him, but he's getting there."

Julia murmured sympathetically. "But what about you, Aaron? How are *you* holding up?"

"You know, I'm okay. I don't have to tell you divorce is hard, but Dirk and I are moving through it. We've come out on the other side as better friends than ever. I have a loving family and supportive coworkers, and I know just how lucky I am. But I won't lie, it's still hard sometimes... and lonely."

Julia's heart squeezed in empathy. "Don't let yourself stay lonely. I still intend to hold you to your word."

He tilted his head. "My word?"

"About hanging out more often. I can even introduce you to William. You can see for yourself why I have zero chill where that man is concerned."

He rolled his eyes, but he was grinning. "Duly noted."

The server appeared to take Aaron's drink order and both of their food orders. After she left, Aaron folded his arms on the tabletop and pinned Julia's eyes with his. Julia recognized that look from her months of working for him. It was his *let's get down to brass tacks* look.

"Since you mentioned him, you know William has zero legal rights here, don't you?" he began.

"You mean paternity rights?" The little bit of legal research Julia had managed to conduct over the past few days had prepared her. "Yeah, I got that impression."

"Were you hoping for some other outcome?"

"I was hoping William would get a chance to know his son. To spend time with Robert and help raise him, and be a second dad to him. But can Kevin keep him from interacting with Robert?"

"Not during *your* custodial time, unless, of course, he can show that William is a danger to Robert."

"Well, he can't."

"But William would still have no legal rights of his own to Robert.

That means if you and William broke up again, and you decided you didn't want him to see Robert anymore, William would have no recourse. Depending on the circumstances, that might actually be a good thing. But it also means if, God forbid, you were to die while Robert was a minor, and Kevin wasn't inclined to allow William access to Robert, then William would still have no legal recourse."

Julia leaned back in her seat, fidgeting uneasily with her fingernails. "Okay, but let's say William and I got married someday. In that situation – if I die while Robert is a minor – would William have any recourse?"

"Not even then."

"Even though William is the biological father?"

"William's opportunity to establish himself as the *legal* father expired on Robert's second birthday. But since he didn't, and Kevin's name is on the birth certificate, Kevin is the father – period, end of statement."

"But William didn't even know about Robert's existence until now, much less that he was Robert's father."

Aaron sighed, unwrapped his silverware, and draped his napkin in his lap. "Listen, Julia... if you and William are really determined to establish him as the legal father and blow a ton of money and emotional energy on a long shot, William could argue before a court that you and Kevin willingly defrauded him. In other words, if it weren't for you and Kevin concealing Robert's true paternity, William would have stepped up and made a claim for custody. But even then, he'd almost certainly lose. And you can just imagine the potential ramifications for you and Kevin, being accused of fraud."

Julia twisted her own paper napkin into a tight rope. "Yeah, no, that sounds terrible."

After a beat or two, Aaron asked, "Have you stumbled across California Family Code Section 7611 yet?"

Julia frowned down at the tabletop. "Yeah."

"Then you already know – there's a presumption that if Kevin is on the birth certificate, he's the father. The presumed father has rights over the biological father, as long as he's the one who's been raising and supporting Robert all this time. And by the way, it also means Kevin can't get out of his obligations, including financial support."

"I don't see Kevin trying that; but then again, he's surprised me before."

"Well, if he did, he'd also lose his rights to Robert." After a moment's pause to allow it to sink in, Aaron gently added, "Kevin is the only dad Robert has ever known."

Julia sighed. "I know, and I don't want to interfere with their relationship; I really don't."

"On top of that, Robert and Paige have grown up together as siblings. If everyone can set aside their egos and come to terms with what's best for Robert, I think you should all agree that William is Robert's other dad, and he gets to spend time with Robert during your custodial time. It wouldn't be legally binding, of course, but as it stands, there's nothing Kevin can do about it. Now – *how* you do that? That's what a family therapist is for."

"Luckily, we already have one. Clio's the best."

After a moment's hesitation, Aaron added, "How do you think William will feel about having no rights here?"

"He already knows that's probably the case. And he also gets that Robert still needs Kevin in his life, and he's totally fine with it."

"Good. And how do you think Kevin will react to hearing that William is back in the picture?"

"No clue," Julia admitted. "I mean, now that we're divorced, he shouldn't see William as a romantic rival. I'm just not sure how threatened he'll feel, knowing William is Robert's biological dad. Or how much resentment he still feels over the relationship William and I had when he ran off to Brazil."

"I wish I could help you with that."

"Aaron, you've been super helpful. It sounds pretty cut and dried."

"Pretty much. But listen, keep me posted if any more questions come up – and for Christ's sake, don't go through my receptionist next time."

Julia grinned. "Okay, if you insist; but you may come to regret that offer."

Aaron grinned right back. "Okay, but if so, I'll just block your number."

THURSDAY, MAY 10, 2012

Thursdays were Julia's therapy days, literally and figuratively. Her individual therapy and parent coaching with Clio happened every Thursday at five-thirty. Julia had found Clio several months ago, after Paige's disastrous attempt to steal from Cardone's. It was a minor miracle when Julia managed to snag not just one, but two coveted weekly appointments with Clio – one for Paige, and one for herself.

Under Clio's guidance, Paige and Julia had both grown exponentially. So every Thursday, after closing the shop, Julia took the bus to the Mission. Clio's office was only a short walk from William's apartment.

After her session with Clio, it was another short walk to the studio on Valencia Street where she took her weekly dance class. And dance had become just as essential to Julia's mental health as Clio had. Thankfully, Julia's mother gladly took on childcare duty every Thursday so Julia could tend to herself in this way.

That Thursday, when Julia emerged from the bus and checked her phone, she found a text from William had come through while she had no reception.

Happy to meet up after your class. What
time? And would you like to meet at the
taquería?

Is 8:30 too late? If not, then ✅ to taquería.
☺

Never too late for you. See you at 8:30 at the
taquería.

Smiling privately to herself while she walked, Julia texted back a kiss emoji, then took a moment to savor his last two texts. Everything was still so new, and it still didn't feel real. It had only been five days since Julia thought she would never see him again.

A little past eight-thirty, Julia stepped through the open door of the taquería. William had already claimed a booth and was watching the doorway expectantly. When he spotted her, he rose and took a step forward, his eyes riveted to her, his mouth curving into an almost bashful smile. As she reached him, they exchanged a quick peck on the lips.

He guided her into the booth beside him, and they spent a few moments simply holding hands and smiling deliriously. Clearly he had showered after work, because he smelled delicious – something vaguely spicy, warm, and masculine that Julia couldn't place.

"You look…" His eyes swept over her, as if he might find the right word somewhere on her body. "…stunning."

Heat pooled between Julia's thighs. "I was just thinking the same thing. About you, I mean. In the dictionary under 'good enough to eat,' there's a picture of you." When he flushed, she turned toward the door and waved. "Bye-bye, filter."

He smirked. "What filter?"

"Touché. Sorry about that." She gave him another quick peck on the lips and started to scoot out of the booth to go order.

But he stopped her by tugging her closer and caressing her cheek with his thumb. "You know, you don't have to apologize for who you are. To me, or to anyone else."

Scrambling for a witty reply, Julia gave a breathy, nervous laugh, instead. But she gulped it back when he rested his palm on her cheek – a tender, steadying hand.

"I fell in love with you with no filter, and I still love you with no filter," he continued quietly. "So please, never apologize for who you are."

Swooning, Julie murmured, "If I promise not to maul you again, will you kiss me with tongues?"

With a soft laugh, he pulled her even closer and dipped his head, pausing just before their mouths met. "I thought you'd never ask."

The kiss was far from chaste, but not enough to get them kicked out of the taquería. Afterward, Julia went to order. When she returned, she said, "Sorry I was a little late. I took a few minutes to freshen up after class." Snuggling against him with her head on his shoulder, she added softly, "But I could never compete with how scrumptious you smell right now."

"I do?" His voice was a little deeper, his tone knowing.

"Mm-hmm." She took his hand in hers. "Even better than birria."

He laughed. "I've never been compared to birria and come out on top."

"So you're saying you've been compared to birria?"

"Come to think of it, no. That's a pretty original compliment."

With her head still on his shoulder, she threaded her fingers through his, and he stroked her hand with his thumb. The chaste caress sent electric impulses directly from her hand to her nether regions, leaving her speechless in their wake. Julia would never understand how such a tiny spark, delivered from this one man's fingers, could ignite her libido into a towering inferno. But she was beginning to seriously doubt her ability to keep her own touches chaste.

"This was your dance class, right?" asked William, his tone a bit husky now.

"Yeah. It's kind of my second therapy."

"Honestly, I get that. What kind of dance?"

"Bollywood."

His eyebrows lifted, and he smiled. "Why Bollywood?"

"I made a good friend in San Jose named Savreen. She's from India, and she dragged me along to her Bollywood lessons. It helped me rediscover my love for dance."

At that moment, an employee delivered their food. William squeezed Julia's hand once before releasing it, freeing her to gnaw off an impressive bite of taco; and she chewed while he smirked across the table at her.

"What?" she said around a mouthful of food.

"I'm just remembering what my brother Mike used to say about tacos."

"What?"

"Are you sure you really want to know? This is Mike we're talking about here."

"Against my better judgment? Yes."

He performed a fair impression of Mike's ape-like posture. "'If God didn't want man to eat pussy, why did he make it look like a taco?'"

In spite of the libido-killing impersonation, Julia's body threatened to spontaneously combust, knowing *that's* what William was imagining as he watched her eat. But she played it cool. "I could be wrong, but I'm pretty sure it was Bette Midler who said that first."

William laughed so hard, his face resembled a stop light. "Oh God, I hope so, because if I ever talk to that bastard again, I'm going to roast him so hard for quoting Bette Midler."

Julia couldn't help laughing with him – Mike quoting Bette Midler *was* hilariously out of character. But she still couldn't stop her nether regions from responding warmly to the mental image of William between her thighs, indulging his appetite for her with as much relish as she indulged in these tacos.

Finally, William unwrapped his burrito, and they spent a couple minutes eating in companionable silence – until she remembered. "I guess we should talk about what we came here for."

"You spoke with Aaron."

"Yes, and also with Clio, our family therapist." Wincing under the pressure of her nerves, Julia nevertheless plunged right in. "I need to break the news to Kevin before the kids talk to him on Saturday."

"You mean because the kids have already spent time around me?"

"Yes, and of course, I can't ask them to hide anything from their dad. Can't, and wouldn't." She shook her head in dismay. "I know the way the kids met you wasn't ideal, so I want to be as sensitive as possible in how I explain it to Kevin. Not just for his sake or mine, but for the kids' sake, too. I know that whatever helps Kevin's peace of mind also helps the kids."

"Will this change anything with Kevin's paternity rights, or mine?"

Julia recounted everything Aaron had told her the previous evening, wrapping up with, "So this is really just about telling Kevin we're back together, and that Robert will be spending time with you. All of that, plus ideally – eventually – I'd like to fold you into our family as Robert's other dad. That's not something that can happen overnight. Clio said we'll need to prepare Robert by having him spend plenty of time with you and me together. That way, he feels safe with you when we do finally tell him. And she also said when the time is right for that major conversation, it would be great if you, Kevin, and I all come to her office with Robert. Ideally, Kevin would tell Robert that he has permission to love both of his dads equally."

William nodded slowly, considering. "All of that makes perfect sense."

"But first things first – telling Kevin." At the mere thought of it, Julia suppressed a groan. "He usually has internet and cell phone access on Friday evenings, when he gets into town, so I thought I might call him tomorrow."

William's eyes drifted to the ceiling, and he rubbed his jaw. "What are you afraid will happen when you tell Kevin about this?"

"Honestly, I have no idea; but my worst fear is that he'll feel threatened, and sic his high-powered legal team on us."

"From what you said earlier, it sounds like Kevin has no control over whether I see Robert during your custodial time. But still, maybe you could start by reassuring him that neither of us wants to take Robert away from him – that he's still Robert's dad, he still has all the rights, and he'll still have just as much time with him. You can tell him I'm happy to work with all of you to come to an arrangement that includes me in Robert's life, but doesn't diminish Robert's relationship with Kevin."

Julia's heart fluttered at how evenly William discussed something undoubtedly very painful. "That sounds like a good plan."

"What kind of phone or internet service does Kevin have out there in the Galapagos?"

"By Galapagos standards, it's top-notch. I can't say his calls never drop, but not much more than they do here."

"That's good. You wouldn't want to lose the call in the middle of a conversation like that."

She squeezed his hand. "How are you feeling about all of this?"

"None of it really surprises me," he admitted. "Since I did have time to think about it and prepare, I'm okay. Maybe I'm still a tiny bit bummed on some level that I'll have no legal rights, where Robert is concerned; but honestly, I understand. It *is* what's best for Robert, assuming Kevin's been a good dad; but I guess..." He trailed off, and he tapped his foot beneath the cover of the table until he dragged his eyes back to hers. "I guess I'd be lying if I said I'm not a little sad right now."

Tiny cracks formed in Julia's heart, and her voice came out as a croak. "I can imagine a lot of reasons why you might feel that way, but I don't want to put words in your mouth."

After another moment's hesitation, he admitted, "Honestly, I'm just sad I missed out on being his first dad. His *only* dad."

Julia detected no resentment, and he didn't pull his hand away. Nevertheless, she prompted, "Only sad?"

Gently, he reassured her, "I'm not angry anymore, if that's what you mean."

"But if you were... I mean, even if it was just running in the background... that would still be completely valid. I hope you know I would understand."

"I've had to deal with some baggage, where Kevin is concerned. And not just because of this, but for years now, ever since..." Again, his voice trailed off, and she didn't miss the way he looked down at his left forearm – the one with the mermaid tattoo. His sleeve covered it at the moment, but he stared down at his arm as if he had X-ray vision.

Then his forehead creased, and he pushed his food aside.

Gently, Julia reached for his left arm, her eyes still riveted to his. For the moment he avoided her gaze, dragging his free hand over his mouth and beard. She pushed up the sleeve of the flannel shirt he wore unbuttoned over a T-shirt, exposing the mermaid on the underside of his forearm. He didn't draw back, so she gently stroked the skin over his tattoo. After a minute, he dragged his eyes back to hers. They were dry, but his forehead was still creased.

To Julia's horror, her throat constricted, and tears pricked at her eyes. She gulped down a breath, trying to stop them. "I'm sorry," she whispered.

"No, *I'm* sorry."

They gazed at each other a while, and then she pushed up the right sleeve of his flannel shirt. She ran her fingertips over the compass tattoo on the underside of that forearm, and he obligingly wriggled out of the flannel.

The flash of color on his bicep, peeking from beneath the hem of his short sleeve, caught her eye. She lifted the sleeve, exposing the new tattoo.

It was some kind of bird, stabbed straight through the center of its body with a knife. And a banner over it read *Avery*.

Julia's alarm must have registered plainly on her face, because William quickly explained, "It's a classic sailor tattoo – a swallow with a dagger. It's meant to commemorate a fallen comrade. I got it in memory of a fellow deckhand, Matt."

"Oh." Julia hesitated. "But... I mean... it says Avery."

William laughed awkwardly. "All of us on the boat called him that because there were two Matts in our crew. It can cause deadly mix-ups on deck if there's two guys with the same name, so each Matt had his own nickname."

In spite of herself, Julia couldn't help feeling relieved that Avery wasn't a woman. She quickly squashed that thought and asked, "How did he come by the nickname Avery?"

"His last name was Averyanoff, but the other guys were too lazy to learn to pronounce it. So they just shortened it to Avery."

Julia studied the tattoo again. It was quite beautiful, actually, with its intricately-graded shades of red, blue, and black.

Six years earlier, William showed her some photos he took during his years in Alaska; but he never spoke of his time there, or even of the people he met. Now, tentatively, Julia ventured, "And Matt passed away?"

William's face warped with some intense emotion. "The truth is, Matt pushed me out of the way of a falling crab pot. Those things are eight hundred pounds, you know. It only glanced me and fractured my skull – but it fell on him. Crushed him to death."

Julia put her hand to her mouth. "Will... you never told me."

"Because I had survivor's guilt for so long. I mean, I didn't cause the accident, but I still felt guilty that he lost his life saving mine. He had Ash to support, and I had no one."

His voice trailed off, and she clasped his hand in both of hers. "Ash?"

"Matt's son. Actually, Ash is the son of *two* good friends of mine."

At a loss, Julia waited for him to elaborate. Finally, after a tense silence, William added, "It, um... it has to do with a relationship I had. It was after you and I broke up the first time, back in '95."

Slowly, Julia nodded her understanding. Whatever William saw in her face must have reassured him.

"My first sort-of girlfriend after that was my tattoo artist."

"Oh," Julia blurted, and he shot her an uneasy look. "No, it's okay. I just hadn't pictured your tattoo artist as a woman. Please – go on."

He shifted his weight in his seat. "Well, after I kind of spiraled downward – you know, with the alcohol and so forth – Haze is the one who suggested I go to Alaska to work on the fishing boats."

Julia raised an eyebrow. "Haze?"

"Well, that's not her real name," William laughed. "It's Serafima. But everybody used to call her Haze. She lived up there in Alaska for a while. That's where she met Matt – Ash's dad. By the time Haze and I dated, she and Matt were divorced, but Haze was the one who suggested I get a job with Matt on one of the sober boats up in Alaska."

Julia gave a short laugh. "The sober boats?"

"Yeah, that's what we called them," he said, chuckling awkwardly. "Boats run by captains who were teetotalers. That way, I wouldn't be tempted back into some bad old habits. And during my five years in Alaska, Matt became a very good friend. He was my best friend, in fact."

"Jesus," murmured Julia. "I had no clue."

Blinking, he took a moment to collect himself, then quietly continued. "After Matt died – after I came back to California – Haze and I reconnected for a while; but sadly, it was really Ash that I loved. Not in some weird way," he added hastily, with a self-conscious laugh. "I just mean I loved that kid like my own son. Still do. But I couldn't keep stringing Haze along when I didn't care for her like she deserved. After that, she moved to Alaska again so Ash could grow up closer to his dad's family."

Julia turned her eyes down to his swallow tattoo, running her hand along it again. "Did Haze give this to you?"

William nodded, and Julia's mouth twisted into a coy smile as an idea occurred to her. Without warning, she shifted herself onto his lap, straddling him. She paused just long enough to enjoy the stunned look on his face before shifting out again, this time settling on his left side.

He shot her a look of complete consternation. "What are you up to?"

But she refused to answer – she just grinned and took his left arm. Touched the mermaid tattoo on the underside of his forearm. Ran her fingers across it.

"Oh, I see now," he said softly, and her pulse stirred at his knowing tone.

He watched her keenly as she kissed her way up his forearm and ran her hand along his bicep. She slipped her fingers beneath the hem of his shirt sleeve and lifted it, exposing the new tattoo on his left bicep.

A red rose, blooming from a green stem with leaves and red thorns. And a dagger plunged through the heart of the rose.

But now that Julia looked carefully, the rose itself was vaguely in the shape of a heart. A single petal dropped from it, and that was the flash of red she had seen below the hem of his sleeve. But again, as she looked closer, the falling petal could also have been a drop of blood.

Her own heart aching with regret and longing, Julia shamelessly ran her hand over his rose-heart. Traced its outlines with her fingertip, and planted kisses along them.

William dipped his head, bringing his face that much closer to hers. After a minute, he touched her chin, tilting her face up. He hesitated just long enough to catch her eye before nudging her mouth open, his tongue lightly skimming hers. When he broke away, his mouth still hovered over hers, his breath warm on her lips; and he stroked her hair with his hand.

Her pulse stampeded out of control – she remembered that wolfish look all too well.

After a moment, William said, "Let's get out of here."

"Where would we go?"

The obvious answer was *his place*. She knew that; and from the way he hesitated, she knew he did, too.

"We could," she whispered.

He swallowed past the lump in his throat. "It's very tempting, but at the moment, I'm probably not thinking with the right head." He leaned into her again, lightly tangling his fingertips in her hair. "But I do know one thing, Julie – you deserve better."

She frowned. "What do you mean?"

"I mean you deserve an entire night in a nice, warm, comfortable bed," he continued gently. "And a shower, and a kitchen where I can make you breakfast. You deserve better than getting bent over the back of my couch and leaving fifteen minutes later. Especially for our first time."

Her heart swelled, then dissolved into a puddle of goo. "Okay, fair enough. But consider this a deposit. I reserve the right to get bent in the future, and it had better be over your couch. A voucher for a coucher."

He groaned, but humored her with a pity-laugh. "Deal. Just show me where to sign."

She winked. "Oh, I will."

"Did you drive here?" he asked.

"No, I took the bus from my shop. I have a dedicated spot there, and it's free."

His eyes widened. "You weren't planning to take the bus back, were you?"

"Why not?"

"Well, I mean... taking the bus at this time of night?"

"*You* do it."

"Yeah, but..."

"Oh, I see. 'Yeah, but I'm a man.'" She winked so he would know she was only teasing. "What, you don't think I can handle the crazy?"

"I just think you have no idea what level of crazy you're talking about," he said, snickering uneasily.

"I do this every Thursday, you know."

"That doesn't mean you should."

"Oh, come on; it's not that bad! Not anymore."

"Some areas have gentrified, but let's put it this way – any time I come home after dark, I have to run the gauntlet of the working girls at the end of my block. They usually congregate in front of one of the meth houses. Emphasis on *one* of the meth houses."

Somehow, Julia was actually laughing now, when only a few minutes ago, she had been on the verge of tears. At the sight of it, William's face softened.

"I'll come with you," he said. "For the sheer entertainment value. We can bring our food with us. And then, if you don't mind, you can drive me back to my place."

FRIDAY, MAY 11, 2012

The Galapagos Islands were one hour ahead of Pacific Time, and Julia knew Kevin usually got into town every Friday around four o'clock. From his hotel room there, he Skyped with the kids every Saturday.

But this Friday, she waited until five o'clock Galapagos Time to give him a chance to settle in, and then she placed the call.

"Hey." Since their divorce, his tone was always flat and neutral when he picked up her calls.

"Hey. How's it going?"

"Fine. Just getting ready to grab dinner. What's up?"

He knew she never called on Fridays unless she had some urgent business with either their lawyers or their kids. "Um, well... do you have a few minutes, or would you rather eat first?"

"That bad, huh?" he said drily.

Julia gave an awkward laugh. "I hope not."

"Okay, shoot."

"There's something I need to tell you before you talk to the kids tomorrow."

"What did Paige do this time?"

Again, she coughed out a nervous laugh. "It's not about Paige. Well

– I guess it is, kind of; but it's not anything she's done. She's doing pretty well, actually. I think Clio and the school are really helping," she added.

"So what's up?" Still all business.

She drew a deep breath for courage. "What I'm about to tell you changes nothing for the worse, where you and the kids are concerned. And I really hope it changes nothing between us, in terms of co-parenting. At least, from my perspective, it doesn't." Then she winced at how condescending and patronizing it sounded, coming out of her mouth. It had sounded so good in her head while rehearsing it, over and over, all day long.

Kevin's slightly sharper tone confirmed her fears as he replied, "Sure, Julia, but I think you should just say what you called to say. No need to soften any blows, if that's what you're worried about. I'm used to it by now."

She ignored his passive-aggressive jab, as well as the twinge of annoyance it triggered. "What I wanted to tell you is, William and I are in a relationship."

Silence.

Julia squeezed her eyes shut, grimacing in actual, physical pain as she waited for the other shoe to drop. In fact, she waited so long that she glanced at her phone screen, worried that the call had dropped. "Are you there?"

"I assume you mean *the* William, right?" His voice was calm. Deadly calm. The calm before a storm.

"Yes."

Another silence. "And I assume the only reason you needed to tell me this before I talk to the kids tomorrow is because they've already met him."

"Yes, but that happened by accident."

He gave a single, rueful laugh. "How does something like that happen by accident?"

Julia cringed. "What I mean is, I didn't plan for them to meet that way."

"What way?" She didn't miss the slight uptick of agitation in his tone. He didn't have to say anything – she knew he was imagining that they had caught Julia and William in bed together. Just as Paige had, six years ago.

After Julia and Kevin reconciled, Paige came to him one day, asking why Mommy didn't want her to know that Daddy had come home. That's how it all came out – while Kevin was still missing in Brazil, Paige had stumbled upon Julia and William in bed together. In the darkness, Paige assumed that her father had finally come home. Julia tried to somehow convince Paige that it wasn't her father, without admitting to what Paige had really seen.

When Kevin heard the story from Paige, it strained things between him and Julia irreparably.

Despite the jab of defensiveness in her chest, Julia understood his anger – she really did. Besides serving as the nail in the coffin of her marriage, the whole incident hurt and confused Paige, and damaged her trust in her parents. If Julia had been stronger – if she had been able to resist the tiny sliver of comfort and joy William offered during a time when darkness swallowed her whole; or even if she had just found a way to be honest with Paige about what she saw – maybe she could have headed off at least some of Paige's suffering.

It was one of her greatest mistakes in life, and her greatest regret as a parent. It had taken Julia six years of therapy to stop self-flagellating, if only to free up enough headspace to make things right for Paige.

But these days, if Julia lacked anything in the self-flagellation department, Kevin supplied the difference. It took all her internal strength to pull herself together and explain as calmly as possible how the kids managed to meet William *by accident*.

When she finished, Kevin spat out, "So let me guess: Robert already knows that William is his *real* dad."

"No, of course not."

"But William knows about Robert," he continued, his tone still strained.

"Yes, but–"

"And you couldn't have just asked to meet him somewhere else? Maybe another day, or another time? You had to actually invite him into the house, with our kids?"

She cringed. "I know, but I wasn't thinking clearly in that moment. I was shocked, and overwhelmed."

Kevin scoffed. "Is that something you do? Let random people come into your house with the kids when you're shocked and overwhelmed?"

In spite of herself, Julia's brows pinched and her fingernails dug into her palms, but she was determined not to dignify that with a reply.

"I'm sure William was shocked, too," Kevin persisted, "when he discovered we had been keeping his son from him all these years. I'm sure he has no feelings about that whatsoever."

She forced her tone to remain placid. "Kevin, you have all the rights, where Robert is concerned. William knows that, and he gets it, and he agrees that's what's best for Robert."

"Yeah, because he has no other option. If he did—"

"Neither of us wants to interfere with your relationship with Robert. You're his dad, Kevin, and he needs you in his life. The last thing any of us wants is to hurt Robert." He had no immediate response to this, so she gently added, "You'll still have every bit as much time with him as you ever did. And like I said earlier, you have all the legal rights."

"So now what?" demanded Kevin. "How are we supposed to explain this to Robert? Or are we just going to keep hiding the truth from him for the rest of his life?"

"No."

"So what, then? Does William get to be 'Dad Two' now? Or no – I bet he gets 'Dad One' status, and I'm number two, right?"

She closed her eyes and drew a deep breath through her nose so she wouldn't raise her voice against his petulance. "You're still Daddy to Robert, and you always will be. But Clio has some ideas about how we can all work together to make this as smooth as possible for Robert. To start with, she'd like to give you a call and talk with you. Would that be okay?"

He gave a huff. "Why not? Just know I'll be consulting my own people, too."

"I understand."

"Good." Another long silence followed. Then he let out yet another heavy sigh, but this one was longer – softer. Like sadness. "I guess I always knew this would happen... you and William, I mean."

She hummed, wondering how he could know a thing like that; but she was afraid to poke the bear by asking.

"I'm just surprised it took seven whole months. I figured he'd be back in your bed as soon as the ink was dry on our divorce. From the very beginning, I knew I was your honorable mention. He was always the grand prize."

Julia clamped her lips together, even as her hackles rose.

"You're a walking Crystal Gayle song, Julia," he persisted. "You talk in your sleep."

At least his tone wasn't dickish anymore. In fact, it was just the opposite. It was almost... compassionate.

Another long silence followed before he quietly continued. "The first time you came to me – you know, in the hotel room, after your grandmother died... I had wanted that for so long. Aside from the day Paige was born, I still count that as the best day of my life. And then you came to me again and told me that perfect day had made us parents."

At his confession, the floor dropped out from underneath her. Tears pricked Julia's eyes as a tidal wave of sadness, remorse, and compassion nearly drowned her. That was not at all what she had expected him to say.

"Kevin..."

She felt like the worst person on the planet because she had never been able to reciprocate the love he felt for her – at least, not to the same degree. And it hadn't been for lack of trying. She had desperately tried to convince herself that she was over William after her attempt at reconciliation – the letter she sent him in Alaska – came back marked, "Return to Sender."

She had sent it in December of 1996, after learning he had gone to work on the crab boats. Her abject terror for his safety drove home just how far she was from being over him. But when her letter came back, she assumed he didn't want to hear from her anymore.

In retrospect, Julia knew now that she had been depressed. The uncles and grandmother who had truly raised her were gone. She still woke up a few nights a week with William's name on her lips. Neither Santa Barbara nor the marine biology field turned out as expected, her GPA was in free-fall, and every grad school she applied to rejected her.

So when her grandmother passed away in March of 1996, Kevin drove her all the way from Santa Barbara and accompanied her to the funeral. Kevin had comforted her so sweetly, and she needed comfort then, more than anything else. Which is why she came back with him to his hotel room, even though she hadn't been on the pill in over two years.

When she missed a period and started vomiting a month after Gran's funeral, it was all too easy. Kevin was already her best friend in Santa Barbara. They were both marine biology students, they both loved aquariums, and they both grew up Catholic in the Bay Area. Julia didn't feel the spark for Kevin that she had for William, but with a foundation like theirs, she figured it was only a matter of time. So she walked the stage in June to accept her diploma, and then a week later she walked to the altar to accept Kevin's ring.

But she still kept William's modest diamond in that shoebox, along with the mermaid necklace he had given her. And all the therapy and couple's counseling in the world couldn't transform Kevin into someone who spoke her love languages – who soothed her spirit or sent it rocketing into the cosmos.

And now, all she could think to offer him was a pathetic, "I'm sorry."

"Not nearly as sorry as I am for failing you and Paige. I'm the one who ran away when the going got tough. But at the same time…" She listened to his uneven breathing as he grappled for words. "The couples' counselor taught us to use I-statements, so I'm going to use my I-statements now."

Julia gave a short, joyless laugh and waited, her stomach sour with dread.

"The first time I heard you say his name in your sleep, I wanted to die," he continued. "I wish I could say I'm being melodramatic, but there were only two things that stopped me then, and every time since then. One was Paige. And the other was the hope that maybe one day, I would be enough for you. But every time I heard you say his name, or I watched you close your eyes and knew you were thinking of him, my heart died a little more. So I may seem angry, Julia, and I guess I am. But at the root of it all is this love I once had."

The tears poured down Julia's cheeks now. But once again, all she could think to say was, "I'm so sorry, Kevin."

And then her heart cracked open a little more to hear him sniffing on the other end of the line – to hear his voice break as he said, "I'll talk to Clio, and I'll do the right thing for the kids. I love both of them, equally."

"I know you do." And she really did.

On Saturday morning, Julia took Robert to his T-ball game, and after lunch, Julia gave the kids privacy while they Skyped with Kevin. But afterward, during their weekly aquarium maintenance, Paige confirmed that sure enough, Robert spilled everything about the whale-watching trip and Mom's new boyfriend, William.

Internally cringing, Julia set aside the weekly water testing supplies. "Do you want to talk about it?"

Paige continued siphoning detritus from the bottom of the tank. "Dad handled it fine, I guess. I could tell he wasn't thrilled, and he changed the subject as soon as possible."

Julia nodded. Then she scanned her daughter's face for any sign of trouble. About ten minutes into the Skype call, Julia had taken Robert aside so Paige and Kevin could talk privately about everything that had happened in 2006, and about Phoebe's revelation of Robert's paternity. But now, after that conversation, Paige's face seemed placid enough – a hopeful sign.

Of course, that could have been because Paige loved working with Julia on the aquarium, almost as much as she loved painting. In fact, she derived a lot of inspiration for her art from it, since both the aquarium and her easel were in the den.

"How did your own conversation with your dad go?" Julia tried.

"Okay, I guess."

When Paige didn't elaborate, Julia prompted, "How are you feeling about it right now?"

"Fine." Before Julia could probe any further, Paige suddenly straightened, still holding the bulb syringe she was using to clean debris from the sand. "Oh, guess what? Dad says he'll be home from the Galapagos in time to take me and Robert for the Memorial Day weekend!"

"Oh," said Julia in genuine surprise. Kevin had not mentioned anything about that on the phone yesterday; but then again, given their conversation, maybe it was no wonder it had slipped his mind.

"Now we won't have to stay with Grandma Beale." Paige's grimace signaled how she felt these days about her monthly visits with Kevin's parents. "Dad's going to fly up to get us on Friday morning, and then fly us home Monday afternoon."

Thanks for running that by me first, Kevin. But Paige's revelation reminded Julia – she would have all of Memorial Day weekend to herself.

"That should work just fine." *Just fine indeed.*

After the weekly aquarium maintenance, the business of preparing for dinner distracted Julia even further. William would come over that evening with the salmon from Cardone's. In the meantime, Julia and the kids harvested green beans, shallots, and herbs from her mother's garden. Then Robert accompanied Julia to the farmer's market to buy cherry tomatoes, since they weren't bearing fruit yet in her mother's foggy garden. By the time they got home, there was only enough time to start prepping the vegetables before William was due, at five. And William was the most punctual person she had ever known – nothing filled him with more existential dread than running late.

Sure enough, at five on the dot, the doorbell rang. Robert dropped his kid-safe knife and hopped down from his stepstool by the kitchen counter, where he had been chopping basil. "Diego! Diego! It's Diego!"

As he careened from the kitchen, Julia laughed and called out, "Hey, come back here! You know you're not supposed to answer the door yourself. Besides, you look like a Martian, with all that basil juice on your hands."

Robert begrudgingly returned. "Hurry, Mommy, before Diego leaves!"

She chuckled, and after they finished wiping their hands, they went together to the front door. There was William, his guitar slung across his back, bearing a brown-paper-wrapped package. Diego sat alongside him, his tongue lolling from his mouth.

Without so much as a hello to William, Robert dropped to his knees and threw his arms around Diego. Paige came bounding down the stairs and brushed past both Julia and William to join her brother.

William grinned at Julia. "Who's chopped liver now?"

"Guys," Julia admonished. "Did we forget that manners are also for people, not just dogs?"

Both Paige and Robert laughed their apologies and greetings to William, then turned their attention right back to Diego.

"It's okay; I agree – Diego is much more interesting," laughed William, handing the package over to Julia. "First catch of the season, fresh off Uncle Frank's boat."

"Is he still fishing?" marveled Julia, ushering him into the house, followed by Diego and the kids.

"Of course. He'll never pack it in. Besides, he's not that old."

"William," interrupted Paige, "can we bring Diego out back to the patio? Grandma's out there, too."

William assented, and while Julia closed and locked the front door, he unleashed Diego and retrieved the dog toys from his backpack.

After the kids and Diego went out back, Julia beckoned William upstairs. "I'm just getting dinner ready. Wanna keep me company?"

"I can do better than that. Give me a job."

In the kitchen, Julia showed William where her father kept his filleting knife, and William got right to work on the salmon.

"What's for dinner?" he asked.

"Oh, it's this one-pan salmon dish I make, with orzo." Holding up one of the glass prep bowls, she added, "Tomatoes are involved."

Laughing softly, he set down the filleting knife and came to give her a peck on the lips. "You know me too well."

She beamed up at him, but judged it best not to distract him any further – not with sharp kitchen implements and open flames nearby.

"Back to work, chef. The kids get hangry if I serve dinner much later than six."

After Julia plated dinner, William carried them out to the patio table. By the time Julia brought her own plate downstairs, Paige and William still lingered in the in-law unit, where he marveled over Paige's latest artistic endeavor, still drying on her easel. It was an oil painting of the splendid dottyback in their aquarium.

Spotting Julia, William said, "You told me Paige is talented, but I had no idea you meant *this* talented."

"Every bit of artwork in this room is something she painted," Julia replied.

Wide-eyed, William crossed the room to the framed serigraph of an octopus. "Paige... you made this?"

"Yeah. I actually prefer making serigraphs over this kind of stuff," Paige said, gesturing to her easel.

"She's won tons of awards," Julia added, "and she already has some of her art in galleries around the city."

"I've even sold four pieces," Paige admitted.

"This is incredible." William turned to Paige as if she had just leveled up yet another notch in his esteem. "But doesn't it take special equipment to make serigraphs?"

"Yeah, but it's too messy and takes up too much space, so I make my serigraphs at Aunt Brigid's studio."

William gave a quizzical tip of the head. "Aunt Brigid?"

"Yeah, she's..." Frowning, Paige turned to Julia. "Mom, how is she my aunt, again?"

"She's your grandpa's sister," Julia clarified, "so technically, she's your great-aunt." For William's benefit, Julia added, "She's also my cousin Aaron's mom."

"She runs this amazing art studio and teaches all these different classes," Paige added. "We have a monthly membership."

"I'm always amazed at people who have artistic gifts like yours," William replied.

"Oh, come on – you're a brilliant photographer," Julia pointed out.

"But photography is a completely different art form. I'm talking about people who can see something so clearly in their mind, or even just bring it to life from a model in front of them. My brother Mike can do that, but I draw like a four-year-old."

"You and me both," Julia laughed.

At her mother's prompting, the three of them filed out to join her and Robert at the patio table. Diego came to sit patiently at Robert's feet, poised to salvage any errant food scraps. He had learned quickly during his previous visit who his most likely supplier would be.

Julia's mother poured wine for herself and Julia. William spent a while catching up with Robert, who regaled him with a play-by-play of his tee-ball team's victory that morning. William listened attentively and celebrated Robet's home run with a high-five, then prompted him to take a breath just long enough to sneak in one bite of dinner.

While Robert chewed, William turned to Julia's mother. "I take it Paul is at work?"

"Oh yes," Julia's mother replied. "I keep suggesting that maybe it's time to retire, but he says when you retire is when you die."

William gave a short laugh. "How does he figure that?"

"Oh, who knows," Julia's mother replied with an exaggerated wave of her hand. "So then I nag him to hurry up and hire a new sous chef so at least he can take off Saturdays, as well as Sundays. But he keeps saying he can't find anyone good enough; and besides, he insists the head chef is the one who's supposed to work on Saturdays, not the sous."

"He's not wrong," Julia interjected.

"I know that, dear. You may remember, I helped him run that restaurant for over forty years," her mother snapped. To William, she added, "Maybe he'll listen to you if you try to talk some sense into him."

William got that deer-in-the-headlights look, so Julia intervened. "Mom, Dad's ego makes Gordon Ramsay look like the Dalai Lama. If *you* can't even get through to him, how is William supposed to?"

"Because I'm merely his wife," she retorted sardonically before once again giving a dismissive wave of her hand. "Anyway, how is your mother doing, William?"

Recovering from the whiplash of the abrupt subject change, William replied, "She's hanging in there. Still processing through the stages of grief. Now that it's been two months, people aren't visiting as often, so she has more time to sit and stew on it."

"My goodness, has it already been two months since your father passed away?"

"Yeah; it was March 8th."

Julia's mother clicked her tongue in dismay. "Well then, I'm glad we're going over there tomorrow. I'm long overdue for a visit."

"I'm sure she'll enjoy that. Kelly and I have been trying to give her the space she needs to grieve, but at the same time we encourage her to stay active, at least a little. But I have a feeling something is going on, because when I came over today, I saw a lot of taped-up moving boxes in the living room."

"Oh," Julia's mother said, breathless. "Is she moving to Treemont already?"

"I don't know. She was pretty evasive when I asked about it."

Julia couldn't help noticing her mother's distraught look, and she reached across the table for her hand. "It's okay, Mom; even if she's moving, it's only a mile or two away."

Julia's mother set her fork down, and her chin quivered. "I know; I just can't help feeling like it's the last straw. The last of the old guard, abandoning this neighborhood. We're the lone holdouts now."

Julia glanced at William, who wore a sheepish look – he hadn't known the topic would upset Julia's mother. Julia offered him a faint smile of reassurance.

"Mrs. Dunphy, I know Mom would love to have you over as soon as possible," William interjected. "And you know she's never stood on formality, especially with her good friends; so you can drop by any time you want."

"And besides, Mom – you and Dad aren't the 'lone holdouts' around here. There's Diane, and the Vecchios, and–"

"I know, I know," her mother grumbled. "I just remember when you and Alison were kids, you would run in and out of each other's houses. The doors were always open. And now, everybody's doors are closed, and nobody around here even speaks English anymore..."

Julia's mother dissolved into tears, much to her grandchildren's shock. Julia did her best to hide her annoyance, while at the same time refusing to dignify her mother's racism and xenophobia by pointing out that young white families were starting to move back into the neighborhood. Besides, her mother would just argue they weren't the right kind of white families. And if you asked her what *that* meant, she would answer with some variation on "good, wholesome, practicing Catholics."

For Julia's aging, increasingly frail mother, change was terrifying. Julia knew her mother was grieving the monthly, sometimes weekly loss of lifelong friends – some by distance, others by death. Friends whose children she had practically helped raise, and who had helped raise hers. Friends she had gone to church with and played bridge with for fifty years or more. Whose weddings, baptisms, and now funerals she attended.

Robert climbed out of his chair and rounded the table to wrap his arms around his grandmother's neck. "Don't cry, Grandma. If you're lonely, Jacob will talk to you."

Through her tears, Julia's mother gave Robert a quizzical look. "Jacob?"

"He lives across the street, and he's almost a grownup."

Smirking, Julia clarified, "He's in Kindergarten."

Julia's mother gave a ragged laugh and blew her nose into her napkin. Then she tugged Robert into her lap. "Okay, little Tadpole – I'd love to meet Jacob. But we should introduce ourselves to his parents first."

Julia figured it wasn't the best time to mention that Jacob's parents didn't speak English. "Mom, no matter what happens with friends and neighbors, Alison and I will always be right here in the city. We're not going anywhere."

William cleared his throat. "Mrs. Dunphy–"

"Karen," Julia's mother corrected, wiping her eyes and nose on her napkin. "You know you don't have to call me Mrs. Dunphy anymore, William. You're an adult now, and you're practically family."

He and Julia exchanged bashful glances before he continued, "Then maybe you'll understand why that goes for me, too – if you or Paul need anything, I'm at your service. I'm positive I can speak for my sister Kelly, too. She's staying put, and she's only three blocks away."

"I know, kids. I'm sorry," admitted Julia's mother. "I didn't mean to break down in front of everyone."

Julia took her mother's hand and squeezed it. "It's okay, Mom."

Her mother squeezed Julia's hand right back. Then, glancing around at the tabletop, she heaved herself to her feet. "Whoops! You forgot the saltshaker, Paige."

"I'll get it, Mom." Julia started to stand, but with a faint wink, her mother stopped her with a firm hand on her shoulder. Julia got the message: her mother just needed a minute to collect herself. After her mother retreated into the house, Julia lifted her eyes to William's, and they offered each other an apologetic little wince.

Straightening in his seat, William cleared his throat and said, "Hey, guys, guess what I saw today on the boat?"

He recounted how a mother and baby gray whale swam right up to his boat. Paige and Robert both bemoaned that it hadn't happened on their Tuesday excursion, so William retrieved his phone to show them a video one of his customers shared. As the kids watched, he looked up and caught Julia's eye. She offered him a grateful smile, and his eyes softened and lingered for several long seconds. Once again, Julia's cheeks flushed with heat – but this time, it wasn't from embarrassment.

Until Robert brought the moment to a screeching halt. "Hey Mommy, do baby whales come out of their mommy's blowhole?"

SUNDAY, MAY 13, 2012

Other's Day began like any other Sunday. Julia woke at six, before the kids, to practice the latest Bollywood dance steps she had learned. Her father had long since left to get Dunphy's up and running for Mother's Day. So at seven, after a quick shower, Julia made a pot of oatmeal – just enough to tide them over until brunch.

Julia startled when her mother appeared in the kitchen, her puffy eyelids and yawn betraying that she had just woken up.

"Oh, you're awake," Julia commented, heading straight for the coffee maker to brew a cup for her mother. Even in retirement, her mother had retained her night-owl tendencies from working in the restaurant. She usually didn't get up until nine.

Julia's mother dropped heavily into the banquette seat at the kitchen table. "I decided to attend the early Mass, since brunch is at eleven." Shuffling some papers on the kitchen table, she added, ever-so-casually, "Maybe Robert and Paige would like to go with me? Give you some time to yourself?"

Julia shot her a good-natured stink eye. Her mother had never quite given up hope of bringing Julia back into the fold; and if not Julia, then at least the kids.

"All right, all right. Hope springs eternal," her mother conceded, chuckling. "Did you know Paige is already up and painting?"

"Really?" Julia considered a moment. "She must have woken up and gone downstairs while I was in the shower."

"She's really excited about her new painting."

Julia poured the coffee, then delivered her mother's mug to the table. "It's a good one. Will was kind of blown away when he saw it."

Julia didn't want the oatmeal to get any colder, so she went downstairs to wake Robert and announce that breakfast was ready. From there, the nauseous quivering in her stomach over their post-brunch visit with the Quinns crowded out all other thoughts.

Julia took particular care with her appearance that day – curling her hair and swiping a fresh coat of paint on her toenails. Putting on a tad more makeup than her usual lip gloss, eyebrow pencil, and mascara. Choosing the most spring-like thing in her wardrobe – a white sundress with a full skirt and a pattern of large rosettes – and pairing it with silver metallic kitten heels. And of course, for extra warmth against the San Francisco fog, she topped it off with a light cashmere cardigan, a straw cloche hat, and a rose-colored silk scarf.

When Julia came downstairs to inspect Robert's sartorial choices, she found him in full pirate costume, playing with his Beyblades. Before she could say anything, he looked up at her with wide blue eyes. "Wow, Mommy, you're so pretty!"

Her heart melting, she lowered herself carefully to the rug beside him and squeezed him around the shoulders. "Thank you, Tadpole! You look pretty *arrrrgh-mazing*, yourself." He giggled and *arrrrgh-ed* back at her, and she added, "You're wearing that to brunch?"

"Yep."

"Hmm..." *Well, why not?* "Good choice for a seafood restaurant."

Paige emerged from the bathroom, and Julia sucked in a sharp breath. Paige had streaked her choppy dark hair with magenta dye and rimmed her eyes with heavy black eyeliner. She had pulled on a slashed-up pair of black skinny jeans and Doc Martens, and wore a black pleather jacket over a magenta tank top that clung to her curves. Not only that, what looked like a silver hoop glinted against her right nostril.

The expression in Paige' eyes as they locked on Julia's was an unspoken challenge. But Clio's endless refrain looped through Julia's consciousness – *pick your battles.*

So even as Robert's *whoa* jerked Julia out of her stupor, she cleared her throat and calmly said, "Did you pierce it, or is that one of those clip-on things?"

"Clip-on," Paige mumbled, sniffing as she strode casually through the den and back upstairs.

It would be an interesting brunch at Dunphy's, with both Captain Jack Sparrow and Nancy Downs from *The Craft*. And it would make for an even more colorful reunion with the Quinns tonight.

To Julia's shock, Dunphy's was half-empty. On Mother's Days long past, customers waited an hour or more for a table, if they could even get one. And yet, almost twenty minutes passed before the sullen waiter brought Julia and her mother's mimosas. Even then, if there was any champagne mixed in with the orange juice, it was undetectable. After that, it still took another forty-five minutes to get their food.

In years gone by, Julia's mother would have marched right into the kitchen to personally excoriate the staff; but these days, none of the employees even knew who she was. Eventually Robert and Paige got so bored – not to mention fed up with all the octogenarians glowering at their fashion choices – that Julia took them out of the restaurant for a walk down the Embarcadero.

After her mother finally texted that the food had arrived, they returned to a nearly inedible meal of lukewarm poached eggs, soggy French toast, incinerated bacon, and weak coffee. Robert pushed morsels around his plate, and Paige complained for the eighteenth time about being dragged here every single year.

And then a loud volley of profanity careened all the way from within the kitchen, out into the dining room. Among the offenders, Julia recognized her father's voice. The next moment, the kitchen door swung open violently, and a rotund, red-faced man in a white coat and skull cap stalked through it, right into the dining room. Back through the still-swinging door, he loudly entreated Julia's father to suck his dick.

After the cook stormed out, Robert leaned into Julia, wide-eyed. "Mommy, I think that man said a bad word."

The entire ordeal had already swallowed up two and a half hours of their day, and by that point, Julia's mother was on the verge of tears. From all the shouting and swearing, a virtual mutiny was underfoot in the kitchen. One by one, patrons left in a huff without paying. Julia's mother stayed behind to help pick up the pieces, entreating Julia and the kids to go home without her.

Now, at five o'clock, Julia was working on her Halloween costume for that year. What she had in mind would take her the entire five-and-a-half months between now and then. Paige worked nearby on her splendid dottyback painting, and Robert provided the soundtrack with the same three guitar chords, over and over again.

Julia's mother finally appeared in the in-law unit, stooped beneath the weight of the day. Catching Julia's eye, she jerked her head in the direction of the staircase – a silent summons.

"So, you quelled the beast?" Julia prompted after they sat at the kitchen table. She referred, of course, to her father.

"Not really."

Her mother sagged, the corners of her mouth drooping; so Julia got up again to make them both a cup of tea. "Who quit in a huff, this time?"

"Everyone."

Julia whirled around, nearly dropping the teacup she held. *"What?"*

"I mean, the one you saw was the new sous chef. At least this one lasted a whole three days. But after you and the kids left, the entire restaurant quit en masse."

To hide her shock, Julia faced the counter and filled the infuser with loose leaf tea.

"Julia, you've got to help me," her mother blurted. "You and Alison. He won't listen to me."

Julia poured the hot water from the electric kettle into the teapot. "What are we helping you with?" she asked warily.

"It's time for your dad to retire. Sell the restaurant, or close it, or hand over the reins to someone new. But he gets so belligerent if I even mention it."

"I think, in his heart of hearts, Dad knows you're right. He knows both he and the restaurant are past their prime, and it terrifies him. I don't think he knows what he'd do with himself in retirement. It would help if he had something already lined up."

"Like what?"

Stumped, Julia fell silent.

"Exactly," her mother doubled down. "That restaurant is his whole life. I need you and Alison to help me, if we want to convince your dad it's time to call it a day. I like your idea of brainstorming other pastimes we could tempt him with."

"What about traveling?" Julia suggested. "You two have never taken time off to travel."

Her mother's mouth drooped again. "I'm seventy-five, Julia. I can't go traipsing around the world. With my heart, I need to stay close to my doctors."

Julia's own heart sank at the reminder of her mother's heart failure. But there was no time to belabor the subject.

"I'll talk it over with Alison and give it some thought. But right now, we have to get ready to go to the Quinns'."

And with that, Julia's anxiety ricocheted back to the forefront.

She was about to face William's family for the first time since she had saved their home and business. And the Quinns were about to meet William's son – Ann's grandson. Kelly's nephew. William had reassured Julia over and over that they would welcome her and Robert with open arms. But after the fiasco of six years ago, she keenly felt the need to make as good of an impression as possible.

Her mother retrieved the bottle of Cinsaut her friend Diane had given her. Julia packed it with their other offerings of food and flowers. Downstairs, she found Robert still in his pirate costume, and Paige still wore her emo-slash-scene-girl garb. But it didn't matter – this was them. Julia, herself, had always been quirky. It was one of the things William had always loved about her. The rest of the Quinns could either take them or leave them. For her part, Julia would not borrow trouble.

With a clear head and heart, she set out from their house with her mother and kids in tow, a bouquet of flowers in one hand, and a bag stuffed with food and wine in the other. She confidently strode the three blocks from the Dunphy house to the Quinns'.

William's parents' house – where she and William had lost their virginity to each other. As it came into view, she silently asked herself – how many nights had she spent in their in-law unit, curled against William's body in his extra-long twin bed? It was impossible to know.

Fondness clutched at her heart. The last time she was here – three months ago, when she came with a proposal to sue their unscrupulous health insurance company – Ann Quinn had met her at the door with a scowl. But this time, it was William who sat on the front step, following their approach with his eyes, Diego fast asleep at his feet.

An irrepressible smile curved Julia's mouth. William's stylishly faded black jeans were a bit more tailored and dressier than usual. His button-down shirt was still blue plaid, and still untucked, but not flannel. It was more of a pressed Oxford-style, and again, more fitted than usual. He had left the top two buttons undone, treating her to a glimpse of his Saint Peter pendant nestled into a hint of chest hair; and he had rolled the sleeves up to his elbows. The flash of black from the tattoos on his forearms drew her attention – but not as much as the two bouquets he held.

As they drew closer, his own mouth twisted into a lopsided smile – the kind he wore when he was trying not to let it overtake his face too much. The color rose to his cheeks as he rose to his feet. Diego scrambled awake with a curious look at William, followed by a comical double-take when he caught sight of the rest of them. And the whole time, William's eyes stayed riveted to Julia. They drank her in – all of her – from hat to heels.

Flushing, she glanced down at her sundress and back up again. His full smile finally broke through, and his nearly-aquamarine eyes usurped every shred of her attention. For just a moment, all of existence narrowed down to just this: the two of them, really seeing each other for the first time, all over again.

This man, right here.

If there had ever been any doubt in her mind, it ended here.

William was her person. Her soul mate. Her perfect ten. Her forever, and ever after.

Families, kids, exes, jobs, money... it would all work out. She was certain of it, right down to the marrow of her bones.

And then, her surroundings snapped back into focus when Robert barreled between them, flinging his arms around William's legs with enough enthusiasm to nearly knock him over.

"Hey, you!" William's laughter jerked out with the force of Robert's impact. Shifting both bouquets into his right hand and wrapping his left one around Robert's head, he bent toward Robert in greeting. And then, almost immediately, Robert relinquished William and squatted to accept face licks from Diego.

His sparkling eyes returning to Julia's, William finally stepped forward. "Happy Mother's Day," he said, relieving her of the bag she carried and holding one of the bouquets out to Julia. Greeting her with a hug and a kiss on the cheek. Leaning into her ear, and whispering, "You take my breath away."

He kissed her once more before pulling away. She beamed up at him, happier than in years, and the corners of his eyes crinkled as he offered another bashful smile. She plunged her nose into the flowers – peonies, her favorite – and her gaze tracked him as he offered Julia's mother a bouquet of pink roses. Julia watched her mother's face light up and heard her exclamation of delight, but the steady drum of her heartbeat drowned out everything else.

Paige returned William's greeting with an awkward wave. And then William placed his hand on Julia's lower back, igniting tingles up and down her spine as he led the way inside.

The post-war Doelger-style house William had grown up in was a mirror image of Julia's childhood home, with its gated-off tunnel entrance leading into a ground-level, indoor hall. Like the Dunphys, the Quinns had long ago converted their garage into an in-law unit, accessible from the entry hall. Meanwhile, a staircase from the entry hall led up to the main level of the house.

Mouth-watering odors greeted them when William opened the front door. So did the young voices coming through the open door of the in-law unit.

"That sounds like my nephews," said William as he led them into the in-law unit's den. Much to Julia's astonishment, the photos William had taken – the ones Julia had framed for him over eighteen years ago – still hung on the walls. The last time she had been here in February, to talk with Ann, Julia had been too nervous to notice.

But before she could take that in, she found herself blinking at the two boys sitting on the floor in front of the television, thoroughly engrossed in a video game.

"Hey guys," William called out. "If we were snakes, we would have bitten you."

The older boy paused the game, while the younger one turned with a grin. "Sorry, Uncle Will."

"We have guests," William continued, and the boys rose to their feet.

William had once told Julia that Xavier was twelve-going-on-thirteen, but he looked at least fifteen. He was a cute kid, with slightly-outgrown corkscrew curls, light brown skin, and a smattering of freckles over his nose and cheekbones. Heavy blinking accompanied what little eye contact he made; and he performed all the requisite greetings, but in a flat tone.

The younger boy, Zach, was maybe seven or eight, with medium-brown skin, short twists in his hair, and an adorable, dimpled smile. He took one look at Robert and demanded, "Why are you wearing a pirate costume?"

"Because I'm the Dread Pirate Robert."

Zach gave this explanation a single moment's consideration, then shrugged and invited Robert outside to play.

"You can't leave, Zach," Xavier balked. "We haven't finished our game yet."

Zach started to argue, and William opened his mouth to intercede – but Paige beat him to it.

"I'll play with you, once I'm done meeting everybody."

Paige gaped at Xavier as she said it, her cheeks slightly pink. When he turned to blink at the tops of her shoes, she explained, "I love the Sims."

Xavier's eyes lifted and snagged on Paige's for just a moment. He blinked rapidly several times in a row before his eyes darted away again. "Okay."

Crisis averted, William turned anxiously to Julia, mouthing the word, "Ready?"

A flock of butterflies took wing in Julia's belly, but she nodded. Turning to follow him upstairs, she immediately stopped short, and her stomach bottomed out.

Ann and Kelly already hovered in the doorway.

Ann was much thinner than she had been only three months ago, and her dark hair had taken on more gray. She stood frozen, her eyes glued to Robert. They grew watery as she smiled at him with trembling lips.

Kelly stood just over Ann's shoulder in her usual hands-on-hips stance, but she gazed in wonder at Robert.

Julia's eyes flickered up to William. Smiling, he gently encouraged her forward with a reassuring hand on her lower back. To Julia's amazement, Ann stepped up and gathered her into a tight embrace. Ann may have looked older and thinner, but her hugs were just as hearty as ever.

After a moment, Ann clasped Julia's arms and gazed up at her. She was definitely fighting back tears, and now, so was Julia. Ann's trembling lips curved into a warm smile that conveyed everything: forgiveness, gratitude, and hope. "Thank you," she finally murmured, nodding.

A single, fat tear rolled down Julia's cheek. In a shaky whisper, she replied, "Thank *you*. For my son's father."

Once more, Ann nodded, her trembling lips still pressed together in a smile, her eyes still shimmering as she accepted Julia's offering of tulips.

Julia pulled a tissue from her purse to dab her eyes and nose, then dragged her gaze to Kelly. They exchanged nods in place of words. Julia beckoned Paige forward, and Kelly – who had supervised Paige during her amends-making shift at Cardone's – accepted Paige's flower bouquet graciously.

Finally, it was time for Ann and Kelly to meet Robert.

William gently guided Robert forward. "Mom, Kelly... this is Robert. Robert, this is my mother Ann, and my sister Kelly."

William's voice was quiet, almost reverent. Julia saw that he, too, was blinking back tears, and with that, there was no hope left for Julia – her own waterworks breached the levee.

Stooping, Ann extended her hand to Robert. "Hello, Robert. I'm *very* happy to meet you."

Glancing at Julia for reassurance, Robert shook Ann's hand and said, "Nice to meet you, too, Mrs. Quinn."

"Such nice manners, young man." Ann beamed in approval.

Once again, Robert's eyes skittered over to Julia before saying, "Um... you have nice manners, too, old lady."

Against Julia's will, a loud cackle erupted from somewhere deep in her belly. Thankfully Ann and everyone else burst into laughter, too. Robert grinned the way kids do when they don't understand why everyone is laughing; only that they were the cause.

"Kids," Ann remarked. "They keep you humble."

Julia's laughter caught in her throat as Ann stepped toward Paige. The only time Ann had ever seen Paige was four months ago, in January, when she overheard Paige swearing loudly in the middle of Safeway. It was the same day Ann first clapped eyes on Robert, and instantly realized he was her grandson.

But now, Ann greeted Paige warmly, and thankfully, Paige was as pleasant as she had ever been.

With the most nerve-wracking introductions out of the way, Ann and Julia's mother wrapped each other in a tearful, lingering hug, exchanging private whispers. Julia watched from her peripheral vision, dabbing her eyes with her tissue and blowing her nose, until Kelly stepped closer.

Clearing her throat and shoving her hands into her pockets, Kelly asked, "Is your sister still coming?"

Julia offered Kelly a watery smile. "She should be here any minute. She's just closing up her bakery."

Kelly nodded, her eyes looking everywhere except at Julia, but Julia sensed she was trying her best. "Pilar and I wanted to talk to Alison about a wedding cake."

"I'm sure she'd love that!"

"The wedding is only a month away. We only got engaged a month ago, so we haven't had much time to plan; and any place that makes decent cakes is already booked."

"Well, of course I can't speak for her, but knowing her, she'd find a way."

Again, Kelly nodded, and then her eyes swept to Robert. She crouched down with as warm of a smile as Julia had ever seen from her. Offering Robert a fist bump, she said, "Hey there, little man."

Robert returned the fist bump. "Hey there, big woman."

Julia ran a hand down her burning face, then peeked through the gaps between her fingers. Grinning at Ann, Kelly said, "You're right, Mom; they do keep you humble." In high school, Kelly had been very athletic, if big-boned; but now she sported the same stout figure her mother once did. Until very recently, the only thing distinguishing daughter from mother, besides fewer wrinkles, was Kelly's asymmetrical, undercut hairstyle.

"Come outside, guys," Kelly called, still chuckling. "Come meet my fiancée and her family."

Kelly led them all through the sliding glass door onto the back patio. There, at the table, Julia recognized the Ochoa men. With a stab of panic, she realized she had forgotten their names. Two young women sat across the table from a third, extremely pregnant one – obviously Pilar. They all rose in greeting, and even Pilar tried to heave herself to her feet.

Kelly rounded the table and rested her hands on Pilar's shoulders, gently settling her back into her chair. "Everyone, this is Pilar, my fiancée."

With a bright smile, Pilar placed her hands on her belly. "Sorry for not standing. I'm a little weighed down these days."

"And these," Kelly added, gesturing to the two women standing across the table, "are her sisters, Flora and Emilia."

Pilar graciously re-introduced the rest of her family at the table: Pilar's grandfather Gustavo, her father Sergio, and her teenage brother Rafael.

As everyone got acquainted, Julia's eyes drifted again to Pilar, who still sat with Kelly's hands on her shoulders. She was a pretty young woman with deep brown skin and hair in cornrows, the long ends trailing down her back. Pilar must have sensed someone watching, because her eyes flitted to Julia's. Her smile bloomed warmly, revealing perfect teeth and two endearing dimples.

Julia liked her immediately.

But Kelly and Ann were already herding everyone back inside and upstairs to meet the rest of Pilar's family. Delfina and her mother-in-law, Socorro, emerged from the kitchen to greet them. Lucía, a girl around Paige's age, trailed behind.

Amid all the greetings, Julia glanced around the Quinns' living room and noticed two things. First, the space had changed drastically since the last time she had seen it. At some point, the Quinns had removed the dark, seventies-era wall paneling, lava-orange shag carpeting, and dingy mustard-yellow drapes. In their place, they had painted the walls a fresh, clean white, replaced the drapes with plantation shutters, and refinished the original parquet floors. Not only that, the sagging avocado-green furniture was gone, with more modern styles taking their places.

The second thing Julia noticed, though, were the two taped-up moving boxes stacked against the wall, with *Ann Quinn* scrawled on each one.

At that exact moment, her mother blurted, "Ann! Are you moving?"

Ann froze, wide-eyed. Then she turned to Kelly with a frown. "I asked you to put those boxes in the bedroom."

Julia's mother looked back and forth between Ann and Kelly, who suddenly wore a hangdog look. Bracing herself, Julia's mother rested a hand on the back of the Quinns' sofa. "You *are* leaving."

Ann's shoulders sagged as she heaved a sigh of resignation. "I didn't want you to find out this way. It all happened so suddenly..."

Julia came to place a reassuring hand on her mother's arm and glanced over at William for clues, but she found none in his sober expression.

"Oh, no," whispered Julia's mother.

Kelly took a few paces forward. "Mrs. Dunphy – Karen – Mom's right. It was only late Friday that the property management company called to say they had an opening, but she has to move in by Tuesday.

You know how competitive these places are in the city – we had to jump on it while we had the chance."

Julia wrapped an arm around her mother's shoulder, guiding her to the sofa, and Ann came to sit on the other side. Kelly offered Julia's mother a box of tissues. The Ochoa women retreated silently back to the kitchen.

"Karen..." Ann's tone was almost mournful. "I'm so sorry you're finding out this way. I just didn't know what to do. It's not the kind of news you deliver over the phone, and I haven't had a single chance to come tell you since we found out on Friday."

"But *why?*" Julia's mother demanded; and despite Julia's compassion for her mother's grief, she winced a bit at her shrill tone. "*Why* are you leaving?"

"Oh, my sweet friend." Ann grasped one of Karen's hands in her own. "Kelly and Pilar are about to add two more members to our family, and they already have two boys. Our house is a carbon copy of yours, so I don't have to tell you that three bedrooms and 1500 square feet just isn't enough."

Julia's mother glanced around herself, then straightened and blew her nose. "Oh, I'm sorry, everyone. It's a sin to submit to despair."

"Despair?" Ann said gently, putting an arm around her friend's shoulders. "Why despair?"

"It's just... everybody's leaving, or dying. I don't know anyone around here anymore."

"Well, *I'm* not dying," Ann pointed out with a soft chuckle.

"And as far as leaving," William interjected, "don't forget it's only two miles away."

Julia's mother gave William a watery smile and stretched out her arm, offering her hand. He came forward and took it. Turning to Ann, Julia's mother said, "This young man has always been like the son Paul and I never had."

William gave Julia's mother a kind smile. "I'm not such a young man anymore, but if you want to call me young, I won't argue."

Chuckles circled the room, and then Ann said, "Karen, you'll be the first friend I invite over, I promise."

Julia's mother dabbed her eyes and blew her nose again. "You're sweet, dear. Thank you. But enough of this blubbering from me. What are you making for dinner? Can I help?"

As the women filed into the kitchen, Paige went to play the Sims with Xavier, and Robert followed Zach outside to play. That left Julia and William alone in the living room. He jerked his head, beckoning her into the corner furthest from the kitchen.

He stood very close to her, leaning against the wall, and whispered, "I'm so sorry; I only found out moments before you did."

"How?"

"The same way: I saw the boxes all piled up. They couldn't deflect my questions anymore."

She ran a hand down the sleeve of his shirt, snapping off a loose thread from it. "How are *you* feeling about all this?"

He looked around himself. "I won't lie; I'm kind of sad – watching my mom getting older and frailer, and moving out of the house she and Dad raised us in. But I'm glad she has a great new place that's so close. And I'm happy for my sister and Pilar."

"I get it. I never really appreciated how much of an emotional upheaval it is, watching your parents age."

"And losing them."

For several moments, Julia rubbed William's arm as he stared, unfocused, in the direction of the stairwell. After a minute, a smirk gradually overtook his frown. "We've made some nice memories here, you and I. Haven't we?"

A poignant ache seized Julia's chest, but she reached up and touched the side of his face. "And we'll make lots more, in new places."

He took her hand and kissed it, a knowing sparkle in his eyes. In response, she grasped both of his hands and stilled a moment. Her head dropped in mock defeat, and she shook it.

"Penny for your thoughts?" prompted William, his tone laden with concern.

"Oh, I was just remembering…" She proceeded to recount for him the brunch debacle at Dunphy's.

"My God," he muttered. "I knew it had gotten bad over there, but I didn't know it had gotten *that* bad."

She peered up at him quizzically. "How did you know?"

"Remember my cousin Stephen? The deckhand on your whale watching trip? He started working at Dunphy's when he was a teenager, just like I did. In fact, I'm the one who convinced your dad to hire him. He went to cooking school, then came back to Dunphy's; but he quit almost immediately."

"Because of Dad." Julia didn't even have to ask.

"And from there, he worked his way up to sous chef at another restaurant."

"So why is he working as your deckhand?"

"I offered him the job when his last restaurant shuttered a few months ago. No fault of his, of course; just the toll of trying to operate a restaurant in this city. But Stephen's dad is a fisherman, so he knows his way around a boat; and since we used to work together at Dunphy's, I already knew he's a good worker."

A light bulb went off in Julia's head. "Do you think he'd be open to coming back to Dunphy's?"

William huffed out a laugh. "Not as long as your dad is there."

"No, I mean as head chef."

William's eyes widened. "Is your dad retiring?"

"Yes; he just doesn't know it yet. Now that the entire restaurant quit in a huff, maybe he'll finally see the light."

William chuckled. "Yeah, good luck with that. But honestly, I don't think Stephen is quite ready for prime time yet. Give him another few years, though, and he will be."

Julia gave a thoughtful hum as they carried the food, wine, and flowers she had brought into the kitchen. Delfina stood at the stove, stirring something dark, fragrant, and smooth in a pot. Kelly and Lucía flanked her on either side; and the matriarch, Socorro, supervised them all with a proud smile. Ann and Karen arranged flowers and appetizers at the kitchen table.

"What are you making?" asked Julia as Kelly came to relieve her of the pastry boxes.

"It's called mole de tichinda," replied Delfina. "I've been teaching your sweetie to make it."

"Yeah, and no matter how many times I make it, it never turns out as good as Delfina's," retorted William with a grin. "I'm convinced she's holding out on me."

Delfina gave him a coy smile, then turned to pinch Lucía's cheek. She said something in Spanish, then giggled at William's look of dismay.

"She just admitted it," William explained to Julia with a good-natured snicker. "For her daughters' eyes only."

"Rightfully so," Julia said, with a wink at Delfina. "It looks and smells amazing, but what is it?"

"It's a mole with mussels," William explained.

"Traditionally it's made with a special type of mussels called tichin-das," added Delfina, "but you can only get those from the mangroves of coastal Oaxaca. So we just make do with whatever we find here."

The doorbell rang, and Julia turned to William with a smirk. "Brace yourself – that's probably Alison."

She didn't miss the flicker of dread in his eyes, and no wonder. Alison's loud, boundless energy had always flustered him. Admittedly, she was a lot.

But he gamely volunteered to answer the door, and Julia followed him. The moment he swung the door open, his eyes bugged out of his head before he quickly diverted them to the floor. There stood Alison in all her glory, balancing her usual load of pink-and-white-striped pastry boxes. She had bleached her pixie-cut hair platinum-blond and traded the hoop in her nose for a tiny, sparkly stud. She also wore a pair of cat-eye sunglasses with white frames and sky-high heels; but the showstopper was the low-cut, sleeveless yellow dress that was one strip of fashion tape away from a wardrobe malfunction. The way it wrapped her curves screamed *cougar on the prowl*.

Julia knew she had donned it all in the vain hope that Mike would show up.

While a frazzled William relieved Alison of some of her pastry boxes and retreated upstairs, Alison peered over their rims of her sunglasses at Julia.

Julia shook her head. Deflating, Alison mouthed, *Fuck!*

"How are you standing upright in those stripper heels," demanded Julia, "much less walking?"

"I prefer the term 'fuck-me pumps,' thank you very much."

The corners of Alison's mouth drooped, and Julia almost felt sorry for her. "You got his number the other day. Did you reach out?"

"Of course. I called and texted. *Repeatedly*. Radio silence."

"Huh." Julia knew Mike could never resist a booty call from Alison. If he wasn't answering Alison's texts, it could only mean one of two things – either the number had been disconnected, or something was very wrong.

Julia wondered if it would be wise to mention this to William. It seemed clear that he was enforcing boundaries with Mike – that he was done cleaning up Mike's messes.

Her eyes skittered over her sister again. "I hope you brought a sweater; otherwise, you'll freeze to death when the sun sets."

"I'm already freezing to death. I just didn't want anything covering the canvas that is *this*." Alison gestured up and down the length of her own body like a game show hostess presenting a prize.

Julia opted not to respond, instead taking the remaining pastry boxes from her sister. As they climbed the stairs, Julia glanced down once through the cellophane window of the top box – her sister's strawberry tartlets with lemon curd and vanilla pastry cream. Julia's favorite.

They carried the boxes to the kitchen. William was busy rearranging things in the fridge to make room, but everyone else's eyes goggled when Alison made her grand entrance, wholly unfazed, even when their mother breathed a mortified reproach.

To divert attention from Alison, William offered to help Delfina.

"Oh, no; there's already too many people in here as it is. ¡Vete, vete!" laughed Delfina; shooing him away with a sweep of her hands.

Closing the refrigerator door behind him, William grinned at Julia. "I'm being evicted."

"Only so you can attend to your beautiful *novia*," Delfina replied cheerfully. To everyone else she added, "And that goes for all of you – ¡Sáquense a la chingada de la cocina! Kelly, go take care of my daughter; and Ann; go get to know your little–" Her eyes widening, Delfina caught herself just before blurting the secret. "...your *guests*."

After Julia and Alison stored their pastry boxes in the refrigerator and poured themselves glasses of Cinsaut, William ushered them from the kitchen. As they crossed the living room, he blew out a breath.

Placing a hand on the small of Julia's back and leaning into her ear, he whispered, "That was close."

"A little too close for comfort," Julia agreed. Luckily, neither Paige nor Robert was in the kitchen at the time. Julia didn't think Lucía knew about Robert's secret, but if she did, she had not picked up on the near miss.

As he descended the stairs behind Julia, William's quiet voice derailed her train of thought. "She's not wrong, you know."

"Who?"

"Delfina, of course. I *do* need to attend to you." They reached the bottom of the stairs now, and he gently turned her to face him. He took her hand with a crooked smile that sent those butterflies alight in her stomach again. Bending to kiss her cheek, he whispered, "And you *are* beautiful."

"Get a room," teased Alison, derailing Julia's more agreeable thoughts on how, exactly, William might attend to her.

"Get a hobby, besides harassing me," Julia sneered.

Alison shot back a playful grin, shameless as ever; and then a movement in Julia's peripheral vision sent her stomach swooping. Sure enough, Ann, Kelly, and her mother had overheard the entire exchange. Thankfully, they bit back their amusement and said nothing; but still – Julia would make sure to trip Alison later in those Louboutin knockoffs.

They all filed through the den, past Rafael sprawled on the couch, scrolling through his phone with a bored look. Past Xavier and Paige, still engrossed with the Playstation. They spilled out into the crisp evening air and seated themselves around the enormous rectangular patio table. The Quinns' back yard was no larger than the Dunphys', but the table could have seated twenty people. Clearly, with all of William's aunts, uncles, and cousins, the Quinns entertained a lot. And now they were about to add the Ochoas and the Dunphys to the mix.

Pilar and William flanked Julia at the table, and Kelly sat across from them. Sergio and Gustavo smoked at the other end of the table, while Flora and Emilia set the table for dinner. Ann crossed the patio and dragged a chair closer to Robert and Zach, who drew pictures on the concrete with sidewalk chalk.

Ann's two grandsons.

Two cousins who didn't even know they were cousins yet.

Everyone eavesdropped, almost holding their breaths, as Ann spoke to the boys in low tones. She focused especially on Robert as he prattled at length about his future prospects in the pirating industry.

Beneath the cover of the table, William's hand slid over Julia's. She seized onto it for dear life and laced her fingers through his. The tears pooling in her eyes spilled over, so she swiped at her cheeks and turned a trembling smile on him. His own suspiciously-watery eyes met hers, and he returned her smile.

Everyone around them tried not to notice Julia and William having a moment, instead focusing their attention on Ann and Robert. Julia knew those two shouldn't have to get acquainted in a fishbowl, so she turned to Pilar and cleared her throat.

"How long have you and Kelly known each other?" she began.

Pilar aimed her megawatt smile at Julia. "Two years. We met when Kelly visited Will at his apartment."

"She invited me to join her roller derby league," Kelly chimed in, "and the rest is history."

"Courtship on wheels," quipped Pilar. Placing her hands on her belly, she added, "I haven't been on skates in a while, though."

"When are you due?" asked Julia.

"September 16th."

Holy cow. Pilar still had four more months to go? The poor woman. It occurred to Julia that if she had ever been pregnant with twins, she might have been twice as sick with HG.

She could smell her own sour puke, along with the hospital antiseptic. Her stomach quivered. Her pulse fluttered ominously in her throat.

Thankfully, at that moment, Delfina came to the rescue with a tureen of mole, and Lucía trailed her with a bowl of rice. Julia offered to carry things to the patio, so Delfina had her set smaller bowls of mole in front of Robert and Paige.

"These are less spicy," Delfina explained. "Just in case."

William grinned at her. "Just say it, Del – it's gringo mole."

Amid the laughter, Delfina explained to Julia, "Mole de tichinda is much spicier than the moles most people are used to."

"Why is that?" Julia asked.

"Well, it's..." Delfina faltered a moment. "It's from the coast of Oaxaca. The milder moles come from the central areas and other parts of Oaxaca."

Pilar's sister, Flora, interjected something in Spanish, and Julia noticed that her family received it with varying degrees of dismay and amusement. Emilia, sitting next to Flora, rolled her eyes and said, "Híjole; here we go..."

Flora turned to Julia. "The food of Afromexicanos – Black Oaxacans... it's spicier than the rest of the state."

"Mija..." Delfina sighed.

Flora ignored her. "The escaped slaves who settled the coast brought their spicy stuff with them."

Delfina added, "Flora is majoring in Sociology at Berkeley." As if that explained everything.

Frowning at both her mother and Emilia, Flora replied, "I, for one, am proud of my heritage."

"So am I," Delfina balked.

"Right, mamí; *that's* why you always try to hide the fact that we're Black and Mexican."

Julia got the impression that Flora was the Paige of the Ochoa family – the force of nature kid, as well as the social justice warrior, in its best and original sense.

Pilar bolstered this impression by placing a hand over Flora's with a chuckle. "Slow your roll, manita. It's Mother's Day, remember?"

"Speaking of hiding things, Delfina," William intervened, "maybe you wouldn't mind disclosing to Julia the magic mole ingredients you've been holding out on me? I'm sure your secrets are safe with her."

"Nice try," Delfina deadpanned, finally taking her own seat.

The earlier reminder of Paige now had Julia swinging her eyes in her daughter's direction, only to stall there when she found Paige and Xavier deep in conversation. From the snippets that reached Julia's ears, they were conferring over digital animation and video games. With growing dread, Julia watched Xavier retrieve his phone from his back pocket and pull up God-knows-what for Paige to see.

"Will tells me you got the school district to reimburse you for the cost of Paige's school."

Kelly's low voice yanked Julia out of her anxiety death spiral. Tearing her eyes from Paige and Xavier, Julia returned them to Kelly and forced a smile. "It was by no means an easy process, nor a cheap one. It helped a little that I was a paralegal back then, but my experience wasn't in special education law, so I still hired an attorney."

Kelly nodded. "I hear from all the other parents I've talked to and all the support groups online that I'm pretty much going to need one."

"Are you thinking of going for it? For Xavier?"

"I am. After what Will told me about Janus Academy, I went and toured the campus. I still can't believe there are places like that for 2-E kids."

"The district isn't going to tell you about them, that's for sure," grumbled Julia.

After Julia texted her special education attorney's contact card to Kelly, the rest of the meal went off without a hitch. When she wasn't savoring Ann's joy as she interacted with Robert, Julia got to know the young woman sitting beside her. Pilar was twenty-five, had once been in the Coast Guard, and was currently on leave from her job as a real estate appraiser. As Pilar chatted, Kelly listened attentively with a tiny but worshipful smile.

Meanwhile, William ate in comfortable silence beside Julia, listening to everyone's conversations and availing himself of every chance to hold her hand beneath the patio table. Julia was constantly, acutely aware of his physical presence – his warm palm; his fingers brushing hers affectionately. The little squeezes he gave her hand when she turned to smile at him, and he smiled back. If she ever needed her left hand, he placed his palm on her thigh instead, over the fabric of her dress. Currents of electricity radiated from his hand through the rest of her body; and the further his palm crept up her thigh over the course of the meal, the more the tingly sensations converged between her legs.

When blue twilight descended on the patio and the cafe lights blinked on overhead, Julia caught William already looking at her. With a hint of a smile playing at his lips, he mouthed the words, *I love you.*

I love you, too, she replied, also silently, and didn't even try to hide her beaming smile.

The way he looked at her was everything. Love. Lust. Cherishing. Aching. She knew if he held a mirror up to her right now, she'd find that same look on her own face.

And then, in her peripheral vision, she noticed Ann, smiling across the table at both of them. Clearly, she had been watching for some time.

Busted.

But as Julia held her gaze, Ann's smile widened into something like gratitude. Like a silent blessing.

MONDAY, MAY 14, 2012

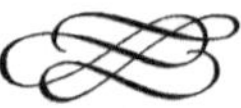

On Monday after lunch, while driving to her afternoon aquarium servicing appointment, Julia's phone rang. She glanced at the screen just long enough to determine it was her next client, Lars. As soon as she found a good spot to pull over, she called him back.

"Hello, Julia?"

"Yes, hi, Lars! I was just on my way–"

"Hey, you know what? I'm really sorry about the timing, but I've just learned that my wife forgot to call you. Meg and I have decided to go with a different company."

"Oh…" Julia's stomach bottomed out. Lars and Meg were by far Julia's biggest account. They had five saltwater aquariums dispersed throughout their nine-thousand-square-foot, mid-century modern masterpiece – more, even, than Julia and Kevin kept at their peak. "I'm sorry to hear that. If you have a minute, may I ask, was there anything in particular that persuaded you to go with a different company?"

"You know, we've enjoyed working with you, Julia. It's just that the new company's vision aligns better with ours."

The new company's vision aligns better with ours. What kind of bull-shit corporate-speak was that?

No doubt misinterpreting Julia's silence, Lars quickly added, "I'll pay you through the end of next month, per our contract."

Julia cleared her throat, mentally grasping for ideas on how to salvage this. "Would you be open to me stopping by today anyway, for a final consultation? To help transition your tank to its new caretakers? I'm only asking because I care about the welfare of the fish in your tank."

A pause. "What do you mean?"

"Well, different companies have different methods of caring for fish. So, for example, I use products that are as clean and gentle as possible for both the fish and the environment. Depending on what you're shifting to, you may need to give the fish a while to gradually adjust. Saltwater fish in particular are very–"

"Yes, well, Julia, I think this company knows what they're–"

"And also, most companies source their fish from places like Indonesia, where fishermen use toxins to paralyze them. That makes them easier to capture, but it also damages the coral reefs. I get my fish from fully-vetted, sustainable breeders here in the U.S."

"I understand, and I think that's very noble, which is why I hired you, but–"

"All of that means it's going to take just a bit longer to establish your tank and get it looking as vibrant as what you and Meg are going for. But I can show you videos of my clients' tanks after twelve months–"

"The thing is, Julia, we're hosting a campaign fundraiser for the President at our home in September, and he'll be there, so we can't wait twelve months for the wow factor we're going for."

In truth, this news stunned Julia to silence. A fundraiser for the *President?* She closed her eyes and allowed herself to imagine it for just one moment – the attention and business she would get when billionaires, politicians, and journalists clapped eyes and cameras on her aquariums.

She knew she could do it using the bad old methods – the ones that a lack of alternatives had limited her to until recently. She could get Lars' house looking like the freaking Monterey Bay Aquarium by September.

But Julia had made a solemn pledge to both herself and Paige to stick with sustainable breeders and the cleanest products and methods.

What else was there to stay in this business for, if not to educate people and be one cog in the machinery gradually shifting toward better practices?

But that *vision*, to borrow from Lars, was not compatible with his hard-on for overnight razzle-dazzle. And Julia had no intention of breaking her pledge to herself, Paige, or the creatures in her care.

Swallowing past the dry lump in her throat, Julia forced the words out: "I'm sorry, Lars. If you need your aquariums looking that finished before September, I'm afraid you're right – my services aren't the best fit. But I'm still happy to come by for a final consulta–"

"That's okay, Julia; the new company's got it covered. In fact, they're here right now."

He had already mentally checked out and moved on to the next item on his to-do list. Aggravation welled in Julia's chest like hot acid. But she somehow managed to say calmly, "Good luck with your fundraiser, Lars. And thank you for your business these past two months. I hope you and Meg will keep me in mind for your future–"

"Sure thing, Julia. Take care."

The line clicked dead, and with a string of choice curses for tech bros everywhere, Julia threw her phone into the passenger side footwell.

Thankfully, though, her phone had an indestructible case and screen protector, because her next impulse was to text William. It was Monday, which he usually reserved for his days off, and she knew he had no chartered excursions that day.

> Just lost my biggest account b/c they wanted me to deliver the Great Barrier Reef overnight, and I refused to compromise the very principles they hired me for. 🥺

The moment she concluded he must be busy, and put her key in the ignition, her phone rang. His name popped up on the screen. She answered immediately with, "Plus, they actually forgot to let me know, so I was already on my way to their weekly appointment when Lars called to fire me."

"Julie, I'm so sorry." His voice was low and soothing. "That's just shit."

"That's more than half my income at the moment, and no other prospects in sight." She told him the whole story, tying it all together with the cringey "vision" comment and how Lars hung up on her.

"Prick," William spat out, and Julia immediately felt better, simply knowing he was in her corner. "Where are you? Can I meet you somewhere?"

Julia stilled. "You mean now?"

"If you're free."

It *would* give her a chance to test the waters and get a sense of how William might receive the news Alison had shared with her about Mike. "You know, since Señor Douche Canoe fired me, there's nowhere I absolutely *have* to be until six. I should definitely get some work done at the shop, but I'd much rather hang out with you." She glanced down at her grubby work clothes. "Are you at the pier?"

He was.

"Does Cardone's still have showers for employees? I always keep a change of clothes with me. I'll still look like a mechanic, but at least I won't smell like fish and aquarium chemicals."

"Like you haven't kissed me plenty of times when I stank of fish?"

She considered. "Good point. Payback time."

"Besides, if your goal is to *not* smell fishy, I'm not sure showering at a fish processing plant is your best bet. But you could shower at my place."

Her heart leaped into her throat, followed promptly by the swish of her pulse in her ears. "Um–"

"I promise, I won't touch," he laughed softly.

The thing was, now that he mentioned it... she kind of wanted him to touch. Vivid memories of them showering together came flooding back, deluging her loins with heat.

"Julie?"

"Yeah," she blurted. "Sorry. I was just... letting my imagination wander a bit too far."

Again he laughed, low and rumbly; but this time, there was no awkwardness behind it. "Me too."

Oh, shit. "I think this is a very dangerous idea."

"For now, maybe. But not forever."

She stilled, listening to the sound of his breath and her own as his words hung between them, laden with meaning. But she couldn't resist the offer, and twenty minutes later, she parked her work van a few blocks away from William's apartment. It was no mean feat, considering the van's monolithic proportions and the scarcity of parking. She texted William to let him know where she was, and he met her halfway to accompany her.

Despite the funk clinging to her grubby, utilitarian work clothes, he practically beamed as he watched her approach. And even though she insisted on waiting until after her shower to kiss him, *he* insisted on at least holding her hand as they walked and talked about everything and nothing. It felt so good, and once they were in his apartment, she was that much more tempted to just keep holding it, all the way into the shower.

She stopped short and smacked her forehead. "Crap!"

He startled. "What?"

"I left my change of clothes in the van! I can't believe I did that." But actually, she could. Talk about a Freudian slip.

He held his hand out. "Give me your keys and I'll go get them while you're showering."

"No; I can't make you go all the way back there!"

"It's three blocks, Julie," he chuckled.

"Four."

Julia watched a light bulb go off behind his eyes. "I'll loan you a shirt and, I don't know... a pair of drawstring pants, or something? You can wash and dry your clothes while you're here. I share a washer and dryer with the Ochoas." At the dubious look on Julia's face, he added, "We can still sit out on the patio. Just talk."

She considered his offer. "I guess that works."

"Toss your dirty clothes outside the bathroom, and I'll throw them in the washer."

"Okay, but no peeking at my underwear."

He acknowledged orders with a smirk and a salute. "I'll get you a clean shirt and shorts."

As he went to an espresso-colored dresser against one wall, Julia took the opportunity to look around. For the first time, she noticed it was a studio apartment – hence the dresser in what she had previously assumed was just a living room. Without even thinking, she searched for any sign of a bed, but saw none. Mentally smacking her forehead for letting her thoughts wander in that direction, she turned instead to the framed photographs on his walls.

Along one wall were landscapes, rural townscapes, and cityscapes in what looked like some time-forgotten part of the Mediterranean. A gracefully-weathered village with tile roofs, perched fortress-like on a rocky, scrubby hill. A narrow balcony-lined alleyway, terminating in a glimpse of a domed cathedral. Centuries-old vineyards flanked by Italian cypresses. Flashes of azure and turquoise sea.

Another wall had the local cityscapes – an upward-looking shot of the Transamerica Pyramid from the street level. Vibrant Mission District murals, and the mission itself. The Peace Pagoda in Japantown, and strings of red lanterns zigzagging above the streets of Chinatown. And of course, the obligatory shot of the Golden Gate Bridge.

And a third wall featured the ocean shots, clearly snapped from a boat – probably William's. There were whales, dolphins, and sharks. Fishing boats, and sailboats, and even cargo ships. Sunsets over the Farallones, and over the empty horizon.

Meanwhile, William scrounged diligently, first through his dresser, then through an armoire along another wall. Now, carrying a small stack of folded clothes, he joined her by her side.

"My customers took these photos."

Julia looked up at him in some surprise. "Really?"

"One of the trips I offer is an ocean photography class. I have to drive the boat, of course, so I have a photographer on board to teach that one. But once we're out there, I sometimes step away from the helm for a few minutes. These are some of my favorites from over the years."

"And what about the others?" she asked, gesturing around the room at the other walls.

"I took those."

"Wait–" Julia crossed the room to the wall with the Mediterranean photos. "You took *these?*"

"I did. In Sicily."

"Will! When did you go to Sicily?"

"Back in 2004." He came to stand beside her again, gently igniting electric sparks between her shoulder blades with his palm, and pointing to the mountaintop village. "Believe it or not, that's where my nonna's parents came from."

Julia's jaw dropped. "That place is stunning. And you went into the village and looked around?"

"I did, and I actually found distant family still living there."

"Get out!"

"I'm serious," he laughed. "Mom gave me a family tree, and I just went around with a Sicilian dictionary and phrase book and asked if there was anyone descended from Cataldo Salvaggio or Elira Cuccia. And of course in an ancient, isolated place like that, everyone is related, and everyone can recite their family history going back five hundred years. I found a whole bunch of third and fourth and fifth cousins."

"That is so impressive." After another moment of gazing at the impossibly picturesque hamlet, she said, "So you went with your mom?"

A two-beat rest. "Actually, I went with my girlfriend back then."

The floor dropped out from underneath her. "Oh."

An awkward silence settled between them. Julia's eyes glazed over until she was no longer really seeing the photo. But she forced herself to keep staring at it anyway, in case her face betrayed any sign of discomposure.

2004.

It must have been the old girlfriend who confronted Julia at MacGowan's, back in 2006. The tall, dark-haired knockout who sneered at Julia's reflection in the ladies' room mirror. The one who snarled, "Do you think you're the only woman he's written a song for?"

No wonder William never mentioned that trip.

Julia squeezed her eyes shut in a vain attempt to expunge the memory. Whatever her name was – and Julia had never learned it – she was ancient history. A history as ancient as the village in this photo; or it may as well have been. And Julia had grown beyond her petty insecurities since those days.

Hadn't she?

William's gaze made a wary circuit of Julia's face. Clearing her throat, she forced a smile and gestured to the clothes he had brought her. "You must be Will, from the wardrobe department."

He grinned in obvious relief as he handed them over. "Hopefully you'll find something here that works. Nothing that fits perfectly, I'm sure; but it's just the two of us."

Yes. Yes, it *was* just the two of them, in that tiny studio apartment. Staring heatedly into each other's eyes.

Julia pointed to the patio door. "Out."

He laughed and went instead to a different door. Opening it, he flipped the bathroom light on for her. "I'll be back in a couple minutes to get your dirty clothes."

It was Julia's turn to salute before locking herself in his bathroom.

It was clean and masculine, with a similar palette as the rest of his apartment. Luxuriant memory foam bathmats buffered Julia's feet from the cold porcelain tile. She turned the shower faucet all the way to hot and allowed it to run a minute. She was cold-natured, and she preferred a steamy bathroom before shucking her clothes. Finally naked, she unlocked the bathroom door, opened it as little as necessary, and tossed her dirty clothes on the floor outside.

She closed and locked the door, started to turn back to the shower – and promptly unlocked the door again.

Just in case.

Standing under the spray of hot water, she entertained fantasies of William sneaking in and joining her. But there was nothing she could do with those thoughts right now. He wasn't going to sneak in, and she didn't want to keep him waiting while she attended to her urges. With a frustrated groan, she bypassed the chance to use William's body wash, which smelled so much like him, as her own personal lubricant.

Afterward, running the fan to clear the steam, she picked through William's offerings and chose one of his plaid flannel shirts. It was so big that even with her long legs, it fell almost halfway down her thighs. All his drawstring pants were so big, even cinched to their tightest, that she decided to forego pants altogether. She was nice and toasty now anyway, and she strongly suspected he wouldn't mind.

Rolling up the cuffs of his sleeves, she unwound her hair from the towel and combed through it with her fingers before finally leaving the bathroom. Padding barefoot and pantsless through the living room, she gazed through the glass patio door. William sat at the patio table, facing her, working on his laptop.

She slid the door open, and the second his eyes made contact, they widened, traveling the length of her body. Lingering especially on the bare skin of her legs.

He slowly closed his laptop and pushed it aside.

"Like what you see?" Julia asked, her voice husky.

"Uh, *yeah*." He swallowed, his Adam's apple bobbing in his throat. His pupils dilating as he finally met her heated stare with his own.

She lifted an eyebrow. "You like it when a woman wears your shirts?"

"I don't think there's a heterosexual man alive who doesn't like that."

"I've never been a flannel kind of girl." She hugged herself in the soft, warm fabric. "But after today, that might change."

He looked at her like he'd rather relieve her of the flannel and warm her up, himself. More fantasies intruded, this time of him sliding his warm palms up her bare legs; and of the raw heat darkening his gaze when he cupped her backside, only to discover she was going commando.

As badly as she wanted it, she also knew they weren't here for that. Instead, she lowered herself into the chair opposite him and oh-so-casually inspected her fingernails. "Remember Holly's Halloween party, back in '93?"

He huffed out a laugh. "Is that a serious question?"

She lifted her eyes to his. "I remember, when you saw me in that mermaid costume, you looked at me the same way you're looking at me now."

"How am I looking at you?"

"Like you want to cover me with hot fudge and whipped cream and lick me clean."

"Huh. Is that right?"

She nodded. "Absolutely."

"Well... can I?"

"I mean, yeah. You can also cover me with nuts if you want; but I can't offer you a cherry because you already took mine."

He flopped back in his seat and wiped a hand down his scarlet-red face. "Don't hold back, Julie." But he was laughing silently behind his hand.

"I never do, and you love it, by your own admission. You created this monster."

Still laughing, the skin bunching around his eyes in the way she had always adored, he lowered his hand from his face and stretched it across the table. Without hesitation, she met it with her own.

"Julie, you're the furthest thing from a monster that I can imagine. You are so heart-stoppingly beautiful, it..." He hesitated, his breath hitching. His brow furrowing with the effort. In a near-whisper, he finished, "You bring me to my knees."

For once, she couldn't tease him about his choice of words. In fact, she couldn't find any words, herself. She brought his palm to her face and leaned her cheek into it.

"Will," she whispered. "It's so hard, not being able to touch you."

"You *are* touching me."

She let out a ragged little laugh. "You know what I mean."

His breath stuttered again, and his forehead still creased with emotion; but he said nothing.

She brought his palm to her lips and closed her eyes. She wanted him so intensely, even her salivary glands responded.

He groaned. "Your pantslessness will be the death of me."

She couldn't help giggling a bit. "I swear to God, none of your pants fit, no matter how tight I cinched them."

"Maybe bringing you here was a mistake."

That threw a bucket of ice water over her libido.

"Shit." He straightened in his chair. "I didn't mean that the way it sounded. Don't get me wrong, I'm beyond thrilled you're here, but that's just it – I'm a little *too* thrilled. I really thought I could keep it together if I just remembered all the reasons."

"Yeah... what were all those reasons again?" she quipped. "Do you have a jumbo size chip clip?"

"A..." He blinked. "What?"

She bit her lips to suppress her giggle. "Or a binder clip, or even a large, heavy-duty rubber band? I could try and gather the waistband of your pants together, just enough so they'll stay up."

She followed him back into the apartment and watched from the safety of his sofa as he rummaged through his drawers and cabinets. Finally, he came up with both a jumbo chip clip and a large rubber band, and she returned with them to the bathroom. When she emerged a few minutes later, she had managed to cinch the waist of one of the pairs and pin the spare fabric together with her jerry-rigged contraption. The bunched-up slack resembled a phallus jutting from her navel, and William couldn't stop laughing.

"Screw this," she giggled as she returned to the bathroom to shed the pants. When she emerged again, she asked, "Do you think we can sit on opposite ends of the couch without mauling each other?"

"I don't know, but I'm happy to try."

So they settled on their respective ends of the sofa and spent a while talking about what Julia and Kevin had discussed during their Friday evening phone call.

"The good news is, Kevin and Clio have already spoken. She couldn't give me any details, of course, but she sounded upbeat when she mentioned it this morning, so I take that as a good sign. And also, she wanted me to run a date by you."

"A date?"

"For us to meet with her. Just you and me, to start; but eventually, it will be with Kevin, too."

He retrieved his cell phone from his back pocket and opened his calendar. "What date?"

"How about this Thursday at 5:30? And, for that matter, every Thursday at 5:30, until further notice?"

The hand holding his phone slowly lowered as his eyes lifted to hers. "Isn't that *your* regular appointment?"

"There's really no other day or time I can make it work. I'm giving up my individual appointments for the next few weeks so we, the parental units, can work all of this stuff out. And knock on wood, it's only until we get things settled with Robert."

Glancing at his calendar again, he rubbed the back of his neck. "It will be tight, and we'll have to come and go separately; but yeah, I can make it. And then maybe we can grab dinner nearby. A friend of mine who used to cook at Dunphy's works at a restaurant in that area, and he says it's amazing."

"It's a date!"

William cleared his throat. "How do you think Kevin will react to meeting me? Or... I guess, re-meeting me."

Julia squirmed, recalling the one and only time William and Kevin had met, in September of 1995. She wouldn't call that a proper meeting, though – it was more like a pissing contest.

William had surprised her with a visit to Santa Barbara. When he saw Kevin hug her a few seconds too long, he accused Julia of cheating on him – an accusation he leveled right there, in front of her dorm. With all her dorm-mates walking past, pretending not to eavesdrop.

Of course, she hadn't been cheating, and the humiliation was the final nail in the coffin of their relationship. Between his jealousy and her anxiety around her flagging grades, they had both been too young and insecure to weather the strain of a long-distance relationship.

Still, that was then, and this was now. If any jealousy lingered in William's heart, it didn't show. Anxiety was the only emotion marring his features.

"The bottom line is, Kevin says he'll do whatever is best for the kids," Julia finally answered. "And Aaron says if that's really the case, Kevin will come around, especially once his lawyer tells him he doesn't have a legal leg to stand on."

"What do you mean?'"

"You know – like if he wanted to keep you away from Robert, or something."

William nodded, digesting this. "I won't let myself stress about it. We'll cross that bridge together, if we ever come to it."

Together. That single word made Julia's heart expand within her chest, revealing itself in the smile on her face. The idea of them doing things *together* from now on – solving problems *together...* it still felt like a miracle.

Still, emotional support didn't translate to money. And neither of them was exactly raking in the dough. "I just pray Kevin doesn't change his mind and decide he *doesn't* have the kids' best interests at heart. Because I can't afford the attorneys' fees, especially now that Lars and Meg dropped me."

William straightened. "Have you thought about asking Holly and Aaron if they'd let you set up an aquarium in their reception areas?"

"Holly lives in Boston now." She played with the ends of her still-damp hair. "Maybe I should have reached out to Aaron long before now. You know – no stone unturned. But I don't know; I guess I felt like it would be taking advantage of our family relationship."

"You're the only one that knows what's best, where mixing business and family are concerned. I was just throwing it out there."

She lifted her eyes to his face. "By the way... I'm not sure if I'm doing the right thing, but I thought I should let you know what Alison said last night."

One eyebrow lifted. "Alison?"

"She told me Mike hasn't responded to any of her calls or texts."

She instantly regretted her decision when William's brows pulled down. "It's like I said before," he muttered. "This is what Mike does when he's using. He cuts everyone off. Once he's run out of ways to manipulate or steal from them, I mean."

Despite their no-contact rule, she scooted closer and took his hand. Gently she said, "I'm sorry. I shouldn't have brought it up."

His brow unfurrowed, and he took both of her hands in his. Dipping his head just enough to catch her eye, he said, "Julie, you can talk to me about anything. *Anything*, okay? Nothing is off limits."

Touched, she slowly nodded her understanding. He drew a breath, and she sensed he was gathering his thoughts.

"You know my dad was a high-functioning alcoholic, right?" he finally asked.

"I kind of figured that out over the years, yeah."

"He would work all day and drink himself to sleep every night. What Dad died from – esophageal cancer – it's common among alcoholics and smokers, and he was both. Uncle Frank is an alcoholic, too; and then of course, Jimmy died of a heroin overdose. The addiction gene is strong in my family, which is why I try really hard to avoid alcohol now. I hate to bring this up again, Julie, but during those few months in '95 and '96, after we split up, alcohol and weed were my poisons." Seizing her hands in his again, he quickly added, "The only reason I'm telling you this is because I may not be able to do anything about the genetic side, but I can do something about the environmental side. And I don't want our son to grow up watching people cope with life by using substances. That's how I grew up; but Robert? He won't."

"I know, Will," Julia said, keenly aware that he had just referenced their future together as a family, and feeling her whole body flush in response.

"Well, you shouldn't be so confident." When Julia flinched, he explained, "Managing this disease of addiction takes constant vigilance, and you deserve to go into things with your eyes open. I still have a sponsor; still check in at AA meetings from time to time. So I guess what I'm saying is... once we have a home of our own, we can't keep alcohol around. Like, at all. I hope that doesn't sound like a tyrannical proclamation; it's just a reality and a limitation of living with me, and you deserve to know that up front."

Julia freed one hand to brush it across his hair, then traced her fingertip down his jawline. Softly, she said, "Is that all you're worried about?"

He gave a rueful chuckle. "I wish. But on top of all that, I won't be able to take you to places that serve alcohol. At least, not places that focus on it, like bars, or wineries. It's a big part of why I stopped playing with a band."

"I don't need to go to those places. Or if I ever do, I'll just drag someone else along. I can take it or leave it."

"And that's exactly what I'm afraid I wouldn't be able to do – leave it. So like I said, I might allow myself a single sip of champagne during my sister's wedding toast; but after that, you're stuck with this boring teetotaler for the rest of your life."

She freed her hand from his grasp and, together with her other one, framed his face. "Will... imagining a future with you is the least boring way I can think of to spend my time. Being stuck with you for the rest of my life sounds like nirvana. A second ago, I said I can take alcohol or leave it. What I can't leave off, though, is how much I love you and want you."

Her declaration seemed to take his breath away, along with his voice. As she continued clasping his face in her hands, his eyes flitted between hers, then dropped to her mouth. His smile sneaked in sideways as heat infiltrated his gaze.

She had never felt this with anyone but him – this ache that was almost painful. This confluence of love and lust that threatened to unravel her.

She lowered one hand from his face and allowed her fingertips to brush against his, resting on his knee. Still staring into his eyes, swallowing past the lump forming in her throat, she whispered, "I love you so much, I can't breathe right now."

She thought she heard a little gasp as his eyes rolled shut – as he absorbed the impact of her admission. He took her hand from his knee and pressed it against his lips, holding it there. "Me too," he whispered finally against her fingers.

"I can't believe I'm here, looking at you," she admitted. "What have I ever done to deserve this?"

His eyes opened, and he pressed her hand against his wildly flailing heart. With the fingertips of his free hand, he traced the side of her face. "You're brilliant, and loving, and funny. You're the most beautiful woman I have ever laid eyes on." He tucked a lock of hair behind her ear. "I've never once stopped loving you. Not for a second. Not even a little."

His breathless confession melted her soul and set her body ablaze. She was so turned on that she squirmed, and she didn't even care that he could see it. The way he swallowed hard in response only poured fuel on the flame.

She whispered, "We could."

His eyes fluttered closed. Clearly torn, his brow furrowed, and his nostrils flared as he exhaled a puff of air. But he said nothing.

"Considering my track record with the pill, I got an IUD a few months after Robert was born, and I still have it. The irony is..." Her voice trailed off a bit, her next thought dumping a bucket of ice water over her libido. But his eyes were open again, searching hers. "It turns out, I, uh... I never had any need for it. And, um... that also means I don't even need to be tested."

It only took him a few seconds to grasp her meaning. He looked down at her hand and petted it, caressing her fingers. She felt a lump rising in her throat, and quickly gulped it down.

Breathless, she whispered, "What about you?"

He lifted his eyes with a quizzical look. "What *about* me?"

"Has there been anyone in your life over the past few years?"

He brushed her cheek with the tip of his thumb, but said nothing. She put her hand over his and said, "It's okay. I know I was at a really insecure place six years ago, but that's long since behind me."

"Julie... there's been absolutely no one since you. Not even once."

She gaped at him in utter disbelief, but his eyes told her he wasn't joking. Her chest flooded with a familiar warmth.

The tops of his ears reddened, and he gave her a shy smile. "Is that really so hard to believe?"

"Yes!" blurted Julia, and after a startled moment, they both burst out laughing. "Surely you had plenty of opportunities?"

While his eyes flitted back and forth between hers, his thumb caressed her lip. "I learned my lesson a long time ago. In the long run, meaningless encounters only make me more miserable. And I sure as hell wasn't ready for anything like a relationship when I still wanted you so much." His voice trailed off into a whisper.

The warmth in her chest rocketed straight southward, fully rousing the long-dormant fire-breathing dragon in the pit of her belly. Speechless, she nuzzled his beard with her hand. The revelation that he had gone without sex just as long as she had – that he was probably aching for it just as badly – obliterated all room in her brain for anything else.

He still caressed her lips, and as his eyes flickered to her mouth, she lightly kissed the tip of his thumb, her tongue darting out to taste him. His pupils dilated until the blue of his irises nearly vanished, and he drew a sharp breath before sliding his thumb a little further into her mouth. She sucked, swirling her tongue around it, her eyes still riveted to his – a preview of coming attractions.

And then he tangled his hand through the hair on the back of her head, crushing her mouth into his. She opened to him on a moan and his tongue probed deep, tangling with hers, together with his thumb.

Almost frantic. She let her hand stray up his thigh, between his legs. Stroked him through his jeans, and found him already fully erect.

He seized her by the waist and stood, lifting her like she weighed nothing at all, and setting her feet on the rug. After a frantic scuffle, their clothes littered the floor. He clasped her hands in his and stepped back to take in the sight of her naked body, and she took in the sight of his.

The beauty of him sucked the air from her lungs. His body had always been breathtaking – devastating, really – but never in all their time together had he been this fit, lean, and toned. Not in some artificially-carved, gym-rat way; but naturally, in the way of a man who lived an active life.

She seemed to have the same effect on him as his eyes slowly traveled her, memorizing her. His lips parted, and the rise and fall of his chest further deepened. Then he pulled her into him again, and they both sighed with the pleasure of their bare skin pressed together, of putting their hands and mouths all over each other's bodies.

"Oh, God," he gasped, his eyes rolling back as she wrapped her hand around his erection, stroking. He was so hard for her that it stood almost straight up.

Desperate, she glanced around, whispering, "Where's the bed?" And then she laughed as he hurled the sofa cushions across the room and yanked a strap, unfurling the sofa-bed with the sheets still on it. He literally swept her off her feet again before gently laying her down on the mattress. He hovered over her, his lips still parted; and she yelped in surprise when he gripped her behind the knees and yanked her bottom to the edge of the mattress.

She craned her neck up to watch, licking her lips in anticipation, her sex flush scorching her skin all the way to her scalp. He held her gaze as he knelt on the floor and draped her legs over his shoulders. Her head dropped back onto the mattress, and she groaned in relief at the first touch of his tongue. At the same time, he slipped a fingertip inside of her and stroked her with a come-hither motion. With his other hand he grasped and kneaded her breasts, each in turn.

He had lost nothing in the past six years – he still knew her body inside and out, as if by muscle memory or even instinct. As if he had thought about her, and about this, every day of his life since. Tiny sounds of relish escaped him, as if he were slowly desiccating in some desert and the taste of her was the only thing that would quench his thirst. And she was only too happy to oblige – within less than a minute, her back arched and she cried out, sending her screams up to his ceiling as she flooded him with her orgasm.

He waited until the writhing and gasping finally slowed and her body came to a rest. Then he climbed up and over her. Grasped her face in his hands. Feathered kisses all along her face, trembling with restraint until she nodded her readiness.

"Julie," he whispered, hoarse with longing. "I want this more than I've ever wanted anything in my life."

She breathed as he sank into her, sweeping away all the years of solitude, of waking at midnight, desperately trying to claw her way back to sleep where he was still waiting. Everything else around them faded as well, and the only thing left was this rapture of moving together.

AFTERWARD, he slid his palm between her back and the mattress and rolled them both onto their sides. They faced each other, tenderly kissing, her leg slung across his hip; and their eyes roamed each other's faces. He slid his hand to her bottom, pushed her hips into his and stayed inside of her as long as humanly possible.

"I love you," he whispered after a while.

"I love you so much," she murmured in reply.

He kissed her again, his tongue sliding lazily along hers. Then he whispered against her lips, "Why does it always feel so good?"

Her mouth twisted into a wry smile. "A six-year dry spell will do that."

"No, it's always been like this with you. Nothing and no one turns me on the way you do."

The overwhelming adoration nearly incapacitated her, but she managed to whisper, "Same, sweetheart." She kissed him again and stroked his hair; but when she pulled back, his eyes were troubled.

She touched his face. "What's the matter?"

After a moment's hesitation, he admitted, "I wasn't exactly planning to do this so soon."

She propped herself up on her elbow and gazed at him. "Are you sorry?"

He tucked a lock of hair behind her ear. "I could never be sorry for this."

"Then why do you look like a kid on his last day of summer vacation?"

He humored her with a halfhearted smile, but said nothing. She took his hand and pressed it against her heart, and finally he admitted, "After this, I don't know how I'm supposed to let you go."

"Let me go?" She ran the back of her fingers down the side of his face. "What are you talking about?"

His brows came together, as if he, himself, were confused. "Well, at the very least, I don't know how I'm supposed to let you go home, not knowing when I'll see you again."

"Oh, that's easy – tomorrow. At dinner."

He gave her the stink eye. "You know what I mean."

"Yes, I do. You mean 'see' as in 'know.' And you mean 'know' in the Biblical sense." He laughed, and she added, "So what else?"

"Come again?"

She nodded enthusiastically. "Yes, please."

He tickled her in retaliation, and she whooped with glee as she batted his arms away.

"Let me rephrase," he laughed, and then froze. "Wait – where did we leave off, again?"

"Letting me go."

"Oh, right. That's a downer. No wonder I blocked it out of my memory."

"Yeah, nice try, but you're not getting off the hook that easily." He grinned, and she persisted, "So what else do you mean when you say you don't know how you're supposed to let me go? Because I'm far too full of myself to believe you'd dump me *now*."

"Not if you keep doing the things you just did to me."

"What, making lame jokes?" She wiped her forehead in facetious relief and flicked away imaginary beads of sweat. "Thank God – I have a never-ending supply of those."

He took her fingers in his hand and kissed them. His eyes crinkled up at the corners in the way she had always loved.

"Letting me go," she persisted, more gently this time. "I'm gonna take a wild guess here – you mean if I leave you. As in, for good." He said nothing; just looked at her poignantly. She seized his hand and kissed it, again and again, blinking back the ill-timed tears that stung her eyes. "Now I'll tell you what I've told practically everybody, except the one person I should have told it to long ago."

"Who?"

"*You*, of course. Ready? Here goes." With a shaky laugh, she admitted, "I'm terrified."

"What?" His eyes widened. "Why?"

"Because I've grown attached. Maybe too attached; and maybe too soon. Not just to you, but to the hope that you're going to stay with me. Like, forever. And every time I remember how many hurdles we still have to clear – when I remember it's only been a few *days*, for Christ's sake – I'm terrified. But at this point, I just give up – I love you too much. You're the very heart and soul of me, Will. You always have been."

"Julie," he whispered raggedly, his face suddenly red, his forehead creased with emotion. He drew her closer and rolled onto his back, gently pulling her head down on his chest. He held her tight against his side and stroked her hair.

Finally, he admitted, "My feelings... I don't think I could have said it any better, myself. How you feel is exactly how I feel. What you want is exactly what I want. It's all I've ever wanted for sure in life – to share it with you."

She propped herself up on his chest. Looked into his eyes. "I know there's a lot of trust that needs to be rebuilt."

"Julie." He touched the mermaid pendant dangling from its chain around her neck. "Please don't say that."

"I mean..." She played with the St. Peter pendant on the chain around his own neck while she chose her next words carefully. "It's like I said before. Maybe I have no right to make you any promises, after everything that happened last time, but–"

"If you mean the last time we broke up, it's time to let that go." When Julia's eyes widened, he stroked her hair. "I hold no grudges for the choices you made. Most of them weren't even choices; not really. There was nothing different you could have done when you were so sick, and unable to function, and completely vulnerable, and your daughter was so unhappy… I've let it go, and I think you should too."

"Will… the point is, I want this to work with every fiber of my existence, but it would be naïve if I swore with any certainty that it will. The kids' well-being still has to be my number one priority, of course. But otherwise, I plan to proceed as if you're non-optional. Because that's exactly how I feel."

"Me too," he whispered. He cupped the back of her head with his hand and pulled her down for a deep kiss, and Julia breathed in his heady cologne of soap and sweat and sex. And later she wondered if they might have gone another round, had they not heard the scratching on William's patio door.

William grinned against her lips. "Diego knows we're home."

"The whole house probably knows." Julia snickered, blushing at the sudden recollection of how loudly she had screamed his name.

"Do you mind if I let him in?"

"I don't know if I'm ready for your dog to see me naked. It feels like a big step, this early in our acquaintance."

He quirked a single eyebrow. "I'm sure he can wait while you get dressed, if you're that priggish about it."

"Nah; on second thought, it's bound to happen eventually. May as well get it over with."

Still grinning, he got out of bed to retrieve his boxers from the haphazard pile of clothes on the floor. Safely reinstalled in them, he peered through the vertical blinds to make sure there were no humans on his patio. Then he drew back the blinds and slid open the door, and Diego bounded in, the entire back half of his body wagging with unrestrained joy.

While William squatted to rub Diego's ears, Julia sat up in bed. She couldn't help snickering at her own absurd self-consciousness as she tugged the sheets and blankets up over her breasts. At her movement, Diego's ears pricked, his jaw snapped shut, and his head whipped around, searching. When he spotted Julia, his tongue unfurled, and he hurtled himself onto the bed. Julia yelped with glee as he nearly tackled her with face licks. Finally abandoning all attempts at modesty, she allowed the covers to fall, and vigorously rubbed him along both flanks.

William climbed back into bed with a tender smile, his eyes riveted to Julia's face as she wrestled with Diego and giggled like a maniac. Finally, after a couple of minutes, she lifted her eyes to his.

"What?" she snickered, acutely aware again of her literal and figurative nakedness.

He tucked a lock of hair behind her ear and cupped her chin in his hand. "A little over a week ago, I believed I'd never see you again. I had reconciled myself to being alone for the rest of my life. And now look at you – you're here. With me. In my bed. And you're more beautiful than ever."

Love and tenderness threatened to overwhelm her. She didn't know whether to smile, cry, or laugh; she couldn't even summon words. But apparently the look on her face was enough, because he leaned over and touched a soft kiss to her lips.

Her eyes drifted to the new tattoo on his left bicep. She touched it and said, "I see you learned what it means."

He gave a quizzical tip of the head. "What *what* means?"

"My middle name. Róisín."

"I've always known what it means," he said, "and it suits you."

"It was my Gran's name."

"I know that, too, Little Rose."

Her smile flashed across her face before quickly fading. "I'm afraid to even ask what it's about."

He looked down at it and said quietly, "It's also based on an old sailor tattoo. A dagger through a rose meant a sailor was loyal."

"But it looks like it's more than just a rose."

Suddenly bashful, he pointed to the stem and said, "See how all these little thorns are arranged?"

Now that Julia looked, the tiny thorns' arrangement wasn't haphazard, like she would expect on a real rose. Most of them occurred in pairs that flanked either side of the stem. Two singleton thorns, one on top of the other, flanked only the right side. And the bottom two pairs jutted from the stem at an angle.

"Does that remind you of anything?" William prompted.

Julia frowned, inspecting it even closer, but she drew a blank.

"Have you ever heard of the Ogham script?"

Julia's eyebrows raised, and she lifted her eyes to his. "The ancient Irish alphabet?"

He nodded.

"You mean this spells something?"

"Some*one*."

Her hand went to her mouth as she started to grasp his meaning.

Reddening a bit, he looked back down at the tattoo. "There wasn't really an Ogham letter for J. So I spelled it the Italian way." He pointed to each letter in turn, going vertically down the stem. "G-I-U-L-I-A."

"Oh my God," she said, her heart threatening to slam right through the wall of her chest.

He peered up at her through his lashes. "Should I not have told you?"

"No! I mean yes – *yes*, you absolutely should have told me. I just..." She grunted in frustration with herself. "I'm sorry."

"For what?"

"Well, for..." She gestured to his rose-heart, stabbed through with the dagger. "For hurting you."

"Is that all you got from that?" He shook his head, smiling. "Didn't you hear me when I said it means loyalty?"

"Yeah, but... it's also shaped like a heart."

"Sure. But you know what my mom said: I have a loyal heart."

"And she'd be damned if she let me anywhere near it again."

"But that's not something she's ever had any say over. You've always been there, no matter what she or anyone else thinks about it. I love you more than anything, Julia – except, now, also, our son."

"Will..." His name escaped as a whisper. She kissed him, her heart contorting with poignant feelings. "I love you."

"And I want you to stay with me tonight, but I know you can't. So in just an hour or so, I'm going to have to say goodbye and let you walk out my door, and I'll have to come back to this bed alone. Do you have any idea how hard that is for me?"

She reached between his legs, over his boxers. "Apparently only half-way-hard?"

"Oh my God, you're shameless," William groaned through a laugh, grabbing her around the waist and lifting her into his lap, facing him. In response, Diego barked and sprang to his feet, assuming it was playtime again. Julia and William both laughed and petted him; but after a minute, William said, "Diego, *abajo*." Diego obediently jumped down from the bed and curled up on the floor to wait.

"I *am* shameless," Julia admitted, "but I swear I wasn't trying to trivialize what you said. You know me – I just can't resist a good setup."

"Yes, I know you," he said softly.

He kissed her deeply for a while, sliding his palms over her bare backside and up her torso, her ribcage, her breasts; and as she straddled his lap with her arms hooked over his shoulders, she could see where things were headed.

He broke the kiss, put his lips to her ear and murmured, "So what are we going to do about this? Us sleeping together, I mean."

At the warm tickle of his words against her ear, Julia's skin erupted into a million goose bumps. "Hopefully, more."

He laughed softly as he nibbled her earlobe. "But how?"

The goose bumps dispersed. "I don't know. I'm not sure I'd feel good about imposing on people to watch the kids while we sleep together. Certainly not on anything like a regular basis."

He pondered this in silence for a minute. "You didn't say never, though."

She grinned up at him. "I mean, maybe once a month?"

He considered some more. "I know my mom and sister would love spending time with Robert – getting to know him. I bet he'd have a blast hanging out with Xavier and Zach, too."

"And my sister is Paige's absolute favorite. Paige is always on her best behavior when she's over there; and I think Alison has a knack for bringing out the best in Paige, too."

"And then there's your parents. And, eventually... Kevin." The name landed between them with a thud. "How often do you think he'll have the kids, once he's back in Santa Barbara?"

"Aaron says it will most likely be one weekend a month, like before."

"Well then... there's that."

"And then, once he's defended his dissertation, he's coming back to the Bay Area permanently, and he'll get fifty-fifty custody. But that probably won't be until September."

She was powerless to conceal the note of strain in her voice. He looked down at her, scanning her face. "You're sad."

"At the prospect of missing out on half of the kids' childhood from now on? Yeah."

"Oh..." He gathered her up in a tender hug, stroking the hair that tumbled down her back. "I'm sorry. I hadn't even considered that take."

"It's hard," she said, her voice still strangled. "But I have to admit – it would be much harder if I didn't have you. I'm just afraid to contemplate what that says about me as a mother."

"What *what* says?"

"That in spite of my sadness at the idea of not having the kids every day, some part of me is actually looking forward to some time to myself. To *our*selves." She squeezed his arm for emphasis at these last two words.

"It says you're a flesh-and-blood human being with independent needs and interests. And I think it's actually healthy for your kids to see you attending to those things."

Julia smirked up at him. "It's healthy for them to see their mother indulging her libido?"

"Stop," he laughed, poking her ribs lightly, making her giggle. "You know what I mean."

"Oh! And then there's Kevin's parents. The kids spend the last weekend of every month with them in Atherton. I mean, you and I could even bump our little slumber parties up to *twice* a month, since Kevin's parents are already a standing monthly appointment."

His mouth twisted into a coy little smile. "I fully intend to do as little slumbering as possible on those occasions."

TUESDAY, MAY 15 – FRIDAY, MAY 18, 2012

As penance for her Monday self-indulgence, Julia spent the rest of the week at the shop, head down, playing catch up. Behind only caring for the fish, marketing became Priority One-Point-One. If she ever hoped to recover from losing Lars and Meg's account, she would have to win new ones.

Between all of this, plus cleaning, ordering, bookkeeping, inventory, and, of course, customers – Julia found precious little time to reflect on the soap opera playing out in her personal life.

But every night that week, William came over for dinner. On Tuesday, he even did the cooking – a mild version of cold sesame noodles that even the kids loved, garnished with cucumbers and peanuts. And every night, he spent an hour teaching Robert and Paige more chords – Robert on his preschooler-sized guitar, Paige on a guitar he bought for her from an estate sale.

On Wednesday night, William accompanied Julia and Robert to tee-ball practice; and then on Thursday, he met Julia at Clio's office in the Mission for a productive session. Afterward, they walked to the fancy-schmancy New American restaurant William's coworker had recommended.

"Wow; you weren't kidding – this place is outstanding," Julia remarked as the restaurant hostess ushered them to their table.

Julia took in the warm, wood-paneled dining room, the inviting bar with its fully-stocked shelves bathed in amber light, and the stamped-copper tile ceiling. She admired the grain in the tabletops' honey-colored wood, and the chairs with their leather seat cushions and woven-rattan backs. It was thoroughly classy without being over-starched.

Julia's dad could stand to take a page or two from this restaurant's playbook. She had been to some of the best and most expensive restaurants in the world with Kevin and his family, but this place somehow managed to combine special occasion vibes with the feeling of entering a friend's home.

After taking their seats and ordering their non-alcoholic drinks, William reached across the table for her hand. "Have I told you how beautiful you look in that dress?"

Julia sat back just enough to peer in disbelief at her solid red dress, with its V-neck and cap sleeves. "It's just one of those non-wrinkle things. Something I can fold down to the size of a credit card and change into after dance class."

But his smile only widened as his eyes swept over her, lingering on the mermaid pendant resting in the hint of cleavage above the V-neck-line. "So I guess that's what *you've* been doing."

"Doing...?"

"To stay fit. You asked me last week what I was doing to keep in such good shape." He ran his fingertips up her arms, coaxing goosebumps from the skin there. "Bollywood dance is obviously what *you've* been doing."

Julia smiled. "That, yes; but my job is a workout in and of itself. I carry around some big jugs."

He laughed out loud at this. His stunning eyes were an even more unreal shade of blue in this light, and her pulse fluttered at the intensity of his gaze. She wondered if he, too, was thinking of what happened Monday.

He said, "I have a surprise for you."

"What is it?"

"Well, if I told you, it wouldn't be a surprise, would it?"

She harrumphed. "Lame."

"So, don't take this the wrong way, but for me to show it to you, we'll have to go back to my apartment." His coy grin sneaked in from the side. "I don't mean we have to go *inside* my apartment. Just *to* it."

"But I thought going inside was part of the plan," she said. "I brought my bundling board."

He pretended to search underneath the table. "Does your bundling board fold down to the size of a credit card, too? And besides, isn't it a bit too late for bundling boards? I mean, considering our Monday extracurriculars."

"It's a *figurative* bundling board, and tonight, we're gonna be chaste as fuck."

"Oxymoron much?" William retorted, and at the same time, their server arrived with their drinks. From the smirk on her face, it was obvious she had heard every word; and after she left, Julia and William spent the next five minutes snickering behind their hands like teenagers, until tears stung their eyes.

After rolling their eyes in ecstasy at their bourbon-glazed pork chops and South Carolina-style shrimp and grits, they staggered, bloated, to William's apartment. Julia rested her head on William's shoulder, groaning in pain and trying very hard not to burp or fall asleep standing up.

They crossed Van Ness, and William led Julia around the corner and up the block, until he stopped directly in front of his apartment. He stood there on the curb with a little smile, as if waiting for her to notice something.

"What?" she said, looking all around. She saw nothing out of the ordinary.

That's when he placed his hand on top of a silver Jeep parked along the curb. "Here she is. All mine."

Julia gaped, first at the Jeep, then at him. "Wait – you bought a car?"

"Not a car. A Jeep."

She walked around the Jeep, taking it in – a Wrangler. "Why?"

"Um… because I'm a very big boy now?" he joked. He shifted his weight, as if self-conscious. "I realized I'll be doing a lot of back and forth between my apartment and your house. And if I ever want to bring Robert anywhere, I'll need a safe way to chauffeur him. For that matter, sometimes I might want to chauffeur *all* of you." He hesitated, fixing his keen gaze on her. "Plus, I hope this doesn't sound incredibly chauvinistic, but I worry about you taking the bus on Thursday nights from the Mission to the Castro. I mean, *I* didn't even feel comfortable riding with you last Thursday." He patted the roof of the Jeep again. "So now I can take you myself."

Who knew that watching a hot guy turn into a family man would be such an aphrodisiac? Clearly, she was getting old. "Okay... wow. But do you have a driver's license?"

He startled her with a loud guffaw. "Is that a serious question?"

"I mean, I know you have one for a motorcycle, but–"

Sliding his arm around her waist, he yanked her right up against him and silenced her with a firm kiss on her mouth. "Yes, dork. For a car, too."

"Well," she said, still smiling, still breathless from his kiss, "I mean, you've never owned a car before, have you?"

"No, but that doesn't mean I've never driven one." He retrieved a key from the pocket of his jeans, unlocked the passenger door, and held it open for her. "So get in."

"Wait – I thought we were going back to your apartment to practice safe chastity."

He laughed, but his look was apologetic. "I hate to admit it, Julie, but I'm pretty wiped. It's been a long week, and my busiest day is tomorrow." He tucked a lock of her hair behind her ear, peering earnestly into her eyes. "Plus, you look pretty tired, yourself."

"Gee, thanks," she said, smiling up at him so he would know she wasn't really offended.

"Well, aren't you?"

"Tired?" In truth, she was about to fall asleep standing up. "Sure, but only because making out isn't on the menu. If it was, I'd be getting my second wind right about now."

He grinned, shifting his arms around her waist a bit tighter, but said nothing.

"Wow, look at us, turning into geezers!" But she cast his new Jeep some serious side-eye again.

"Oh my God, woman; do I have to lift you and put you in there myself?"

To her own dismay, the mental image of him cave-manning her into his car inflamed her libido all over again. "Yes."

He laughed and swept his hand toward the car in an *after you* gesture. "Get in, you menace."

"Aye aye, cap'n."

FRIDAY, MAY 25, 2012

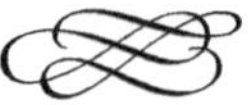

The next week went by much as the previous one had, with one glaring exception – Kevin's looming return from the Galapagos.

All week, an electric current pulsed through Paige and Robert as they counted down the days. And an anxious energy thrummed through Julia and William when he came over in the evenings.

To William's credit, he kept his cool each time Robert mentioned his excitement that "Daddy" was coming home. Maybe William, like Julia, found some small measure of consolation knowing that at least they would enjoy an entire holiday weekend alone.

As for Paige, her answering scowl each time Robert mentioned Kevin spoke volumes without words. Julia made sure to email Clio with plenty of heads-up for her Thursday evening session with Paige. Julia had sacrificed her usual appointment time in anticipation of Paige and Kevin's Friday reunion.

On Friday, Julia trudged through work in a thick fog of anticipatory lust. She closed shop early that day to pick the kids up from school, so why did it feel like the longest workday of her life? The kids' bags were packed and waiting at home, and Julia's was in the trunk of her Subaru. She had a few non-perishable groceries in her trunk already, and she would run by the market in the Mission before letting herself into William's apartment with the key he had given her. She planned to surprise him – not only with herself, but with dinner already cooked and waiting.

Still, it was with almost crippling trepidation that Julia answered the front door. Julia and the kids had not seen Kevin in the flesh in almost a year – certainly not since Julia's reconciliation with William. She had no idea what kind of greeting awaited her.

Kevin's wary eyes flickered briefly over her as he pushed his heavy black-rimmed glasses up the bridge of his nose. He had lost some weight, and a hint of scalp peeked through the thinning curls on the crown of his head. New flecks of gray stippled his dark beard and hair.

Julia nodded in greeting and held the door open. Kevin cleared his throat, but said nothing as he crossed into the foyer. Julia had barely closed the door before Robert surged out of the in-law unit with an exuberant shout. Beaming, Kevin hoisted him in the air, and Robert wrapped his arms and legs around Kevin's torso with a whoop of glee: *"Daddy!"*

Julia's heart gave a poignant squeeze at the reminder that this man was, after all, the only daddy Robert had known. And Kevin positively glowed to be holding his son again.

"I missed you so much, Tadpole," Kevin said, burying his nose in Robert's hair. Setting Robert back on his feet, he added, "Look how much you've grown!

"I'm not a tadpole anymore," Robert agreed, and Kevin's laugh was unadulterated joy.

Paige appeared in the doorway to the den, where she had been waiting with Robert. Looking a bit uncertain with her arms crossed, she leaned against the door frame, staring, unfocused, at the umbrella stand by the front door.

"Paige," Kevin breathed out, taking a tentative step toward her. "Look at you! You've grown so much, too."

"Too bad you weren't here to see it happen." Paige pinned her father with a defiant glare, but behind the challenge, Paige's pain was clear to see.

Kevin's smile evaporated, and he swallowed thickly. "I was planning to take you guys for dumplings before we head to the airport. Does that sound good?"

Dumplings were Paige's favorite. She gave a noncommittal shrug, but she bolted upstairs to fetch her shoes and jacket. With that, Kevin offered Julia a sheepish smile, which Julia returned with an encouraging one of her own. Kevin may have been flawed in many ways, but until now, he was the only father figure the kids had; and he was trying.

After her mother came downstairs to offer a polite greeting, Kevin left with both kids. Now with a one-track mind, Julia drove across the city and parked around the corner from William's apartment, stopping at the small Mexican grocery to buy the perishable ingredients for dinner.

TWO HOURS LATER, chicken tinga was keeping warm on the stove, the fresh ingredients for tacos were prepped and ready to go, and Julia herself had showered and changed into a fresh slip of a dress. She curled up on William's couch, trying in vain to read a book pulled from his shelf. After re-reading the first page over and over without absorbing a single word, she realized that she had forgotten what book she had chosen. She closed the cover and examined the title – *East of Eden*.

It was useless – an electric current pulsed through every inch of her skin and every hyper-aware nerve ending.

And that's when she finally heard Williams's key turning in the front door.

Her heart in her windpipe, she stopped herself just short of leaping to her feet. Instead, to channel her nervous energy, she went to fidget with the place settings at his little table until the front door swung open.

He pulled up short at the sight of her. Shock had apparently stolen his voice, too, because all he could do was gape.

She gestured theatrically at the table, like a housewife in a campy fifties commercial. "Welcome home, honey!"

He shifted his sunglasses to the top of his head. He was a god in nothing more than a three-button maroon henley with the sleeves hitched up, and a pair of worn jeans.

Swallowing hard, he finally blinked. "You're here!"

She made cheesy jazz hands, and then he stared long and hard at the table, laid out with candles and placemats and cloth napkins and good tableware and scrumptious-smelling food. His forehead creased; his eyes wore a conflicted, pained expression.

Her pulse accelerated, and she swallowed hard. "Are you hungry?"

He lifted his eyes to hers again, then raked them down her tiny dress with its spaghetti straps, and her bare legs that stretched beneath its hem.

"Am I hungry?" His jaw ticking, he dropped his bag on the floor with a thud, then crossed the room in a handful of resolute strides. "Yes."

"Thank God," she breathed the second before he snatched her up; and his ravenous growls as his mouth took hers matched his wolfish leer a moment ago.

Her dress roughly parted ways with her body as he yanked it up over her head. She answered by ripping his shirt over his head just as aggressively; and then he jerked her strapless bra down.

His aqua irises darkening to cobalt, he stared at her bare breasts for one reverent second before dipping to devour them, grunting like she was the best thing he had ever tasted. Holding his head against her, she closed her eyes on a moan and turned her face up to the ceiling. Tenderly he traced the margins of her nipples with his tongue; then she hissed in satisfaction as he sucked their hardened peaks between his lips.

Falling to his knees, he kissed his way down the underside of her breasts and her stomach, tapping his tongue into her navel before trailing it to the waistband of her panties. With his teeth, he dragged them to the floor.

And then, without warning, he tossed her thigh over his shoulder and buried his face between her legs. She groaned so loudly that the whole neighborhood would have heard, had he not reached up with one long arm to cover her mouth.

But more than anything on the planet, she needed to feel him filling her, the ragged edges of his breath skittering across her skin. She needed that more than she needed oxygen itself.

So she snatched his hand and tugged him to his feet. He gazed down at her, his eyes a question she answered by fumbling with his belt, her hands shaking uncontrollably with need. He quickly lost patience and flicked it open himself. She jerked his zipper so roughly that the tab broke off. Grunting in approval, he seized the fabric of his fly with both hands and ripped it open the rest of the way.

Dropping to her knees, she yanked his pants and boxers down in one movement, and took him into her mouth with a greedy, guttural sound. He swore and tangled his fingers through her hair; and as her mouth and hands took the measure of him, he groaned out a string of profanities so long and loud, she was positive the whole neighborhood heard this time.

After only a few seconds, he murmured, "No, no, no," and his fingers gently nudged the underside of her chin; so she released him with a final swirl of her tongue and a parting kiss. Before she could get to her feet, he swept her up, wrapped her legs around his waist, and walked her backward.

"I need it," she moaned, so out of her mind that she didn't even know what she was saying.

"What do you need, Julie?" he rasped out against her lips, still walking her backward.

"You," she pleaded. "Inside."

He granted her wish as soon as her back hit the wall. "Tell me how," he gasped against her cheek as he thrust into her. "How do you need me?"

"*Hard*, Will."

He delivered in spades. "Tell me you need it as bad as I do."

"I need it," she practically sobbed, her fingers curling at the sensation of him hitting so deep. "I need *you*."

As she dug her nails into his sweat-slickened back, he drew a shaky breath and hissed the word *yes*. If it was possible for him to pound into her even faster, he did.

"Tell me you've been thinking about me all day," he ground out.

"God, yes, Will; you're all I can think about."

His warning sounds stuttered against her cheek, along with his breaths. His whole body tensed and trembled.

He shouted her name just before unleashing a volley of near-screams, and she arched her hips, making herself concave. She wanted to absorb everything he gave her, as much as possible, for as long as possible. She wanted to absorb his entire body inside of hers.

Gradually his cries subsided into helpless moans, but he continued to pulse into her rhythmically until his grip loosened. As he slipped out of her with a grunt, he summoned the last of his energy to carry her to the bed.

He laid her down on the mattress, gently cradling the back of her head with his hand until it sank into the pillow. Then he lowered himself on top of her, kissing her tenderly, gazing into her eyes with something akin to awe.

"I love you," he said in a whisper.

"Will," she whispered back, stroking his hair, her eyes flickering back and forth between his. "I love you so much."

He kissed her once more; then, with an enormous sigh of relief, his eyes rolled shut and he lowered his forehead onto the pillow beside her head. She heard him whisper, "Julie.... nothing has ever felt this good."

Melting, she turned her head just enough to brush her lips against his cheek and the shell of his ear. "Same."

"I don't want to stop for anything."

"Not even for dinner?" she teased.

"I'm sorry; you were so sweet to cook for me." He was already kissing down her jaw, her neck. Her breasts. "And I certainly don't want all of your hard work to go to waste." He licked and gently nibbled his way down her stomach, past her navel. Shifted himself between her legs as she squirmed in anticipation, and lifted his eyes to hers. "But right now, I want *you* for dinner."

She arched her back with an ecstatic moan as his tongue zigzagged up the center of her, parting her. Tasting. Flickering. Gradually circling in on the most sensitive part of her, the part that screamed most insistently for its attention. Occasionally it strayed a bit lower, the tip of his tongue swirling her arousal with his own release, smearing it around her tender nub. It was erotic, and a little filthy, and he always remembered that she loved it.

She was panting now, the sweat beading on her flushed skin, her hips rocking in sync with his attentions. She reached down to fist some of his hair in her hands like she always used to, but it was too short now; so with a groan, she seized his whole head and ground herself into his face. She didn't even care anymore that she was probably suffocating him.

And then, finally – *finally* – his mouth zeroed in on its target, sucking, humming; and he slid two fingers inside of her, then three, curling them.

"Oh my God, Will – yes... *Yes!*"

She went blind as the ecstasy spiraled through the core of her and came blazing out through her fingertips, her toes, the top of her head. While her whole body convulsed, she dug her heels in and slid them along the mattress and fisted the bedsheets and screamed *oh my God, yes,* over and over again.

Some tiny corner of her consciousness marveled at how long the shockwaves surged through her, with no sign of slowing. But as the intervals between inevitably lengthened and their intensity ebbed, she savored every precious pulse and shudder, in case it was the last.

Then she lay there a long while, utterly paralyzed, her neck still craned backward in its orgasm reflex. Her eyes were still closed, her mouth open and breathing.

William still lay between her legs, his entire head moving in slow circles, caressing all of her with his whole face. She whimpered in appreciation at the erotic sounds his mouth made as he kissed and gently sucked where she was still so tender. At first, that was all her brain could process – pure sensation.

But after a geologic age, she became aware again of her surroundings – the buzz of his refrigerator; car engines zooming past on the street; dogs barking in the neighborhood.

The slow, rhythmic breathing of the best lover in the galaxy.

She peeled open her eyes and lifted her head to peer down at him. He pressed one last soft kiss between her legs, then grinned up at her, clearly very pleased with himself.

"Welcome back to Earth," he said, his voice deeper than usual – huskier. He climbed back over her and sealed his mouth over hers, offering her a taste of her own pleasure. She lazily wrapped her arm around the back of his head, pressing his mouth and tongue into hers. She felt him twitch against her hip and realized he was already hard again.

"I can't move," she offered by way of apology, her voice hoarse from screaming. "That was by far the best orgasm I have *ever* had."

"That's okay; I don't want your dinner to get any colder than it already is." He pressed another sensuous kiss to her mouth, then grinned. "But I have plans for you later, so don't even bother getting dressed."

"As long as you're willing to abide by those terms, yourself."

Over dinner, they fielded all sorts of grand possibilities for the next two evenings after William got off work. But Julia already sensed that none of those would happen. Instead, they would grab some takeout and end up right back in William's bed, both nights, for the entire night. And that was just fine with her.

THURSDAY, JUNE 7, 2012

On a Thursday nearly two weeks later, as she trudged through work in a fog of nerves, Julia renewed her prayers to the god of male egos to spare Kevin and William. All too soon, it was time to lock up and take the bus to the Mission. Then she was in Clio's waiting room with Kevin, who sat ramrod-straight in his chair, legs uncrossed, gripping the armrests with white knuckles. He lifted his eyes and, finding only Julia, blew out a breath of relief.

Julia claimed her own seat without a word. She pulled her phone from her purse and pretended to scroll through Facebook, but she could see nothing on the screen through her anxiety. Thankfully, Clio emerged a minute later, her warm voice and reassuring smile soothing Julia's nerves as she ushered them into her office.

She was impeccably dressed, as usual, in a flowy pants set with an orange, brown, and yellow geometric print. Clio once told Julia she had bought it in Nigeria while exploring her ancestral roots.

Julia's eyes lingered on the scarf around her neck. "Is that the one I gave you a few months ago?"

Clio's perfectly-tinted lips curved into a radiant smile. She touched the matching plum-colored muslin, with its delicate thread-like tassels and its subtle flecks of sparkle. "I still can't believe you made this for me."

"It looks great on you."

Clio had rearranged the furniture, pushing the sofa back against the wall and arranging three comfortable chairs around the room instead. All three chairs sat at a slight angle to each other, facing Clio's. The placement was deliberate – it offered everyone plenty of personal space, and they could see each other easily with a slight turn of the head; but no one was forced to stare anyone down, head-on.

"Julia, I thought you might like to sit here," she suggested, gesturing to the middle chair, and Julia suppressed a grim smirk. She knew it was a prudent arrangement under the circumstances, but ironically, it formed a real-life love triangle. It also put Julia directly in the line of fire, should the two men decide to throttle each other.

As Julia took her seat, Clio invited Kevin to choose whichever chair he preferred. After offering beverages, Clio finally dove in.

"First of all, I want to compliment you both for being here. It takes courage and wisdom, not to mention a lot of love for Robert and Paige. I just want to acknowledge that."

She paused to let her words wash over them. Julia nodded faintly, while Kevin cleared his throat and mumbled a stilted, "Thank you."

"I just want to review the plan," continued Clio. "First, when I hear the door chime, I'll go greet William in the waiting room and prepare him, just like I'm preparing you now. Then I'll bring him in and offer him something to drink before we start the introductions. Kevin, you said you'd feel comfortable with Julia introducing William, but you'd prefer not to shake his hand. Is that still the case?"

Kevin nodded, and the relentless bouncing of his knee was the only clue to his state of mind.

"When I spoke to William, he agreed to that, but I'll remind him in the waiting room," Clio continued. "After introductions, I'll guide us on some intention setting. From there we can start problem-solving on how to reach your goals as a family. Does that sound like what you were both expecting?"

Julia and Kevin both signaled their assent.

"Now, some quick guidelines to keep us headed in the right direction. First, don't talk over each other. I'll guide the conversation, giving each person their turn to speak. Please don't interrupt anyone else's turn. Try to focus on genuine listening, and not planning your next response. So far so good?"

Julia and Kevin murmured their agreement.

"If you need to talk about difficult feelings, just remember to use I-statements – when *blank,* I feel *blank.* But otherwise, let's try to keep the focus on problem solving – how we plan to explain things to Robert, and how you can keep the peace going forward, for everyone's sake."

Julia and Kevin agreed to those terms as well, and then Clio led them in a relaxation exercise. By the time they had finished, it was only another minute or two before they heard the telltale chime of Clio's door.

Clio turned her placid smile on both of them. "Are you ready?"

Julia glanced over at Kevin, who stared down at the rug. His Adam's apple bobbed in his throat, but he nodded his assent, and so did Julia. They agreed to continue with their silent mindfulness exercises after she left, and then Julia tried to spend the next ten minutes or so in meditation, eyes closed. But even if her exterior looked placid – and Julia was far from certain it did – her pulse jackhammered in her throat and swished through her ears.

The air grew stagnant with apprehension. This was it – the first time the two men would face each other since the confrontation, seventeen years ago, that doomed Julia and William's relationship. And now that the stakes were exponentially higher, they would all find out if those same two men could set aside their hurt feelings for the kids' benefit.

All too soon, Julia heard the creak of Clio's door, followed by Kevin sucking in an anxious breath. Her eyes flew open, and there he was, stepping into the office with his hands jammed into the pockets of his jeans.

William's gaze landed on Julia before flitting to Kevin. He ducked slightly, like he did when he wanted to appear non-threatening, and nodded toward Kevin in greeting.

"Please, make yourself comfortable," Clio prompted him.

William murmured something and quickly took his seat. Clio offered him a beverage, which he politely declined; and then she turned to Julia with an encouraging smile.

"Would you like to make the introductions?"

Julia shifted awkwardly in her chair as she introduced the only two men she had ever been with in her thirty-six years of life. They made brief eye contact and exchanged quiet, cursory greetings. And that was that.

Once again, Clio commended them all for being there, then gently steered them into intention-setting. They all agreed that they wanted what was best for everyone – for the three adults in Robert and Paige's lives to accept and respect each other's presence and involvement.

Then Clio led them into more perilous waters – the question of how to broach, with Robert, the subject of his paternity.

"I just don't want my history or my future as Robert's dad to be diminished in any way," Kevin explained when Clio prompted, his brows drawing together. "He calls me Dad now, and I always want him to think of me that way. Of course, William can be a dad to him, too. I just mean I don't want to set up a dynamic where one dad gets pitted against the other."

After a few moments to confirm that Kevin was finished, Clio thanked him and prompted William to take his turn.

William looked directly at Kevin. "I want the same thing. I don't want to replace or subvert you as Robert's dad. I only hope to be introduced to him, eventually, as his other dad, and to have the role of a dad in his life, too." Leaning slightly forward in his seat, he quietly added, "I don't want to take anything from Robert; I only want to add. I want him to feel safe and loved."

Biting the corner of his lip, Kevin nodded and diverted his gaze to the rug in front of him.

"Also," William continued, "this should go without saying, but almost all of that goes for Paige, too – except, of course, I'm not trying to be her other dad. But as long as I have any role in her life, I'll do my best to make her feel safe and loved."

Kevin lifted his eyes from the rug to William's face. "I appreciate that."

To stymie her tears, Julia had to draw on every tool at her disposal. So far, this was going far better than she could ever have dreamed. In fact, she was starting to wonder why she had ever gotten herself so worked up, in the first place.

And then all eyes drifted to her. With a ragged laugh, she admitted, "I'm not sure I can keep it together, but..." She reached for a tissue on Clio's coffee table and twisted it into a rope. "Like both of you, I want Robert to feel happy, safe, and loved. I also want to make sure the way we tell him about this doesn't hurt or confuse him. I want him to know he's allowed to love both of his dads equally, and no one will get mad at him for it."

Kevin and William both nodded their agreement. Then Clio invited them each to name the strengths they believed their parenting team brought to the table – strengths they could draw on in aligning actions with intentions.

"It seems like we all want what's best for the kids," observed Kevin.

"I agree; it seems like we're all willing to set aside any personal agenda, and prioritize the kids," said William. "I think the more people they have to love them, the better off they are."

"Once again, I could hardly have said it better," agreed Julia.

So then Clio invited them to share any challenges they foresaw – and the room fell silent.

Kevin's expression soured, while William put his elbows to his knees and stared down at his shoes. Tension stole the oxygen from the room.

"Kevin?" Clio said gently.

Kevin shifted his weight, avoiding eye contact with everyone. He cleared his throat. "Like I said, I want the kids to feel safe, and..."

After several long seconds of heavy, painful silence, Clio asked, "Do you worry that the kids will be unsafe?"

"Honestly... yeah."

Indignation welled in Julia's chest, but she stemmed it by focusing on her breathing.

"What are your concerns, Kevin?" Clio prompted.

Kevin drew a long, slow breath. "I swear I'm not trying to be a jerk, but..." He scratched his eyebrow. "The first time I ever encountered William, his behavior had me afraid for my safety. And then in 2006, when Julia and William... reconnected... my attorney learned some things about him that gave me pause."

"This may be painful for all three of you," Clio admitted, "but I think it's important we get it out in the open – that we make sure we're all on the same page, in terms of what we're talking about. Kevin, none of us has any way of knowing what, for sure, you're referring to."

William lifted two fingers, drawing Clio's attention. "If it's okay with Kevin and everyone else, I'd like to own up right now to my past. If there's anything else Kevin has heard, he can add it."

"How do you feel about that, Kevin?" Clio asked.

Kevin shrugged. "I mean... yeah, okay."

William squirmed a bit, but he looked Kevin straight in the eye. "I've always dealt with anxiety, and after Julia and I broke up in '95, I went through a major depression. I self-medicated with alcohol. I also smoked a lot of marijuana, and yes, unfortunately, I slept around – all in a misguided attempt to take the edge off my depression and anxiety. After I got that DUI, I cleaned up and went to work on the crab boats in Alaska. While I was there, I only worked for captains who ran a clean boat, and I attended AA meetings every time I was in port. I've been going to therapy and taking antidepressants ever since. I can count on one *finger* the number of drinks I've had in the past sixteen years. And no drugs."

Kevin blinked at William, digesting.

"It's a lot to take in, I know," admitted William, "but I wanted to be thorough. If there's anything else you've heard about me, I'd still be more than happy to address it."

"No," Kevin admitted. "I appreciate your candor. Does the no-drugs thing include marijuana?"

"Yes," William confirmed. "No marijuana."

"Any guns or other weapons?"

"No."

Kevin shrugged, and glanced over at Clio.

But William piped up again with, "I'd like to address what happened back in '95. You know... the first and only time we've met, before now."

Slowly, Kevin nodded.

"I owe you a long-overdue apology," William said. "My behavior that day was abhorrent, and I felt that way about it even then. I've never started a fight–" He pulled himself up short, and a slow grin snaked its way onto his face before he suppressed it. "Well, okay, I've started one fight in my whole life. But he deserved it, by his own admission; and after that, he became my best friend."

To Julia's surprise, Kevin's smile flashed briefly across his face before he seemed to remember himself.

"The point is," William continued, "I'm sorry for the stupid, boorish way I acted that day. But I am not a violent man."

Again, Kevin nodded slowly. "I'm not a violent man, either. But I would become one if anyone hurt my kids."

Clio opened her mouth to intervene, but William beat her to the punch. "I'd expect nothing less."

For a tense moment, the two men stared each other down, until Kevin gave a final nod and turned back to Clio. Only then did Julia dare to breathe.

Clio let Kevin's mild posturing slide. In an even more soothing tone, she said, "William, what about you? Anything you foresee that might get in the way of aligning your actions with your intentions?"

William drew a long, contemplative breath through his nose, then blew it out through his mouth. Crossing his ankle over his knee, he said, "I'm guessing there are still some hurt feelings on all sides, but for Paige and Robert's sake, I hope we can let bygones be bygones. I'm optimistic we can get along and co-parent peacefully."

Clio allowed his words to settle. Then she turned to Julia, lifting her brows by way of invitation.

"I feel like a broken record," admitted Julia, "but yeah – what they said. I just worry we'll forget to set aside our personal agendas for the greater good."

"I'll stop you right there," Clio broke in, "because I can assure you that absolutely *is* going to happen. I hate to rain on everyone's parade, but you're all merely human. There will be times when you behave with less-than-perfect decorum. But I already get the feeling those will be the exceptions, not the rule. And we can talk about how to do some repair-work when it *does* happen."

They all murmured their agreement. Clio surveyed the group with a smile. "Well then. Let's start planning this conversation with Robert!"

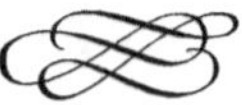

The next week stole by in a flurry of activity. William came over every evening he could, always bringing Diego. Every night after dinner, William schooled Robert and Paige on the basics of guitar, and then Paige schooled William on the basics of her Playstation.

Julia urgently needed to woo new clients – ones with deep enough pockets to replace Lars and Meg's. Luckily, she had two free and eager sources of child labor to exploit. In the evenings after dinner, Xavier walked the three blocks to their house with his laptop, where he and Paige were more than happy to design new graphics, flyers, and posters for Julia's business. And over the weekend, Julia chaperoned them to her Aunt Brigid's studio, where they printed the posters they had designed.

It was summer vacation, so on weekdays, Paige accompanied Julia to the aquarium shop. Together they restocked shelves, counted inventory, and chatted with Mitch and José, the gray-haired couple who dropped by every week to reminisce about Rob and Tim. When they came in, Paige always found some excuse to linger and eavesdrop. It tugged at Julia's heartstrings, knowing that Paige was curious about the two men who practically raised her.

Wednesday evening, during a lull in conversation at the dinner table,

Julia's father took a hefty gulp of Cinsaut, then drew a deep breath and released it slowly. Her mother, meanwhile, sat right beside him, a reassuring hand on his shoulder. The tension Julia had witnessed between them in recent weeks seemed to have subsided.

"I wanted to tell you all," her father began, pinning his flat stare on each person at the table, "that after giving it some thought, I've come to realize Karen was right."

Julia's eyes widened. Without meaning to, she exchanged incredulous glances with William. That might have been the first time she could ever remember her father admitting out loud that he had been wrong and someone else had been right. Too bad no one besides Julia's mother seemed to know what he was talking about.

"Right about what, Dad?" Julia prompted.

"That I don't want to sink this restaurant I worked so hard to build, or see its name – *my* name – become a laughingstock," her father continued. Then he paused to consider a moment, frowning. "I guess it's too late for that last part. But all the more reason to concede it's time to hand over the reins."

"You mean sell the restaurant?" asked William.

Paul shook his head. "I'd still be the owner, at least for now, but I'd bring on new blood, like you said. A new head chef. And... I guess we'll have to change the restaurant's name."

While Julia's mother hid her knowing smirk behind her wineglass, William offered Julia's father a sympathetic look. He seemed to understand, as well as Julia did, just how excruciating this was for him.

"I don't suppose you have any suggestions?" her father asked William.

"Suggestions?"

Her father waved his hand impatiently. "The new chef. Do you know anyone?"

For a moment, William looked like a deer in the headlights. Then he shot Julia an uneasy look before saying in a low voice, "Marisa."

To Julia's consternation, her mother winced at her before quickly looking away. Her father shifted awkwardly in his seat. "Marisa?" he echoed.

William nodded slowly. "Marisa Zunino."

"I know who you mean, William. I'm just not sold on the idea."

"She's the obvious choice," William persisted. "She's a known quantity. After she left Dunphy's, she worked her way up in some of the best kitchens in America, and now she's the head chef at Zeneize. You must have heard how she turned that place around."

Julia's father still said nothing; he just held William's gaze with a skeptical expression. Or was it a wary expression?

Her mother, on the other hand, was trying a little *too* hard to avoid looking at Julia.

After several uncomfortable seconds, William's face reddened a bit. "I don't work at Dunphy's anymore, Paul."

Utterly bewildered, Julia glanced back and forth between the two men, searching for clues. Finally, her father said, "Can you put me in touch with her?"

William shook his head. "Just call Zeneize."

With a sinking feeling, it finally dawned on Julia. Clearing her throat, she excused herself under the pretense of going to the bathroom. William watched her go with an almost hangdog look.

In the bathroom, Julia retrieved her cell phone from her pocket and sat down on the toilet seat lid. Opening a browser window, she started typing.

Boom.

Marisa Zunino. With pages and pages dedicated to her on the internet, all emblazoned with superlatives like "rising star" and "culinary goddess." Breathless reviews from smitten food critics with overwrought headlines like "Zesty Zuppa with Zeneize's Zunino."

She tapped the *Images* tab on the search results.

Marisa Zunino. Tall, with long, sleek, dark hair and large, dark doe eyes. The facial bone structure and pouty mouth of a supermodel, with the body and the luminous complexion to match.

Marisa Zunino. The same bombshell who, six years ago, dropped a bombshell on Julia at MacGowan's. Who warned her not to let William get her pregnant because he wasn't the marrying type, then vanished back into the nowhere she came from.

The same woman who marked the beginning of the end for Julia and William back in 2006.

Julia closed the browser and locked her cell phone. Tried to catch her breath and gather her wits about her.

She thought she had left the past firmly behind. Thought she had long since reconciled herself to the less-savory aspects of William's history.

So why did this new revelation twist itself like a dagger in her heart, all over again?

Surely it couldn't matter anymore that he had past relationships. Many relationships, in fact. Of course a brilliant, sweet, sexy man like William would have no trouble getting laid. Even with drop-dead-gorgeous hotties like Marisa Zunino.

Marisa Zunino. The acclaimed head chef of a highly-reviewed, sought-after dining experience in the Mission District, one of the trendiest neighborhoods of San Francisco. *William's* neighborhood.

Julia sprang from the toilet seat lid to inspect herself in the mirror. Surprise, surprise – staring back at her was the same oblong, freckled face as ever. The same too-small gray-green eyes; the same slight overbite that even the most expensive orthodontists in San Francisco had been powerless to remedy. The same B-cup boobs, and the same three gray hairs, which she promptly ripped from her scalp.

She turned sideways to appraise her best feature – her cute, round, perky butt that William had always relished so thoroughly. Even that didn't offer its usual consolation. After a conquest like Marisa Zunino, what appeal could Julia possibly have?

Julia hid in the bathroom as long as she dared, until she feared her mother would assemble a search party. When she finally emerged, her parents and William still discussed the inevitable improvements Marisa could bring to Dunphy's. As she rounded the corner into the dining room, the conversation at the table stopped short, and everyone turned to stare. Julia's eyes zeroed in on William's somber ones, peering at her. Waiting for her next move.

Without a word, she retreated downstairs, through the in-law unit, and out to the back patio.

She pulled up a seat at the patio table. Took several breaths of fresh air, and listened to the gentle peal of her mother's wind chimes. Watched the pinwheels in the garden do their hypnotic thing.

Marisa Zunino. Jesus, even her *name* sounded infinitely more alluring.

After a while, the patio door scraped open. William's eyes snagged on her with that same somber expression, but neither of them said anything as he approached, trailed by Diego.

He drew up a chair across the table from her, and they sat in silence for a minute while Julia absent-mindedly rubbed Diego's ears. Diego's tongue unfurled in appreciation, but the expression on William's face never changed. It was curious and concerned, but he waited calmly for her to do the talking.

"It's my hang-up to get over; I know that," she admitted finally. When he still watched her, unruffled, she added, "It won't ruin things. I won't let it, I promise. I mean—"

"Julie." He reached across the table for her hand, and she gave it willingly. She squeezed his hand, her heart jackhammering, rendering her mute. They sat in silence a few minutes, and Diego happily curled up again at William's feet.

"Did you already know who she was?" he asked gently.

Julia shook her head, too embarrassed to meet his gaze.

After a while, William explained, "Marisa was a high school soccer teammate of Kelly's. I met her once or twice back then, but I didn't really get to know her until she came to work at Dunphy's. It was her first job after culinary school. Kelly told her to apply."

He paused, gauging her reaction so far. Whatever he saw must have reassured him, because he continued, "She's half-Italian and half-Irish, like me. We grew up in the same neighborhood, and we both enjoyed cooking. It seemed like it ought to be a good match, on paper, but it was toxic."

"Toxic? How? I mean—" Cringing, she rushed out, "I'm sorry; that's none of my business."

"No, it's okay." Still holding her hand, he dragged his free one over his mouth and beard. "Well, she's a force of nature, I'll give her that. She has ambition in spades, and she didn't understand how I could be content to stay at Dunphy's as a line cook. She wasn't very nice about it; and when she told me she was pregnant, I knew it would be the worst lie if I asked her to marry me – if I committed to anything more than helping raise the baby. She was angry because she thought I had deliberately misled her about my feelings."

"And you didn't?"

"No. Or at least... not deliberately." When Julia gave him a searching look, he frowned and shook his head. "It was more about my own lack of self-awareness. I was trying to move on with my life, and just... not succeeding. I know that's not much better, but there was no malicious intent. The pregnancy was unplanned. We had never discussed marriage or children or any of that. It would have felt like a betrayal – not just of myself, but also a betrayal of Marisa and any child we brought into the world. We would have set a terrible example of what a loving relationship is supposed to look like. So I told her I'd support the baby and be fully involved as a dad; but I couldn't stay with her as a partner. In the long run, she decided she couldn't go through with the pregnancy, and it all ended very acrimoniously. I moved out, she left Dunphy's, and I haven't talked to her since."

"And after all that, you think she'd be willing to come back to Dunphy's?" Julia pointed out delicately.

"For the right price? Yeah." Again, he shifted his weight. "I've heard about her rise in the culinary world over the years. I respect her talent. And as combustible as our relationship was, she worked well with your dad. She's exactly the right chef to save his restaurant."

"Then I guess he'd better hire her," she reflected drily.

With a rueful smile, he added, "It helps that I don't work there anymore."

"Maybe; but I *do*. I come in every week to maintain the big saltwater aquarium in front. And now, she knows who I am – or at least she knows what I look like, and my history with you."

William stared soberly across the yard at nothing in particular. A muscle ticked at his temple as he pondered this dilemma.

After a minute to think, Julia reflected, "I guess if Dunphy's folds, I won't have an account there, anyway, and I'll lose that income. So if she's as good as everybody says, I'll put on my big-girl panties. But how do you think she'll react to seeing me? She didn't seem too thrilled that one time."

"To be honest, I don't know. Jealousy was a thing with her, back then. But it's been eight years." They sat in silence for another minute, until he said, "If it helps – if it's okay with you, and it's not too weird – I'd be willing to reach out and try to talk to her. Maybe even set up some kind of meeting between you two, to clear the air."

"It would be *very* weird," Julia admitted, "but if she agrees to even consider the job, I'd be willing to do it."

He dipped his head and captured her eyes with his. "You have nothing to worry about. I hope you know that."

"I know that up here," she acknowledged, tapping her head with her free hand.

"But not here," he finished for her, placing his hand over his own heart. "Julie... you looked her up when you were in the bathroom, didn't you?"

Julia dropped her eyes to the tabletop. "I sat on the toilet and Googled her name like a loser. I won't lie... for a second, I felt inadequate. And not just because she looks like a Victoria's Secret Angel." To her own disgust, her eyes started to burn. Still glaring down at the table, she bit her lips and blinked furiously to keep the tears at bay. Finally, she gave in and allowed them to flow, looking up again through watery eyes. "But I also know what I see and feel when you look at me, and when you touch me. I see the things you do for me and the kids. *That* is real. You leave me in no doubt of your love for me."

He scraped his chair around the table, setting it next to hers, and gathered her into his arms. Pressing a kiss into the crown of her head, he murmured, "And you leave me in no doubt of your love for *me*. You have this endless inner beauty to complement all of your outer beauty. And by the way, it's not just lip service when I say you're the most beautiful woman in the world. If you could see the heads you turn, everywhere we go... how proud I feel, in a very unevolved, possessive way, having you on my arm. Sometimes I think my chest will burst from puffing out so much. And no, that's not an *Alien* reference."

Julia couldn't help but cackle, even as she wiped tears away. "No, that's just your inner cave man fighting to get out."

He took her hand in his and pressed it to his lips. "I love you, Julie. I admire you as a person. I lust after you. Even in the years we were apart, not a day passed when you didn't cross my mind. Honestly, I've never wanted anything as much as I want to be with you, and love you, and make you smile, and make you come. Preferably all at the same time."

She aimed her heat-filled gaze at him. "Quit making me horny when I can't do anything about it."

His lips twitched in amusement. Moved beyond expression, Julia could only give him a poignant look. He reached across the table for her hand, and she gave it willingly. She squeezed his hand, her heart too full for words.

FRIDAY, JUNE 15, 2012

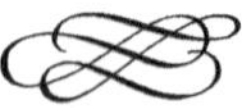

That Friday, after an uncharacteristically busy morning, Julia checked her phone and found a missed call from Kevin. With looming dread, she put the phone to her ear to listen to his voicemail.

"Hey, Julia." Kevin's voice sounded hoarse. "Um.... welp... it's flaring up again. The Crohn's."

For much of his life, Kevin had suffered from Crohn's Disease. It came and went in waves, sometimes with months or even years between.

Now, on the voice mail, Kevin chuffed in frustration. "I'm so sorry, Julia. Sorry for doing this to everyone, yet again. You have no idea how broken up I am to miss Father's Day with them. Please, if you don't mind, can you have the kids call so I can apologize? That is, if Paige will even speak to me." Another long pause; then, his voice dull with resignation: "I've scheduled an appointment with a new specialist at Stanford."

That was the end of the message. Her mouth going dry, Julia slowly lowered the phone from her ear.

"Mom?" Paige's voice, coming unexpectedly from the open doorway of the office, made Julia jump. "Is everything okay?"

Forcing a smile, Julia faced her daughter and deflected. "You know what Aunt Brigid told me? She wants me to bring you back to the studio next Saturday so she can finish your encaustic lesson. Would you like that?"

Paige clapped her hands and squealed. "Oh my God, I'd *love* that!"

Thankfully, Paige seemed to have forgotten entirely about Julia's turn of expression. Instead, Paige spent the rest of the day grinning to herself, no doubt daydreaming of finishing the encaustic painting she had started the week before. Julia dreaded having to crush her spirits later when she told her Kevin wasn't coming for her tonight.

Plus, she dreaded crushing William's spirits when she told *him* not to come over for dinner. He did not need to witness one of Paige's melt-downs – at least, not yet. At the moment, he was aboard *The Albatross*, but she knew she needed to let him know as soon as possible. She also knew she would still be too busy to take his call when he got back to the pier at four o'clock. So she dashed off a quick and apologetic text message.

Once they got home, she dutifully gathered her mother, Robert, and Paige in the living room to deliver the news. Paige's brows dropped, and she slumped in her seat on the couch.

"Oh, that's too bad, kids," clucked Julia's mother. Then, in a too-chipper tone, she quickly added, "But don't worry, we'll make it a fun day, anyway!"

Julia put a gentle hand on Paige's arm. "Your dad wants to apologize to you and your brother on the phone."

Paige glared. "That's what you were listening to at lunch, wasn't it? A message from Dad, flaking on us yet again."

Gently, Julia said, "Your dad isn't feeling well, Paige."

"You really believe that?"

"I do. I know that doesn't make it easier to miss out on time with him, but–"

"Why didn't you just tell me, then?"

Julia blinked. "Tell you–"

"When you heard the message at lunch. Why did you wait until now?"

"I wanted you to be able to take some space if you needed to."

"You think I'm going to get all hysterical again, don't you?" demanded Paige as, ironically, her voice rose in pitch.

"Hysterical? No. Sad, angry, upset, though? Those would all be valid f–"

"*Shut up!*" Paige screamed. "Just *shut the fuck up* already with the stupid validating crap!"

And then, of course, Julia's mother burst out with, "Paige! Watch your language, especially in front of your brother!"

"Mom," Julia hissed. Beside her, Robert whined and clapped his hands over his ears, then fled downstairs to his bedroom.

Roaring in frustration, Paige sprang to her feet and stormed off to her room, slamming the door behind her.

"Are you just going to let your daughter speak to you that way?" blurted Julia's mother, her voice shrill. "In front of your five-year-old?"

"Mom," Julia seethed through clenched teeth. "Not the time or the place."

"When will it ever be the right time?" her mother demanded. "It doesn't seem like these expensive therapists and schools are helping much."

Maybe her mother was right – maybe it was all a huge waste of time and money if Paige still found herself losing her temper at the most inopportune moments.

But no.

Things weren't flawless, but they were so much better. Besides, as Clio kept reminding her, perfection was never the goal – only progress. Paige hadn't run away or stolen anything since she started seeing Clio; and Julia and Paige's communication had vastly improved – today notwithstanding.

What Julia needed, right this second, was to give Paige some space, and to do some repair work with her son.

She found Robert in his usual hiding spot under his bed. The duvet served as a curtain, covering the gap between the bed frame and the floor, so she laid down on the rug and lifted it. She found him curled up with Bodgie – his battered, treasured blanket – and Prince, the stuffed frog Kevin had given him. He sucked his middle and ring fingers like he used to when he was younger.

"Hey, Tadders," she said gently. "I am so sorry about what happened up there. I know it felt scary, but I promise, you're safe, and so is everyone else."

After a minute to think about it, Robert popped his fingers out of his mouth and crawled out from under the bed. Julia sat up, and Robert climbed into her lap. Julia kissed the top of his head and huffed his unique scent – a mixture of watermelon-scented shampoo, sunshine, and dirt. He wrapped his arms around her neck.

"Paige was mad," he observed simply.

"She sure was," Julia agreed, rubbing his back. "We all get mad sometimes, and that's okay; but it's not okay for us to yell at each other. The thing is, when we make mistakes like that, we usually figure it out later, after we calm down. So, I'm giving Paige some time to calm down, and then I'll talk to her."

"Well... I guess Mr. Chen says everybody makes mistakes."

Mr. Chen was Robert's preschool teacher. "Mr. Chen is very wise."

"Like today – I made a *big* mistake."

"You did? What did you do?"

"I ate a bug."

Julia quirked an eyebrow at him. "You *what?*"

"I was picking cherry tomatoes with Grandma, and I put one in my mouth when she wasn't looking, and it had a bug in it, and it tasted like poop and throw-up."

"Ew!" laughed Julia. "Poop *and* throw up?"

He nodded soberly. "Mixed together."

"Okay, but how do you know what poop tastes like?"

"'Cause one time I scratched my butt, and–"

"Okay, never mind! Just don't do that again, okay?"

"The poop, or the bug?"

"Either. And for goodness' sake," she added, tickling his ribs until he squealed, "don't scratch your butt and put your fingers in your mouth! Or at least, wash your hands first. That's what you call learning from your mistakes."

"Yeah; and Grandma told me not to eat tomatoes without letting her look at them first."

"Wow. Grandma might even be wiser than Mr. Chen." Julia pulled him in for another hug. After another minute, Robert drew back and looked her in the eye.

"Mommy, why doesn't Daddy just take some medicine?"

A tiny cracked formed in Julia's heart, but Robert giggled as she lightly tickled him again. He absolutely loved being tickled. "Working on it, Tadpole. Sometimes it takes a while to find the right medicine."

"Why?"

"Would you believe people have been learning about bodies for thousands of years, and we *still* don't know exactly how they work?"

"Thousands of years?" He scratched his face. "That's longer than you've been alive, right?"

"Tadders, that's even longer than Grandma and Grandpa have been alive. But don't worry – Daddy's doctors are working hard to find the right medicine." She patted his back. "Hey, sweetie, do you want to watch a show while I talk to Paige?"

He gave a whoop of glee and scrambled to his feet, and she set him up in front of the Octonauts. Then she trudged upstairs, her dread building by the moment. From the sound of it, her mother was banging around the kitchen, making dinner. Julia wasn't ready to face her yet, annoyed as she still was. Instead, she hurried down the hallway, hesitating at the door to the bedroom she shared with Paige. Even from the other side of the door, Julia could hear tinny sounds blasting from Paige's earbuds.

Drawing a few slow breaths, she knocked loudly.

"Come in."

When Julia opened the door, Paige paused her iPod and removed her earbuds. Sitting on her bed, she looked calm enough.

"Are you ready to talk?" ventured Julia. "Or would you like more time?"

Paige sniffed, setting her lap desk aside, along with her angry anime sketches. "Now is fine."

Julia went to her own bed and lowered herself on the edge. "Do you want to say anything first?"

"Nope."

"Okay," Julia said slowly, remembering to breathe. She hated this feeling of walking on eggshells. "I'm sorry."

Paige pulled a thread from her blanket and wrapped it around the little fuzzball she had been working on for months. The fuzzballs were like her version of a worry stone, or a fidget toy. "What for?"

"Everything. For what happened just now in the living room. For your dad getting sick again. I know how hard you worked on those neckties and how much you were looking forward to giving them–"

"It's fine," Paige interrupted flatly.

Julia didn't try to say anything else just yet – she just stayed present with her daughter for a minute or two. Eventually, she asked, "Would it be okay if I gave you a hug?"

"No," Paige said immediately.

The old familiar helplessness crushed Julia under its weight. She took several more deep breaths, and made herself vulnerable.

"Sometimes, when I feel like I can't help you, I get scared." At this, Paige briefly glanced up, but her expression was an enigma. Julia allowed her confession to hover between them for a few seconds. "I have to remind myself to sit with that fear, and not run straight into problem-solving. To admit I'm afraid I'm a bad mom because I can't fix everything for you."

Paige gave a slight eye roll. "You're not a bad mom," she droned, as if reciting a well-rehearsed mantra.

"Oh, I know," Julia quipped, and felt her shoulders relax a bit when Paige rewarded her with a begrudging laugh. "It's just hard to remember it's not always my job to fix things. I just want you to know I'm always here for you."

"I know," Paige said, this time more quietly and with more sincerity. She pulled another thread from her blanket and wrapped it around her rapidly-growing fuzzball.

After a minute, Julia tried again. "Would it be okay if I talk about your dad for a second?"

Paige heaved a world-weary sigh, but consented.

"Remember how Clio taught us that two seemingly contradictory things can be true at the same time?"

Paige grunted.

"I know you're angry with your dad, and that's valid. At the same time, I really do believe it breaks his heart when he can't have his time with you and your brother." Paige scoffed, but Julia doubled down. "I believe him when he says he's doing everything he can to get better."

"Like what?" Paige snapped.

"He made an appointment with a new doctor, for one thing. A specialist at Stanford he's never seen."

That silenced Paige for the moment, and she went back to weaving threads into her fuzzball.

"When you're ready," Julia ventured, "and you're open to talking on the phone, I think he'd like to tell you himself."

"Okay, but I'm not ready."

"And that's perfectly fine."

Paige stared down at her frayed blanket, on its very last leg.

"If you put that thing over your head," Julia suggested, "you'll look like a swamp monster, draped in algae, rising from the primordial ooze."

Paige grinned, and to Julia's delight, she draped the blanket over her head. With her eyes peeking through its gaping holes, she moaned and curled her fingers and clawed at the air.

Playful Paige made increasingly rare appearances, and Julia was *so* there for each and every one.

After leaving Paige's room, Julia reluctantly wandered back to the living room. Thankfully, her mother must have still been in the kitchen, because the living room was empty. So she ventured back downstairs to the den, where Robert's eyes were still glued to the Octonauts.

With a pang of guilt, Julia decided to just let him watch TV. When Julia was feeling like a failure as a mom, as she did right now, she usually found it soothing to gaze at the aquarium or get a little sewing done. But neither of those were getting the job done.

It had always been Kevin's abandonment – real or perceived – that had triggered Paige's downward spirals. She had been doing so much better lately. She hadn't tried to run away in five months. And now here they were, rebooting the whole cycle, all over again.

But this time, Julia didn't have to cope alone.

Locking herself in the bathroom, she retrieved her phone from the pocket of her joggers and tapped William's name in her Favorites.

"Hey, gorgeous." His face and gentle baritone over FaceTime were a salve to her spirits.

"Hi, sweetheart." From his bare shoulders, she could tell he was shirtless. Droplets of water clung to his hair and his collarbones. She quirked an eyebrow. "Um, what are *you* up to?"

He chuckled. "I just got out of the shower, and now I'm getting ready to grab some dinner."

"I'm so sorry," she groaned. "You could have been having dinner with us right now."

"It's okay," he murmured. "There will be other dinners."

She beamed. "God, you're a sight for sore eyes."

His own eyes and smile were as wide as hers as he settled onto his couch. "So are you."

She lifted an eyebrow and craned her neck forward, as if that would somehow help her see further down the front of him. "Are you wearing anything at all there?"

He tilted the phone down, momentarily revealing a lovely broad chest that tapered down to a narrower waist, followed by loose athletic shorts riding a bit low on his hips.

Her salivary glands twinged, as only William could do to her. "You seriously look good enough to eat. Luckily, now I'm allowed to."

Lifting his phone camera back to his face, he growled a little at her innuendo. "Yes please."

She shook her head to clear it. "I would love to relive the glory days of our youth and indulge in some hot phone sex right now."

His smile widened. "The new, improved version, complete with visuals."

"But I'd rather save all this pent-up frustration for when we're in person."

With a low growl, he warned, "I'll take you pent up or any way I can."

She wiped a hand down her face. "So! How was *your* day?"

His knowing laughter shimmered through her body. "Not as eventful as yours, apparently."

The reminder deflated her spirits, dumping her right back onto Planet Earth. "I should have seen it coming."

He sat up a little, his smile straightening. "What do you mean?"

She explained Kevin's pattern of falling ill at the worst possible times and the effect it had on the kids, especially Paige. "I feel so powerless to help her. I can barely contain my own anger. I mean, Kevin has a chronic autoimmune disease that causes him severe pain, and he has no control over when it decides to flare up. So why can't I find it in my heart to feel more compassion?"

Gently, he said, "Because you're a mother, and those kids are your living heartbeat. Anything that hurts them launches you into mama bear mode."

"Okay, my brain knows this; so why does my gut tell me I'm a horrible, selfish woman?"

He reeled back in surprise. "How does feeling protective of your kids make you a horrible, selfish woman?"

"Because I can't seem to get a better grip on my anger toward Kevin, not even for the sake of my kids' mental health."

"Julie, as much as you'd like to be superhuman, and often seem to pull it off, the truth is you're only human after all. Come roll around in the muck with the rest of us mortals."

"Roll around in the muck, huh?" She could only grin across the ether at this man, adoration cinching tighter around her heart. Making it hard to breathe, in the best possible way. "Any time, any place."

And then, as if that weren't enough, his eyes and his tone both softened. "Julie, I told you six years ago – I'll never interfere in Paige's relationship with her dad; but I'll love and care for her as if she were my own. I already do. You'll never be alone in this ever again."

She hoped the heat of her own gaze came through over FaceTime, branding him. Claiming him. She wanted to slurp those little droplets from the divots in his collarbones. "And after I get my hands on you, you'll never walk again."

"Hmm... I accept those terms."

They sniggered like teenagers for a minute, then fell back to just staring, drinking each other in.

Julia sighed. "I love you, Will."

His gaze softened as he touched his fingertips to his lips, then briefly to his phone camera. "I love you, too, sweetheart."

SUNDAY, JUNE 17, 2012

$\mathcal{D}$unphy's was still closed – no Father's Day brunch, this year. So that morning, Julia's dad accompanied her mother to Mass. Then, with her mother's help, Julia spent the entire day making her father's favorite dish – osso buco. Paige seemed unusually eager to help, prattling cheerfully while insisting on assembling a zucchini and white bean salad, all by herself.

It wasn't until Paige redirected the conversation that Julia realized why she was in such good spirits. "Are you *sure* Xavier likes beans and zucchini?"

Julia bit back a smile. While Kelly, Pilar, and Zach went to the Ochoas', Ann and Xavier were coming to the Dunphys' to celebrate William's first Father's Day. "Yes, honey; I told you I talked to Kelly last night and confirmed that Xavier would eat everything we're serving."

"Everything?" Paige echoed skeptically. "Even Grandma's octopus salad?"

"Even that."

Paige had made it clear she disapproved of any culinary desecration of her spirit animal. Now, Julia's stomach tightened as she watched her daughter's face darken – the first sign of impending trouble.

"'Cause you know Xavier is a vegetarian, right?" Paige said sharply.

"Based on what Kelly said, I think he might be more of a flexitarian. Besides," she added, pointing with a spoon to Paige's salad, "you're making a great vegetarian dish for him. High in protein."

Paige grumbled something unintelligible, but returned to her own salad in a darker mood. Her brooding didn't even let up when Alison arrived – probably because Alison brought a rhubarb coconut pie. It was a favorite of Julia's father, but Paige found its tartness intolerable.

It wasn't until William arrived with Diego, Ann, and Xavier that Paige perked up. Paige rushed downstairs to greet Xavier, and they promptly settled in front of the PlayStation to try a brand-new game called Minecraft. Ann had also brought what she described as an Italian gazpacho, which she placed in the refrigerator before settling on the sofa to catch up with Julia's parents.

Soon, at Julia's prompting, Robert came upstairs with a package for William.

"Hey, Tad." William stopped tuning his guitar and set it aside. "What's this?"

"Coasters," blurted Robert before William even had a chance to open it. Oblivious to Ann's snort of laughter, Robert added, "I made them all by myself. And I wrapped them, too."

Turning the package over in his hands, William inspected the adorably sloppy results. "I can tell, because it's wrapped with love."

Diego put his paws on William's thighs, conducted his own inspection, and sneezed his approval. Then William tore into the package and pulled out one of the "coasters" – two squares of fabric, loosely sewn together.

"A frog print!" exclaimed William. "Perfect!"

"Robert's nickname is Tadpole," Julia explained aside to Ann.

Ann chuckled. "Where'd he get that from?"

"When he was a toddler, he pronounced his name 'Ribbit.' From there, his nickname went through several iterations. Tadpole is the one that stuck."

"Look, that's not all," Robert continued, diving into the package himself and thrusting another coaster right in William's face. "Whales!"

William had to lean back to see it. "Sure enough!"

"And fish, and cameras," Robert persisted, yanking each one from the package in turn. "Mommy says you like cameras."

"That's right." William flashed a quick smile at Julia before adding, "You did great."

Julia held up her hands. "Don't look at me; that was all Robert, with only a little help from my mom."

"Good job, Tadpole!" exclaimed Ann.

Peering anxiously at William, his voice suddenly shrinking, Robert asked, "Do you like them?"

"Are you kidding? I love them!" William gathered Robert into a hug and kissed the top of his head. "I'll use them every day. Thank you, buddy."

"You mean Tad," Robert corrected, and William rewarded him with by rumpling his hair.

Soon everyone gathered around the table, with Julia's father at its head. Julia had seated William between herself and her father. Beneath the table, Diego turned in three circles before settling at William's feet, smacking his jowls and heaving a contented sigh. The females of the family occupied themselves with serving, and Julia's father hummed in satisfaction at each offering.

Across the table from Julia, Paige set her own zucchini and bean salad directly in front of Xavier. Beaming her prettiest smile, she announced, "I made this for you, because you're a vegetarian."

Xavier glanced up briefly at Paige, and Julia could have sworn she saw him blush before immediately casting his eyes down again. For the first time since Julia had known him, he smiled.

"You remembered," he said quietly.

"At least *somebody* around here cares about your dietary preferences." Paige aimed a triumphant sneer at Julia. "Try it first, before you try anything else."

Julia's face flared at her daughter's imperiousness. Beside her, Alison placed a reassuring hand over Julia's with a sympathetic smile.

Xavier obediently scooped a helping onto his plate. After sampling, he gave it a thumbs up.

"Is it good?" Paige persisted, her smile widening even further.

Xavier glanced at her just long enough to register Paige's beaming smile before gulping his bite down awkwardly. Not awkwardly as if he didn't like the salad, but awkwardly as if Paige's smile flustered him. This time, his face unmistakably reddened. "Epic," he mumbled.

With another look of triumph, Paige resumed her seat; and Julia spent the next few minutes studying Paige and Xavier in dismay as they traded furtive glances and smiles.

Until that moment, Julia had not fully appreciated how much Paige was starting to look like a teenager, nor how remarkably pretty she had grown. She boasted her father's dark hair, light olive skin, and big brown eyes, together with her mother's smile.

But a few minutes later, Paige's mood soured again when Xavier sang the praises of the octopus salad. In a wounded tone, Paige demanded, "How can you eat that? I thought you were a vegetarian."

Evidently oblivious to Paige's distress, Xavier replied, "Not a hundred percent, honestly. I like octopus, and Cardone's is good with its sourcing." Turning to Julia's mother, Xavier added, "That's where you got this from, right? Cardone's?"

"It is," Julia's mother confirmed.

In a callback to Paige's earlier snark, Julia's father said, "At least *somebody* around here has good taste."

Paige, in turn, glowered down at her osso bucco, stabbing it with her fork; but she said nothing more. An awkward silence settled over the table.

Until the doorbell rang.

Beneath the table, Diego yipped and scrambled to his feet. Frowning at Julia, her father asked, "Were you expecting anyone else?"

Julia sprang to her feet. "No, but maybe Aaron decided to come, after all. I invited him, since he said he was going to be alone."

She rushed downstairs, but when she threw open the front door, the face that greeted her on the other side sent her pulse rocketing into her throat.

Kevin.

Her whole world reeling, Julia stepped out onto the front porch and quickly shut the door behind herself.

"What are you doing here?" The question fell from Julia's lips before she thought better of it.

Creases burrowed into Kevin's forehead. "Nice to see you, too." He looked like death warmed over – thinner than ever, and a bit green. He wrapped his arms around his belly, a stance Julia recognized all too well from his previous flare-ups of Crohn's.

With a pang of guilt, Julia rushed out, "I'm sorry; that was rude. I just... wasn't expecting you."

"I texted," he balked. "Several times."

She started to contradict him, but the words died on her lips as she retrieved her phone. He had, in fact, sent several texts. Not only that, he had called a couple of times. And left voice mails. "I'm sorry, Kevin. I've been insanely busy."

"Why don't you ever turn your ringer on?" Kevin snapped. "Or at least put it on vibrate?"

"I'm sorry," Julia said, a bit defensively. "I get six billion robo-calls a day."

"I told you to put your number on the Do Not Call list."

"I did, but–" Suddenly alarmed, Julia's eyes made a quick circuit of his face. "What's wrong?" What else, besides bad news, would bring Kevin to her doorstep when he was clearly still so unwell?

Kevin sagged, as if all the fight suddenly went out of him. "It's Father's Day, Julia. I just really needed to see the kids."

"You... needed to see the kids," Julia echoed. Irritation coiled behind Julia's sternum. "Kevin, you're obviously in a lot of pain."

"I just miss them." He sounded exhausted. "So much."

"So you flew all the way up here, feeling like that?"

"No; I flew in on Wednesday, before I got sick. I was already staying with my parents, planning to fly the kids to Santa Barbara on Friday. And then last night, my parents decided on a whim to go to New York. I can't be all alone today, of all days. Not again." His voice breaking, Kevin added, "The kids are growing up fast, Julia. I don't want to miss out on any more time with them."

"Kevin, you can't just show up without confirming it's okay first."

"I tried!" he practically shouted.

"I know, and I'm sorry I didn't see your texts. But I had no reason to expect you to text or call, much less drop by. Yesterday you were barely able to speak. Plus, like I said, I've been swamped, getting things ready for Dad and Wi–"

She gulped down the bombshell just before it dropped: William was there. Celebrating Father's Day. With the kids.

But her sudden shift in expression did not go unnoticed, and something like fire kindled behind Kevin's dark eyes. "And who, Julia?" His voice was calm, but its tremble betrayed his agitation.

Julia sighed. "Kevin..."

Kevin's nostrils flared, and he stepped closer. Instinctively, Julia retreated, pressing her back against the door. Kevin saw it and stepped back again, some of the fire dissipating from his glare. But with the same ominous calm, he said, "So you're telling me that William is in there right now, with *my* kids. On Father's Day."

Julia squared her shoulders. "I don't need your permission to include him in family gatherings, especially ones you weren't even planning to be at. William is a part of my life now, which means he's going to be a part of the kids' lives from now on, too."

A seismic shift transformed Kevin's features. All the fire went out, replaced by several beats of mute shock. Then he whipped his glasses off and buried his face in his other hand.

To Julia's horror, she realized he was crying. "Kevin..." She didn't know what to do. Offering a hug didn't seem like the right move.

"Goddammit," he choked out, a little too loudly, repeatedly pounding his fist against the exterior wall. She prayed the kids hadn't heard. Thank God the windows were shut, and double-paned.

Before Julia could shush him, the front door burst open behind her, and William filled the doorway with his full six-feet-four-inches. Julia gave a tiny shake of the head, but he was too busy glaring at Kevin to notice. Julia had never seen William like this – nostrils flaring, wound tight, and ready to spring at a moment's notice.

At least, not since they were twenty, when he confronted Kevin in exactly the same way.

"It's okay," she whispered, taking advantage of the chance to wrap her hand around his bicep.

William's eyes snapped to Julia's. "He was swearing at you."

"Not swearing," Julia rushed out. "Well, okay, *mildly* swearing; but not at me. Just at the situation."

"What situation?" William stepped out onto the porch and shut the door behind him. Glowering again at Kevin, he demanded, "What was that loud sound? Were you hitting her?"

Jabbing a finger at William, Kevin snarled, "*Fuck* you, okay? I was sad and upset when I found out you're spending Father's Day with my kids. I hit the wall. I'd never hit Julia, or anyone for that matter. But you know, for the second time in our short, unpleasant acquaintance, I'm not sure you'd stick to the same code."

William tensed even further under Julia's grip. "Hey asshole, I thought I was protecting Julia *and* the kids. You're welcome."

"Holy fucking shit, this is hot!"

The new voice yanked their attention to where Alison leaned against the door jamb with a cheeky grin. Julia hadn't even heard the door open.

"I can't even remember the last time two dudes fought over me." Jerking her thumb back into the house, Alison added, "Can you just hit pause a sec? I need to grab the popcorn."

Mortified, Julia pinched the bridge of her nose, until she realized that her sister's outburst had produced an outcome that was both unexpected and desirable. With her hand still wrapped around William's bicep, Julia felt the tension drain from his muscles. And then Diego barreled outside, nails clacking on hardwood and concrete. Clearly, he was no guard dog, because after a few assessing snuffles around everyone's legs, he unfurled his tongue and flopped down at William's feet.

William ran a hand over his scalp, his eyes wild and unfocused. Then he turned to Kevin with a contrite look.

"Shit... I'm sorry."

Julia watched Kevin's shoulders drop. "Me, too."

"I misunderstood." William bent over to clasp his knees, practically wheezing, and Diego scrambled up again to lick his face. "Oh, Jesus..."

"It's okay," Kevin reassured him. "Actually, if the situations had been reversed, I hope I would have done the same."

"My work here is done," declared Alison, dusting off her hands before retreating into the house and shutting the door behind herself.

William ran both hands through his hair. Unable to look Julia in the eye, he stared at his shoes instead. "God, Julie; I'm so sorry."

"It's okay," Julia whispered. In truth, her sister was right. She had never been one to go for the knight in shining armor thing, but the way William rushed headlong into what he thought was danger? She wanted to pull him into the bushes and have her way with him.

Kevin stepped forward, his wary eyes glued to William. "Are we good?"

"Yeah." William puffed out a breath of relief. "Yeah, we're good."

"Then if you two can coexist in the same space," Julia interjected, "come with me to the in-law unit. We need to chat."

Their hangdog looks might have pulled a laugh from her, if she weren't still so embarrassed. Both men followed her inside, with Diego trailing behind.

Kevin still slumped as he continued shaking his head. "I shouldn't have come here."

William turned to Kevin. "I want to say again how sorry I am. You know... for over-reacting out there."

Kevin buried his face in his hands, muffling his voice. "You reacted exactly as you should have, if you thought I was being violent. In fact," he added, finally lifting his head to look William in the eye, "thank you."

Julia looked to William, who gave a tiny, imperceptible nod, as if reading her mind. To Kevin, she offered, "You could join us for dinner. Could you eat?"

Kevin's eyes widened in surprise. "Probably not. And I don't want to intrude."

"It's not an intrusion," William broke in. "Not from my perspective."

Kevin glanced at William. "Thank you. But what about Paige? Isn't she still pissed at me?"

"She's pissed at the whole world," Julia replied drily.

After a moment to reflect, Kevin tentatively said, "Are you sure? I really don't have t–"

"Positive," William interjected.

Julia offered William a grateful smile, then led them both upstairs, feeling like she was in a surreal Terry Gilliam film. Never in a million years would she have foreseen Kevin and William seated around the same table, enjoying the same Father's Day dinner. The whole incident had scrambled Julia's brain so thoroughly, it never even occurred to her to prepare her kids. Not until she reached the top of the stairs and watched Paige's mouth fall open.

While everyone else jumped up with surprised greetings, Robert rushed forward to throw his arms around Kevin's legs with a delighted shriek. But Paige stayed riveted to her seat, her expression darkening by the second. Finally, in a surly tone, she blurted, "Mom, why is Dad even here? I thought you said he was sick."

"He is," Julia answered. "But he was sad about missing Father's Day with you guys. As it turns out, he texted and called to ask if he could drop by, but I didn't see his messages."

"Well, you should have just stayed away," Paige groused, glaring at Kevin. "No one wants you here."

"Paige," Alison said sharply, and Paige's eyebrows scrunched together. Alison rarely rebuked her niece.

"*I* want him here," Robert protested, and Paige's head whipped around, her eyes flashing with barely-contained rage.

"What do you care? He's not even your real dad!"

It seemed like every adult in the room gasped in unison. Even Diego woofed in alarm.

Paige crossed her arms and doubled down. "And even if he *was* your dad, it's not like he gives a fuck about either one of us."

But her defiant scowl evaporated when it landed on Xavier. Only when Paige registered his look of horror did she realize what she had said.

"What do you mean he's not my real dad?" Robert's tiny voice yanked Julia from her stupor.

Alison dropped a steadying hand on Julia's shoulder. "I've got Paige," she whispered. "You take Robert."

What Julia really wanted in that moment was to get her hands around Paige's neck, which is why she shot Alison a look of gratitude for intervening. And the icing on the cake was, Paige had said it in front of William's mother.

"Come on, Tadpole," Julia said, studiously avoiding Ann's eyes, her voice tight with fury despite her best efforts. She steered her son into her parents' bedroom, since Alison would most likely take Paige to the other one.

Tears streamed down Robert's face. "Mommy, what did I do?!"

"Oh, Robert…" She squatted to lift him, and he wrapped his legs around her waist and his arms around her neck. She sat on the edge of her parents' bed, where she rocked him in her arms, shushing him gently. Tears pricked at her own eyes to think he blamed himself. "Sweetie, you didn't do a single thing wrong. None of this is your fault, not even a little."

"Then why is everyone so mad?" he demanded through sobs. "Why did Paige say Daddy isn't my real dad?"

"It was wrong of her to say that." Julia could only pray that Robert was too young to pick up on the subtle nuance in her phrasing.

But Robert drew back to look her in the eye. "Is it true?"

Julia placed a gentle hand on the back of his head and snuggled him back against her shoulder. What was she supposed to say now? He was so smart, like his father. Like *both* of his fathers.

Her mind whirled. Robert would know if she answered with anything but a resounding *no*. On the other hand, if she wasn't honest now, he would feel betrayed when they finally *did* tell him the truth.

Miraculously, despite Robert's gut-wrenching sobs, Julia managed to choke out, "Hey, buddy, let's breathe. Remember balloon breathing?"

His crying eased somewhat, and he nodded against her shoulder.

"Okay, let's do it. Ready?"

She led the way, prompting them both to inhale a slow breath through their noses. They expanded their hands apart from each other, as if clasping an inflating balloon, before slowly releasing the breath through their mouths.

Already, hiccups had replaced Robert's sobs. "Good!" Julia praised. "Let's do it again."

They repeated this exercise a few more times until all the tension drained from Robert's body, and he sagged in her arms. She rubbed his back and tenderly shushed him for another minute or two.

Finally, she said, "I know all the yelling was scary. For now, I just want you to know you're safe, and you're not in any trouble. None of this is your fault."

Robert pulled back again, his face streaked red. He searched her eyes with his own heart-stopping turquoise ones. He had never looked more like William than he did in that moment.

Julia smiled gently. "Remember how we talked about families the other day when William and I were tucking you in?"

"You mean how there's all different kind of families?"

"Exactly. Well, what if I told you our own family is like that? What if you actually have two daddies? What if Daddy *is* your real daddy... but so is William?"

"You mean they both planted the seed in your tummy? The one that grew up into me?"

Julia gulped down a guffaw. Clearly, their rudimentary birds-and-bees talk had taken root. "No, they didn't both plant the seed that grew up into you. Besides, there's a lot more to being a dad than just that."

He tilted his head, puppy-dog style. "Like what?"

"Well... like taking good care of you. Loving you, and keeping you safe. Teaching you things. And sometimes – if a kiddo is *really* lucky – they get more than one dad to love them."

"And that's me," he deduced. "*I'm* a lucky kiddo."

"That's right!" She rumpled his already-tousled hair. "The point is, there are lots of ways to be a dad, not just the, um... the seed-planting part."

No-nonsense as ever, Robert said, "Well, Daddy's the one who takes care of me." After another moment to think, he concluded, "But so does William, now. And he looks more like me, so maybe he's the gardener?"

Laughing again, Julia took both of his hands in hers. "You're so smart. But I want you to know something, and this is super important, so listen up."

"What?" he demanded excitedly.

"The reason you never met William before is *not* because he didn't want to be your dad. And it's not your fault in any way. The truth is, Tadders... William only just found out he was your dad."

Robert searched her face a moment before asking, "Why?"

"Oh, Tadpole... I want to answer that for you, and soon, I will. I wish I knew how to answer it right this second, but it's one of those super-confusing grown-up things. But this much I can tell you: if William had known he was your daddy, he *totally* would have been a part of your life, all along. And now that he *does* know, we were all just trying to figure out how to explain it to you without confusing you, or making you think it was your fault. And I'm just so sorry you had to find out this way, instead."

Robert's lips twisted as he considered. "So I guess this means I'll have two daddies from now on, just like my friend Rowan."

Julia laughed out loud now. "Yeah, but we won't all live in the same house, like her parents do."

"Why not?"

"Um, well... I get the feeling Rowan's mom loves both of Rowan's dads, and that's why they all live together."

"Oh. But you don't love Daddy anymore, so..."

A spike of sadness drove through Julia's heart as she stroked his hair. "Your daddy and I were in love once, and we still care about each other."

"But now you love William."

Julia's heart flip-flopped. "Yes."

"And he loves you." He said it like it was an obvious fact. "So why doesn't William marry you? Why doesn't he live with us?"

Julia kissed the top of his head. As always, at the mere thought of living with William, an invisible blanket of warmth surrounded her. "Someday he might, but not yet. First, we all have to make sure it's the right thing. And you get a say in that, too."

Robert's brows came together. "Hey Mommy, is William Paige's gardener, too?"

Julia's nerves were so rattled by this point that her stomach felt like a pinball machine. These were prime migraine-triggering conditions. After this, she would have to pop a migraine pill prophylactically.

Gently, she said, "No, Tadders."

"So... who is?"

"Daddy is, sweetie."

He did that puppy-dog head tilt again. "Why?"

Julia reached out to sweep a blond curl away from his eye. He was overdue for a haircut. Shame knotted itself around her heart. How could she possibly explain something so complex, so *adult* to a five-year-old? They hadn't gotten that far yet in their planning sessions with Clio. Julia wanted her explanation to be honest, but age appropriate. The last thing she needed was to confuse or traumatize him.

Sighing, she admitted, "That's another one of those things that's hard to explain right this second. But I promise, we will explain someday very soon. For now, I just need you to know that you are so loved. By me, and by Daddy and William, and by your whole entire family."

At that moment, Julia heard a tap on the bedroom door. "It's me," came her mother's voice from the other side. "Can I come in?"

Julia looked to Robert. "Is it okay if Grandma comes in? Or do you need more time in here, just the two of us?"

In answer, Robert went to open the door, and Julia's mother closed it behind herself before joining them on the edge of the bed.

"All's quiet on the western front," she reported to Julia. "Your father is downstairs talking to the men. Xavier is watching TV in the living room."

Julia heard no more shouting. "Paige?"

"Still in your room with Alison." Her mother brushed the hair back from Robert's forehead with an affectionate hand. "You two take as much time as you need in here."

"I don't need any more time," Robert chirped, bouncing off the mattress by his butt and landing on his feet. "I already know about my two dads."

Her mother's shocked eyes locked on Julia. "Wha–?"

"Hey Mommy," Robert broke in, already halfway to the door, "can I watch TV with Xavier?"

"Upstairs only," Julia called after him, but he took off without even waiting for her answer. To her mother, she quietly added, "I'll explain later."

After popping her migraine pill, she swept past Xavier and Robert, watching *Avatar: The Last Airbender* in the living room, and found her dad downstairs in the den with Kevin and William. Both younger men slumped on the sofa, as if drained of all life force, but they straightened when she appeared. Immediately Kevin doubled over again, hugging his torso in pain.

Julia nodded to her dad, who silently left the in-law unit, closing the door behind himself.

"I hope Dad wasn't a jerk," Julia offered with an uneasy snicker, stepping further into the room.

"Does he know?" William asked soberly.

It took Julia a few beats to register that he was talking about Robert, not her father. Julia closed her eyes in resignation. "Yes."

Still doubled over, Kevin groaned. "This is all my fault."

Julia sat in the armchair her father just vacated. "It's no one's fault. And surprisingly, Robert seems totally fine now. It's almost like he's *excited* to have two dads. He shrugged it off like it was nothing and asked if he could watch TV."

William barked out a laugh, but Kevin remained slumped over, shaking his head. When he buried his face in his hands again, Julia asked, "Is there anything I can do? For the pain?"

Kevin rolled his head back and forth. "Never is; never was."

"Do you need to go to the hospital?"

Once again, he shook his head emphatically. "I'm actually on the upswing, believe it or not. That's why I thought I could handle this – seeing the kids, I mean."

"But you're doubled over in agony."

Kevin waved her concern away. "It's the stress. It'll calm down. Besides, I still need to talk to Robert about everything. We all do," he added, glancing up at William. "And then I need to give Paige a piece of my mind."

"She needs a day or two to re-calibrate," countered Julia. "And we should at least consult Clio first."

Kevin bowed his head again. "Yeah, you're probably right."

"But I *will* go get Robert."

The moment Robert appeared in the den, Kevin steepled his fingers against his lips, his eyes suspiciously glassy. William scrubbed his hand over his jaw and mouth and sniffed a couple of times.

Robert's eyes snapped to Kevin with solemnity so far beyond his years, it would have been funny under any other circumstances. "It's okay, Daddy; I still love you, even though you're not my gardener."

Julia winced, and Kevin's brow furrowed in confusion. "Your... gardener?"

"I'll explain later," Julia whispered aside to Kevin.

"But you're still my Daddy, aren't you?" added Robert.

"Of course I am," Kevin said hoarsely, folding Robert into his arms. "I will *always* be your daddy, Tadpole. And I'll never stop loving you."

"Me either." Robert squeezed him around the neck before bursting apart and running to throw his arms around William's neck. "I'm glad you're my daddy now, too."

Closing his eyes, William wrapped his arms around Robert like his life depended on it. "Me too, buddy."

Julia snuck a peek at Kevin, but his expression betrayed no resentment – only discomfort, tinged with sadness.

"Mommy," Robert chirped, wriggling out of William's grasp, "can I go now? Xavier paused the show for me."

Julia smiled and rumpled his hair. As he sped past, she playfully swatted his backside, and he unleashed a volley of giggles that reached them even from the top of the stairs.

Things went miraculously well after that. Julia's mother had taken all the food back to the kitchen and kept it warm or cold, as needed; so for the most part, everything still looked and tasted good. Julia's father chatted pleasantly enough with Kevin about his upcoming dissertation defense, while Julia's mother commiserated with his fruitless job search in the Bay Area – including his unsuccessful application to a local marine mammal conservation center.

After dinner, they adjourned to the patio. William and Xavier helped Julia's mother in the garden, while Kevin played Velcro darts with Robert on the ancient board Julia had grown up with. She redis-covered it a few days ago while helping her mother clean out the attic – a long-overdue chore that Julia suspected her mother had tackled with her own impending mortality in mind.

Ann, meanwhile, helped Julia with the dishes in the kitchen.

"I'm sorry," Julia said quietly as she dried and put away the soup tureen. "I'm afraid some of the interactions you've had with Paige have been less than stellar."

Ann waved away her concern. "Will told me about her Asperger's diagnosis." With a sly, sidelong glance at Julia, she added, "I guess that's one more thing she and Xavier have in common."

"You mean besides their mutual passion for art, video games, anime, and just about everything else?" Julia's tone dripped with amusement.

"Including each other?" Sensing her reply had taken Julia aback, Ann quickly clarified, "I just mean there's an obvious puppy love blooming between them. Nothing serious."

That wouldn't be weird at all, thought Julia. After all, there was a decent possibility that Paige and Xavier would be step-cousins one day. "I'll keep an eye on it."

"Yes," Ann murmured knowingly. "That might be wise."

ALISON, who had stayed in the bedroom with Paige for most of the evening, finally emerged solo. She beckoned Julia with a wave and a rare, sober expression. Julia excused herself to follow her sister downstairs to the den.

"Paige is incredibly embarrassed and ashamed," Alison said right off the bat. Then, with a smirk, she added, "Though to be honest, I have a feeling she's more worried about what Xavier thinks than anything."

Julia laughed, but there was no genuine humor in it.

Alison's eyebrows pulled together. "Take it easy on her, Julie. She was already so worked up about everything else, she forgot you hadn't told Robert."

Staring down at her shoes, Julia could only shake her head in resignation.

Alison's frown vanished, and she moved to gather Julia into a hug. Then she drew back, still clasping Julia by the shoulders. "I'm sure you remember, when we were kids, I was a master manipulator, and I put up a good front of not caring what anyone thought. It wasn't until I was an adult, and I finally got my ADHD diagnosis, that I understood it was a mask – armor, really."

Julia quirked an eyebrow. "Armor?"

"Against rejection. Against constantly being labeled a fuck-up or an idiot for things I couldn't help. The point is, don't let the mask fool you. Paige may be thirteen, but she's still just a kid. And a neurodivergent one, at that."

Julia chewed her lip, considering. Finally, she said, "It's really helpful, hearing your perspective. And Al... I never thought you were a fuck-up or an idiot. I'm sorry if anything I said or did gave you that impression."

Alison blinked once or twice, then grinned, the mask sliding seamlessly back in place. "That's okay. What are sisters for, if not to keep each other humble?"

Paige spent the next half hour tearfully apologizing to Julia in their bedroom, while Diego consoled her. When the three of them finally emerged, Paige apologized to Robert and everyone else, as well – including, Julia couldn't help but notice, Xavier.

She accidentally eavesdropped when she came to refill her father's wineglass. She found the bottle of Cinsaut still on the dining table, and as she poured, Paige and Xavier's voices drifted from the kitchen.

"I know what that's like," Xavier was saying. "You know my other mom isn't even in the picture anymore, right?"

"No, I didn't know," Paige murmured.

"She might even be dead. Last anybody heard, she was living in a tent under the freeway. She chose drugs over me and Zach."

"Oh," murmured Paige. "I'm so sorry."

"What your dad did back then, running off like that... that was shit," Xavier acknowledged. "But he's trying; anyone can see that. I gotta be honest, Paige – listening to you complain about your life feels like a slap in the face."

Clearly taken aback, Paige breathed, "What?"

"I mean, you have three whole parental units that love you and give you everything you need. And on top of all that, your dad is filthy rich, you're smart, you're talented, and you're, um..." Xavier's voice grew thin and strained. "...you're ridiculously pretty."

The ensuing silence told Julia that his confession stunned Paige just as much as it stunned her.

But Julia hadn't meant to eavesdrop for this long. And with the silence stretching longer and longer, it occurred to her to wonder what they were doing in there. Snapping out of her trance, Julia swept into the kitchen with her father's wineglass.

Paige and Xavier both jumped in their seats, but it wasn't like Julia had caught them sticking their tongues down each other's throats. They sat on opposite sides of the kitchen table, both of their faces flushed red.

"Hey!" Julia said brightly. "I was just coming to get another San Pellegrino for Will."

After recovering from the initial shock, Xavier stared at the tabletop, repeatedly blinking and sniffing. Paige, meanwhile, chewed her fingernails, but she, too, said nothing. Julia wagered they were both trying to work out how much Julia had overheard.

"Are you guys still hungry?" Julia tried. When they both shook their heads, she added, "I think the Playstation is still free downstairs, if you want to pick up where you left off. You know... smashing pyramids, or whatever it is you do in that game."

Paige rolled her eyes, but at least it was a good-natured eye roll. The eye roll of the long-suffering teen who secretly finds it funny, how out of touch her parents are.

Back outside, Robert and Kevin had grown bored with Velcro darts and made their way back to the patio table. When Julia joined them, depositing Paige and Xavier at the Playstation along the way, she pulled up short at the scene before her: William, seated at the patio table with Kevin, engaged in stiff but civil conversation.

Wonders never ceased, because then Paige and Xavier spent the rest of the evening teaching William to play Minecraft. At one point, Julia caught William's eye and gave him a grateful smile, which he returned with a subtle nod.

By then, it was well past Robert's bedtime. Julia found him curled in his aunt's lap, his lids suspiciously heavy as he unleashed a ferocious yawn. Alison handed him off to Julia and bid farewell, Kevin drove back to Atherton, and Kelly and Pilar picked up Ann and Xavier. That, in turn, left Julia and William to put Robert to bed.

"You know it's okay to feel whatever you feel about Daddy and

William," Julia murmured, smoothing Robert's hair back from his forehead as William tucked him under the covers.

His brow scrunched up. "What do you mean?"

"I mean about having two dads. Happy, sad, confused, excited, mad... it's all normal and okay. And it's okay to feel different things at different times."

"Hmmm..." Robert tapped his lip thoughtfully. "I think I feel curious."

Julia chuckled. "That's a great word."

"Curious, and sleepy," he added around a yawn.

"Tomorrow you can ask as many questions as you want," William reassured him, "but for now, sweet dreams."

Robert tugged his stuffed frog, Prince, under the covers and wrapped his arms around him. His mouth stretched around a final yawn as his eyelids sank shut.

"Love you, Tadpole," Julia whispered, kissing his cheek; then she kissed Prince and added, "You, too, Other Tadpole."

After William kissed Robert's forehead, he turned out the bedroom light and gently closed the door. Taking his hand, Julia pulled him into the den and invited him to sit. Then, reaching into the closet, she finally retrieved William's gift.

She had used the same taupe wrapping paper with navy-blue ticking stripes that Robert had used. But she had done a much tidier job and topped it with a navy-blue, satin-edged arabesque ribbon, tied in an ornate bow. She brought it to William on the sofa, sitting beside him.

"What's this?" he asked, turning it over in his hands, inspecting it.

"It's a Father's Day gift, silly."

His cheeks pinked up a bit, and he gave her one of those shy smiles that made her heart do gymnastics. Then he tugged at the ribbon, peeled away the paper, and uncovered the two flannel shirts.

Shooting her a quizzical look, he unfolded the one on top. "Wait. Isn't this...?"

"Yours?" she finished for him, with a sly grin. "I may or may not have stolen it from your closet. But it was for a good cause," she added, gesturing to the second shirt.

He set the first shirt aside and unfolded the second one. In a tone of wonder, he asked, "Did you make this?"

"I used the stolen shirt as a pattern."

"I already guessed that part. It's just..." He flipped it around to look at the back. At a loss, he simply cupped the back of her neck with one hand and smiled warmly.

Suddenly unsure of herself, she leaned into his touch. "I've never seen you in green plaid before, and this flannel is so incredibly soft – really good quality. So I thought..."

His gaze softened, and he blinked several times. Then, with his hand still at the nape of her neck, he drew her to him in a soft, lingering kiss. His lips were warm and full on hers, and her pulse fluttered erratically, her skin turning fizzy.

When he finally broke the kiss, he whispered, "It's perfect. Absolutely perfect. Thank you."

She put her hand over his heart and found it drumming a steady rhythm. Her eyes swept between his, and his face flushed again. This time, she cupped the back of *his* neck.

Their tongues swept together, and they both drew sharp, surprised breaths through their noses. With one hand on his neck and the other on his chest, she felt his heartbeat swell to a crescendo.

She suddenly flashed back to earlier when he barreled outside, practically feral with protectiveness. To know that this soft-spoken gentle giant, capable of infinite tenderness and patience with children – capable of rocketing her body to so many heights of pleasure – that he also had the will and ability to keep them all safe? And yet he also had the self-control to rein it in and admit when he screwed up? And on top of all that, he had the maturity to spend the rest of the evening treating his erstwhile nemesis with civility?

Once again, some prehistoric part of her brain lit up, igniting her body into a conflagration.

She broke apart and rested her forehead against his, practically gasping for air. "It's been way too long," she chuckled.

"Twenty days, six hours, and–" He glanced at his watch. "–twelve minutes."

"But who's counting, right?"

He nipped the shell of her ear and whispered, "Only five more days to go."

Goose bumps erupted over her body as she contemplated an entire weekend in bed with him – at least, when they weren't enjoying Kelly and Pilar's wedding festivities. After all, it was the kids' weekend with Kevin's parents.

Leaning into his ear, she whispered back, "Don't forget the protein bars and Gatorade."

By the time Julia and William dragged themselves out of bed on Kelly and Pilar's wedding day, it was almost noon. Achy and bleary-eyed, they refrained from reenacting the previous night's sexcapades and managed a chaste shower together. Afterward, William ceded the bathroom to Julia. When she finally emerged an hour and a half later, she was not surprised to find him already waiting at the table with his laptop open, probably sneaking in some work.

But she was not prepared for how the sight of him in a suit would stop her in her tracks and make her heart stutter so violently. And when he turned in response to her tiny gasp, he reacted similarly – eyes flying wide-open, fingers frozen over the keyboard.

When he remembered himself, he slowly stood, revealing his full glory to her, and drinking in all of hers.

Not once, in all their time together, had Julia seen him in a suit. Suit-William irrevocably spoiled her for Anything-Else-William. Suit-William blew yesterday's Rehearsal-Dinner-Esquire-Model-William out of the water.

She had never seen anything as beautiful as this tall, fit man in his tailored black suit, crisp white dress shirt, and royal blue tie. He had trimmed his beard without making it *too* clean; and the beginnings of his loose dirty-blond curls required no product to look perfectly rakish.

As she leered, William's eyes devoured her in turn, starting with her loosely-curled hair. She had pinned the right side half-up with a beaded clip, leaving the rest unpinned to sweep over her left shoulder.

From there, his eyes took in her rose lip color, then swept over the silver mermaid pendant he had given her long ago, now glinting against her collarbone.

Finally, his gaze stalled on the new dress she had sewn, just for this occasion.

"Julie..." He let out a shuddering breath as he took in her black sheath dress, with its spaghetti straps, darted bodice, and airy overlay of sheer black tulle. But what made it suitable for a wedding, despite the color, were the spring-like pink roses and green leaves scattered all over the tulle. Julia had embroidered them herself. From there, William's eyes raked down her legs to the rose-colored strappy sandals that showed off her French pedicure.

His forehead creased with emotion, his eyes fixing on hers with something like gratitude. "I've said it before and I'll say it again: you are the most beautiful woman on the planet."

Her heart dissolving into goo, she came forward to slide her hands up his chest. "I'm no Helen of Troy."

He settled his hands on her hips, leering shamelessly at the way the dress hugged her willowy figure, form-fitting but not excessively so. "Helen of Troy's got nothing on Julia of the Sunset," he declared, toying with a lock of her copper hair for emphasis on *the Sunset.*

Julia beamed. Now that she stood this close, she noticed the subtle neat-motif strewn across the royal blue silk of his tie. She also noticed that he clearly had no idea how to actually *tie* a tie. She fiddled with it a moment, then redid it altogether.

When she finished, she lifted her eyes to his. Her pulse fluttered at the undisguised adoration she found there. She straightened his collar, then smoothed her hands over his chest again.

"Thank you," she whispered.

"For what?" he said, his voice still raw.

She ran his tie lightly through her hand. "For coming back to me."

Since he couldn't kiss her without messing up her lipstick, he ran his fingertips along the line of her jaw. "I could never stay away."

~

It turned out Julia was the person most skilled at pinning on boutonnieres and corsages. That's how she found herself at the church, performing that exact service for the entire wedding party. Of course, she saved the best for last, pinning William's boutonniere to his lapel while trading secret smiles with him.

"Have I told you yet how handsome you look?" she whispered finally.

His smile widened further. "Nope."

"What the hell is wrong with me?"

"Good question."

She laughed. "You look so incredibly handsome today. Not that you don't always look handsome; but today?" She gave a chef's kiss, which he returned with a real kiss on her cheek. Finally, straightening his tie and lapels, she whispered, "Knock 'em dead, stud-muffin."

Leaving a flustered William with Kelly and the rest of her attendants, she returned to the vestibule. But there was no more time for mingling, because the wedding was about to start. The weather-beaten sixty-something usher offered his arm with a familiar grin, as if he knew her; and after a moment's confusion, she blurted, "Uncle Frank!"

"As I live and breathe," chuckled William's uncle.

"Oh my God; it's so good to see you!" gushed Julia. Frank had taken Julia and William out on his fishing boat during their senior year of high school, allowing Julia to interview him about a fading local industry for her school report – while also allowing her and William an opportunity to steal their first kiss.

"How are you doing?" she asked breathlessly.

"Ornery as ever," Frank confirmed cheerfully. "On my fourth wife now. Nina."

"I assume you brought her, right?"

"Much to my kids' chagrin," he quipped. "They're all here, too."

Julia couldn't help but laugh as he started to escort her to the front pew on Kelly's side. "Well, I can't wait to meet her. And see all your kids again."

Since Ann had not taken her seat yet, Julia was surprised to find two people already there. Surprise turned to bewilderment when she recognized one of them as her sister. Sure, Alison had made the wedding cake, but that didn't exactly entitle her to a front row seat with Kelly's family. Even Julia had been reluctant to accept their invitation to sit with them, considering how new everything still was between herself and William. Kelly and Ann had to practically browbeat her into accepting.

Julia took in the wraithlike figure beside Alison. His well-worn, too-casual clothing sagged on his frame, as if he had recently lost weight but couldn't afford replacements. For one moment, Julia wondered if Alison had picked up a homeless guy.

Beside Julia, Frank gasped. "Holy shit – *Mike?*"

Julia's confusion turned to shock. Sure, it was partially because Mike had never RSVP'd, so no one had accounted for him in the seating arrangement. But it was mostly because no one who had known Mike before would recognize him now.

Mike Quinn – formerly of the bulky biceps and shredded abs. Plurally-tattooed, lip-licking, lasciviously-grinning haunter of seedy gyms everywhere.

Now, the brittle remains of his dark hair hung in faded wisps over his forehead and sunken temples. His cheeks were hollow; his eyes bugged out of bony sockets. Having recovered somewhat from the initial shock, Julia finally registered the other thing that was missing – the veritable arsenal of piercings that used to adorn his face. He still wore a single silver hoop in one nostril and a single plug in each earlobe, but that was it.

Julia was supposed to be the first into the pew, and then she would scoot over so Ann could sit by the aisle. But since he was here, Mike should be the one sitting beside his mother.

Julia did not want to have to step across him and Alison to get to their seats. "Go around the front," she whispered to Frank. "I'll sneak in from the side aisle."

Frank silently complied, his normally-jovial face as sober as a judge;

and Julia slid into the pew, beside Alison. Mike acknowledged both Julia and Frank with a wave and a sheepish half-smile.

Julia leaned into her sister's ear. "What the hell is going on?"

Alison frowned. "Um... Kelly's getting married?"

"You know what I mean."

Slowly, as if Julia were a toddler, Alison explained, "And, um... Mike is Kelly's brother? So, like... he's here?"

"And you're his plus-one."

"Bingo."

But now was not the time for further grilling, especially not once the processional music started. She spied Uncle Frank leading Ann to her seat. Clearly even Ann had not expected Mike, because she let out a yelp of surprise, then snatched his hand, unleashing a volley of whispers in his ear. Devastation marred her usually upbeat features. For his part, Mike just looked... embarrassed. Closed off. His shoulders slumped, and he avoided his mother's worried frown. Gone was the swaggering peacock Julia had known, replaced by this fragile shell of his former self.

But then, a minute later, Julia thought her heart would pound itself right out of her chest as William escorted the maid of honor down the aisle. His eyes flitted to hers, lighting up briefly before darkening when they landed on Mike and Alison. He quickly shifted his focus to Kelly at the front of the church, and Julia followed his lead.

Pilar had gifted Kelly a white linen guayabera with exquisite royal-blue embroidery flanking its front pintucks. Kelly had paired it with a cream-colored blazer, matching slacks, and tan loafers.

Xavier and Zach processed in turn behind William, each escorting a taller, adult bridesmaid, much to the guests' amusement. After Kelly and Pilar's final attendants escorted each other down the aisle, the music swelled, and the guests rose in anticipation.

With her parents flanking her on either side, Pilar embodied the definition of "radiant." She wore her burgundy-dyed hair in Sisterlocks, curled and rolled into a forties-style half-up. A filmy veil floated down her back from a tiara pinned in her hair.

Through the illusion lace against her décolletage, the sweetheart neckline of Pilar's white dress offered a hint of cleavage. The lace extended to her shoulders, cap sleeves, and halfway down the tulle overlay that draped her baby bump. A lacy, gauzy cathedral train trailed behind, and she carried a simple bouquet of white roses.

Delfina's chin quivered, and Sergio was the picture of paternal pride as they escorted their daughter down the aisle. As during the rehearsal, Pilar beamed down the aisle at Kelly; and Julia had never seen Kelly smile so widely. Grinning beside her, William offered his misty-eyed sister a handkerchief and rubbed her arm fondly. Then he caught Julia's eye and held it as they shared a small, secret smile.

Even though she barely knew Kelly and Pilar, Julia found her eyes pricking with tears. She had no idea what these two women had endured to be together, but the love and acceptance their families offered today was beautiful to witness.

Pilar seemed determined to stand through as much of the ceremony as possible, even though it quickly became clear that it would be a long, mostly-traditional Catholic wedding, celebrated alternately in English and Spanish. The Unitarian-Universalist minister must not have cared which denomination's liturgy they used. Of course, there were times when Pilar and Kelly were supposed to kneel; but Pilar sat instead, with Kelly kneeling alongside her.

During the vows, Julia's heart turned somersaults when she caught William watching her again. His blue eyes gleamed as he held hers unflinchingly. The corners of his mouth lifted almost imperceptibly. Warmth blossomed behind Julia's sternum, and the scene before her shifted. It was only a moment – a split second in time. But during that second, their surroundings disappeared, and it was just the two of them, together at a wedding.

Their wedding.

Smiling wider, he slowly blinked. She knew he saw it, too.

And then it was time for him to retrieve the wedding rings from his pocket, and the spell was broken.

WITH THE DANCES OVER, the cake cut, and the bouquets and garters dispensed with, it was time to see Kelly and Pilar off to their new life. At last, after saying their goodbyes, William and Julia made their escape.

Every nerve ending in Julia's body vibrated with delicious anticipation as William placed a hand on her lower back, steering her toward his Jeep.

Until a voice called out William's name, stopping them dead in their tracks.

Julia felt William stiffen and heard him swear under his breath. Just as they both turned, she realized who it was.

Sure enough, Mike cautiously approached on the sidewalk. Alison stood a ways down the sidewalk, illuminated by the corner street lamp, scrolling through her phone.

William stood rigid beside Julia, waiting for Mike to speak. She gestured toward her sister. "I'll just go–"

"No. Stay." William stopped her with a hand on her arm, his steely gaze never leaving Mike. "This won't take long."

Mike cleared his throat, shuffling on his feet. "Um – hi, Will," he said quietly, and once again, it struck Julia how unprecedented *quiet* was for Mike. Then he turned a faint smile on her. "Hi, Julia. Good to see you."

Before Julia could respond, William barked out, "What do you want, Mike?"

Mike flinched, understandably. William's sharp tone even took Julia aback.

Mike scratched his nose, unable to meet William's glare. "Um... I was hoping we could talk privately, but if now's not a good time–"

"Are you using?"

Mike blinked. "Wh-what?"

"I said *are... you... using?*"

The way William snarled the question through clenched teeth made Julia's stomach quiver. Evidently she had underestimated his anger toward Mike. Maybe even William had.

After a moment to digest his brother's question, Mike's face reddened, and a hint of a frown etched his brows. He lifted his hands and took a step or two backward.

"You know what? Forget it."

Spinning on his heel and shoving his hands into his pockets, he strode back to Alison, who looked up from her phone in shock. Before Julia could see more, William steered her away with a hand on her back.

Julia walked briskly to keep up with his long strides, but she waited until they were safely in his Jeep before speaking. Even then, she held off another minute as he locked the door and draped his forearms over the steering wheel, pressing his forehead into them.

He said, "He's still using."

Gently, Julia asked, "Are you sure?"

William sighed. It wasn't an exasperated sigh; just an exhausted one. Sitting up, looking her in the eye, he explained, "The weight loss, the sores on his face... Trust me when I say I know an active meth user when I see one. Thanks to Jimmy, I learned to be hypervigilant."

Guilt coiled around Julia's heart. "I know. I'm sorry." Reaching over the console, she placed a gentle hand on his arm. "I can see you're still really angry, with *both* of your brothers."

William frowned thoughtfully. "I guess you're right."

She stroked his hair before adding, "You should absolutely keep those healthy boundaries, and also... just don't forget what you said in your best-man speech. About being a family who loves with fierce loyalty."

William's frown slowly unfurled as her words hit home. "'We screw up, we hurt each other, and sometimes we even take a break. But we always come back to love.'" He reached over to tuck a lock of hair behind her ear, then clasped her chin between his thumb and forefinger. "Yes, I wrote all that. But Julie, it was *you* I was thinking of when I wrote it. And this is exactly why."

Julia tilted her head. "*What* is?"

Leaning across the center console to clasp her face in both hands, he whispered, "You always guide me back to myself."

Without waiting for her reply, he captured her mouth with his. With a murmur of surprise, she clasped his face and kissed him right back. Their tongues swept together frantically, their breaths crescendoing until William abruptly broke the kiss.

"You are so fucking gorgeous tonight, Julie," he said, his voice raw. "I don't want to talk or think about anyone but you right now. I need to take you home and taste every inch of you."

"Oh my God, Will," Julia said with a breathy laugh, her thighs clenching involuntarily. "When you say things like that, I don't know if I can wait that long."

"You can and you will," he ordered, cranking the Jeep's ignition and throwing it into gear. Casting her a playful sidelong grin, he added, "But only because I can't lay you out like I want to in here."

~

WILLIAM SPED home as fast as traffic and safety would allow. But once he got her inside his apartment, he found the self-control to take his time with her – self-control that had eluded him last night, their first night together in a month.

Sitting on the edge of the bed, he bunched the skirt of her dress around her waist, exposing her black lace panties; then tugged her into his lap, straddling him. They shared lazy, sensuous kisses as she relieved him of his tie and unbuttoned his shirt. He reached behind her, found the top of her zipper, and slowly dragged it down her spine. With his palms, he swept the spaghetti straps from her shoulders, then peeled the bodice down her torso, revealing her strapless black lace bra. He broke their kiss long enough to admire the view, then looked into her eyes, his forehead furrowing with raw emotion.

"You are *everything*," he rasped out.

Heat bloomed red over her skin. Her eyes drifted shut, and she tipped her head back with a murmur of longing. He responded by pressing warm, wet kisses to her throat. She had forgotten how to breathe, or even move. She could only savor the way every nerve ending answered his touch with a shower of sparks.

As his lips traveled to her collarbone, he tugged at the clasp of her bra. It was a sturdy contraption with three hooks, so she reached behind herself to assist, popping it open. Tunneling beneath the cups, he scooped her breasts into his warm palms, sending the bra tumbling to the mattress.

The hands gripping her trembled with restraint as he leaned forward, flicking his tongue first to one nipple, then the other. Sucking them into his mouth, lavishing equal attention on both.

"Your nipples are my favorite things to put in my mouth," he said after, his breath hot against her skin. Then, putting his lips to her ear, he whispered, "Besides your clit, I mean."

She unleashed a ragged moan, grinding like a feral thing against the impressive bulge in his pants, making him hiss with pleasure. Still, he took his time undressing her the rest of the way, almost reverent with each new part of her body he uncovered. Laying her down on the mattress, he seized her dress, still bunched around her waist, and tugged it down her legs, discarding it on the floor.

When his fingertips hooked into the waistband of her panties, she shuddered in anticipation. And then he was inching them down, his eyes riveted between her thighs where she ached almost painfully. He made her feel powerful and sexy, his pupils blown wide as they drank in the evidence of her desire.

Grasping her knees, he gently pried them wider, his heated stare still fixed between her legs. Then he crawled backward off the bed and simply stood at its foot, raking his eyes across her naked, exposed body. He bit his clenched fist, his gaze tinged with awe and disbelief. His suit trousers were utterly useless to conceal the massive erection straining against them.

Nearly all the blood had vacated her brain, but she cobbled together two brain cells and pretended to pout. "No fair. I only got your shirt halfway undone."

Laughing softly, he answered her with a maddeningly slow strip-tease. At last, he stood there like a well-endowed Michelangelo sculpture in the flesh, his arousal on full display.

"I want to touch you," she whispered, sitting up, reaching for him.

But he crawled over her and gently urged her back down. "Soon," he promised, kissing her lips, "but first, please let me be selfish. My mouth has been watering ever since you came out of my bathroom wearing that dress. I can't wait another second."

His words alone had her arching up off the bed. She couldn't fathom how her body would react once he followed through on his promise. "Please do it, Will."

As he kissed his way down her stomach, she drew a sharp breath through her teeth – a hiss of anticipation. His hands swept along her curves, lifting her body to his lips. She trembled as he knelt between her legs, his eyes locking on hers.

With the first swipe of his tongue, her legs quaked violently. To her astonishment, she was already on the razor-sharp edge of an orgasm, shouting as stars gathered behind her pupils.

But just as quickly as he got her there, he ripped the proverbial rug out from underneath her, denying her the sweet relief she chased.

The sadist actually had the nerve to grin up at her as she panted, writhed, and cursed him. When her explosion was no longer imminent, he dove in again – sucking and nibbling, licking and feathering. Dipping, swirling, and tapping. Careening her right back to the edge before once again pulling up short with a smirk. She lost track of time as he repeated this dance over and over, leaving her sweating, writhing, and pleading for release.

And all of that was before he even added his fingers.

When he finally did, her raucous orgasm snatched her right from this plane of existence, wrenching her body inside-out. Powerless to stifle the shrieks tearing out of her, she thrashed in the wake of each tsunami of pleasure.

When the last wave finally ebbed, leaving her a whimpering puddle, she couldn't even open her eyes. She grew heavy, sinking into the mattress, while at the same time lighter than air, floating up to the ceiling. Never in all her thirty-six years of life had she experienced a more powerful, transcendent, life-altering orgasm.

She wanted him to give her that every day, in their shared bed. In their shared home.

Every. Single. Day.

The epiphany hit her like a clap of thunder. But before she had time to process it, he was climbing up her body again, his heavy-lidded gaze dark with need.

Still, he was in no rush, settling alongside her and turning her so they faced each other on their sides. His relentless erection prodded her thighs as they shared languid kisses, their hands roaming each other. Finally, she reached between them, wrapping her hand around him, and his resounding groan broke their kiss.

Slinging her leg over his hip, she opened herself to him again, caressing the most sensitive part of herself with his tip. His unrestrained grunts and moans told of his own pleasure, rocketing her within seconds to another orgasm.

He was shaking now – positively vibrating with need. She nudged his chest, rolling him onto his back, throwing her other leg over to straddle him. He was an absolute vision beneath her, his blue irises eclipsed in pools of black, his short curls wild from her fingers. A sheen of sweat set the tattoos on his arms aglow and highlighted his beautifully carved chest as she raked her fingernails through the hair there. He put one hand on her hip. With the other, he reached between their bodies, guiding himself to her.

"I'm going to marry you, Julie," he gritted out, his voice hoarse with longing.

"I'm going to let you," she murmured, sinking down onto him. Sharing his pleasure, compounding it, and making it more than the sum of their two bodies.

MONDAY, JUNE 25, 2012

On Monday afternoon, Julia serviced the aquarium at Dunphy's; and it was eerie to see her father's restaurant quiet and shuttered at that time of day. The change in the environment perturbed even the fish, and she made sure to spend a little extra time there with them.

She got home with just enough time to shower before Kevin's parents dropped the kids off. Julia gave a silent prayer of thanks when they departed mere moments before William arrived.

When he did, the kids talked his ears off about their impromptu weekend in New York. Stranded in the kitchen making dinner, Julia could only listen helplessly to their relentless prattle, floating in from the living room.

"Grandma took me to the zoo in Central Park," Robert announced.

"Hmmm," responded Julia's mother. "Did you go, too, Paige?"

Paige scoffed. "Hell no. Grandpa took me to the Met."

Julia cringed to know how this must sound to William. It was a constant battle, trying to keep the kids grounded in reality when Kevin and his family were multimillionaires. Reminding them that nearly one hundred percent of humanity couldn't summon a private jet to any destination in the world on a whim. Staving off entitlement, when John and Phoebe Beale believed entitlement was their birthright.

Thankfully, that was one point on which Julia and Kevin had always agreed. They had made the conscious decision to live far below their means in neighborhoods that weren't wealthy enclaves. They had sent their kids to public schools, at least until Paige could no longer get the services she needed in hers. And they had dragged the kids – kicking and screaming, if necessary – to volunteer at home and abroad. In fact, they never traveled without incorporating service into at least half of their itinerary, exposing Paige and Robert to the world's realities, and to the obscene privilege they enjoyed by comparison.

But although she knew this, William did not. And right this moment, the kids sounded almost boastful. Plus, she couldn't help wondering how William felt, being forced to hear about his once-rival's parents and their boundless wealth.

To rescue William, she summoned the kids into the kitchen to help with meal prep. But even after gathering around the patio table for dinner, Paige and Robert refused to let up.

"Mommy, how come you never take us anywhere, like Daddy does?" Robert demanded.

"Yeah," Paige seconded, "you haven't taken us anywhere in, like, *ages.*"

Julia cast a self-conscious glance around the table. "We haven't taken any vacations recently because I run a business now, and because..." She made silly jazz hands. "...money doesn't grow on trees. Dun-dun-*dun!*"

"Yeah; it comes from credit cards and amen machines," Robert concurred with a sage nod.

"*ATM*, you dolt," snapped Paige, smacking Robert on the back of the head.

"Paige!" Julia snapped, before drawing a deep, calming breath. *Opposite action,* admonished Clio's voice in her head.

Thankfully, Julia's mother intervened. "Speaking of entrepreneurship, I believe your father has something to report."

Julia's father looked up in confusion before registering his wife's meaning. "Ah. Yes." To William, he said, "I met with Marisa at Zeneize."

In spite of herself, Julia's stomach bottomed out at the mention of Marisa. William's face reddened as he studiously avoided Julia's eyes.

But before he could reply, Paige interjected, "Zeneize... Why does that sound familiar?"

"It's a restaurant," Julia said flatly.

Paige's face lit up. "Oh yeah, right! Grandma and Grandpa Beale took us there."

Zeneize didn't sound like the kind of restaurant Julia would take kids to. "They took you and Robert to Zeneize?"

"Well, us and Dad."

That was news. "When was this?"

"Just last month. It was super-cool. You know the chef there is getting that new show."

At Paige's little bombshell, Julia's throat clamped shut. She wasn't sure she really wanted to know, but when Paige didn't elaborate, Julia prompted, "What new show?"

"You know... the reality show where she's going to take over bad restaurants and make them good again?"

"Zeneize's chef is going to do that? Marisa Zunino?" The name tasted like ashes in Julia's mouth.

Paige snapped her fingers. "Yeah, that's her name! She's supposed to be really great."

"Well, your grandfather is thinking of handing Dunphy's over to a new chef," Julia's mother explained to Paige. "Maybe that new chef could be Marisa."

Julia's father cleared his throat. "Marisa was intrigued. She said she'll propose Dunphy's to the show's producers. Obviously nothing is set in stone, but there's a chance that, for the first season of her show, Marisa will rebrand Dunphy's as *Zeneize at Fisherman's Wharf.*"

"Oh, well, that makes sense," Paige said around the bite of food she shoved into her mouth. "Did you know she actually used to be, like, a *Sports Illustrated* swimsuit model or something? Dad says she'll boost ratings by luring male viewers."

Julia's stomach lurched at the glimpse of William's beet-red face. Not to mention the way he studied his plate as if there would be an exam on it tomorrow morning. Suddenly queasy, Julia lowered her fork and closed her eyes.

After several seconds of painful silence, Paige glanced around the table. "Why is everyone acting so weird?"

"Excuse me," Julia mumbled, springing from her seat and fleeing indoors, where she locked herself in the in-law unit's bathroom.

Because of *course* Kevin thought William's ex-girlfriend was hot.

And of *course* William's ex-girlfriend was an actual supermodel, on top of everything else.

How had Julia missed this little detail when conducting her online intel? And then she remembered – she had "safe search" enabled on her browser, in case Paige ever got around her lock screen.

Retrieving her phone, she disabled safe search, then typed *Marisa Zunino* in the browser.

Sure enough, there were several grainy online photos of a barely-legal Marisa, her ample bosom threatening to explode from a teeny-tiny string bikini. To add insult to injury, they didn't even look like fake boobs – she was just naturally that stacked. The top's white triangles barely covered her nipples, and she had an almost freakishly tiny hour-glass waist to go with it. Marisa might not have been the cover model, but who cared? She had made it into a *Sports Illustrated* swimsuit edition, for Christ's sake.

A moment later, Julia heard a light tapping at the bathroom door. "Julie, you had better not be looking her up in there."

With a shaky, joyless laugh, Julia opened the door. William regarded her with another one of his sad puppy-dog looks.

"How did you know?" she asked.

He shook his head in dismay. "Why do you keep doing that?"

She lifted an eyebrow. "You mean to tell me you've never cyber-stalked Kevin? Not even once?"

His answering silence spoke volumes.

"Speaking of Kevin, does he know Marisa is your ex?"

He held up his hands, as if to reassure her. "I have no clue. It's prob-ably just a coincidence. Zeneize is pretty hot right now." Immediately, he looked like he regretted his choice of words.

Julia glowered down at her phone. "When I see how genetically-gifted she is, on top of being brilliant and famous, it's hard not to wonder how I'm supposed to compete."

"Compete?" Seizing her elbow, he murmured, "Come with me. No one on the patio can eavesdrop if we talk upstairs."

She allowed him to lead her upstairs, where he sat on the sofa and patted the cushion beside him. She obeyed, and then he wrapped his hand around one of hers.

"Julie, I'm not sure how to adequately convey just how dysfunctional my relationship with Marisa was, but I'll try." Clearing his throat dramatically, he slowly enunciated each word for effect. "*Marisa was not a nice person.* Frankly, at times, she was downright cruel. For most of our time together, she treated me with thinly-veiled contempt."

"Then what do you think the attraction was, on her side? Besides, obviously, that you're one of the few humans hot enough to be in her league."

After a scoff of denial, he took a minute to consider her question. "Honestly? I think it's because I never pursued her. For one thing, I thought she was Kelly's ex-girlfriend."

Julia barked out a laugh. "Why?"

"Because when they were in high school, they spent a lot of time quote-unquote 'doing homework' in Kelly's room, with the door locked. They even went as Xena and Gabrielle one Halloween. But Kelly set me straight– no pun intended. Turns out they were just smoking weed in there, supplemented with the occasional six-pack of Zima. She says she made a valiant effort to get into Marisa's pants, but Marisa shot her down."

"Ouch."

"Anyway... I think Marisa didn't know what to make of my initial indifference, and it intrigued her. I think she's one of those people who only wants what she thinks she can't have."

Julia tried and failed to stifle an eye roll.

"Yeah," William agreed with a dry, humorless laugh.

Julia gripped his hand tighter. "I'm sorry if I'm frustrating you with all my obsessing about Marisa."

His gaze softening, he brought her hand to his lips. "I'm not frustrated, sweetheart. I just want you to feel comfortable."

"Thank you," she whispered, planting a soft kiss on his mouth.

"And I know I will. I promised myself I'd communicate with you, even if it felt scary."

He squeezed her hand with a tender smile. "Thank *you*. That's all I ask."

THURSDAY, JUNE 28, 2012

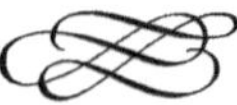

The rest of that week was no less frenetic than Monday. Between scheduling and attending appointments with therapists and meeting with Aaron – not to mention routine work and parenting duties – there simply weren't enough hours in the day. By the time dinner ended each night, Julia was practically sleepwalking. She was sorely tempted to cancel the individual therapy she had scheduled with Clio for Thursday and just rest, instead; but she knew she needed Clio's input. And sure enough, between Clio and her dance class afterward, Julia felt much better, like always.

That is, until William told her his news over dinner.

"I got in touch with Marisa today," he announced quietly, lifting his eyes from his plate to assess her reaction.

The bite of burrito Julia had just swallowed stuck in her throat, and she took several sips of water to clear it. "Sorry," she muttered.

"No, *I'm* sorry," William replied with a rueful chuckle.

"So, how did that go?"

"Better than expected, I guess. I had prepared myself for the worst, but it wasn't like that. Though she did seem a little cautious at first."

"Cautious?" Julia hoped her tone sounded less ruffled than she felt. "How so?"

"For one thing, after meeting with your dad last week, when my number popped up on her caller ID, she figured it couldn't be a coincidence. Later, she admitted she initially thought I was calling to ask for a job." He wiped his hand down his face with a rueful snicker.

"So what did you find out?"

"Long story short, they haven't settled yet on a restaurant, but she sounded pretty optimistic about Dunphy's prospects. It would make a good storyline, considering it's where she got her start. It would be like coming full circle – an 'apprentice is now the master' kind of thing."

Julia gave a wry laugh. "As much as the Sith Lord shoe fits, we'd better not frame it that way to Dad."

He laughed along with her before reaching across the table to take her hand and growing serious again. "She said something else that might interest you."

Julia's heart stuttered, even though she had no idea what it could be. "Okay?"

"She told me she was actually grateful to me for ending our relationship."

Julia barked out a laugh. "Wow. That's... okay."

"She wasn't hateful about it," he said with a nervous chuckle. "She just says she knows now that if we had started a family, she never could have achieved the things she has. She also says that after a lot of therapy, she realizes we were never compatible, and neither of us was ready for a healthy relationship. She admits that none of those epiphanies occurred until after she saw us at MacGowan's that day."

Julia hummed thoughtfully. "So you talked about me, then."

"I told her Paul is your father, and you're still the one who maintains the aquarium at Dunphy's. I thought she should know, if she was considering taking over, and of course Paul didn't think to tell her."

Julia huffed out a laugh. "No surprise there."

"The bottom line is, if the production team ends up selecting Dunphy's, she'd be happy to meet with you to clear the air."

Contemplative, Julia nodded slowly. William squeezed her hand and dipped his head to catch her eye. "I was hoping you'd feel a little more at ease, knowing she has no lingering interest or regrets, any more than I do. And that she feels no resentment toward you."

Julia smiled. "It does help. Thank you. And I'm still happy to meet with her, too."

The next evening, as Julia drove her to Clio's office, Paige was ambivalent to learn that she would not be spending July Fourth with her father, as previously planned. Clio had promised to try to get Paige to open up about her feelings regarding Kevin, and to explore some more the events of Father's Day; though of course Clio could not divulge any of Paige's confidences. But just knowing that Clio, with her gentle ways and the excellent rapport she had built with Paige, would probably get as close to the truth as possible – that reassured Julia's mom-heart considerably.

With how overwhelmed Julia was, it wasn't until her relatively quiet Sunday morning that it dawned on her – she hadn't heard from Alison all week. Normally they texted at least twice a week, if only to trade funny memes. But now Julia realized that since the post-wedding dust-up between William and Mike, which Alison had witnessed, it had been radio silence.

A pang of guilt speared through Julia, despite knowing the estrangement between William and Mike was their business, not hers or Alison's. But Julia wasn't angry, and she didn't want to leave Alison with the impression that she was. So she drew her phone from her pocket.

> Hey, Sis! Sorry I've been quiet all week. It wasn't intentional, I promise; I've just been slammed with work and life. I hope you'll be at dinner tonight, because I'd like to talk about what happened at the wedding. 😬

She distracted herself from her worries by roping Paige into the weekly aquarium maintenance. Not that it was that hard to convince Paige to help with their beloved pet fish. And it was a good distraction for Paige, too, who positively vibrated with the anticipation of seeing her favorite aunt.

But when Julia still hadn't heard back from Alison by one o'clock, she sought her mother out in the garden, where she and Robert were hauling in the season's first tomatoes. When Julia appeared, her mother shielded her eyes from the rare mid-summer sun and peered up at her.

"The heat this year is unbearable!" her mother complained. "But it's great for the San Marzanos. Best crop I've ever seen. Show Mommy, Tadpole!"

The basket Robert came running with nearly overflowed with brilliant red tomatoes. "William's gonna love these!"

"Ooh, look at those beauties! I bet he's going to make us the best batch of tomato sauce you've ever tasted."

"Tonight?"

Julia couldn't help but grin. She found it so heartwarming and poignant that Robert loved tomatoes every bit as much as his father did. "Maybe not tonight, but very soon. Why don't you carry those into the kitchen?"

Julia waited until he disappeared into the house before turning back to her mother. "Hey, have you heard from Alison?"

"Mm-hmm."

"Today?"

Her mother turned from the Roman cages and peered at Julia from beneath the brim of her sunhat. "Yes, today. Why?"

"Huh. She didn't answer my text. Is she coming to dinner?"

Slowly and methodically, her mother snapped a single tomato from the vine, all the while studying Julia with narrowed eyes. "Yes, she's coming tonight. Is there a problem?"

"No, no problem," Julia said with forced cheeriness. "Just making sure."

It would be the first time William saw Alison since the wedding. Julia had no idea how Alison might react to William in the aftermath of those events. Julia and William had talked about it already, and he was prepared for anything.

But when Alison showed up earlier than usual, before William had even arrived, the first thing she did was drag Julia into the den.

"There's something I need to tell you," Alison began after shutting the door to the in-law unit. "I've been talking all week with Mike."

"Okay," Julia said slowly. "How is he?"

"He's clean and sober, for the moment. That's not why William hasn't seen Mike over the past few months."

"What do you mean?"

Alison gestured to the sofa. "Maybe you should sit down."

Startled, Julia nevertheless took Alison's advice, and Alison sat beside her.

"There's a secret that Mike has been keeping for a long time now," Alison began. "He gave me permission to tell you because William is going to need a shoulder to lean on after he hears it."

"Okay," Julia said hesitantly. She wondered if this was just more of Alison's histrionics that she occasionally indulged in. "Hears what?"

"Mike is HIV-positive."

Julia's stomach plummeted to her toes, and she put her hand to her mouth. So, definitely not histrionics. "Oh my God."

"I'm sorry to be so abrupt, but I wanted to tell you before William gets here, so you'd have time to process it first."

"Why?" Julia dropped her hand from her lips. "Wait – Mike's not here, is he?"

"No," Alison denied, as if offended Julia would even consider such a thing. As if Alison hadn't been completely oblivious to other people's feelings only last Saturday, when she and Mike showed up unannounced to the wedding.

"Then why couldn't this wait for another day? Why did you have to spring this on me right here, right now?"

"Because Mike only just this afternoon gave me permission to tell you, and I'm afraid he'll get cold feet again."

Julia frowned. "It sounds like he didn't really want to share that information. Have you been pressuring him?"

"No, Julie, I swear that's not what this is. He wants to tell William. He's wanted to all along. Mike looks up to William. He sees how successful William has been at maintaining his sobriety, and he really wants his own sobriety to stick this time. He was trying to reach out to William the night of the wedding, but William's reaction was so... angry."

Julia had to admit, William's harsh response to his brother's overtures had shocked and intimidated even *her*. And she didn't even have any real stake in the outcome.

But did Alison?

"Alison... you and he... you're not still..." She waved her hand in the air, gesturing vaguely between Alison and a hypothetical Mike.

Alison shrugged. "Well, if nothing else, there's very little danger in letting him eat me out."

Julia cringed. "Oh God, Alison! TMI."

"What? You asked! I mean, if nothing else, he's literally the only guy I've ever known who can keep up with me and my appetites. With the medications, his viral load is undetectable now; and I was already taking PrEP, anyway." She fixed Julia with a sharp look. "You know that's a thing now, right?"

"What?"

"The medications. HIV isn't a death sentence anymore; and with an undetectable viral load, he can't transmit the virus."

"Of course I know that," Julia snapped.

Alison held up her hands. "Okay!"

To Julia's horror, tears stung her eyes and nose. She gulped them back almost furiously. "Rob and Tim dying was the defining moment of my childhood. You don't think I've kept on top of every single treatment development since then?"

Alison frowned. "Well, how was I supposed to know?"

Julia sat in stunned silence a moment, and then her shoulders sagged. "I'm sorry. I don't know why I'm being so defensive."

Alison's brow unfurrowed, and she pulled Julia into one of her signature bear hugs. "Hey. It was a huge trauma for both of us. I get it."

After a moment, Julia disentangled herself and swiped at the lone tear that had escaped. "So you're doing all that, for Mike? Taking PrEP, I mean?"

Alison waved her hand dismissively. "Not *just* for him. You know me, Julie – I'm Princess Polyamory. But I've always cared a lot about Mike."

At a loss for words, Julia said simply, "Wow."

Alison scoffed at Julia's reaction. "I mean yeah, he's a mess personally. But he'll also give you the shirt off his back. You can call him at four in the morning when no one else is there for you, and I speak from personal experience here. He's always smiling, even when he's hurting. Not a cruel bone in his body. As much of an animal as he is, he's never once made me feel cheap or disrespected me. In fact, he's one of the few guys who's ever made me feel good about myself."

"And you... *care* care about him?"

Alison squirmed, and it floored Julia. She had never seen her sister like this when talking about a man. "I mean..."

"Alison. This is me you're talking to. Your loving and beloved sister."

Alison's eyes slid back to Julia's. "Yes. I *care* care about him. Does that surprise you?"

It was Julia's turn to fumble for words.

Again, Alison laughed. "Okay, I know he's not the most intellectual guy, but that's not because he's stupid. You know he's actually pretty fucking smart, right?"

Julia couldn't help coughing out a laugh. "No, I did not know that."

"Well, he *is*."

To Julia's dismay, Alison seemed a little offended. "Okay, I admit I don't know Mike very well. So tell me."

"Well, for one thing, I'm ninety-nine percent sure he has undiagnosed ADHD."

Julia frowned, considering. "Will told me it's bipolar disorder."

"Yeah, but I think they've been treating him for the wrong thing all these years. For one thing, he told me the only time he ever feels like a normal person is when he uses meth. Meth is a stimulant, and I know from personal experience that many people with ADHD self-medicate with stimulants. Also, Mike never really gets depressed, like people with bipolar disorder do. He's one of the happiest people I know. The only time he gets depressed is when he fucks up some relationship, like with William. Or me."

Julia studied her sister, unblinking. "So he returns your feelings?"

"Is that really so hard to believe?"

"No, of course not! I just didn't know Mike was capable of feeling that way about anyone."

Alison lobbed her most withering stink-eye at Julia. "Just because we're extremely polyamorous doesn't mean we're incapable of love."

"Love," Julia echoed. "Alison! Do you mean to tell me that you and Mike Quinn are in *love*?"

Alison grimaced. "Neither of us would use that terminology, exactly."

Julia caught her jaw dropping and snapped it shut, but she wasn't fast enough.

"What, Julia? He's creative. He's funny. He's fun. He's sexy as fuck."

"That's a matter of opinion."

"Fine; *I* think he's sexy as fuck." A sly grin twisted her mouth. "And holy mother of God, the things he can do with those piercings..."

"Nope." Julia clapped her hands over her ears. "Nope, nope, nope."

Alison cackled, and Julia couldn't help grinning, herself. She knew that Alison enjoyed shocking her.

"But yes, Julia," continued Alison, "he really is quite smart. He can fix anything mechanical you put in front of him. He can imagine something incredibly detailed and draw it flawlessly the first time. He can play any song on virtually any instrument after hearing it only once. He has perfect pitch. And the lyrics he comes up with, even though he reads at a second grade level... but that's not his fault. With undiagnosed ADHD, and as hyper as he is, it's no wonder he never did well in school."

"Has he ever been tested for ADHD?"

"Not yet, but I'm going to make him, so he can get on the right meds, finally. He did that for me once, you know?"

"Did what?"

"Oh come on, Julie; you know this! I went through a pretty hard-core meth phase."

"Al," Julia gasped. "I swear to God, I did not know that. I mean, I knew you tried it once or twice..."

Alison scoffed. "Once or twice? Julie, when you and I first met the Brothers Quinn, I was on the fast track to becoming a full-blown tweaker. Mike was the clean and sober one back then. He brought me with him to his Narcotics Anonymous meetings. And without him, my life would have gone a very different direction."

Flabbergasted, Julia tried to think back to that time in their lives. She was Alison's sister and, in many ways, her best friend. But even she had been totally clueless. "I didn't know it got that bad."

"It did. I still think he saved my life. He came and got me one time when I thought I was OD'ing at a rave and I didn't trust anyone I was with. He stayed with me the whole night and the next day to make sure I was okay. Then he convinced me to get into treatment." Her face fell. "It's why I was so heartbroken when I realized he had started using again, back in 2006. We almost lost him back then."

"I know." Julia thought back to that long night in the ICU waiting room, holding William's hand. "But you hadn't been in touch for a long time before that."

Alison shrugged. "Things got complicated. We had an understanding that we weren't exclusive; but then he started acting jealous. I never had any aversion to a romantic relationship with him; I just never wanted to be monogamous."

"And what about now?"

"Honestly?" After a moment's consideration, Alison admitted, "I don't know. I mean sadly, at my age and with my weight gain, I get fewer offers, anyway. Men are assholes. But Mike actually seems to dig my new curves, and when I'm with him I don't feel like I'm missing out. He really is a fucking god in bed."

Julia stuck her fingers in her ears and gave a little ululation. But once Alison's laughter died down, she nudged Julia's arm. "What about you? You seem to be walking around with a certain glow these days. Speaking of the Brothers Quinn."

Julia couldn't stop either the flush or the stupid grin from spreading across her face.

"There must be something in the water at the Quinn house," Alison observed. "They need to bottle it and make their first million."

"Alison, there aren't enough superlatives in the English language. I'd say it's the best sex of my life, but of course I only have Kevin to compare it to, so that's not saying much."

Alison choked on a guffaw. "Ouch!"

"So instead, I shall boldly assert that it's the best sex ever had in the history of womankind."

"That *is* a bold assertion, especially considering the woman you're making it to."

"I'm serious, Al. These orgasms have the capacity to punch a hole in the space-time continuum and create wormholes to another dimension. And they come so easily, pun fully intended."

"Jesus, okay! I get the idea already."

"Oh come on, don't tell me *that's* your limit."

"No; you're just making me jealous. Be careful or I might steal him from you."

"Nah; I doubt he's freaky enough for your taste. You'd better stick with his brother."

"Well, at least help a girl out – what, exactly, is he doing to put that perma-grin on your face?"

Julia couldn't help snickering a bit. "It helps that he looks like Will. Oh, and also that he sounds like Will, and smells like Will, and just generally *is* Will. Basically, I'm Willsexual."

"Hmm. Sounds a little vanilla for my taste. I'll take your advice and stick with the cayenne-spiced brother."

Julia laughed with her, but after a minute, Alison's smile straightened again.

"Julie, remember when I told you people wear masks like armor?

That sometimes it's easier to just go along and act like the idiot everyone thinks you are?"

"Are you saying that's what Mike does?"

"I *know* that's what he does. Or at least, he used to. But I think he really means it this time when he says he's done with the mask."

Julia remembered how different Mike seemed at the wedding – not just in terms of his appearance, but also his entire demeanor. Gone was the bro-ish posturing and the cretinous jackhammer-laugh of yore.

"I just really don't want to violate Mike's boundaries, Al. Are you really sure he wants me to tell William?"

"Yes. His hesitation wasn't about telling William; it was about William's reaction after the wedding. I think it's important for Mike to have someone besides just his sponsor to turn to. Someone he cares about who's cheering him on. And Mike loves William; he really does."

Julia sighed. "Listen, I won't betray William's confidence by speaking for him. And I can't make any promises about the outcome. But I will talk to him."

"I understand. Thank you."

"Just don't mention anything about Mike, yourself. Not tonight. Not if you want the best possible outcome."

Alison mimed zipping and locking her lips, then tossing the key.

"And don't act all angry or weird around him, either."

Alison grinned. "Should I sit in the corner all night?"

Julia grinned back. "It couldn't hurt."

"Oh, shut up."

Laughing, Julia grabbed her by the arm. "Come on. Let's guzzle some of that Cinsaut before my sexy teetotaler gets here."

WHEN WILLIAM ARRIVED AN HOUR LATER, his eyes landed on Alison with a wary edge. But his shoulders relaxed when she smiled and greeted him, if not warmly, then at least cordially. Her easy demeanor continued to assuage his discomfort through the rest of the evening, until she bowed out a little earlier than usual.

"I have to get home to Tallulah Bankhead," she explained, rising from the patio table.

William lifted an eyebrow. "Tallulah Bankhead?"

"Yeah; she's diabetic and needs her insulin. For that matter, I'm sure Cyd isn't happy with me, either."

"Cyd?"

"She poops in my fuzzy slippers if I stay out too late."

While Paige and Robert literally collapsed on the ground in a fit of giggles, Julia leaned over and whispered in William's ear. "Tallulah Bankhead and Cyd Charisse. They're her cats."

"Of course they are," he muttered, and while Alison took leave in her usual cloud of noise, Julia giggled at the bemused expression on William's face.

But once Alison departed, dread of the task her sister had charged her with took up too much real estate in her brain. By the time they finished putting Robert to bed, the gravity of her dread had swelled to black hole proportions.

"Are you okay?" William whispered after they closed Robert's door and returned to the den. "You seem a bit preoccupied."

Julia gave a low, humorless laugh. "I've been charged with delivering a message."

William's brows shot up his forehead. "A message?"

Julia scratched the side of her nose. "Sorry; I, uh..." Suddenly sweaty, she adjusted the scarf around her neck. "Would you like to sit down? This might take a minute."

William's eyes scanned her face with obvious worry. *Shit.* She was already screwing this up.

"I'm sorry," she said again, forcing a smile until she realized that if it felt fake to herself, it undoubtedly looked fake to him. "Sorry."

"Julie." He gently clasped her elbow. "Stop apologizing and relax. It's just me."

"Yeah, exactly," she said drily. "It's you."

"Whatever you have to say, I'm right here. Always."

"But I don't like to be the bearer of bad news. Especially to you."

"Bad news?" His alarm increased by the minute. "Julie, what's wrong?"

She smacked her clammy forehead. "God, I'm a disaster." Yanking her scarf off completely, she gestured with it to the sofa. "Let's sit."

He obeyed, never once removing his worried stare from her face. They sat side-by-side, angled toward each other, and she took his hands in hers.

"Um... it's about Mike."

Something in his gaze hardened a bit, but beneath the armor, she detected a hint of something else. Something like fear.

No, not fear – pain. Or maybe both.

"Alison told me she's been talking with Mike all week," she continued, "and, um... she seems to think he really is clean and sober. Apparently he's in a sober living environment, for now."

William glowered at a corner of the room and echoed, "For now."

"She seems to think he's really committed to sobriety this time."

"Yeah, he's said that before." His tone grew sharper by the minute.

"I know, Will," she said, gently squeezing his hands, "but this time, he's had a bit of an extra wake up call."

He fixed her with a sharp, questioning stare, and there was nothing left to do but recount what Alison had told her.

By the time she got it all out, he was resting his head in his hands, with his elbows on his thighs. She rubbed his back in slow circles and waited for him to finish processing.

Finally, William lifted his head and fixed his eyes on hers. A watery sheen turned them an almost unnatural electric blue.

Julia scooted closer and enfolded him in a hug. "Sweetheart, I'm so sorry."

After she had comforted him in silence a few minutes, William pulled back and clasped Julia's shoulders. "I'm willing to hear Mike out, but I need to talk to my AA sponsor first."

"That sounds smart."

"And I won't make any promises about what I can or can't do for Mike. I can't help anyone if I don't keep myself healthy and sane first."

"I get that, too. Whatever your decision, I support you." She placed her palms on his cheeks. "And Will? You told me this once, and now it's my turn to remind you: you'll never have to be alone in this again."

He tipped his head. "In what?"

Julia gestured all around herself. "*This.* Life. Challenges. Hardship. I'll be right there with you through all of those."

Smiling, he leaned forward to plant a soft kiss on her lips before murmuring, "And in the joys, too, I hope."

She beamed. "That goes without saying."

In her dedicated parking spot behind Castro Aquarium Service, Julia sat in her work van and cried.

It had been a horrible day at work – maybe the worst of her life – so when she finally got it out of her system, she was tempted to call William and kvetch. She glanced at the time on her phone screen: almost four o'clock. In only an hour and a half, she and her parents were meeting William and his mother for dinner at Ann's new condo. They were all long overdue for a visit, and Alison had volunteered to take Paige and Robert to dinner so it would just be the grown-ups.

Julia exchanged her work van for her Subaru and raced home as quickly as traffic allowed. After a speedy shower, she allowed her hair to air dry and threw on a casual maxi dress and scarf, just in time for Alison to ring the doorbell.

While Paige ran out to Alison's car and Robert ran circles around his mother and aunt, Alison's worried gaze lingered on Julia. "Are you okay?" she whispered.

Julia tried, and failed, to force a brave smile. Her shoulders sagged instead. "Not really. I'll call you later."

Alison's eyes widened in alarm. "Is it because of William? Because of what I asked you to tell him?"

"No!" Julia stroked Alison's arm and managed a real, if faint, smile. "It has nothing to do with that, I promise. I'll tell you about that later, too."

Alison puffed out a breath. "Thank God."

Julia forced a smile, and then Alison caught Robert around the waist as he ran by, sweeping him over her shoulder like a fifty-pound sack of flour. "All right, you beast! You're more like an overstimulated chihuahua than a tadpole."

Dangling upside-down over Alison's shoulder, Robert squealed with delight as she stomped out the front door. Julia laughed heartily, thanking her lucky stars for her free-spirited sister.

Once Alison and the kids departed, Julia shuttled her parents to Treemont. After dropping them off at the entrance and finding a parking spot, Julia joined them in the foyer, where they appraised their surroundings.

While working for an estate lawyer in San Jose, Julia had visited her fair share of retirement communities and nursing homes. All too often, their twee Victorian or stately Georgian aesthetics were meant to evoke a distant, reassuring past. But Treemont had a more mid-century vibe. The building itself dated to the fifties, with its clean lines and concrete planes; but a central atrium allowed natural light to pour in. Green plants, thoughtfully-spaced wooden accents, and tasteful pops of color did the rest. There was nothing fancy or hip about the place, but it didn't look worn, dated, or cold.

Julia bit her tongue – she didn't want to give her parents the impression she was trying to influence them one way or the other.

"Ready?" Julia gestured to the elevator. "Will said Ann's condo is on the fourth floor."

The elevator dumped them out into a carpeted hallway. Grasscloth in a muted seagrass-green papered the walls, and modern art between each front door provided more pops of color. They followed William's directions to a door numbered twenty-three, and knocked.

"Come in, come in!" Ann greeted them with her warmest smile, swinging the door open wide and waving them in. After inviting them to hang their sweaters in the hall closet, she beckoned them further inside. "Will's just finishing up dinner. Let me show you around."

Once again, Julia's parents craned their necks around, absorbing their surroundings as Ann led them into the living room. A countertop separated the living room from the kitchen, where William turned from the stove to wave hello. "Sorry, just wrapping up here; give me one minute."

Julia winked, and he winked back before turning back to the stove. But if her parents heard him, they didn't show it, because Ann's guided tour had them enthralled. The space was small but didn't feel cramped, with its vaulted ceilings and skylights. Sliding glass doors led out to a balcony overlooking the restaurants and shops of the Inner Sunset. There were no steps in the condo to trip over. The bathroom was wide enough to accommodate walkers and wheelchairs. It had a walk-in shower with grab bars and a seat. In spite of all this, it didn't feel like an "old folks' home." Everything in the condo was freshly updated with clean, transitional-style finishes.

While her parents settled on the sofa, catty-corner to Ann's recliner, Julia drifted to William in the kitchen. He was plating dinner, but when she joined him at his side, he smiled and bent to plant a quick peck on her lips.

"What did you make?" she asked.

"Pasta alla norma."

"Can I help?"

"You already are." He offered a quick wink before whisking the plates to Ann's small dining table. Julia delivered the salad, and together they poured wine for their parents.

"You know you don't have to abstain on my account," he said quietly when he saw her pouring a glass of mineral water for herself.

"It's on my own account," she reassured him with a tired smile. At the sight of it, he froze, wine bottle in hand.

"Are you okay?"

"I had a rough day at work," Julia sighed. "Would you mind if I told you about it later?"

His eyes made a concerned circuit of her face, but he nodded. Without another word, they carried the beverage glasses to the table, and William summoned everyone to dinner.

"Just like your nonna used to make," Ann praised William, her smile poignant as she pointed to the pasta alla norma with her fork. He offered a complaisant smile in return, and then Julia's mother lifted her wine glass.

"To grandmothers."

They echoed her toast, and each took a sip before returning to the subject of Ann's new home. Ann described how the residents regularly got together for barbecues in the courtyard, workouts in the community gym, and parties in the community center. In addition, they enjoyed regular outings to the theater, museums, the local senior center, and more. She shared all the juicy gossip she had gleaned so far on each of her neighbors.

While they talked, Julia found her mind wandering back to the day's events. She didn't realize her expression had soured until she caught William watching her with a worried frown. She straightened, plastering on a feeble smile, but from the deepening furrows in his brow, he wasn't buying it.

After dinner, Julia cleared the table and washed dishes, while Ann took Julia's mother to meet a neighbor. William and Julia's father watched a baseball game on TV, sharing silent space in the living room. When Julia finished the dishes, she ventured out onto the balcony to get some fresh air, take in the view – and give William an opportunity to join her. He took the hint within a minute, sliding the balcony door shut behind himself.

"Your dad is happily engrossed in the Giants game," he assured her in a low voice as he stopped just behind her shoulder and slid an arm around her waist.

She sighed. "Sorry about my glum mood tonight."

They never actually looked at each other; just stared out over the neighboring rooftops at the corner grocery stores, shops, and Asian restaurants of Irving Street. He said, "Do you want to talk about it?"

To Julia's dismay, tears pricked again at her eyes. She thought she had gotten them all out of her system in the van. "I got sexually harassed at work."

His wide eyes snapped to hers. "What?!"

She shushed him, peering through the sliding glass door to make sure her father had not heard.

William gently clasped her shoulders and turned her to face him. "What happened?"

The tears spilled over. "You know how Mondays are my aquarium servicing days, right?"

"Yeah?"

"Well, my last client of the day is an insurance office, and it's one of the more lucrative of my remaining contracts – nowhere on par with Lars and Meg's account, but a distant second. The lead agent is nice enough. Kind of dull; but at least she stays out of my way. But she has this forty-something son who's waiting to take over the agency when she retires. And every week, he kind of hovers over me–"

"What do you mean, hovers over you?"

Julia could tell he was doing his best to stay calm, but his tone carried a definite edge. "Hanging around, asking questions about everything I'm doing and how everything works, and just generally being annoying. It's why I save their account for the last of the day: it always takes the longest to finish, with Chad's constant interruptions."

William gave a single, rueful laugh. *"Chad?"*

"Right? And he's a total Chad, too. Pastel shirts and chinos, spiky blond hair... The thing is, I'm used to this crap from men, like they don't really believe I can do the job. Usually, they chill out after they see how capable I am, despite my two X chromosomes. But Chad... he's just been relentless. I couldn't tell if he was genuinely interested in saltwater aquariums, or if he just doubted my competence."

"What did he do to you?"

Sighing, Julia studied the people and cars on the street below. "He wasn't in the office when I arrived, but he came in when I was about to siphon the old water from the tank. And he was wearing a golf visor, no less – go figure. Anyway, he comes over and starts asking what I'm doing, like usual. He's never seen me do it." Peering up at William in a wary, sidelong way, Julia asked, "Do you know how that works? The siphoning?"

William shook his head.

She looked out at the street again, without really seeing anything. "It's just a basic gravity siphon. Nowadays there's all kinds of fancy equipment you can use, but I still do it the old-fashioned way. You have this tubing, and you stick one end into the dirty water. The other end of the tube sticks out of the aquarium, over the top edge. You put your siphon bucket on any surface that's lower than the aquarium's water level. You get the water flowing through the tube, and gravity does the rest."

"Okay... so what does this have to do with *Chad* sexually harassing you?" he asked, heaping extra contempt on the *Chad*.

"He kept asking me how you start the water flowing through the tube. He acted like he didn't know, but I'd bet my life savings he knew *exactly* how."

With a bewildered frown, William asked, "Okay... how *do* you start the water flowing through the tube?"

Again, Julia pinned William with a wary look. "You suck on it."

As understanding slowly unfolded, William's expression morphed from confusion, to horror, to outrage.

"Exactly," Julia said drily. "I did everything I possibly could to avoid using the word 'suck.' Like for example, I said, 'You use your mouth.' But he just kept saying 'I don't understand,' or 'How do you use your mouth?' And then he said something like, 'But isn't that dirty?' And like an idiot, I said, 'Not if you know what you're doing.' And then he said..." Her heart rate picked up, remembering, and her voice grew strained. "He said, 'Well, I can certainly tell you know what you're doing, Julia.'"

"Piece of shit," William snarled.

Wincing, Julia admitted, "That's not all, though. He said something like, 'I'm still having a hard time visualizing how that works. Can you demonstrate?'"

"Fuck," William spat out. "What did you do?"

"Nothing. I froze up." Julia was shaking now, her vision blurring with tears. "So I demonstrated, because I didn't know what else to do or say. And then he said, 'So what you're telling me is, you *suck* on it, Julia.'"

"I'm going to kill him." Julia knew he didn't mean it literally, but he was positively vibrating with righteous anger. "Please tell me you dumped his account and walked out of there."

"It takes a lot of time to pack and re-load all the stuff I bring with me," Julia said, her voice quavering. "It's not like I can just abandon all my expensive equipment right there in the lobby with some jerk-off whose fragile ego I just bruised. Besides, they're currently my most lucrative account. If I lose them, on top of Lars and Meg, I may as well fold."

"Julie, there's got to be a way."

Julia had to close her eyes and pace her breathing so she wouldn't say anything she would later regret.

"See, this is what men don't understand," she began, her voice steady, if strained. "Almost every woman deals with crap like this at work; and then we have to figure out how to walk that razor-thin line between maintaining professional credibility, versus blowing up our careers because we refused to give some guy a blow job. And not only that, we have to navigate that line with only a moment's notice. Because nobody sent me a daily agenda that said, 'Nine A.M.: Dunphy's aquarium. Twelve noon: lunch. Two P.M.: get sexually harassed.' I didn't have all morning to plan how I was going to respond; I had to figure it out on the fly. Men don't have to deal with this crap anywhere near as often, and that's one more reason it's so much harder for women to compete professionally."

The whole time she was talking, William's expression underwent a series of transformations: from angry, to chastened, to clarity, before finally settling on sadness. He reached for her and folded her against his chest, hugging her tightly. Rubbing circles over her back and kissing the top of her head.

"I'm so sorry, sweetheart," he murmured against her hair. "I'm sorry you've had to deal with this."

"Me too," she said, her voice muffled against his shirt. "I have no clue what to do."

He continued comforting her for another minute. Then, he pulled back to look at her. "You said earlier that if you dump Chad's account, you might as well fold. But you still have the shop."

"The servicing side of my business is what keeps the brick-and-mortar side up and running."

He frowned. "I don't understand."

She swiped at yet another tear sliding down her cheek. "The shop's rent is biggest component of my overhead. And then inventory alone is twenty-five thousand."

"A year?"

She barked out a rueful laugh. "A *month*." When his mouth dropped open in shock, she added, "The aquarium servicing side is more affordable – you can start with just a few thousand dollars of equipment. After that, it's just a van, insurance, cell phone, and gas."

"So why not shift to a service-only model?"

"And close Rob and Tim's shop?" Julia was growing impatient with her apparently endless well of tears. "Mitch and José would be so heartbroken."

He tipped his head. "Mitch and José?"

She waved her hand. "Regulars. They knew my uncles."

A hint of amusement twitched at his lips. "So you want to keep the shop open, for Mitch and José."

The corners of her mouth pulled down, and she refused to answer. He gathered her into another soothing hug. "Okay. Can you hire an employee or two to staff the shop while you do the servicing side?"

"Yeah, but that would cost even more money."

"But you would also bring in more money if you're servicing aquariums five days a week, instead of only Mondays."

"It's not just the wage I would be paying, though. For every employee I hire, there are a lot of other incidental business expenses. Accounting, insurance, tax..."

"Okay, what does that amount to?"

"Roughly, for each employee? Double the hourly wage, plus five dollars. And that's per hour."

"Okay, but have you ever really sat down and crunched those numbers to see what you would take home at the end of the month?"

Julia frowned. "Not really."

Pulling back to look at her, he ran his hands up and down her arms. "I can help with that, if you want."

"It's not just the money, though. If I hire an employee, I have to worry about what they're doing while I'm out and about. Or vice versa, if I staff the shop and they do the servicing stuff. But since the servicing side is my bread-and-butter, I would never trust that to anyone else."

Once again, a hint of a smile played at his lips. Then he reached into the pocket of his jeans and retrieved something wrapped in a handkerchief. She watched, frowning, as he unfolded it, then gasped when he opened his palm to reveal her uncle's watermelon tourmaline.

When she looked up again, her mouth agape, William's hint of a smile bloomed into a full-blown one. "Remember what you said when you gave me this? Watermelon tourmaline unblocks the barriers to your heart and brings balance. You said your uncle wanted you to open your mind and heart to the unexpected. To make peace with the forces that were beyond your control. You gave me this because I was afraid of screwing up our fresh start. You said, *for now*, it had done its magic for you. Well, *for now*, it's done its magic for me." He turned her hand palm-up. Placed the watermelon tourmaline into her open palm, and closed her fingers around it. "I've carried this everywhere, but I'm not afraid anymore. So now, I'm returning it."

Clenching the stone, her tears spilling over, Julia wrapped her arms around his waist and rested her cheek against the soft flannel shirt she had sewn him. He rubbed gentle circles on her back and kissed the top of her head, his warm lips lingering.

"Oh my God, son; don't tell me you're already making her cry!"

Ann's muffled voice jolted them apart, but they laughed when they found their mothers grinning from the other side of the sliding glass door.

"It's a good cry, I promise," Julia assured them, sliding the balcony door open and wiping the tears from her cheeks.

"That's good," her mother remarked. "We got back from our walk to find you blubbering and your father completely oblivious. So much for chivalry."

Julia's father looked up from the baseball game. "Did you say something?"

With a tiny wink at Julia's mother, William lied through his teeth. "I was just telling Julia, what this condo complex needs is an aquarium in the community room. For that matter, I think there's a pretty good market for aquariums in retirement communities, senior centers, and memory-care units."

"You know, you're right," Julia's mother seconded; and she and Ann retreated to the sofa to discuss the possibilities.

A smile warmed Julia's face and cheeks, and he returned it in that sexy way that crinkled the skin at the corner of his eyes. "As for me," William continued in a low voice, "I've always wanted to learn more about saltwater aquariums. Next Monday, can I shadow you while you take care of the one at Chad's office?"

Laughing, she lightly swatted his arm. "Why, so you can piss around the corners like you did with Kevin on Father's Day?"

"Of course not." He grinned. "I'm going to piss on the fuckwad's golf visor."

Wednesday was July Fourth, and Julia closed the shop for the day. William planned to take Julia and the kids on his boat to watch the fireworks from the bay. And even though they would have to share the night-time cruise with William's other customers, the anticipation radiating off the kids that morning was palpable.

Julia cooked a big breakfast, and while the kids did the dishes, she rewarded herself at her sewing machine with a few more touches to her Halloween costume. It was coming along nicely, but it would still take every bit of the next four months to finish.

Her phone buzzed, and she retrieved it from her pocket. William was FaceTiming her.

"Hey, sweetie." She moved to the couch and fiddled self-consciously with her hair. He sat outside on his patio in a pair of sunglasses, which he tilted to the top of his head.

His eyes widened a bit, as they always did when he FaceTimed her. As if they were trying to soak up every last ray of light beaming her image from his phone screen. "Hi, beautiful."

Julia couldn't help chuckling a bit. She wore no makeup, her greasy hair was tangled in a messy bun, and dark circles ringed her eyes, no thanks to sleepless nights spent fretting over Chad the Fuckwad. She wore a boring white terrycloth jumper and no bra – super comfy for lounging around the house, but hardly fit to be seen in public.

"You are severely biased, but I'll take it." Then she saw him shift anxiously in his seat, and noticed he wasn't smiling anymore. "Is everything okay?"

"Yeah," he confirmed quickly. "Nothing's wrong; just … awkward."

"What's awkward?"

"Um…" He scratched his nose. Looked off to the side. "So I heard from Marisa early this morning."

Her stomach lurched, but she swallowed hard and composed herself. "Oh."

"Your dad did, too. The producers of her new show want her to do a quick run-through of Dunphy's over FaceTime. They just want to get a peek at the layout so they can see what they'd be working with, if they select it. Or so they can reject it outright, if it's obviously not suitable. And since Marisa's own restaurant is closed for the holiday, she thought this afternoon would be perfect."

"Okay…" Then, with looming dread, it dawned on her. "But how does this pertain to you?"

"Well… at the same time, she wondered if you might be open to meeting her this afternoon. I'd be there, too, of course, in the background. For moral support."

Julia laughed. "Moral support?"

Even over FaceTime, Julia could see the tops of his ears redden. "I mean… if you want," he hedged. "I'd give you space to talk, of course."

Honestly, Julia was relieved. She thought he was about to say he was going back to work at Dunphy's – with Marisa.

Julia had planned all along to meet William at Dunphy's at four, then explore the Embarcadero with him and the kids until it was time to board *The Albatross*. So, they just stuck to that timeline. Julia parked in the employee lot and steered the kids through the back door.

The kitchen was eerily quiet, and it smelled different. No wonder, since nobody had cooked there for almost two months. They wound their way around the stations and through the swinging door, dumping them into the dining room. For a split second, Julia pulled up short at the sight that greeted her: William and her father, seated at the same four-top; while at the hostess' station, a busty woman with legs for days and a sleek, coffee-brown ponytail snapped photos of Julia's aquarium on her cell phone.

And just like that, Julia snapped back to the ladies' room at MacGowans, circa 2006: *So you're the flavor of the month.*

Do you think you're the only woman he's written a song for?

Just don't let him get you pregnant.

Oops. A wry grin stole across Julia's face, instantly squelching her looming panic. *Too late for that last part.*

Her smile came just as both her father and William spotted her. They rose to greet her, and Marisa turned from the aquarium.

With a smile that was guarded but not hostile, Marisa came forward, stowing her phone in the back pocket of her skinny jeans. Extra-long skinny jeans, to sheath those extra-long legs. People often complimented Julia on her legs, but they had nothing on the Barbie-esque proportions of Marisa's. The woman was at least six feet tall.

She marched right up to Julia and stuck out her hand. "Marisa Zunino."

Julia could already tell – Marisa was a dynamo. Keenly aware of the two men watching, Julia offered her most disarming smile and shook Marisa's hand. "Julia Beale. Nice to meet you, Marisa."

Marisa glanced back at the aquarium. "I was just admiring your work. When I used to be here, whoever they had taking care of it never made it look this good. And I hear it's environmentally-friendly, too."

A bit flustered, Julia glanced reflexively at William. "Thank you. Yes, environmental stewardship is kind of my niche."

"I can't wait to learn more about it." Marisa was already moving on to greet Paige and Robert. Her eyes lingered, making a circuit of Robert's face, before she grinned at William with a knowing twinkle in her dark doe-eyes. William flushed, clearly uncomfortable, and his eyes flitted to some random spot across the room.

"Kids," Julia said, "maybe you'd like to walk down to the Ferris wheel with your grandpa? Maybe pop into the Musée Mécanique for a while?"

This was their pre-arranged signal: even Robert knew that Julia and William were here for a "boring grownup meeting." And thankfully, despite her vocal resistance at home to "boring kid stuff," Paige followed them out the front door and onto the pier with a minimum of grumbling.

When they were gone, William cleared his throat. "I'll, um... I'll just be in there," he muttered, jerking his thumb toward the kitchen door before stiffly retreating.

Julia watched him go until the door swung closed and she could no longer avoid the inevitable. Shifting her eyes to Marisa, Julia caught her former arch-nemesis already studying her with overt amusement. To Julia's own surprise, they simultaneously burst into laughter.

"Well, this isn't awkward at all," Marisa commented after a minute.

Julia clutched her sides. "Poor Will. I'm sure he can hear us laughing out here."

After another spurt of laughter, Marisa gestured to the nearest table. "Have a seat," she invited, as if she already owned the place.

As Julia took her seat across the table, her heart caught in her throat. She was now face-to-face with the woman who had haunted her nightmares. The woman whose words at MacGowan's sparked a chain reaction, culminating in Julia and William's second breakup in 2006. And that, in turn, was the worst mistake of Julia's life – a scene she replayed every second of in her mind, ad nauseum, for the past six years.

"I don't know what Will has told you about me." Marisa's voice snatched Julia from her brooding. "But it's probably all true."

Once again, Julia barked out a laugh. She had prepared for Marisa to be a lot of things, but funny wasn't one of them.

"Here's something I never told him, though," Marisa continued. "After we broke up, I was diagnosed with bipolar disorder and Border-line Personality Disorder."

"Oh," said Julia, too stunned by Marisa's frank admission to respond.

"Yeah, I know – a double-dose of Crazy Bitch."

Marisa flashed a sporting grin; but Julia knew this couldn't be easy for her – confessing something so deeply personal to her former rival.

"I've struggled with anxiety and depression," Julia admitted. "I've seen how people weaponize the word 'crazy,' especially against women.

And then we don't seek out the help we need because we don't want to be labeled 'crazy.'"

Marisa's mask of cheekiness dropped briefly, baring a hint of vulnerability as she studied Julia. It reminded Julia of Alison.

Finally, Marisa said, "Of course, Will had his own share of things he still needed to deal with." Graciously, she didn't add, *like still being in love with you.* "The saying 'opposites attract' did not apply to Will and me, but I still hadn't accepted that when I accosted you." Pinning her enormous brown eyes on Julia, she added, "I'm sorry for the things I said that day. I hope you'll accept my apology and not feel any awkwardness about working around me, if the producers pick Dunphy's."

Stunned, Julia blinked a time or two before remembering her voice. "Thank you," she managed. "Of course I accept your apology. You'll get no awkwardness from me, either."

Marisa blew out a breath and grinned again. "Good. Because if they *do* pick Dunphy's, your aquarium is the only thing that's staying."

Julia couldn't help laughing again. "Honestly, I don't blame you."

Marisa flicked a critical eye around the dining room. "Seriously – rattan furniture and mauve wallpaper? Hideous, even when it *wasn't* fraying and peeling."

"Is there anything tackier than brass-and-smoked-glass light fixtures, though?"

"Honorable mention to postmodern Art Deco prints of generic coastal scenes."

They cackled until Julia's face burned and Marisa was nearly wheezing. "Well, this went better than expected," Marisa admitted. Nodding toward the kitchen, she added, "You should probably go check on Will before he pulls his fingers out of their sockets. Does he still do that?" She tugged on her fingers and joints by way of explanation.

"Yeah," Julia admitted, still laughing, as she pushed through the swinging door to the kitchen. She found William seated in the office, not tugging on his knuckles, but bouncing his knee up and down. He flinched when she entered, his eyes scrutinizing hers.

"Relax," Julia chuckled. "It went great. I told you it would."

A huge surge of breath exited his lungs, and he sagged in the chair. "You never know."

Julia tipped her head sideways. "She told me herself how things used to be, so maybe I'm not surprised you were worried. But I get the impression she's grown since then, just like you and I have. Hopefully," she added with a wink.

He unleashed a shaky laugh and rose to his feet. Advancing on her, he placed his warm hands on her upper arms. "We never stop growing. *Hopefully*."

She rested her hands on his waist. "Do you know what today is?"

He played coy. "July Fourth?"

She rolled her eyes playfully. "Besides that."

"Oh, you mean the anniversary of me falling in love with you, courtesy of your conversion to Islam?"

Julia tossed her head back in laughter, recalling another Independence Day, nineteen years ago, when William visited her at Dunphy's. She was working the hostess station, and true to her unfiltered self, she overshared about everything from her three-day adolescent dabbles in Islam, to her marine biology summer camp. "Don't forget my enthusiasm for whale fecal plumes. That's what *really* sealed it, wasn't it?"

"That, and watching the fireworks light up your face."

Julia felt the familiar old warmth radiating outward from her chest to the rest of her body. "Wanna make some fireworks of our own? For old times' sake?"

"Excuse me, but I plan to make them for new times' sake, too," he balked. "Just maybe not with Marisa in the next room."

Julia laughed again and pressed her ear to the front of his shirt, listening to his heartbeat accelerate. "Deal."

SATURDAY, JULY 7, 2012

$\mathcal{J}$ulia spent the next few days discerning the next chapter for her business – starting with a quick day trip to Point Reyes on Saturday.

As usual, she brought the kids, hiking up to a bluff that overlooked the Pacific. Today, like most July days, fog swallowed the view. Between that, the chilly wind, and the strenuous hike, almost no one else was there. But Julia and the kids were used to strenuous hikes, and in preparation, they had stopped in Point Reyes Station for smoothies.

Now, Julia placed an envelope with her semi-annual letter to Rob and Tim on their bench, beneath the shade of a coastal cypress. The engraving on the beautifully carved seat back dedicated this bench to the memory of her uncles, with their dates of birth and death.

Twenty years ago, Julia, Rob, and the rest of their family scattered Tim's ashes over this very bluff. That honor and duty fell to them, since Tim's family had disowned him for being gay. The following year, Rob's ashes joined Tim's.

This bluff was where Rob and Tim fell in love. Julia still had the old photo of them from 1969, smiling in this very spot, their whole lives ahead of them. The ocean vista at their backs.

This was where Rob returned on Halloween, nineteen years ago, knowing his own death was imminent. This was where strangers found him, collapsed but still clinging to life, and to his memories of Tim.

The sacrifices Rob and Tim had made to be together were worth it, to them.

That night, over dinner, William was unusually quiet, even for him; but Julia knew he had as much on his mind as she did. He and his mother had spent Friday with Kelly and Pilar, sharing their conflicting feelings over how to support Mike without enabling his destructive tendencies. At the same time, William had respected Mike's privacy by not breaking the news of his diagnosis. He would leave that to Mike.

"I made it clear I want no part in the enabling and codependency that used to play out in our family," William reported, sitting beside Julia in the den after tucking Robert in. "I told them I'm happy to connect Mike with resources to support his sobriety. I'd even help him look for a job. But I won't give him money or pay his bills. I won't babysit him, ever again. I sure as hell won't live with him. And if they allow him to move in, I wouldn't support that – especially if Kelly lets him move in with her kids."

Julia caught herself gaping and clamped her jaw shut. After a few moments to assess, William added, "It may sound harsh, but that's what I grew up with – my parents letting Jimmy and Mike to turn our house into a meth den. Then, my parents and Kelly pressured me to babysit Mike when we were both grown-ass adults. That's what you stumbled into in 2006 when we reconnected – remember?"

How could Julia forget? William and Mike lived together back then, and even played in a band together, just so William could keep an eye on his brother. It was William who made sure Mike took his meds every day; William who tried to ensure Mike stayed on the straight and narrow. And still, despite William's best efforts, Mike wound up in the ICU after OD'ing and going into cardiac arrest.

"We've all been through a lot of therapy since then," William added quietly, interrupting her unwelcome memories, "so luckily, they agreed."

Julia blew out a breath of relief and disentangled one hand to stroke his bare forearm – the one with the compass tattoo. "I'm proud of you. Of *all* of you."

His eyes softened. "Thanks. Me too."

"So what's next?" she asked gently. "With you and Mike, I mean."

Dragging his hand over his beard, William studied Paige's latest painting, still drying on her easel. It was a bioluminescent moth, glowing in vibrant shades of jade, pink, and yellow against a field of midnight stars.

"I guess I'll meet with the asshole," he sighed, and Julia couldn't suppress her resounding guffaw.

Clapping her hand over her mouth, she barked out a muffled, "Sorry!"

He turned back to her with a smile. "Your daughter's artistic talent reminds me of Mike's. He's so much more than his addiction, and in spite of everything he's done, I love him."

Melting at William's vulnerability, Julia drew him in for a chaste kiss. When they pulled apart, a lock of hair escaped from her messy bun, and he tucked it behind her ear. Her heart tripped over itself, like it always did from that simple gesture.

"What about you?" he murmured. "How was your visit with Rob and Tim?"

"Good." She leaned into the warm palm cupping her cheek and closed her eyes for a moment. "They already answered me."

"Answered you?"

She nodded. "I always leave Rob and Tim a letter when I visit. This time, I asked them for some sign of what I was supposed to be doing at work. You know – what we talked about the other day."

"You mean whether to hire an employee?"

"And how to expand the aquarium servicing side. I brought the watermelon tourmaline with me," she added, reaching absently into her cardigan pocket to slide her thumb over its polished surface, "and I told the kids about it. What it meant to Rob, and to me. It reminded me all over again of everything Rob and Tim sacrificed to be together. I mean, Tim sacrificed his teaching career and even his whole family to be with Rob."

William's brows lifted in surprise.

"Not 'sacrificed' in some *Indiana Jones and the Temple of Doom* way," Julia joked. "Tim was born and raised in Fresno. His family was very religious and conservative. They disowned him. They even declined to claim his body when he died, so we handled everything. Thinking of all that reminded me of everything Rob taught me: don't settle for anything less than everything. Believe that you deserve it. If it's meant to be, the details will work themselves out. So on Monday, I'm dumping Chad the Fuckwad, to borrow your eloquent phrasing."

"Aw, you mean I don't get to piss on Fuckwad's golf visor? But I was looking forward to it!"

"I'm pretty sure Rob would rise from the dead and slap me if I kept taking Fuckwad's money. And since I'd like Rob to keep resting in peace, I'm dumping Fuckwad and hiring an employee for the shop."

Smiling, he brought both of her hands to his lips and kissed her knuckles. "I'm proud of you, too, Julie."

"Look at us, growing older and wiser!"

"Speak for yourself. I'm just growing wiser."

She laughed, but when his grin abruptly straightened, so did hers. She rubbed his shoulder, and it seemed to snap him out of whatever zone he had entered. He kissed her hand again. "I'm okay. Just, you mentioning an employee reminded me – Stephen handed in his resignation, effective immediately."

"What?! Why?"

"He claims it's because he got a new sous chef job. But honestly, I think it has more to do with Izumi."

Julia blinked. "Izumi?"

"They've been trying to hide it from me, but they've been dating. I mean, he showed up with her to Kelly's wedding, for Christ's sake. Did they really expect me not to notice? But he was way more into her than she was into him, and I think he got his heart broken."

"So he quit without notice because they broke up?"

Grunting in confirmation, William leaned forward, rested his elbows on his knees, and pinched his mouth and nose between his palms. "And now I have no deckhand for my trip tomorrow."

A jolt of inspiration straightened Julia's spine. "Sure you do. *Me.*"

William lifted an eyebrow. "You?"

"Don't sound so skeptical," Julia laughed. "I hate to bring it up, but Kevin's parents own a virtual fleet of boats. Between that and my college internships, I practically lived on boats during my twenties. Plus…" As if answering a summons, she raised her hand. "Marine biology major? I can back up Izumi on interpretation."

But William shook his head. "No, I can't subject Izumi to yet another awkward situation after she just escaped from one."

"Did you just call me an awkward situation?"

"Absolutely."

She snickered. "So you acknowledge I was right – Izumi's got it bad for you."

William gave a sheepish wince. "After the way she ran out of Kelly and Pilar's reception when she saw us holding hands? I've definitely been keeping my distance from her."

Julia pondered his dilemma. "So what are you going to do about tomorrow, if you don't use me?"

His stumped silence spoke volumes. Finally, he admitted, "I guess I'll have to cancel the trip. And every trip this week until I find a new deckhand."

With a gasp, Julia's face lit up in inspiration.

"Oh, no," William groaned. "I can just hear your gears turning."

"Hear me out, okay?"

"Against my better judgment? Okay."

Steeling herself, Julia said, "Kevin."

William frowned. "What about him?"

"He's in the Bay Area right now because he had an appointment with a new GI specialist at Stanford."

"Oh – no way." William shook his head and lifted his hands, as if to ward off the idea.

"What? I told you, his parents have their own private navy. He practically grew up on boats. And again – marine biology major."

"What part of 'awkward situation' did you not understand?"

"Oh, stop," she teased. "Are you going to sue yourself for creating a hostile work environment?"

"I might. And if not, I'm sure Kevin will."

Julia *tsk*ed. "I thought you two hugged it out."

"Are you psychotic?"

"Yes."

"I know, because you're hallucinating."

"But they're visions for good, not evil."

He actually guffawed. "I have not, nor will I ever, 'hug anything out' with Kevin."

Julia sucked her teeth again and rolled her eyes in mock disdain. "Fine, but still, just hear me out, okay?"

He crossed his arms over his chest and shot her some world-class side-eye. But amusement twitched at the corners of his mouth.

"Look," she continued, "if he's available and willing, maybe Kevin can fill in tomorrow so you don't have to cancel on your passengers and lose that income. Then you'd have all day Monday to search for a permanent replacement."

"I'm sure Kevin is eminently qualified, but even if I felt comfortable hiring him, my liability insurance won't allow me to take someone on who isn't fully vetted and trained. I could lose my captain's license and my whole business."

"But that's what I'm telling you – Kevin *is* fully vetted and trained. He has a bona fide deckhand certification." When William still hesitated, she added, "Surely you can suck it up for one single day?"

Still, he shook his head. "It will take more than a day to hire a permanent replacement."

Sighing, she gently cupped his cheek in her palm. "Just let me talk to him. That way, at least you'll have the option. You don't have to hire him if you still don't want to."

After another moment's hesitation, he gave a reluctant nod, and she kissed him.

Then, after walking him to the door and kissing him goodnight, she drew a deep breath for courage and placed the call to Kevin.

The first words out of his mouth were, "Is everything okay?" Julia rarely called him unexpectedly unless something was up with the kids.

"Yes, everything's fine. I just have a rather unusual question for you. Hear me out, okay?" she added, for the third time that night.

"Okay?"

Squeezing her eyes shut, she dove right in. "Are you available and willing to fill in tomorrow as a deckhand on William's boat?" When

Kevin barked out an actual laugh, she blurted the rest out before she lost her nerve. "And maybe also all of next week?"

"What field, besides the left one, is this coming out of?" But his tone was placid. Amused, even.

"His deckhand quit on him today with no notice. Not because of William," she added hastily. "It was… personal stuff. But the end result is, Will needs someone to fill in immediately, or he'll have to cancel his excursions for the next week. Maybe longer."

"Starting tomorrow," Kevin said flatly.

"Yes, and since you're already in town, and you have a certification… I mean, even if it's only for tomorrow. I know you have to fly back to Santa Barbara after tomorrow."

A two-beat rest. "Actually, I don't."

"Don't what?"

"Have to be back in Santa Barbara next week. Any loose ends I need to tie up on my dissertation, I can do from Atherton."

Julia's mouth fell open. "So you'd actually consider it? Helping William?"

"As long as William is cool with it, too, it might even be fun."

Julia gave a single, incredulous laugh. "William hasn't decided for sure if he wants to bring on a temporary deckhand, but if he does, he's cool with it being you."

"Just let me know the next steps."

"Of course," she rushed out breathlessly. "I'll give William your contact information, if that's okay. And… thank you."

"You're welcome, Julia. Have a good weekend." And for the first time in years, he sounded truly at peace.

The next evening over dinner, Paige and Robert hounded William for intel on Kevin's job performance. Alison, who had joined them as usual for Sunday dinner, eavesdropped in rapt attention, as did Julia.

"He did great," William reported. "He showed up early, and I barely had to train him. It's like seafaring and boats are second nature to him."

"They are," Julia confirmed. "I told you, he grew up crisscrossing the globe on his parents' yachts. That's yachts, *plural.*"

"He was also a great back-up for Izumi, on the interpretation side," William added, and Julia didn't miss the meaningful look gave her. There was a twinkle behind it, and she tipped her head in question before he tore his eyes away.

The moment the kids left the table, Julia pounced on him. "Okay, spill."

William's hand froze in mid-air, still holding the plate he was clearing from the table.

"You're clearly brimming with gossip," she said, "so cough it up."

Chuckling, he resumed his seat and glanced back into the garden to confirm Robert still harvested bell peppers with his grandmother. "I don't think it's exaggerating to say Kevin and Izumi hit it off."

After a loaded beat, Alison clarified, "You mean that super-pretty, super-young naturalist? The one I saw on the pier when you took Paige and Robert whale-watching?"

"Not as pretty as Julia," William hedged, to which Julia responded by singing the chorus of *Smooth Operator.* "But yes, you saw her on the pier that day."

"And when you say 'hitting it off,' I assume you don't mean as professional colleagues, right?" clarified Julia.

"I will neither confirm nor deny," William replied with an exasperating smirk. "I'll only say that when I introduced them, they sized each other up like tourists in Vegas size up an all-you-can-eat buffet. And at the end of the day, Izumi left in Kevin's car."

Julia and Alison exchanged slack-jawed looks, and then Alison grinned like the Cheshire cat. "No fucking way."

Julia jabbed her sister with her elbow, craning her neck to make sure her mother and son hadn't heard. "Maybe he was just being nice? Driving her home?"

Alison barked out a laugh. "That's one way to put it."

Still in denial, Julia blinked repeatedly. "Izumi? And *Kevin*?"

"Oh, come on, Julie," Alison said, "it's not like he's hideous."

Fair enough, but he was no William. Then again, Julia had always been biased, where William was concerned. Meanwhile, thinning salt-and-pepper curls crowned Kevin's five-foot-ten-inch frame. On land, he looked every bit the California professor, with heavy black-rimmed glasses, a full beard, and a slightly rumpled business-casual wardrobe. When hiking or camping, he played the hipster-mountain man hybrid to a T; and while carving the slopes, his pronounced canine teeth gave off distinct yeti vibes.

But she had to admit, after a summer at sea, his skin tanned to a nice golden-brown. And when the weather was warm enough to go shirtless, his chest and biceps spoke to the hours he spent tending aquariums, with all the heavy lifting that entailed.

Besides, he could be charming and charismatic, when he wanted to. It was how he lasted at his father's venture capital firm for seven years. It was also how he first lured Julia into his bed, even though she was still in love with William.

Julia found William studying her closely. Mortified, she snapped her eyes back to her sister. "I just mean Kevin is forty-two and average, while Izumi is twenty-three and gorgeous."

"He's also loaded," Alison pointed out.

"He's not *that* loaded. Not since the Great Recession."

Alison scoffed. "The dude has his own private plane. I think it's safe to say he's loaded."

Julia scowled, flaring her eyes to drive the point home: *Drop it.*

William cleared his throat. "To be fair, I get the impression Izumi has a thing for older guys. I don't know exactly how old her last boyfriend was, but he was divorced with kids, so he probably wasn't young."

In spite of herself, Julia frowned. She harbored zero romantic or sexual feelings for Kevin, and certainly no regrets. So what was her deal?

"Sounds like you've got another impending human resources problem," she said, just to say something. "Sorry I made that happen."

Alison's eyes bounced between Julia and William. He, in turn, tipped his head, staring a question at Julia. Alison apparently took that as her cue, hopping up from her seat. "I'm going to help Dad with the dishes."

Julia waited until she was out of sight, and then William reached across the table for her hand. "You have nothing to apologize for. I'll keep a close eye on it, and if I need to intervene, I will."

Julia stared down at their clasped hands, nodding slowly. "I guess I've been worried about what would happen when Kevin started dating again. You know... how any new girlfriend would fit into the kids' lives, and our family dynamic. And to imagine him dating such a young woman..."

He smiled. "First, we don't even know that they're hooking up. And since they just met today, I think it's far too soon to speculate on dating."

She frowned, considering. "Fair point."

"Besides, don't borrow trouble. Like everything else, we'll cross those bridges when we get there. Yes, Izumi is young, but she's also a bit more mature than your average twenty-three-year-old."

Julia lifted her eyes to his. "Maybe that's why she goes for the older guys."

William gave a noncommittal shrug, but kept his tender gaze glued on her, his eyes making a circuit of her features. "Are you sure there's nothing else bothering you?"

"You mean jealousy or regrets about Kevin? No. Just worried I may have brought you more problems, instead of solving them."

"You didn't," he reassured her, petting her hand with his free one. "Kevin is a great deckhand – better than Stephen. And great with the passengers."

"He can schmooze with the best of them, when needed."

William smirked. "Then they're well-matched."

Julia's brows lifted almost to her hairline. "Are you actually rooting for them?"

"No, you dope," he laughed. "I was teasing, lamely. I just don't want you stressing so much about it."

Grinning, she leaned across the table to reward him with a kiss.

TUESDAY, JULY 10, 2012 – THURSDAY, JULY 12, 2012

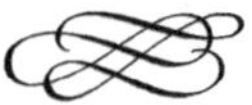

When William still couldn't find a replacement deckhand, he invited Kevin back for Tuesday's whale watching trip.

"How was it?" Julia ventured that evening when William arrived with Diego.

With a faint smirk, he said, "Good. We saw three orcas and a humpback."

Still in the foyer, Julia gave his shoulder a little shove. "Stop playing coy."

He laughed. "I didn't see any smoking gun. Kevin and Izumi were friendly, but professional. And he's still working out surprisingly well as a deckhand and backup naturalist. He doesn't look at me like I'm sprouting horns anymore. He's almost... pleasant."

"Maybe because he's getting some now? With a twenty-three-year-old sex kitten?"

He grinned and rolled his eyes, but he refused to dignify her cattiness with a response.

Kevin worked for William again on Wednesday and Thursday, which made for an interesting Thursday session in Clio's office.

"This is a surprising development," she declared, her eyes ping-ponging between the three of them. "Pleasantly surprising, mind you.

You all seem much more relaxed than you were just a couple of weeks ago."

"I think we've turned a corner," William ventured, looking sheepishly to Kevin for confirmation. "You're a good deckhand."

"Thanks. You're a good captain," Kevin replied with a smile. "And yeah, the dynamic has definitely shifted."

For her part, Julia's beaming smile said it all.

Then Kevin squirmed in his chair and coughed into his fist. "This seems like a good time to mention I've decided to move back to San Francisco before September."

Julia and William both did a double-take. "I thought you had your dissertation defense in August," Julia said.

"I do, but I can fly down for that. I don't need to be in Santa Barbara until then, and I'm tired of being so far from the kids."

Julia's mind and heart were a riot of conflicting feelings. On one level, she had been dreading the day when Kevin moved back and resumed joint physical custody. For a long time, she hadn't known what she would do with herself or how she would fill her time if Paige and Robert weren't there to occupy her every waking minute. The silence in the house would be deafening, and the hole in her heart would feel cavernous.

On the other hand, even before her reunion with William, she consoled herself by remembering how she filled her time, pre-kids, with things like reading, sewing, and aquariums.

Once Kevin moved back to San Francisco, she would have time for those again. Maybe she could create costumes for theater, like she did in high school. Maybe she could take up yoga, or join a hiking group, or volunteer for an AIDS-related nonprofit like the one her Aunt Brigid started back in the eighties.

And now that William was back in her life, she could spend some of her free time with him, too.

After all these months to prepare, Julia knew she had to reframe this time away from her kids as time for self-restoration – for rediscovering and reinventing herself as an individual, distinct from her identity as a mom.

But this week's events had raised another possible explanation for

Kevin's sudden change of plans. And once again, worry niggled at the back of her brain over who else the kids might be spending time with, besides Kevin.

Of course, it was far too premature to broach such questions with Kevin, so Julia swallowed her misgivings and forced a smile. "When are you thinking of moving back?"

"Now."

Julia's mouth went dry, and she studiously avoided looking at William. She didn't trust herself to keep her composure if his expression betrayed the same dismay. "Now? Like – immediately?"

A tiny, almost imperceptible furrow formed between Kevin's brows. "Like, this week."

"But... don't you at least have to pack first? Find a place to live?"

"My condo in Santa Barbara came furnished, and so does my new one in the city."

This time, Julia couldn't stop her mouth from falling open. "You've already found a condo here?" She was about to ask how he had pulled that off, in this housing market, when an unwelcome idea intruded on her consciousness.

But before she could process the thought, they transitioned awkwardly into discussing what coparenting would look like, now that Kevin was moving back. They talked about Robert – how he was processing his new "two daddies" reality, and how they would continue helping him with that.

But despite her best efforts, Julia's mind kept wandering back to the single, inescapable thought that had dropped in on her. The thought that maybe – just maybe – Kevin was moving in with Izumi.

THE WEEKEND FLITTED by so quickly, Julia's head spun to find herself staring down another Monday. And when she scanned the coming week on her calendar, she recalled with a jolt that William's birthday was next Saturday. She hadn't exactly forgotten; the time was just flying by that quickly. And true to form, William had said nothing. He was just going to let her treat it like any other day of the year.

Well, screw that.

Julia spent the next day or two scrambling for a suitable way to celebrate. And by suitable, she meant epic enough to match the adoration she felt for him.

She had plenty of time to search, because even though she and Paige had papered the city with her marketing materials, Julia's phone remained ominously silent.

On Wednesday, after wrapping up her twice-monthly check-in with Aaron, she leaned back in the chair on the other side of his desk and surveyed him. He was a little less put-together than usual. His usually immaculate, long-on-top fade had grown out a bit, and his suit jackets were fitting tighter around his shoulders, as if he were gaining weight. "So enough of all my crap, Aaron. How are *you* doing?"

"Okay," he said, his flat tone suggesting he was far from okay.

"Don't bullshit a bullshitter, Aaron."

He humored her with a halfhearted chuckle, but offered nothing else.

"I know what you need," she persisted. "You need to get laid."

This time, when he laughed, it reached his eyes. "You're not wrong. Let me tell you, the T *does* stuff to a person."

Julia waggled her eyebrows. "So, men? Women? Or 'yes, please?'"

"It's all good," he said, snickering a bit self-consciously. But then his smile quickly faded. "In all honesty, Julia, dating isn't in the cards for me. Like, ever. I'm too busy."

"Aaron..." Julia reached across the desk to give his bicep a reassuring squeeze, then left it there, impressed. "Geez, dude; I guess you weren't kidding about the T. Have you been lifting weights?"

"Rowing," Aaron muttered. "I have plenty of time for it now. And plenty of frustration to burn."

"Color me impressed. It's clearly paying off." So *this* was why his suit jackets fit a little tighter these days.

Aaron deftly shifted the subject back to Julia. "How are things with William?"

"Good," Julia said, careful not to rub it in by sounding too effusive. "Saturday is his birthday, and I'm trying to figure out what to do for him."

He humored her with another polite smile that didn't reach his eyes, at first. But then, suddenly, those eyes lit up.

"Did I tell you Rina is working for Dirk now?"

"You told me she would be, after graduation. What's she doing for him?"

"Apprenticing with the winemaker and maintaining the vacation rental."

Confused, Julia stilled. "Wait – what is Dirk doing these days? I thought he was a wine importer."

"He sold his importing business and bought a biodynamic farm and winery in Sonoma County. He renamed it Fox Glade Farm and Winery."

"Fox Glade..." Julia scoured the dark recesses of her memory. "Where have I heard that before?"

"It's the literal translation of his last name."

"Vosloo means 'fox glade?'"

Aaron grinned. "Kind of badass, huh?"

It finally hit Julia like a thunderclap. "Does Fox Glade bottle a varietal called Cinsaut?"

"It does."

"Mom's friend gave her a bottle of Fox Glade Cinsaut! I had never tried that varietal before."

Aaron nodded enthusiastically. "Dirk's family in South Africa bottled it at their winery. It's always been his dream to introduce it more widely here."

"Well, I can safely say it's our new favorite."

"There's more where that came from. There's a beautiful old farmhouse on the winery that Rina maintains as a vacation rental. You and William could make a weekend of it, just the two of you."

Julia's face fell. "Oh, um... William doesn't drink."

Aaron studied her for a second, but mercifully didn't probe further. "Well, the winery itself is on the other end of the property. All you see from the house is the old orchard and the vineyard. It's a romantic little retreat unto itself."

Julia hummed thoughtfully. "Does it have a big, comfy bed?"

"And a big, comfy tub."

Julia brightened. "Where exactly in Sonoma County?"

"North of Healdsburg. It's a hidden gem that's still relatively undiscovered," he added, a bit wistfully; and Julia sensed the winery had once been his dream, as well as Dirk's.

Julia considered a moment. "That actually sounds really nice, but won't it already be booked?"

"Probably not. Rina actually lives in the farmhouse, so they don't book it for more than seven days per month. And it doesn't come cheap, so it's not in super-high demand."

"Oh," Julia said, deflating. "I mean, I know I divorced a multimillionaire, but you know my current financial situation. How much are we talking about here?"

Retrieving his phone, Aaron waved away her concern. "I'll text you Rina's contact card. Give her a call and she'll hook you up."

"What? No. I can't accept that. It's too much."

They went round and round until Aaron heaved an exasperated sigh. "Julia, with how much you've paid me in legal fees over the years, let me repay you in this small, measly way. You deserve to treat yourself. And your birthday stud, of course."

Julia actually giggled and came around the desk to throw her arms around her startled cousin. "I am *so* going to set you up with someone."

"Fuck, no. I don't trust you within ten parsecs of my love life." But he was grinning broadly as he tapped out his text to her.

"Fine. I'll hover at eleven parsecs."

"It's a vacation rental I found," Julia explained to William the following Sunday over the phone. "If it's anywhere near as nice as the listing photos, you'll love it."

Since William worked on weekends, Julia had arranged for them to drive up to Sonoma County on Sunday evening. They would spend one night at Fox Glade, then drive home again Monday night.

Kevin, meanwhile, obligingly agreed to fill in for Julia on Monday, servicing the aquariums at Dunphy's and the pediatrician's office. He was the only other person she would trust them to. On top of that, Kevin also agreed to keep Paige and Robert at his new place in the city while she and William were gone. It turned out he had not moved in with Izumi, nor anyone else. That wasn't how he found a new condo so quickly – he just lived at a high enough price point to circumvent most of the market's competitors. And in the case of Kevin's price point, the *high* was quite literal – penthouse-atop-a-high-rise literal.

"Where *is* this vacation rental?" asked William. He had just wrapped up his Sunday whale watching trip, and now he was about to drive to her parents' house.

"Nope."

He grunted. "Fine. See you soon."

Chuckling, she hung up and examined herself once more in the full-length mirror. She wore a new kelly-green sundress she made herself, with a fitted bodice and a pinched waist, flaring out to a pleated knee-length skirt. Spaghetti straps and a plunging neckline added sex appeal, and it exposed much of her back, too. Julia knew from experience that William had a serious weakness for her exposed back. Fantasies of him running his tongue up her spine raised anticipatory goosebumps.

She had paired the sundress with strappy sandals that lengthened her legs, and she left her hair down in shiny waves. Her only accessory was the same necklace she wore every day: the simple silver chain and mermaid pendant William had given her nineteen years ago as a promise.

She grinned at her reflection in the mirror. She looked hot.

Half an hour later, when she opened the door to him, he looked positively thunderstruck. His overheated gaze scorched her from head to toe, and she had clearly rendered him speechless.

She flashed him a flirtatious smile and, still holding his gaze, turned to grab her rolling suitcase. It was the smallest one in her arsenal – after all, if their little getaway went according to plan, she wouldn't need a lot of clothes. Therefore, she conveniently had to bend quite a bit to extend its handle. And rather than bending at the knees, she opted instead to bend at the waist.

She felt his eyes boring into her from behind until his innate chivalry won out and he swept the suitcase from her grasp. Setting it right back down at his side, he touched her shoulder, nudging her to face him; and she smiled encouragingly. He wrapped his arms around her waist. Touched his lips to hers, and lingered a long time.

When he finally broke away, he held her by the shoulders and stepped back, his eyes slowly raking over her again. "Wow. You look... wow."

She lifted a saucy eyebrow. It seemed like he wanted to say more, but clearly he was floundering. His face reddened, and he broke into nervous snickers.

In her sultriest tone, she said, "Has the poet lost his words?"

"For his muse? Never." Without warning, he yanked her hips against his, and she yelped. A solar flare erupted between her thighs when she discerned the effect she was having on him. "But I defy even a poet laureate to wax eloquent when his blood is rushing to the wrong head."

"Down, boy," she teased. "Save it for where we're going, and I promise I'll make it worth your while."

He closed his eyes, bit his bottom lip, and didn't even try to hide his groan of frustration. Giggling, she followed him outside, where he threw Julia's suitcase in her trunk. Then, as fast as traffic would allow, she was zipping up 19th Avenue, through Golden Gate Park and the Richmond, and across the Golden Gate Bridge.

He hummed. "North, huh?"

She flashed him a quick grin, just long enough to see him pinch his chin as the gears turned in his brain. "Don't even bother. You'll never guess."

Chuckling, he contented himself with sightseeing – starting with her.

"What?" she snickered when she caught him staring with a wolfish smirk.

"I'd really like to make it to our destination first, but you're making it very hard for me."

Squirming in her seat, she reached over and swatted him. "That's for making me horny while I'm trying to drive."

He tossed his head back in wide-open laughter and seized her hand. For half a second, she wondered what he was going to do with her hand; but he only wove his fingers through hers before resting their joined hands on the center console. Electricity buzzed through every cell that connected them, radiating from their hands through the rest of Julia's body.

Halfway to Healdsburg, William's cell phone rang. Retrieving it from his pocket, he glanced at the phone screen and frowned.

"Who is it?" Julia prompted.

Sliding his thumb over the screen to answer it, he mouthed the word *Mom.* That one word sent Julia's heart plummeting to the floorboard. Ann had always been very respectful of William's space. She never disturbed him when he was with Julia.

"Hey Mom. Everything okay?"

The canned sound of Ann's voice on the other end of the line drifted to Julia's ears, but she couldn't make out any words. However, she could definitely make out William's groan as he dropped his forehead into his palm.

"What?" Julia hiss-whispered; but he held up one finger, still listening. Her imagination ran wild, and the first thing it seized on was Mike. Something must have happened with Mike.

"Yeah, of course," William droned out a moment later. "No, I know you wouldn't, Mom; it's okay. I'm just sorry this is happening, and worried; that's all." Another pause. "Yeah, okay, no problem. We'll head back... See you soon."

After he hung up, she waited on pins and needles for what felt like minutes, but was probably only seconds, before he turned to her with the longest face she had ever seen.

"I'm so sorry, sweetheart," he began, his voice choked with regret. "But we're going to have to go back."

"Is it Mike?"

"Mike? I wish. No, Pilar has gone into early labor. The doctors tried to stop it, but they can't. The twins are coming."

Julia gasped. "Oh, no! But I thought they weren't due until–"

"September," William confirmed, his voice flat. "My new nieces have other plans, apparently."

"Oh, God..." breathed Julia as she exited 101, then made a U-turn heading back south.

"I'm sorry, but I promised when the time came, I would help look after Xavier and Zach. Mom isn't energetic enough to handle the boys herself."

"Of course," Julia murmured. "You don't have to explain."

"And I guess this also means I'll be spending a lot of time at Kelly and Pilar's house for a while," he added quietly. "They'll need all the help they can get while the twins are in the NICU."

Julia considered a moment. "What about Pilar's parents and sisters?"

"They'll help, too, but her parents work full-time. They still have two kids at home, and pay college tuition for two others. Sergio and Delfina just can't afford to take much time off."

"We'll all pitch in." Julia nudged him with her elbow. "Don't forget, we live only three blocks away. And as my mother recently pointed out, we're practically family now."

She peeked at him just in time to watch his cheeks flush red. Facing forward, he tried and failed to smother a delighted smile. The sight of it set a flock of hummingbirds alight in Julia's chest.

But William's smile faded all too quickly. "I'm just so sorry you put this whole trip together, and now I'm bringing it to a screeching halt. You have no idea..." He turned to her, pure agony warping his features. "...*no* idea... how disappointed I am."

Julia reached across the center console and took his hand again. "Sweetheart, I do know. I'd be lying if I said I wasn't disappointed, too, but I'm even more in love with what a good brother and uncle you are."

Yet again, he flushed adorably, and she leaned over the console to give him a quick peck on the lips.

WEDNESDAY, AUGUST 1, 2012

*X*imena and Zuriñe Ochoa-Quinn made their grand entrance only an hour later, and their whirlwind debut on the planet set the tone for next couple of weeks.

Julia, her parents, and William all pitched in to cook meals and clean house for Kelly and Pilar. Other times, Julia and her parents hosted dinner at their house.

Julia even spent a couple of overnights at the Ochoa-Quinns', giving William, Ann, and Delfina a night off. Feeding the boys, transporting them to and from their summer day camps, and tucking Zach into bed at night. Especially for Aspie kids like Xavier, Julia understood the importance of routine.

It was fun to watch the steady, solid friendship blossoming between Paige and Xavier, who shared a love of digital art, animation, and video games; as well as the one between Robert and eight-year-old Zach, who were just close enough in age to play well together.

After three days, the hospital discharged Pilar, but she still spent much of every day with the twins while Kelly returned to work. And a week after that, it was Julia's turn to perform dinner duty at the Ochoa-Quinn house. After work, she picked up the kids, and together they walked over with their groceries.

As they approached Kelly and Pilar's house, a car pulled up to the curb in front. When the driver emerged, Julia gave a start to recognize her.

"Pilar!"

Though she still sported a postpartum belly, all the puffiness had vanished from Pilar's face. For the first time, Julia could really discern her delicate bone structure. Julia swept over to hug her. "Look at you! I haven't seen you since you had the twins! How do you always look so beautiful?"

"Thanks," Pilar said quietly, returning Paige's wave and hugging Robert, her weary smile not quite reaching her eyes.

"But I'm sure you're exhausted," Julia added, draping an arm around Pilar's shoulders, gently ushering her toward the front door. "Get inside and put your feet up."

"I won't lie," Pilar admitted as they walked. Xavier, apparently hearing their approach, flung open the front door, and both Paige and Robert darted inside after him. "I feel like some dystopian dairy-human, constantly pumping around the clock for a few milliliters of liquid gold."

"Been there, done that," Julia groaned, recalling when Paige was born with a poor latch. "Are you doing that finger-feeding thing? Like, where you have to tape a little tube to your finger and let them suck on your fingertip?"

Pilar shook her head, her eyes suddenly shiny. "It's a full-fledged tube feeding. Down their throats."

"Oh..." Mortified, Julia froze right there on the doorstep. "I'm so sorry. I didn't realize..."

Pilar aimed another shaky, watery smile at Julia. "It's okay. It's just, when babies are born this early, there really is no sucking reflex."

"You don't owe me an explanation," Julia said hastily. "You don't have to talk about *any* of this, unless you just want to. But I can imagine you're sick of explaining it, eighty million times, to eighty million different people."

"In a way," Pilar conceded with a sheepish wince. "I know everybody cares, and that means so much to me and Kelly. But..."

"It's exhausting," Julia tried.

With a shaky laugh, Pilar admitted, "A little."

"And when you get home, you just want to relax for a few precious minutes, take a load off, and not have to answer even more questions."

"Yeah." The look Pilar gave Julia was almost searching. Almost like she was seeing Julia for the first time.

"Voice of experience here," Julia said, raising her hand. "I never had premature babies – clearly, since I asked you such a stupid, ignorant question – but Paige was in the hospital once. And so was I, with hyperemesis gravidarum."

"Yeah; Will told us about that," Pilar breathed. "That sounds awful."

Julia waved a hand. "It sucked, but I survived. You, Kelly, and your girls will get through this, too. And we'll all help as much as we can."

"Thanks," Pilar breathed, her eyes shimmering again. Julia wrapped her in a hug, and then Pilar wiped the tears from her cheeks as they passed through the front door.

As she deposited her purse, hat, and scarf on the console in the foyer, Julia peeked through the open door of the in-law unit to find found Xavier and Paige at the desk in the den. Thoroughly engrossed in Xavier's latest animation, they were oblivious to anything else. With a wink, Pilar waved Julia upstairs, where they found William already prepping dinner in the kitchen. Zach and Robert, meanwhile, worked a jigsaw puzzle at the kitchen table.

Wiping his hands on a towel, William stepped away from the chicken he was cutting up and offered Pilar a peck on the cheek. "How are my nieces today?"

"Good. They both gained an ounce over the last twenty-four hours."

"Are they still under the bili lights?"

"Yeah, and they will be for a while."

To Julia, William explained, "The girls have jaundice, so they have to be under these special lights."

Julia hummed sympathetically. "Robert had to be on a bili blanket when he was born, for the same reason."

Zach hopped up from the table to hug Pilar and demand to see the latest photos of his new baby sisters. While Pilar scrolled through her cell phone, William gave Julia a chaste kiss on the lips before returning to his chicken. Kelly, freshly showered and changed from work, strolled into the kitchen to look on with a contented smile, like a queen surveying her realm. Julia caught Kelly's eye and waved, and Kelly answered with a jerk of her head, beckoning Julia into the living room.

"I just wanted to say again how grateful Pilar and I are for all your help since the twins were born," Kelly said in a low voice once they were alone.

Relaxing into a smile, Julia waved her hand. "Of course, Kelly. I'm glad we're nearby."

"I wanted to let you know that I got in touch with the special education attorney you referred me to. Xavier will be starting at the same school as Paige this fall."

Nearly giddy with excitement, Julia actually found herself clapping before forcing herself to stop. She didn't want to overwhelm Kelly *too* soon with her natural exuberance. "I'm so glad it worked out. And I know Paige will be thrilled, too," she added with a wink.

Kelly chuckled knowingly, and then, after glancing awkwardly around the room, she jerked her thumb toward the staircase. "Speak of the devils, I'd better go check on them..."

As Kelly headed downstairs, Julia returned to the kitchen, still laughing. She gave William a quick kiss before nudging him out of the way with her hip. While she arranged the chicken pieces into William's marinade and trimmed green beans, William ordered Pilar from the kitchen so she could grab a quick nap. Occasionally, as he walked Zach and Robert through their puzzle, his gaze snagged on Julia's, and they shared a private smile.

Just as she was ready to dump the seasoned green beans into the sauté pan, Paige burst into the kitchen, gasping for breath as if she had run the whole way, and waving what Julia recognized as her work cell. It buzzed insistently in her hand.

Paige didn't even wait for Julia to speak. "OhMyGodMomHaveY-ouSeenItYet?!"

At the table, William's eyes snapped to Paige in alarm, and Julia quickly wiped her hands. "Paige, what's wrong?"

"*Wrong?* Are you serious?"

"Paige," Julia ground out, "cut the dramatics and tell me what's going on."

Paige gave a scoff of dismay, shaking the still-buzzing phone, as if that explained everything. "You're Instagram-famous!"

"I'm... what?"

"Instagram, Mom! You're famous on Instagram!"

Frowning, Julia excavated the darkest recesses of her memory. "Okay, I give up – what is Instagram?"

Paige scoffed so loudly that Julia flinched.

"It's a social media app," Xavier chimed in from the kitchen entrance. Julia hadn't even noticed him there, wrapped up as she was in Paige's theatrics.

Julia stared at him. "You mean like Facebook?"

Paige's resounding groan ricocheted off the walls. "Mom, I swear to God..."

"Instagram is way better than Facebook," Zach declared matter-of-factly from the kitchen table, snapping a puzzle piece into place.

William stifled his laughter behind his hand, and Julia stuck her tongue out at him playfully. "Okay; so I'm old and out of touch."

"You are," Paige agreed, "but since you mentioned it, I'm sure Marisa has a Facebook page, too."

Julia stiffened, and her smile evaporated. "Marisa?"

"You don't have to download Instagram or anything; just look it up on your browser."

With a jolt, it finally dawned on Julia: "Wait – how do *you* know about my alleged Instagram fame?" After all, Paige did not have her own phone, and was not allowed unsupervised time on computers.

"I was downstairs when your work cell started blowing up. You left it in your purse, on that table in the foyer. So your phone was blowing up, like, massively, and that can only mean one thing: something about you has gone viral on the Internet. So I told Xavier to find out what it was."

Julia looked to Xavier, who nodded in confirmation. "Okay, so how do I see this Instagram notoriety for myself?"

With another grunt of dismay, Paige said, "Just search for 'Marisa Zunino Zeneize Instagram.'"

The call on Julia's work cell had gone to voice mail. She accepted the phone from Paige and pulled up a browser window. Sure enough, there was Marisa's public Instagram page. Ignoring the prompt to download the app, Julia said, "Okay, now what?"

"Now, just look. It's right there, front and center."

Frowning, Julia brought the phone screen closer, and froze. "Wha...?!"

Paige squealed. "I told you! You're famous!"

William, Zach, and Robert all sprang from the table and came to see what the fuss was. "That's the aquarium at Dunphy's," murmured William, pointing to the most recent photo on Zeneize's page.

"But how...?" And then it hit Julia – the photos Marisa had taken of her aquarium on July Fourth. "Why?"

"Click there," Zach suggested, then went right ahead and did it for her.

The caption expanded, and Julia read it aloud. "Beyond psyched to announce I'm teaming up with @stellarproductionsla and @real-lylivechannel for Season 1 of IN THE WEEDS, a new reality show! Each season, I'll give one lucky, crappy restaurant a complete makeover! For Season One, I'm staying close to home and reimagining Dunphy's Restaurant as Zeneize at Fisherman's Wharf! And this INCREDIBLE, sustainable aquarium by Julia Beale of Castro Aquarium Service is the only thing that stays! @intheweedstvshow and @zeneizeatfisherman-swharf for updates – you know what to do! Pound reality TV; pound restaurant life...'"

"Those are hashtags, Mom," droned Paige.

Julia looked helplessly to Zach, mouthing, "Hashtags?"

"Welcome to 2012," Zach quipped, flashing his dimpled smile before returning to the puzzle, trailed by a thoroughly unimpressed Robert. Snickering, William still lingered over Julia's shoulder.

"Did you know about any of this?" she asked him. "That they picked Dunphy's? Or about this post?"

"Nope."

She grunted in frustration. "It's just like Dad to forget to tell any of us. Or *conveniently* forget, as the case may be."

"Mom," Paige broke in, "you missed a huge business opportunity by not already being on Instagram. Marisa could have tagged you in her post, and that would have driven millions of people to your Instagram profile."

"Millions?" Julia echoed skeptically.

"Yeah, Mom. Check out how many followers she has."

"Three-point-two..." Julia's jaw nearly hit her chest. "Does that mean three-point-two *million?*"

"Yep."

"Maybe you could set up a profile right now," William suggested. "You can comment on her post under your new profile. I can send her a quick text and ask her to tag you in it."

Julia gaped up at him. "How do you know about this stuff when I don't?"

"I have a teenage nephew, remember?" He glanced at Xavier, still in the kitchen doorway.

"You have to do it now, though, Mom," Paige insisted. "Opportunity is knocking, and time is of the essence in the social media world."

Julia couldn't help snickering. "If I let you borrow my phone for thirty minutes, could you and Xavier set one up for me?"

"In a heartbeat." She beamed over at Xavier, whose face flushed as he quickly blinked down at his shoes.

A tiny misgiving niggled at the back of Julia's consciousness. She had restricted her daughter's tech access for a good reason – it was how Paige connected, in the past, with the boys she ran away from home with. But after all, Julia would be supervising.

"Okay; but it has to look professional, Paige. I'll text you my business logo and headshot. Keep the colors consistent with my brand."

"I've got you, Mom." The excitement in Paige's voice further stoked Julia's worries.

But again, this was temporary – and supervised. Julia shoved aside her concerns. After unlocking her work cell and handing it over to Paige, Julia watched in dismay as Paige stalked to Xavier and snatched him by the hand. William vacated his seat at the kitchen table so Paige and Xavier could sit there, opposite Zach and Robert. While William took himself to the living room to catch up with his sister, Julia, thoroughly flustered, returned to the stove to finish dinner.

For the next twenty minutes, Paige and Xavier conferred over their task, serious as a heart attack. Paige periodically interrupted Julia, prompting her to approve the creation of her Instagram account, asking a question, or showing her progress so far.

Right as Julia served dinner, Paige bounded up to Julia. Xavier, her ever-present, ever-silent shadow, trailed close behind. "Check it out!" exclaimed Paige, her enthusiasm palpable as a text notification pinged on Julia's personal cell.

Julia retrieved the phone from her pocket and clicked the link Paige had texted. It led her to the new Castro Aquarium Service Instagram page. William and the younger boys gathered around her at the dining table to look over her shoulder.

"Wow," Julia blurted, unable to conceal her surprise. "This is really good."

Her profile picture was her logo. The bio was professional but snappy, almost as if Julia had written it herself. Plus, it included her contact information and a link to her website. She already had several posts up, including three pinned to the top with high-quality photos of both her and her aquariums. Every caption included an enticing call to action.

"Gen Z to the rescue!" crowed Paige.

"You're really good at writing," Xavier remarked, his tone more expressive than usual.

Flushing with pleasure, Paige beamed up at him. "Thanks," she said breathlessly.

For once, Xavier didn't avert his eyes as she studied him. One corner of his mouth hooked up in a rare smile before he noticed Julia watching, and suppressed it.

Another spike of worry chafed at Julia, witnessing their rapidly-growing puppy-love. But after a long pause, Julia discovered everybody was watching her. Overcompensating a bit, she practically squeaked, "Thank you, Paige!"

"You're welcome." Paige was tapping on Julia's work cell again. "Plus, I commented on Marisa's post for you."

Julia's personal cell pinged again. The new link Paige had texted opened to Marisa's post. Sure enough, Marisa had already pinned a comment from @castroaquariumservice.

"'THANK YOU, @marisazuninosf, for spotlighting me and @castroaquariumservice!'" Julia read aloud. "'So excited to be part of the magic that makes @zeneizeatfishermanswharf the hottest new destination in Pound San Francisco! Pound Castro Aquarium Service, Pound Fish Dish–'"

"*Hashtag*," chorused Julia's entire over-the-shoulder entourage.

"Right. Hashtag." Julia frowned over at Zach. "What are hashtags, again?"

"Don't worry, Mom," Paige sighed, "I'll get you up to speed."

Xavier pointed over Julia's shoulder at the phone screen. "Marisa already edited her caption, too."

Sure enough, Marisa had changed *Castro Aquarium Service* to *@castroaquariumservice*.

"Now her three-point-two-million followers can actually find you," Paige explained, followed immediately by, "Oh my God, Mom, look! You already have two new DMs!"

"What?" said Julia, and as Paige shoved her work cell in her face, Xavier reached over her shoulder again to poke the screen, opening her DMs.

Julia read the first one aloud: "'Hi Julia, I saw the pics of your work on @marisazuninosf's post and I know this is probably a long shot, but are you accepting any new clients?'" Julia snorted. "He actually thinks it's a long shot."

"Well, duh, Mom; you're the best aquarist in the city, and you're environmentally friendly, too," Paige declared.

At that moment, Julia's work cell lit up with another call, and tears pricked at Julia's eyes as yet another message popped up in her DMs. "Paige, I'm speechless! I can't believe this."

"Believe it, and get ready. Instagram is a visual platform – perfect for what you do. Now, for the love of Flying Spaghetti Monster, download the freaking app on your personal cell, too!"

"Yes ma'am." Julia gave a snappy salute. "And also? Thank you."

"All in a day's work," quipped Paige.

"Now give me my work cell back," Julia ordered with mock sternness.

"Yes ma'am," Paige echoed, actually laughing. "But first, I'll send your log in and password. You should change those right away."

"Okay. Thanks for the reminder." Julia glanced in wonder at William. Out of Paige and Xavier's line of sight, he silently pretended to clap. "That's very responsible of you, by the way, Paige."

In a coy tone, Paige replied, "How am I ever supposed to get a phone of my own if I don't earn your trust?"

Julia grinned. "We'll talk it over with Clio, but at the very least, consider this a hefty deposit. *If* you keep up the good work, that is."

Later, after everyone sat down to dinner, William leaned into her ear and whispered, "Speaking of deposits, are you ever going to redeem your voucher?"

"For what?"

"Your voucher for a coucher, of course."

Julia swatted him, snickering, and they nuzzled their foreheads and noses together until Paige gagged and Kelly teasingly admonished them to control themselves. When Julia smiled at her, Kelly returned it with a subtle, conspiratorial wink.

AUGUST – SEPTEMBER, 2012

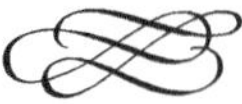

Summer sped by at breakneck speed, like it did every year. Paige and Xavier both started eighth grade at the same school. Julia, William, and Kevin accompanied Robert to his first day of Kindergarten, and as he grinned and waved goodbye without an ounce of trepidation, Julia choked back sappy tears.

That is, until Robert's eyes lit up at the sight of his old friend. "Hey Rowan, look! I have two daddies now, too!"

His boast brought everything within fifty yards to a screeching halt as all eyes followed Robert's. Their audience's reactions varied between shock, disgust, and frank curiosity. Snorting, William smacked his own forehead, while Kevin bowed his head and shook it in dismay.

Julia merely grinned and shrugged. "Never a dull moment."

The truth was, Kevin had integrated into Julia and William's lives more seamlessly than predicted – even if not in the same way as Rowan's parents. Despite finally earning his doctorate, Kevin still struggled to find work. Apparently, all the speculations about him and Izumi had been idle, because she had long since moved on to a new job at a local marine science institute. Kevin still found himself butting his head up against the glass ceiling of ageism, and he refused to exploit his parents' connections to break through. He wanted to succeed on his own merit. That meant Kevin still worked for William, now as the on-board naturalist, since William had long since replaced his deckhand.

August melted into September with no relief from the heat and drought. Filming began on Marisa's new show; and each Monday, when Julia stepped into The Restaurant Formerly Known as Dunphy's, she marveled at the transformation it had undergone in only one week.

On a sweltering mid-September Monday, Julia steered her cartload of aquarium supplies past the office that used to belong to her father. Glancing through the open door, she spied a new employee going over paperwork with Marisa. The moment they looked up, Julia lifted her hand to wave – and stopped short.

"Stephen!" William's cousin, and former deckhand. Julia blurted the classic, obtuse follow-up: "What are you doing here?"

Marisa intervened. "Meet the new sous chef of Zeneize at Fisherman's Wharf."

Julia gaped at Stephen. "No way! You're working with Marisa now?"

"Guilty as charged." With his blindingly handsome grin, Stephen rose to shake Julia's hand. "Good to see you again. How's my cousin?"

"Will's great. He'd want me to tell you hello, and congrats." To Marisa, she added, "So everything's coming together, then?"

"Of course," Marisa said good-naturedly, as if that were a given. And after knowing her only a short while, Julia had no doubt it was.

"I'm just curious, Marisa – do you ever sleep?"

Marisa tilted her head with a look of confusion. "Sleep?"

It took Julia a second to realize Marisa was joking. "Never mind." she laughed.

Marisa swiveled in her chair to face Julia head-on. "Speaking of never sleeping, you're probably not getting much, yourself."

At first, Julia thought Marisa was referring to her sleepless nights with William. Her stomach swooped, until Marisa's self-congratulatory expression clued Julia in to her real meaning. That woman had a healthy ego, but Julia supposed she needed it, in her profession. "Oh, yeah. I actually had to create a waitlist for new clients. I even have an interview next week with the Chronicle. Can you believe it?"

"I absolutely can," Marisa countered. "You're kicking ass and taking names in a male-dominated profession. I know a thing or two about that."

"Um…" With a sheepish wince, Stephen jerked his thumb over his shoulder. "I'll just go cower in the corner now."

Marisa leaned over and pinched Stephen's cheek, cooing, "Aw, the poor wittle fwagile ego!"

Stephen blushed intensely, but he cracked up laughing. Marisa spied Julia's shocked expression and quickly explained. "Don't worry, I've known this kid since we both worked here, in the aughts."

"Oh, right." Julia silently thanked her for not adding, *And also because he's Will's cousin.*

"Anyway," Marisa continued, "why don't you hire an employee so you can take on more clients?"

"I plan to; I just haven't found the right person. I don't trust the aquarium servicing side of my business to anyone but me; and I won't trust my shop to any old reef bro walking in off the street." That's when it hit Julia like a blow to the head. "Oh my God! Kevin!"

Marisa frowned. "Kevin?"

Julia waved her hand. "My ex. Why didn't I think of him sooner?"

Stephen cocked an eyebrow. "You actually *want* to think about your ex?"

"No! Yes. I mean – sorry, I've got to make a call."

Without even waiting for their reactions, Julia dashed off. She steered her cart out of the kitchen and through the dining room to the front of the house before retrieving her phone from her back pocket.

"Is everything okay?" Kevin's voice sounded a bit husky, as if he had been sleeping.

"The kids are fine, but are you?" Julia glanced at her phone screen. "It's two in the afternoon."

"Oh… yeah." He sounded a bit distracted. "I'm fine. Just, ah… having a bit of a lie-down."

"Is your Crohn's flaring up again?"

He barked out a laugh. "I hope not."

Confused, Julia frowned, and then she heard it – a definite female voice, whispering over Kevin's shoulder: "Who is it?"

Julia froze. She heard the telltale rustle of bed sheets as Kevin untangled himself, followed by his footsteps padding into another room.

"What's up?" he prompted, and Julia heard the snick of a door shutting behind him.

Julia's mind was flying at warp speed, yet it took a geologic age to settle on a response. "Sorry if I, uh... interrupted you."

After a two-beat pause, Kevin repeated, "So what's up?"

"Right." Julia cleared her throat. "I just had a brilliant idea. At least, *I* think it's brilliant; I don't know if you will."

"Shoot."

He was getting impatient, so Julia forced herself to focus. "I need to hire someone to cover the shop while I'm out doing my servicing appointments. Do you want the job?"

He coughed out yet another laugh. "That bad, huh?"

Julia frowned. "What do you mean?"

"Oh, no; I just mean it's hard to find good help these days."

Julia rolled her eyes, but she was smiling. "Now you're making me sound like your parents." The jibe was safe because his parents' entitlement and snobbery disgusted him almost as much as it did her. "It's just that you already know everything there is to know, and I wouldn't have to train you. Maybe you could fill in temporarily, until I find someone else?"

"I would, but that schedule would conflict with the job I'm doing for William."

"Oh... right." In her haste, Julia hadn't even considered this. She joked, "So ditch Will and come work for me, instead."

He laughed. "Honestly, I don't think I'd enjoy working in an aquarium shop. Certainly not more than working as a naturalist on a whale watching cruise. Nothing personal."

"Nothing personal taken." After a moment's consideration, Julia asked, "Well, do you at least know someone who can help me? I've already exhausted all connections."

"Let me think about it a day or two and get back to you."

"Sure." In a coy tone, she added, "Enjoy the rest of your, ah... *day*."

"Yeah... you too."

He was giving up nothing, so she hung up, disappointed. Still, she wasn't giving up yet.

That evening over dinner, during a lull in conversation, Julia casually asked the kids, "Does your dad ever bring any of his friends over while you're there?"

"Sometimes," Robert admitted, blatantly sneaking a cilantro-seasoned prawn to Diego, who waited patiently under the table at Robert's feet. Julia's father kept forgetting that Robert hated cilantro.

"Are his friends nice?" prompted Julia.

"Oh," Paige interrupted, turning to William, "that reminds me – remember that girl Izumi? The one who used to work for you as the naturalist?"

Widening, William's eyes flitted briefly to Julia. "Yeah, of course."

"Well, she's one of Dad's friends."

"Oh yeah; she's *sooo* nice!" confirmed Robert. "Sometimes she babysits us."

Paige swatted him lightly. "She doesn't babysit *me*, dufus."

"Yeah, she does," Robert argued. "Last time, Daddy told her not to let you play on the computer."

Paige glowered at her plate. Oblivious, Robert continued, "And Daddy took us to her apartment once."

Julia's stomach lurched, forcing her to set her fork down. "And how was that?"

Not quite grasping her meaning, Robert replied, "Small."

"Only compared to Dad's penthouse," Paige pointed out. "Honestly, I think Dad's dating someone, too. I saw two toothbrushes in his bathroom, and one of them was a pink electric toothbrush. Pretty sure Dad wouldn't buy a pink electric toothbrush. But if he *is* dating someone, I don't know who."

Again, Julia traded knowing glances with William. "Has he ever brought over any other friends?" she asked Paige.

"Yeah; there's his fellow aquarium geeks and marine biology nerds, and even one or two old dudes from his days as a venture capitalist. But Izumi's his only girl friend. I mean – you know. His only friend that's a girl."

The fact that Paige couldn't put two-and-two together and pair her dad with Izumi only confirmed how unusual the pairing would be. Unusual, but far from implausible.

Well, whoever and whatever it was, getting laid on the regular had been good for Kevin. He was much more chill and less sulky. The kids seemed happy and well cared for. And frankly, it had been nice having him back in the city, taking the kids fifty percent of the time. After all, it freed Julia up to spend half her weeknights with William.

William's throat-clearing distracted her from her musings. "Paul, how is retirement so far?" he asked Julia's father.

"Boring as hell," her father growled. Her mother rebuked his mild epithet, and Julia winced. Retirement was a sore topic these days, but William couldn't have known that.

"I keep telling him to volunteer at that AIDS nonprofit his sister Brigid started in the eighties," Julia's mother said. "You know – the one that cooks meals for people living with HIV?"

"Why would I do that?" her father practically roared. "I've never liked that woman, anyway."

Julia's mother reached across the table to pat his hand. "Your sister doesn't work there anymore, remember? She retired and handed the reins over to her daughter."

"I don't even know Maureen," her father stubbornly persisted.

"You don't have to know her to volunteer there, dear."

Julia's father abruptly scraped his chair back, nearly sending it toppling over backwards. "And by the way, you can quit talking to me like I'm a child!"

The rest of them either stared or tried not to stare as he stomped into the house, muttering under his breath. Under the table, Diego scrambled to his feet, nails clacking on concrete as he trotted after Julia's father.

Julia's mother folded her napkin neatly and set it on her plate. With the weary smile of the long-suffering wife, she whispered, "I would, if he'd quit *acting* like a child."

After Julia's mother recruited Paige and Robert to help with the dishes, Julia found herself alone on the patio with William. "So," he said after a moment, aiming a sidelong smirk at her. "That was weird."

Julia burst out laughing. "Yeah."

William slowly nodded, his eyes turning glassy as he grew pensive, until Julia prompted, "Penny for your thoughts?"

"Oh, I was just remembering something your dad once said – that the day you retire is the day you die, or something like that. I see him as the kind of man who needs something to do, and if your parents moved into a place like where my mom lives, they'd have a lot more to occupy their time and their minds."

"I agree, but my parents are in no hurry to leave this house. Every time Alison or I broach the subject, they get defensive and shut it down. Especially Dad."

He grew thoughtful again for a minute. "I know a few months ago, when we first reconnected, you said you have no desire to live in the house you grew up in."

"That's how I felt in May. The only reason I've stayed this long is because of finances. But now that business is booming, I've started looking at the real estate market again, and of course it's only gotten worse."

He peered attentively at her. "So what now?"

She pondered his question for a minute, then begrudgingly admitted, "Now, I'm thinking about making my parents an offer on their house. Either that, or renting it back from them, like your sister does from your mom."

He shifted nervously in his seat. "I've been spending so many nights at Kelly and Pilar's, helping out with my nephews. Thinking long-term, if Kelly and I were neighbors... it might be nice."

He turned to peer evenly at her, and her pulse accelerated. *Thinking long-term,* he had said. *If Kelly and I were neighbors...*

He was imagining a future where he and Julia would live together as a family. And he wanted that family to be within walking distance of Kelly's.

All at once, that was exactly what Julia wanted, too: for their kids to walk to and from each other's houses and attend the same schools. Celebrating holidays together. Enjoying the beach, just around the corner.

Granted, her heart briefly sank to imagine a future where Julia could not offer Ximé and Zuri a little cousin to play with. After all, Robert was five years older than they were.

But it didn't matter: Julia had already made it clear that they could never have another baby, and William had accepted that.

"And also..." William's voice derailed Julia's train of thought. She watched his Adam's apple slide down his throat in a slow gulp, as if he were preparing to say something momentous.

"What is it?" she gently prompted.

"I have to move."

"Move?" Julia's heart thudded behind her sternum. "What, you mean out your apartment?"

He gave a ragged laugh. "Yeah. I was given a month's notice."

"But why?"

"Haze and her son Ash are moving back from Alaska."

"Okay," she said slowly, "but what does that have to do with anything?"

"Well, I mean..." He shrugged. "They need their apartment back."

Flabbergasted, Julia could only stare. "What are you talking about?"

Suddenly understanding, his lips parted in dismay. "Julia. Did I never tell you...?"

"Tell me what?"

"The house I live in belongs to Haze. I live there at reduced rent because I'm her groundskeeper and property manager."

"Oh, that's right! You did mention you live in a friend's house. You just never said it was *Haze's* house."

Almost panicked, he seized her hands. "I'm sorry; I guess it just never came up. I wasn't deliberately hiding anything."

"I believe you, Will," she reassured him, squeezing his hands. "It's not a problem."

He practically deflated with relief. "Thank God. I know, last time..."

She cringed internally, remembering how she had reacted in 2006 when she learned some unsavory details about his past. Specifics that he had never shared of his struggles with addiction, and his past relationships with Haze and Marisa.

I never lied to you, he had said back then. *If you had ever asked me about my past relationships, I would have told you. But really, how helpful or relevant would that have been?*

And of course, he had been absolutely right.

"Last time was the last time," she offered gently. "I was in a bad place, emotionally, when all of that happened. I'm six years older and wiser now. I love and trust you implicitly."

To her shock, his face reddened, and his eyes instantly spilled over with tears. They apparently startled him just as badly, because he gave a shaky, self-conscious laugh and swiped aggressively at them. And that, in turn, opened Julia's own tap.

"You have no idea how good it is to hear you say that," he admitted, his voice strained.

She gathered him up, and they spent the next several minutes letting go of six years of pain, heartbreak, and grief. Julia held on for dear life, rubbing slow, soothing circles over his back. He stroked her hair with an urgency bordering on desperation and planted kisses on the crown of her head.

"William Quinn! I thought your mother told you to stop making her cry!"

Julia's mother filled the doorway, grinning, with a dessert plate in each hand. Her facetious rebuke made them flinch, but rather than break apart, they succumbed to ragged laughter.

"I was going to offer you some of Alison's lemon bars, but I see I'm intruding."

Still chuckling, Julia disentangled herself from William and swiped her cheeks with her forearms. "No, it's okay. We were just wrapping up."

Still red-faced – though now for a different reason – William turned away and scrubbed his eyes. Diego trotted from the house, tongue flopping, and made a beeline for William. He propped his front paws on William's thighs and slurped his cheeks, eliciting more laughter from all of them.

William grabbed Diego's paws. "Is that all I am to you? A human saltlick?"

As Robert and Paige spilled out of the house with their lemon bars, Julia's mother served one to William. Looking up at her, William said, "You know, Paul really seems to enjoy Diego. Maybe he should get a dog of his own."

Overhearing him, Paige gasped excitedly, and Robert pleaded, "Yeah, Grandma! *Pleeeeeease?*"

Julia's mother stilled, pondering a moment. "You know, that's not a bad idea. It's been years since I've seen him smile as much as he does when Diego is around."

Both kids whooped and cheered, until Julia burst their bubble. "Don't get too excited yet, guys. It would be Grandma and Grandpa's dog, not ours."

"Yeah, but we live with them," Robert argued.

"For now," Julia conceded, "but not forever."

Robert's face fell, and for a second, Julia assumed it was at the prospect of no longer living with his grandparents. But he quickly set her straight. "Well, then, can we get our *own* dog?"

Julia's mother cackled, and Julia rumpled Robert's hair, causing it to stick up comically. "We'll see, Tadders." When she looked up again, she found her mother studying her curiously, blinking. Julia tipped her head: a silent question.

Her mother flinched, as if coming out of a daze. "Nothing."

Julia considered pressing her further, but instead, she suggested, "Why don't you guys visit the animal shelter? For that matter, maybe Dad would enjoy volunteering there as a dog walker. It would be a great way to get exercise *and* a shot of doggy-induced serotonin."

Her mother nodded slowly, thoughtfully. "Maybe I'll just sign him up myself and shove him out the door, since he's not likely to take the initiative."

Diego came around to sit at Robert's feet, panting and smiling as he waited for his ration of lemon bar crumbs. "Hey Mom, maybe we can adopt one of Diego's puppies," Robert suggested.

"Boys don't have babies, Tadpole."

"I know, but they can make them," he pointed out sagely.

"Not Diego," William interjected. "He's been snipped."

Robert wrinkled his nose. "What is 'snipped?'"

"Trust me, Tad, you don't want to know."

Amid the laughter that followed, Julia caught her mother studying her again in the same curious, blinking way as before. But her mother's expression quickly cleared, replaced by its typical bland serenity.

~

THAT NIGHT, after William and Diego went home, Julia tucked Robert into bed, then settled at her sewing machine. She was almost finished with her Halloween costume, with over a month to spare. She smiled as she imagined William's reaction to seeing her in it.

She was having a hard time focusing, though. Her earlier conversation with William kept running through her mind.

When she and William reconnected just four and a half months ago, Julia reasoned that it would be at least a year before they even *started* talking about moving in together. And even then, only if he put a ring on it first – proof that some of that Catholic guilt had seeped in, somewhere along the way.

But now, she found herself wondering what they were waiting for. And it reminded her a little too much of the last time she had felt so sure of everything, only to watch it all unravel.

But again, last time was the last time. They were not the same damaged people. They had long since owned their damage, dealt with at least some of it, and were actively working on the rest. This time, they were secure enough to weather the challenges fate flung into their path.

And things really had been going so well. The few times they disagreed, they communicated skillfully and came to a honest resolution, or at least a compromise, that honored each of their needs. And the rest of their time together left her feeling replenished.

Well... except for the lack of sleep.

She grinned just as her mother appeared in the den. "What did I miss?"

Julia smothered her grin and murmured something noncommittal.

One corner of her mother's mouth curved up. "You're thinking about William, aren't you?"

Julia snickered. "Guilty."

"Yeah, I was just thinking about him, too."

"You can't have him," Julia deadpanned.

"Oh, Julia; the last thing I need is another man to take care of. They're worse than kids." Her mother sat on the sofa and patted the cushion beside her. "Sorry for interrupting, but can I borrow a few minutes of your time?"

Julia set her costume aside and joined her mother on the couch.

Her mother took Julia's hand and nodded toward the patio door. "Out there, when you talked about adopting a dog, and you told Robert something about it belonging to your dad and I, but not to you?"

"Yeah?"

"And then you talked about getting your own dog one day?"

Julia's mother had never liked the idea of them moving out. She loved having Julia and her grandkids in the same house, and she was always talking about *that's the way it should be*, or *that's how they did it in the olden days*. Multiple generations living together, under one roof.

Julia loved her parents, warts and all; but living with them as a long-term solution? "Mom, there's not enough space here for all of us," she pointed out gently. "Paige and I are already sharing a bedroom. And one day..."

"When William moves in," her mother finished for her.

Meeting her mother's eyes, Julia slowly nodded. "And I can't expect Paige to share a bedroom with her five-year-old brother."

"I know, honey. That's what I'm saying. The conversation about adopting a dog drove it all home."

"And here's the thing: William just got a one-month notice to vacate his apartment. The friend he rents it from is moving back in."

"And there's no point in expecting him to rent a whole other place, when he could just move in with you."

Her mother stated it like an incontrovertible fact. Julia studied her expression for any sign of disapproval, but to her surprise, she found none. "You think so, too?"

"I do," her mother confirmed, before hastily adding, "The Catholic in me doesn't officially approve, mind you. But the mother in me sees how he lights up when you're in the room. He can't take his eyes off you. And the way he is with the kids... I may not officially approve of him moving in, but I'd question your sanity if you didn't let him."

Julia's laughter was full-throated. "Um, thanks?"

"For what? You're a grown woman. You don't need my blessing."

"But it's nice to have it."

"William has grown up a lot in the last six years, too. Getting his degree, and starting his own business. Getting rid of that damn motorcycle."

Julia barked out a laugh at her mother's rare epithet and didn't bother setting her straight about the circumstances behind the motorcycle's disappearance. Julia had no doubt William would still be driving it, if Mike hadn't stolen it. "But that does mean we have to move out," Julia pointed out.

Julia's mother looked around, taking in her surroundings. Then, she heaved a big sigh. "Not necessarily."

Julia lifted an eyebrow, a tiny pilot light of hope illuminating in her chest.

Turning back to look Julia in the eye, her mother said, "With the kids staying at Kevin's half the time, and you staying with William, your dad and I have really been feeling the emptiness of this house. Besides, we can't keep it up anymore; and I just got word that the Vecchios are moving into Treemont. That leaves only one more two-bedroom unit; and I'd like to have a spare room for the grandkids when they visit."

Julia squeezed her mother's hands. "You mean you and Dad have already decided?"

Her mother huffed out a laugh. "Of course not. This house is your father's hill, and if it were up to him, he'd die on it. But it's not up to him. I'll make him see that moving to Treemont is good for both of us, even if I have to put him in the doghouse first." She waggled her eyebrows. "He won't last three days."

"Mom!"

"What? I would have thought that would give you hope for you and William when you're our age."

Julia grimaced. Even if she wanted to picture her parents getting their groove on in their mid-seventies, she couldn't. In fact, she never could. It seemed more plausible that she and Alison had sprung from their skulls, like Athena. "I can do without that hope, if those are the terms."

Her mother laughed almost gleefully, and suddenly Julia knew who Alison got her ribald sense of humor from.

"Just to clarify..." Julia felt pretty sure of what her mother was hinting at, but she didn't want to be presumptuous. "...how is any of this related to the kids and I moving out?"

Her mother leveled her with a cutting stare. "Do I really have to spell it out?"

"I didn't want to just assume," Julia chuckled. "Here's the thing: I could buy the house from you and Dad, if you prefer. But what if I just rent it back from you, instead? You and Dad would get the income tax benefits, and I get to keep paying your obscenely-low property taxes. Of course, I wouldn't get the tax benefits of home ownership; and you and Dad would have to come up with the money for Treemont from somewhere else."

"What do you think we were planning to do with all that money from the sale of Dunphy's?"

Oddly enough, that hadn't even occurred to Julia. "Really?"

"Of course!"

"Wow. You and Dad could really be living it up right now, if you sold your house on top of all that."

"Julia, with my heart, there will be no living it up," her mother declared, and Julia felt her own heart sink at her fatalistic tenor. "Besides, my version of living it up is staying close to my family and watching you thrive. You, William, and the kids should take the house."

For the third time, Julia's eyes filled with tears. "Wow. I think I've cried more today than I have in my entire life."

"Definitely not. You had colic as an infant."

Julia laughed and reached for her mother, folding her into a tight hug. "I love you, Mom. And not just because you're giving me your house."

"I love you, too, Julie. And not just because you're giving me another grandchild."

Julia jerked back and cocked an eyebrow. "Unless you know something I don't, that's never happening."

Her mother had the audacity to look crushed. "*Never* never?"

"*Never* never."

"Well, then I love you, too, and not just because you're giving me a son-in-law who looks like a young Henry Fonda with bedhead."

"We're not married yet, and you still can't have him."

SATURDAY, SEPTEMBER 29, 2012

The twins came home from the hospital at the end of September, and the following weekend, Julia got to really see and hold them for the first time. Even though they were already two months old, they looked like actual newborns, since it was only two weeks past their original due date.

"I always forget how tiny they are," Julia murmured after Pilar finished nursing Ximé and gently handed her over. Ximé's lids were already sinking as she descended into a milk coma.

"When they were born, I was almost afraid to touch them," Pilar commented. "Their little fingers were so tiny and almost see-through, like fish bones. I was afraid I'd snap them."

William was stretched out on the couch in the Ochoa-Quinns' living room, head resting on a throw pillow at one end, calves propped on the armrest at the other so his bare feet dangled comically. Zuri, the smaller twin, had long since finished her meal. William had promptly scooped her up, and now Zuri was passed out on his chest, her bud-shaped lips forming a tiny O. William looked terrified to move, and Julia chuckled when he shot her an uncertain look – a silent *am I doing it right?*

Julia answered with a tiny nod. Her ovaries practically throbbed at just how right he was doing it. What was it about watching a big, strong, sexy man cuddle a tiny, helpless infant? It almost made her want to go back on her pledge to have no more babies. *Almost.*

Of course, nothing could persuade her to subject herself again to hyperemesis gravidarum, but her heart still ached with something like regret. They would never marvel together over those first ultrasounds. He would never coach her on her breathing, or wipe her forehead in the delivery room, or cry the first time he held his very own child.

Kelly, passing through from the kitchen, dragged Julia out of her daze. "They're here," she whispered, holding up her phone screen by way of explanation.

"Don't worry; I already warned Alison to keep it down," Julia whispered back, not adding that she wasn't sure Alison was capable of lowering her volume. But when the front door swung open to near-total silence, Julia breathed a sigh of relief.

And then she drew a quiet gasp when Mike appeared at the top of the stairs behind Alison. He looked completely different than he had just three months ago, in June. He was almost back to a healthy weight, and his hair was growing back full and dark.

He also looked completely different than he had six years ago, when he was still in the throes of addiction. Of course, colorful and occasionally obscene tattoos still wrapped every inch of exposed skin from his neck down. He still wore a hoop in one nostril, as well as gauge piercings in his earlobes. But he wasn't shifting back and forth with his head on a swivel, like a squirrel on speed; and his black Dead Kennedys tee-shirt and jeans were relatively tame, compared to his historical uniform of silver-studded leather and ripped denim with chains.

His eyes landed immediately on William, and they exchanged tight nods and faint smiles. Then he caught Julia studying him, and Alison weaved her arm through his with a supportive squeeze. He smiled at Julia and mouthed hello, but it wasn't his signature wolfish leer from the past. Julia returned it with a wave and her own friendly smile.

Mike plopped down on a nearby armchair and gently tugged Alison's hand, urging her into his lap. She sat on him at an angle, crossing one knee over the other, and slid her arm around his shoulders. He rested his palm on her thigh, just above her knee; and to Julia's amazement, they looked at each other with something like tenderness. Julia had never seen either of them like this. Julia would have offered Mike a chance to hold Ximé, but for now at least, his arms were full.

At that moment, Zach and Robert tiptoed upstairs with Kelly, whispering excitedly. They crowded around Julia, then William, admiring each baby in turn. Kelly returned to the kitchen to finish dinner, but Pilar lingered in the living room, closely supervising like the first-time mom she was.

Ten minutes later, Kelly announced dinner, and while Robert gently stroked Ximé's black curls, Julia searched the room, frowning. "Where's Paige?"

Robert shrugged as if to say, *I am not my sister's keeper*. So Julia gently handed Ximé off to Pilar, then went to check on her own daughter.

Downstairs, she found the den empty, so she slid the patio door open. Her eyes snagged on a flicker of movement in the rear of the yard. The lot was narrow but deep, so she had to squint a little; but what she saw had her stopping short in her tracks, acid leaping into her throat.

She only caught the tail end, but she thought she saw Paige and Xavier spring apart from each other. Despite that, they still sat very, *very* close – hip-to-hip, in fact – in a patch of clover. They leaned back against the wooden fence, Paige staring over Xavier's shoulder at his phone screen, and it seemed like they were trying very hard to pretend they had been doing that the whole time.

All at once, Julia had two simultaneous epiphanies: first, they were both objectively good-looking kids. And second, although they were still kids, they weren't *kids* – they were thirteen. Xavier was technically younger than Paige, but he was tall and looked considerably older. Historically-speaking, Paige had a weakness for older boys.

Whatever Julia had glimpsed, it was fleeting. Still, as she approached, she resolved to keep a close eye on them.

"Hey guys? Dinner," she called out, just as Kelly and William came downstairs with the first of the serving dishes. As she brushed past William, she whispered, "Keep an eye on those two, will you?"

He shot her a startled look before Julia swept into the house to help serve.

Throughout the meal, Paige and Xavier stayed glued to each other, in their own little bubble; but honestly, there was nothing to see here. Julia knew those two had hit it off as good friends, right from the very start; so she let her guard down. Besides, it was funny to watch Mike get acquainted with his nieces. Alison openly giggled at the panicked look on Mike's face as he gingerly accepted Ximé from her arms.

"She won't crumble to dust," Alison teased. "She's a baby, not an ancient artifact."

"Shut up," he retorted with a good-natured grin, and to Julia's astonishment, he actually *blushed* as his eyes snagged on Alison's.

After Alison coached him on how to cradle Ximé in a football hold, Mike's eyes lifted again to hers, seeking reassurance. She lit up in an answering smile, and they leaned in for a tender kiss.

Julia's sister had long-since made a steadfast vow of childlessness, though certainly not of chastity; so Julia felt pretty sure that's not what this was about. Suddenly, an epiphany bowled Julia over with the wonder of it: this was love, crackling between Alison and Mike. Not just mutual regard. Not just friends with benefits. Not even mere affection.

Love.

And okay – a little lust, too, for good measure. This, Julia acknowledged as their tongues tangled shamelessly for all the world to see. It *was* Alison and Mike, after all.

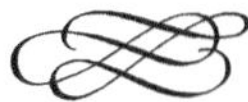

aige and Robert were over the moon when, with Clio's guidance, Julia and William discussed the impending changes: Grandma and Grandpa were moving into the same condo complex as Nonna Quinn. Paige, Robert, and Julia were staying put in the same house; no need to even change schools. And finally – William was moving in.

Granted, they were excited for different reasons – Robert, because he loved William, and his grandparents were still nearby. And Paige, because she would finally have her own room again.

Of course, Julia was excited for her own reasons: no more days or nights apart from William. Their lives and their relationship were moving forward, just like they had always dreamed. Except, of course, that it took nineteen years to get there.

Julia's parents brought their most sentimental belongings and some of their furniture to Treemont, leaving everything else for Julia to deal with as she saw fit. In most cases, Julia sold anything of value, and donated the rest. Her mother's twee taste in decor did not align with Julia's.

During the weeks when Kevin had the kids, Julia helped William pack his Spartan belongings into boxes. With the house now relatively empty, they tore down her mother's old floral wallpaper and repainted. They furnished the house with a blend of William's furniture and Julia's, which had languished in storage for almost a year.

And of course, because Julia did nothing by halves, she had to throw a housewarming party. Not just any housewarming party, but a Halloween-themed costume party with food that looked disgusting, yet tasted delicious. Like Julia's very own kitty-litter cake, complete with Tootsie Roll turds, the ends twisted for maximum authenticity.

By the end of October, Julia desperately needed a break. Luckily, the end of October also brought her birthday; and the Monday night before that, as William slid beneath the covers with her, he murmured, "Clear your calendar next weekend. We have plans."

"But when the kids are with their dad, *you* are my plans," she teased, rolling to face him on her side, already burrowing her hand beneath the waistband of his boxers. "By the way, why are you even wearing these?"

Chuckling, he tugged on her skimpy nightgown. "Why are you even wearing *this?*"

"Because I love the way you take it off," she purred into his ear, delving even further into his boxers.

But he stilled her hand. "I'm serious. We never did make up for the getaway we missed out on when the twins were born. So, I made plans for your birthday."

Her brows lifted. "Really?"

"Of course," he said, his voice growing a little husky as her hand snaked past his and reached its target.

"So," she prompted, planting a soft, sensuous kiss on his lips before continuing, "what are we doing for my birthday?"

"It's a secret," he said, his words turning mushy as she lazily moved her hand along his length.

"No fair," she pouted. "I've literally got your future in my hands. Or at least, I've got your next few minutes in my hands. You had better offer me something in return."

"Oh, I will," he promised against her open mouth, right before silencing her comeback with his tongue.

After a minute, he rolled her on top of him until she straddled his hips, and then he yanked off her skimpy nightgown, exposing her bare breasts to his mouth. "Oooh," she teased in her sultriest tone, "talking about giving me something in return got you all hot and bothered, didn't it?"

He popped off her nipple just long enough to retort, "That, and thinking about the green dress you wore that day."

She lifted an eyebrow. "You mean the sundress with practically no back?"

She gasped in shock when he answered by ripping her lacy thong in two with his bare hands. "That's the one."

Before she could protest the wholesale destruction of her lingerie, he yanked her up toward the headboard and lowered her onto his mouth.

She moaned, rocking against his tongue. "If this is how you react to just thinking about it, I'll definitely be wearing it again next weekend."

Groaning, he rewarded her with the kind of orgasm only he could deliver. The kind that pretzeled her insides and her mind. And afterward, she made sure to return the favor.

Yeah... she was definitely wearing the green sundress next weekend.

*J*ulia was wearing the green sundress.

Maybe that's why there was an urgency to William's driving, as if he were in a hurry to get to... wherever they were going. As much as possible, he held her hand, their fingers interlaced, his thumb caressing hers. That caress zinged through every nerve ending in her body. She repeatedly caught him stealing sidelong glances at her. If she caught him quickly enough, she smiled, and then it was all he could do to keep his own grin from overtaking his face.

She dearly hoped that he wanted to tear her clothes off as much as she wanted to divest him of his.

"Where are we going again?" she tried for the third time that day, then sucked her teeth when he shot her a sidelong stink-eye. "Yeah, yeah, I know – it's a surprise."

Wherever it was, it was north on 101, just like Fox Glade Winery. For half a second, Julia wondered if that was, in fact, exactly where they were headed. But that was impossible. She had never revealed their planned destination because she wanted to save the surprise for another day.

Still, as they passed Healdsburg and approached the exit they would have taken to Fox Glade, Julia's spine tingled.

"You look like you just saw a ghost," William observed.

Julia forcibly rearranged her features into what she hoped was a care-free smile. "Nope! Just still trying to figure out where we're going."

"Hmmm," was his only comment. But the corner of his mouth lifted slightly.

Suddenly, Julia squealed right along with his tires as he jerked the steering wheel to the right, exiting the highway at the last possible second. As they descended the exit ramp, Julia gaped at him, smiling at the same time. "No way!"

He was grinning, but still, he admitted nothing.

"Will! Are you...? Is this...?"

"Am I what?" He shot her an infuriating look of wide-eyed innocence. "Is this what?"

"William Patrick Quinn!"

"Julia Róisín Dunphy."

She made a garbled noise of frustration, but her snickering gave her away. "It is, isn't it?"

"Julia, I really have no idea what you're talking about." But the smirk he was failing to smother told her he knew exactly what she meant. He turned left at the first stop sign off the highway, and from there, they followed a meandering road through vineyard-strewn hill-sides. Julia couldn't remember for sure, but this did seem like the route she had plotted to Fox Glade Winery three months ago.

Finally, after crossing a one-lane bridge over a creek, William steered the Jeep down a dirt road. After that, it was only another quarter of a mile until he slowed in front of a metal gate, on the left.

"This *is* it!" Julia squealed, taking in the inconspicuous sign on the gate announcing the property as *The Fox Den*. "I knew it! But... how did *you* know?"

He grinned at her. "Like I said, Julie, I have no idea what you're talking about."

She swatted his arm as he turned left into the little driveway and stopped in front of the simple, rustic steel gate. "Be serious, Will. How did you find out this was where I was taking you on your birthday?"

"At the housewarming party, I might have mentioned to Aaron that I was looking for something epic to do for your birthday. And he might have asked if we enjoyed our stay at Fox Glade Winery. And I might have said I had no idea what he was talking about. And then it might have all come out about how he hooked you up with a stay here, but we had to cancel when my nieces were born.'"

"When did you find time for this clandestine conversation? I was with you almost the whole party!"

Still grinning, he got out of the car, unlocked the combination padlock, and swung the gate open. After driving through, the Jeep's tires crunched along a lengthy gravel driveway lined with svelte Italian cypresses. Between the gaps in the trees, they glimpsed the orange autumn leaves of the vineyards.

After a minute or two of slow progress along the gravel path, the cypresses yielded to a breathtaking view of gently rolling hills, strewn with orderly rows of grapevines. An unpretentious old white farmhouse with its adjacent tankhouse perched atop one of those knolls, flanked by fruit and olive trees, and more Italian cypresses. Distant tree-covered hills served as a backdrop.

William killed the engine in front of the farmhouse. It was cozy, unadorned, and painted solid white, with peaked gables and steps leading up to a deep front porch. It might have been a hundred years old, or more.

Julia got out of the car and spun in a slow circle, taking it all in, her pleated skirt fluttering in the breeze with her. William came to stand beside her, resting his hand on the bare skin of her back.

Julia closed her eyes. Turned her face up to the warm sunshine. Reveled in the rustle of leaves, the trill of birds, and the buzz of insects. Breathed in the mineral tang of earth, and the sharp zing of chlorophyll.

After a minute, she opened her eyes and followed William's gaze to the vineyards, with their orange and yellow autumn foliage, flanking the rolling fields. There was no other house or human in sight.

"It's perfect," she whispered.

He nodded, his eyes shining, but said nothing. He took her hand, and they turned to admire the house. A white picket fence enclosed a colorful, drought-tolerant garden of native plants, with an old-fashioned birdbath at its center. Silently, he led her around the side of the house to the grove of trees. An oversized hammock stretched between two ancient olive trees. Ripe fruit drooped from apple, orange, and persimmon trees. She plucked a Gravenstein apple, wiped it on the front of her dress, and bit right into it.

Offering it to William, she added, "Here. Just to complete the symbolism."

He laughed and took a bite. Smiling, his mouth still full of apple, he stooped to kiss her. It was a closed-mouth kiss, but she could still taste the apple's sweet juice on his lips.

Still holding hands and sharing the apple, they followed the picket fence all the way around to the back of the house. In the deep, expansive backyard, they spied vegetable gardens. William led her through the gate in the picket fence.

"Look!" Julia gasped, pointing to the tomato vines still bearing fruit, even this late into autumn. They found plum tomatoes, and cherry tomatoes, and colorful heirloom tomatoes in a variety of shapes and sizes.

"Oh, wow. Nothing like a sun-warmed tomato," William reflected, plucking two of the cherry tomatoes and feeding one to Julia. "This reminds me so much of my grandmother's garden. She was a sorceress with plants."

The cherry tomato squirted luxuriantly in Julia's mouth, and she murmured her delight.

"These are good," Willliam agreed after tasting his, "but my grand-mother's were even better. Or at least they are in my memories."

Julia rubbed his back, where his caged albatross still struggled beneath his shirt. The albatross he had gotten all those years ago, after his grandmother died.

The back of the house had its own covered porch with a compan-ionable pair of white wrought-iron chairs on either side of a matching table. Hanging baskets burst with colorful flowers and swung from the rafters in the gentle breeze.

In the very rear of the yard, chicken wire fenced off an area where hens pecked around for their lunch. They found a coop, and William reached into its little door to discover five eggs of varying shapes and colors.

"We should have left the groceries at home," Julia declared. "We can find almost anything we need right here. The only thing missing is a dairy cow."

Outside the fence and some distance to the east stood an old monitor barn, weathered to gray. Beyond that unfurled a wide-open view of neighboring vineyards and pastures, hemmed in by hills.

They stood there in silence for a long time, still holding hands, taking it all in. Watching a red-tailed hawk as it circled over the vineyards. Hearing the soft, contented clucking of the hens and the trills of mockingbirds in the trees. Occasionally, the low of a cow in a distant pasture reached their ears. William stroked Julia's hand with the tip of his thumb, and her heart swelled, overwhelmed by the beauty all around her.

After a while, William reluctantly said, "Speaking of groceries, we'd better get them inside."

Julia nodded, and they wandered silently around to the front of the house. But along the way, they had to pass the old redwood tank house. The original windmill that used to pump water to the tank was still attached to the exterior, at the top. The tankhouse façade bore a double door, and when William tried the handle, he found it unlocked.

Inside, they were delighted to find another whole self-contained tiny house, complete with its own Lilliputian kitchen and bath. A spiral staircase ascended to a low-ceilinged loft with a platform bed, and from there, a ladder led up through a hatch to where the old redwood water tank still sat. They climbed up onto the platform, which offered yet another ideal vantage point for surveying the vineyards.

"This is so cozy!" Julia said once they climbed back down to the loft. "Promise me we'll spend one of our nights here."

Bent at the waist at practically a ninety-degree angle, William couldn't help but grin. "I don't know if I'd fit. But it would be perfect for the kids, if we ever come back with them."

"Share Eden with the kids? Sacrilege!"

He laughed as he followed her back down the spiral staircase and outside. At the farmhouse, they retrieved the grocery bags and coolers from Julia's trunk. William opened the gate in the picket fence, and Julia followed him through the garden and up the front steps to the porch. It smelled delightfully of old redwood, and beneath her shoes, it made the distinct resonant sound of antique floorboards.

The front door was already unlocked, and on the other side, they found themselves in a little entry hall with slightly worn hardwood floors. To the left was a sitting room with a small library; to the right was a parlor with a fireplace; and straight ahead, a staircase ascended to the second story.

They followed the hallway beyond the bedrooms flanking either side. A dining room opened into the kitchen.

The decor and furnishings were antique, rustic, and a bit eclectic, but never gaudy or precious. The walls were either painted a clean white, or covered in muted, block-print wallpaper.

They exclaimed over the kitchen, a relic from the thirties with black and white checkerboard floors, white cabinets, and a vintage Wedgewood range. Even the old General Electric icebox remained, with its Art Deco stylings.

After storing the groceries, they retrieved their suitcases from the Jeep and deposited them on the white matelassé bedspread in the primary bedroom. Julia drew aside the flowing white curtains and flung open the windows to admit the light, sounds, and smells.

After unpacking, Julia returned to the front porch to lean over the railing and survey her temporary realm. She closed her eyes. Turned her face up to the sky. Breathed in the sunshine-tinged perfume of her surroundings.

William came to stand close behind her. As if drawn by a magnet, he rested his hand on the bare skin of her back, just below the back tie of her sundress. He said nothing, but she was all too keenly aware of his fingertips as they traced her spine, up and down the ridge of her back.

Opening her eyes, she gazed out again at the panorama and whispered, "It's just so beautiful."

"Beautiful," he echoed.

She turned her head and found him staring, not at the view, but at her. When their eyes met, he drew a sharp, ragged breath, releasing it just as raggedly; and her pulse quickened at the look on his face. It was a look that encompassed so much at once. His forehead creased, as if with some herculean effort. Finally, he summed it up in a near-whisper: "You are so beautiful, and I love you so much, that it almost hurts to look at you."

She laughed softly. "I'm not quite sure how to take that."

"Take it as me still pinching myself that you're even here. With me."

Her heart turned somersaults and hammered away at her sternum. Still behind her, William slid his arms around her waist, took her hands from the porch railing, and held them in his own. He rested his chin on the crown of her head and spent a long time looking at their hands clasped together, touching her fingers. Brushing his palms across hers.

She did not know how long she watched their hands and fingers slide along each other, like birds engaged in a courtship dance. She saw the knife and burn scars from all the years he had spent cooking in her father's kitchen, waiting for her to come back to him. Her chest flooded with a familiar warmth that she had always known with him; and yet this time she feared it might overwhelm the confines of her heart – fill it to bursting. She couldn't even draw enough breath. She thought it would consume and subsume her.

"This place really is Eden," William murmured finally.

"Yes," she sighed. "Except, I'm getting hungry. I don't think they ever got hungry in Eden, did they?"

"Yes, they did. Remember?"

"Oh, right! That stupid apple again. It ruined everything, didn't it?"

"It didn't ruin this place, apparently. Which is how I know we found Eden again. Who knew it was in California this whole time?"

"Well, that settles it – you *can* get hungry in Eden. Because I'm ravenous."

He touched the mermaid pendant lying against her chest, kissing her tenderly. "I have a solution for that."

He winked and left her there, feeling the breeze caress her skin, listening to him rattling around in the kitchen. Eventually, she settled onto the porch swing until he returned, carrying the picnic basket and handing her the blanket. He led her around the house and into the little orchard. At his prompting, she spread the blanket on the ground in the shade of an ancient olive tree, and they savored the lunch he had packed – fruit and cheese of all kinds, crostini and salami and prosciutto. Olives that they plucked straight from the branches shading them. They washed it all down with sparkling Italian mineral water and a twist of lime from a nearby tree.

Afterward, they climbed into the hammock and dozed off, their limbs entangled. When they woke, by some unspoken understanding, they unbuttoned and untied each other, right there in the hammock. Migrating back to the picnic blanket, they shed their clothes and made love under the olive tree.

Later, as light retreated from the sky, they sat on the front porch swing and admired the palette that the setting sun painted over the vineyards. William cooked dinner, which they enjoyed by candlelight at the dining table. Afterward, they retired to the back porch to marvel at the heavy stars that seemed to hang directly over their heads. Not even the full moon's light could blot them all out. William discovered a telescope on the back porch, and they spent a long time gazing at the celestial spectacle.

They bathed each other in the clawfoot tub, which was cavernous enough for both of them and sported an old-fashioned hand-held shower head. She sat between his legs and leaned back against his chest, luxuriating in the bubbly scented water, resting her head on his shoulder.

"Happy birthday, my sweet love," he whispered into her ear.

"This has been the best birthday of my life," she murmured, turning her eyes up to his. "Thank you for this. All of it."

He kissed her tenderly. "I've loved every single minute so far, as much as you have. And there's more to come."

She sat up, twisted her body a bit to face him. Touched his face, and said, "I love you so much more than you can possibly know."

"I love you, too," he whispered. "Every bit as much."

But she shook her head. "No, I don't think I can ever find the right words to express the love and gratitude I feel for you."

His eyebrows lifted. "Gratitude?".

"For just having you back in my life. In *our* lives."

He touched her chin. Made her look him in the eye. Brushed his hand over her cheek, and whispered, "If it's even one tiny part of what I feel for you and our little family, it's enough."

TUESDAY, OCTOBER 30, 2012

*W*hen William woke Julia with a mimosa mocktail, she felt like she had slept better than in decades. She soon understood why when she saw sunlight pouring through the curtains and glanced at the clock on the bedside table.

She sat bolt upright. "Oh my God! Why did you let me sleep so late?"

"It's only nine," he laughed softly.

"But this is our last day! I want to savor every last second of daylight."

"Resting *is* savoring," he pointed out, brushing the mussed-up hair from her forehead and kissing her there. "You deserve rest, sweetheart."

"*You* didn't sleep in."

"I'm used to waking up at four in the morning, remember? Getting up at seven-thirty felt indulgent. Besides," he added with a teasing smirk and a light smack on her bare butt, "*someone* around here has got to feed us."

She lunged to smack him right back, but he dodged her every attempt. In the end, she lay sprawled out in bed, flushed with laughter, naked for his viewing pleasure. But there was no time for other forms of pleasure, because he had cooked a frittata from eggs the hens laid. He served it on the little white wrought iron table on the back patio.

After that, they spent the day much as they had the previous one – taking long, aimless walks. Harvesting fruit from the orchard and vegetables from the garden. Scattering feed for the chickens, and gathering their eggs. Canoodling in the porch swing and watching the bees and butterflies pollinate the garden out front. Napping in the hammock to the serenades of songbirds. Cooking and eating lunch together.

And of course – sex. Lots and lots and *lots* of sex.

Sex bent over the front porch railing and under the olive tree. Sex on the kitchen counter and in the bathtub. By the end of the day, the sheer volume of sex had reduced Julia to an achey, trembling, waddling wreck. And she was by no means out of shape.

Throughout the day, William snapped so many photos of her that she began to wonder what he could possibly do with them all. Photos of her on the porch swing, crocheting Christmas gifts for Ximé and Zuri. In the hammock with a book, her leg dangling over the side. In the front garden, cutting flowers for their table. In the vineyard, sunhat in hand, her hair blowing loose from her braid, her face without a speck of makeup.

She had to admit – they were great photos.

"Are you going to take pictures of anything besides me?" she teased.

"You're my muse," he replied simply, snapping another photo of her at the white wrought iron table on the back porch. She was sipping a glass of lemonade made from Meyer lemons plucked right from the tree. "The camera worships you, you know."

"Correction – *you* worship me. And it shows in how pretty you make me look in photos."

"No, sweetheart," he said, coming in for a kiss, "that's all you. You're just that beautiful."

"You're smooth with your words," she murmured, kissing him back, "but I'd also love to have some photos to remember this place by after we go home."

So he reluctantly turned his lens on the house, the grounds, and the colorful autumn vineyards. As afternoon waned into evening, Julia spied him in the sitting room, scrawling in the guest book on the coffee table. She peeked over his shoulder and smiled poignantly. He had written, *May I suggest you rename this place Eden?*

"Can you believe Aaron's daughter Rina actually lives here?" Julia came to sit on the arm of the upholstered chair he occupied. "If I lived here, I would never rent it out."

Julia finished signing her own name and set the guest book back on the coffee table. Then William pulled her into his lap, but when his eyes met hers, his smile faded quickly.

"You're sad," he observed.

To Julia's dismay, a lump rose in her throat, and her field of vision swam. To hide it, she forced a laugh. "I'm just not ready to return to the real world. This has been such an amazing little love nest."

He squeezed her. "I'm not ready to leave, either. But we can come back."

Despite her best efforts, the tears spilled over. Forcing another shaky laugh, as if to say *How silly am I*, she swiped at them impatiently. "How? It was so much hassle just to make this happen. I mean, it was supposed to be my weekend with the kids, and for some reason, Kevin is never available anymore to take the kids when it's not his week. Besides, I can't imagine this place comes cheap."

"Cheap, no; but it's maybe not as expensive as you think." He tenderly wiped her tears with his thumb, his eyes flitting back and forth between hers. "It wasn't that much of a hassle. Your sister and Paige have fun together. I bet Alison wouldn't mind hosting more sleepovers with her. And my mom and Kelly were thrilled at the chance to get to know Robert some more. I'm sure he's having a blast at Kelly's with Xavier and Zach."

"I know; but that's all kind of irrelevant, anyway."

A furrow of confusion notched between his brows. "What do you mean?"

She played with his shirt collar. "I mean, we're both small business owners, and our schedules rarely sync. Weekends are your biggest days, so it's not like you can afford to take them off on anything like a regular basis. And I work during the week. I'm not complaining, mind you," she added quickly, stroking a fingertip along his jaw. "I'm just saying, that's the reality of our situation."

"Julie, sweetheart, I'm not as poor as you must think," he chuckled softly, threading the fingers of one hand through hers while circling her waist with his other arm. "I can afford to block off a few weekends per year. Sure, in general, we'll have to plan those at least six months in advance, but I can swing that."

She lifted an eyebrow at him. "Really?"

"I can even afford to block off an entire week," he added. "Maybe not more than once a year, but I can do it."

She considered this for a few moments, staring blindly into a corner of the room, chewing her lip as he traced slow circles over her back with his palm. Finally, she turned to look him in the eye. "You know what? You're right. We shift things around and make compromises. We do whatever it takes to make things work."

"Exactly. And that means from now on, I'll be much more transparent with my finances."

"Me too," Julia vowed. "We definitely should have done that before we moved in together, but at least we're doing it now. I mean, we're partners now, in every way but the piece of paper."

For a moment, he gave her an odd sort of look, and she cringed when she registered what she had just alluded to. But he only cupped the nape of her neck in the palm of his hand and drew her in for a tender kiss.

An hour or so later, as the sun began setting over the vineyards, William appeared on the front porch, where Julia had installed herself in the swing with a book.

"Julie, will you come with me for just a minute?"

She looked up at him in surprise, but then she saw the sly smile on his face. Her heart thumping, she set her book aside and hopped up to accept his offered hand, anticipating that he would lead her to the bed.

But instead, he led her down the front porch steps and through the garden. She followed him out the gate in the picket fence and around the side of the house. He stopped right underneath the ancient olive tree where they had picnicked and made love, and took both of her hands in his.

She looked around for a blanket, but saw none. At a loss, she peered up at him quizzically, waiting.

His forehead creased, and he seemed to be grasping for the right words. "I didn't understand why at the time, but for some reason, I just felt compelled to bring this with me. And now I know why."

"Bring what?" she said, searching again and still spying nothing out of the ordinary.

Then he dropped down onto one knee and pulled a velvet ring box out of his jacket pocket. "Let's try this one more time."

Gasping, she put her hand to her mouth, and touched his shoulder with her other hand to steady herself.

He smiled and said, "I can tell I don't even have to ask, but I will anyway." He opened the box and showed her the ring. "Julia, will you marry me? Will you, finally, be my wife?"

"Yes!" she squealed, and found herself the trope, crying at the same time. "Yes, yes, yes!"

Beaming, he took the ring out of the box. It was a rose gold claddagh ring, filigreed with a Celtic knot pattern. Two hands clasped a crown-topped, heart-shaped diamond in the center.

"I did a little reading beforehand," he explained a bit shyly, slipping it onto her left hand with the crown pointing inward and the tip of the heart pointing outward. "You wear it facing this way when we're engaged. And you wear it with the crown pointing out when we're married."

She spent a while looking at it, swiping at the tears that streamed down her cheeks. "It's so gorgeous."

"Yeah," he admitted, smiling up at her proudly. "But not as gorgeous as you."

She tugged on him then, beckoning him to his feet, and he gathered her up and kissed her.

"Are you really sure?" she whispered.

"Julie, you've given me new life, in every sense. I've never been so sure about anything in my entire life."

"Me neither," she admitted. "My God, I just can't believe this is real. I love you so much."

He nuzzled the hair on the back of her head and kissed her, again and again. After a while, she touched the side of his face and murmured, "When do you want to do it?"

Cautiously, he said, "When do *you* want to do it?"

"As soon as possible," she replied without a moment's hesitation.

He smiled and squeezed her hands. "I'd like our families there."

She beamed up at him, and at the sight of it, his entire being glowed with joy.

"Where?" she asked.

"The Fisherman's Chapel, of course."

"I was hoping you'd say that."

"Small and intimate. Just our immediate families, and maybe my friend Niall, if that's okay."

"I'd like to invite Aaron and my cousin Holly, too."

Smiling warmly, he kissed her again. "We should be able to pull that off pretty soon, without too much hassle."

"Oh no, if it's a wedding you want, it's going to be plenty of hassle, no matter what," she laughed. But she kissed him again, then spent some more time looking at the ring on her finger. He still held her hands in his own, his thumbs caressing her fingers.

Then it occurred to her to wonder, "How are we going to break this to the kids? When we get home, they'll eventually notice the ring on my finger."

"I have a confession to make. While you were out front reading, I went into the backyard and called the kids."

"What?!"

Laughing, he explained, "I called my mother to speak to Robert. And then I called Alison, for Paige. I told them I was thinking about asking their mother to marry me, and I asked for their permission."

"You did not!" But she was smiling.

"I did," he laughed.

"What did they say?"

"They said yes."

"So now I guess your mom and Alison know, too?"

"And Kelly. And your parents."

Her jaw dropped, but she was still smiling. "My *parents*?"

"Of course. I called your dad to ask for your hand."

"Oh, he would have been a complete sucker for that," she snickered.

"I think so, because he also gave his blessing. Actually, to be precise, he said, 'It's about fucking time.'"

Laughing heartily, she reached for him. They spent a while kissing each other, smiling giddily into each other's faces.

It was astonishing how she could never get enough of him, and not just sexually. She never grew bored of his company, even when all they did was sit on a porch swing for an hour like a couple of geezers. She never failed to delight in the thoughtful things he did for her, both great and small, that always hit the mark. And she never tired of finding sweet things to do for him in return.

And yeah – she would never get sick of looking at him, either. His smile was a hard-won prize, but once she coaxed it from him, it was the visual equivalent of a choir of angels singing. And she seemed to have a special talent for coaxing it from him.

And his eyes – oh dear God, those beautiful, intelligent eyes. So intensely blue and full of light that they almost didn't seem real. They gazed down at her with a tenderness he reserved exclusively for her. They had always been her window into his heart, and they still overthrew her.

She thought about all of this as she pulled him even closer, deepened their kiss, and placed her hand on his backside. As she detected the evidence of his arousal, pressing into her belly.

But after a minute, he pulled away. With an exquisitely pained look, he said, "I should probably start making dinner. Don't you think?"

Julia hung her head in mock wretchedness. Laughing, he took her hand and led her back into the house.

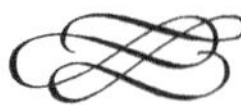

They came home the next morning to an empty house, since the kids were at school. Normally, Julia wouldn't have had time or inclination to throw a pity party over the end of their getaway, because it was Halloween. But for the first year ever, Paige was declining to go trick-or-treating, or even to dress up in costume.

Of course, she was thirteen now, but Julia knew of several thirteen-year-olds who still trick-or-treated. It felt poignant that Paige now believed herself to be too old and too cool for trick-or-treating.

Nevertheless, after months of trustworthy behavior on Paige's part – even with occasional access to electronics, which Paige used to manage Julia's social media accounts – Julia had agreed to allow Paige to stay home by herself while the rest of them went trick-or-treating. In exchange, they would leave a bowl of candy outside, and Paige agreed not to answer the door to anyone.

"Do you still refuse to do the costume thing?" Julia blurted to William after unloading the car and unpacking.

"Normally, yes. But this year, I'm making an exception – for Robert."

"Oh, I see; I've moved down in the pecking order," she teased him.

He smiled and kissed her. "What are you going to be this year?"

She poked him in the chest. "You, sir, will just have to wait and see."

With a hopeful look, he guessed, "A mermaid?"

Julia laughed. "I never want to spoil that precious memory for you by trying to recreate it. Especially at my age."

William scoffed. "What are you talking about? You're the hottest mermaid in the sea at any age."

She laughed again, and drew him closer for another, longer kiss. "The kids will be home from school by three-thirty. Let's plan to greet them at the door in costume. And don't disappoint me."

Knowing they would need every minute between now and then, Julia enlisted William to help set up the rest of the Halloween display in front of the house. Of course, she had already decorated a bit, but she always saved the best for the day of. Afterward, she banished him to the in-law unit while she donned her costume. After putting the finishing touches on her makeup – all except her lipstick – she wandered downstairs again to find him on the couch with his laptop.

But with her first glimpse at his costume, she stopped short in the doorway. "No way!"

He looked up, and his eyes instantly widened.

He was dressed in full pirate garb from head to toe, complete with cuffed blouse and doublet. When he set his laptop aside and stood, she saw the cuffed leather boots over black breeches, the belt with its various pouches, a cutlass with a leather scabbard, and even a pewter mug dangling from one of the belt's many frogs. He had even brushed black dye into his beard and mustache to match the curly wig hanging below his tricorn hat.

Meanwhile, his eyes drank her in from top to bottom, and back up again. "Looks like we had the same idea."

Julia burst out laughing now. "For Robert?"

He nodded.

"Okay, but do you know *who* I am?"

"Besides sexy pirate girl? Nope."

Julia posed like a game show hostess. "Jack Sparrow, meet Gráinne O'Malley!"

"I'm not Jack Sparrow; I'm Bluebeard."

Julia's eyes widened. "And I guess this is where I return your engagement ring, you uxoricidal maniac."

He burst out laughing and came forward to kiss her. She had held off on applying her lip color for this exact reason. She knew that once he got a look at her in this costume, he wouldn't be able to keep his eyes or his lips off her.

"Well," Julia murmured when he finally broke the kiss, "Gráinne and Bluebeard were from two different centuries, so they never would have met, anyway."

"Bluebeard is a fictional character, Julie."

While she laughed, he took a step back and held her by the shoulders, once again raking his eyes up and down her body. She wore a tightly-laced green bodice over a white cap-sleeved blouse, and a short, layered brown skirt with an asymmetrical hem. Julia did not have a bounty of cleavage, but the corset lifted what she did have practically all the way to her chin. She had elaborately braided her hair, and a tricorn hat of her very own crowned her head.

"Uncle Tim would roll over in his grave at the historical inaccuracy of this," Julia admitted. At William's frown of confusion, she added, "Did I ever tell you he was a history teacher before he opened the aquarium shop?"

"No."

"He was, until he got fired for banging a student."

William reeled back in shock. "Really?"

"Uh huh – specifically, my Uncle Rob."

"Oh my God," William murmured. "You never told me that."

"I never knew, myself, until my Aunt Brigid told me a few years ago. It was quite the scandal. Anyway, Tim was positively anal retentive about historical accuracy. But Uncle Rob would tell him to stop being such a bitch, because the look on your face is totally worth it."

"Well then, I owe one to your Uncle Rob." He wiped his hand down his nose, mouth, and beard while stealing one last, lecherous glance at her body. "How are you feeling right now, by the way?"

Julia tilted her head. "Feeling?"

"I remember what today is for you."

Her mouth twisted into a poignant smile. Halloween *was* complicated, ever since Uncle Rob passed away exactly nineteen years earlier. Growing up, it had always been Julia's favorite holiday – a time to show off the costume and makeup skills she had learned from Rob. After all, Rob's first love, besides writing, had been theater.

"It wasn't until Paige was old enough to trick-or-treat that I finally got it," Julia said quietly. "Rob wouldn't have wanted me to mark the day with anything other than total, unrestrained, irreverent joy. Ever since then, I try to honor him by making Halloween as epic as possible."

"Hence the graveyard in front of our house."

Julia laughed. "He would be so proud of me."

She took his hand and led him out front to the spectacle, where they would wait for Paige and Robert to get home from school. They had draped astroturf over the driveway, then strewn it with fake headstones and zombie heads emerging from the ground. Seated around a cafe table, a pair of skeletons with flashing red eyes played poker. On the table in front of each skeleton sat a cheap plastic pint glass stuffed with Halloween candy, and Julia had set a gigantic bowl of Halloween candy in the center of the table. A couple of speakers, hidden in their tiny excuse for a flowerbed, were set to broadcast an epic Halloween soundtrack. And right beside those, a projector would throw ghostly images against the entire front elevation of the house.

"I think the spider really ties it together," William reflected, peering warily at the wedge of glow-in-the-dark webbing that stretched from the upstairs window all the way to the edge of the sidewalk. Perched in the center was a gigantic papier-mâché arachnid that Julia and the kids had constructed the previous weekend.

"That's not a spider, that's Shelob."

He nodded, serious as a heart attack. "Now *I'm* the one having second thoughts about that ring."

As she laughed, William donned his eye patch and his hook; and only a few minutes later, Robert was coming up the street with his friend Jordan and Jordan's mom. Normally, Julia's mother was there to greet Robert and Paige when they got home from school, but today, she had the day off. The residents at Treemont were hosting some kind of Halloween thing for the neighborhood kids.

The instant Robert spotted the waiting spectacle, he crowed and came barreling down the sidewalk. Then Jordan spotted it, too, and took off after Robert.

"Mommy! Will!" Robert screamed on repeat, running back and forth between them and each decoration in turn.

"I think we broke him," Julia murmured aside to William, who put his fist to his lips to stifle a laugh.

Jordan was no less amped up as he pleaded for candy. Julia told him to ask his mom, so as soon as she caught up, Jordan bombarded her with a string of Cantonese. His mom smiled and held up one finger. Once she and Jordan, already devouring his single bite-sized Snickers, crossed the street to their own house, Julia turned to Robert.

"Let's get you into your costume, Tadpole."

"I'm not Tadpole today," he protested. "I'm the Dread Pirate Robert."

"As you wish," Julia quipped, then steered him inside to his bedroom, where she helped him get ready. She knew he could do it mostly, if not entirely, on his own, but it would take longer. Paige would be home any minute now, and she wanted them to be ready.

Sure enough, they returned outside just as Paige appeared at the end of the block. Julia lifted her hand to wave, but her breath caught in her throat, and her hand froze halfway to its destination.

Xavier was walking Paige home.

Granted, as they turned down the block, there was nothing suspicious to see. They kept plenty of space between them. They both looked down at the sidewalk, Xavier gripping the straps of his backpack as he listened to whatever Paige was saying.

Sensing Julia's tension, William rested a hand on her shoulder. "They're just walking home from school together," he whispered.

"Your house is three blocks away," she whispered back, because she still thought of it as William's house, even though it hadn't been for sixteen years. "And it's in the opposite direction from the bus stop."

Tension creeped into the hand on her shoulder, and she turned in time to catch the annoyance flashing through William's eyes. "They're just friends, Julie."

But she didn't have time to analyze that before Robert called out to Paige and Xavier and ran down the sidewalk to greet them. Instantly,

Paige and Xavier froze in place with what looked an awful lot to Julia like guilty faces.

Paige raked a gaze of alarm over Julia, William, and the Halloween display. Cringing, she unleashed the timeless refrain of mortified teens everywhere: *"Mooooooom!"*

William squeezed Julia's shoulder once. "I've got this."

While William defused the situation, Julia summoned Robert back inside the house under the pretense of repairing a ripped seam in his costume. When the front door swung open again, Paige's angry footsteps stomped upstairs, and then Julia heard William's careful tread in the den.

"All done, Tadpole," she murmured, tying off the last stitch in her fake repair. "It's still a bit too early for trick-or-treating. Maybe you can practice your guitar while I finish getting ready."

Robert ran upstairs to do just that, while Julia joined William on the sofa in the in-law unit. He crossed his arms over his chest, pinching his mouth with one hand and regarding her with an unreadable expression. She waited, fidgeting with her fingernails, until finally, William dropped his hand to his lap.

"He was just walking with her. You remember how close our houses are. It's not that far out of his way."

"Is this the first time he's ever walked home with her like that?"

William blinked. "I didn't ask. Does it matter?"

Hot acid rose into her throat, and Julia shifted uncomfortably in her seat. "Both times she ran away, it was with a boy."

His eyes softened. "I know, sweetheart. I know what a huge trauma that was, I really do."

A frown etched into Julia's forehead. "Will, I know you believe there's nothing going on between Paige and Xavier. When you say Xavier is a good kid, I believe that is your honest experience of him, and I have no evidence otherwise. But if I've learned anything in life, it's to trust my gut. It's almost always right; but even if it isn't, I'm still going to press pause and figure out why my gut is sending false alarm bells. Nine times out of ten, it's because they aren't false."

William studied Julia sadly, but behind the sadness loomed a tinge of something else. Something almost resembling... irritation?

He placed his hand on her elbow. "Julie... maybe now would be a good time to go find your uncle's stone."

Julia sat stunned for a moment as heat flared through her face and chest. Her eyes stung ominously, but she tamped down the threatening tears and squeezed both hands between her knees.

Out of the corner of her eye, Julia could see that William was watching her keenly. She took a minute to pace her breathing and use one of the grounding techniques Clio had taught her: five things she could see, four she could hear, three she could feel, two she could smell, and one she could taste. It was a strategy that, for her, never failed to bring her back to center.

Finally, in a steady voice, she said, "I don't need my uncle's stone. When you said that, I felt like you were trivializing what my intuition has been telling me. Whether my intuition turns out to be right or wrong, I'd like to know that when I share it, you'll at least not invalidate it."

She watched the lump rise and fall in his throat as he stared across the room, digesting her words. Finally, he dragged his eyes back to hers, his expression unreadable. "I want to finish this conversation, but now probably isn't the right time. Can we talk about it after Robert goes to bed?"

After a moment's hesitation, Julia nodded; but still, she felt her heart splitting right down the center. It was their first Halloween together as a family, and only one day after William's proposal. It was supposed to be a happy occasion, but instead, she was going to have to compartmentalize her hurt feelings and put on a brave face, for Robert's sake.

Thankfully, William did the same as they walked the three blocks to Kelly and Pilar's house. There, they met up with Kelly and Zach. Kelly wore Ximé in a sling, and Zach wore an elf costume.

"I'm not just any elf," Zach explained when Julia marveled over it. "I'm the Keebler elf."

Julia laughed, and William asked, "Why the Keebler, elf, buddy?"

"Because he makes my favorite cookies," Zach replied, peering sideways at William as if the answer should have been obvious.

Aside to Kelly, Julia inquired, "Where is everyone else?"

"Pilar is staying behind with Zuri and Xavier," explained Kelly.

"Oh, so you have one of those, too, huh?"

Kelly lifted an eyebrow. "One of what?"

"A thirteen-year-old who's too cool now for trick-or-treating," replied Julia.

Kelly grinned knowingly, but it did little to disguise the same poignant feelings Julia was having.

Before they departed, Pilar came to the door with little Zuri in her own sling. "Where do you think you're going?" she demanded of Julia. When Julia froze, startled, Pilar laughed. "I'm not letting you go anywhere until you show me the ring!"

As she arranged her features into a smile and held out her hand, Julia studiously avoided looking at William. Pilar seized Julia's hand and squealed all the right things, until Zach groaned, "Mom, come on! Let's go!"

After bidding farewell to Pilar, the rest of them crisscrossed the neighborhood. Along the way, they joined up with Rowan, her mom, and her two dads. But before Robert's jack-o-lantern bucket was even halfway full, he was already cranky and rubbing his heavy eyelids. From her sling against Kelly's chest, Ximé made ominous noises suggestive of hunger.

"I'd better get this butterball home to her mamí," Kelly observed.

When Zach protested, Rowan's parents gamely agreed to take him along and deliver him safely home when they finished. Then Julia, William, and Robert began the trek home, until Robert cried that his feet were hurting. Julia relieved him of his jack-o-lantern bucket, William swept him up, and Robert wrapped his little legs around William's waist. A minute later, he rested his head on William's shoulder, sucking on his middle and ring fingers. And a minute after that, he was sound asleep.

It should have been a sweet, touching moment, but Julia's heart ached to remember her earlier disagreement with William. And she could tell, from the way he avoided her eyes and the silence he kept, that he knew.

Finally, they reached home to find the bowl of candy out front thoroughly ransacked. Julia placed Robert's jack-o-lantern bucket inside of the bowl and took them both with her as she unlocked the front door. William silently carried Robert into the in-law unit, making a beeline for Robert's bedroom.

Meanwhile, Julia tiptoed upstairs to check on Paige. The lights were on in the living room, but Paige was nowhere to be found. The kitchen was dark, but Julia checked there anyway before setting the Halloween candy on the table and making her way to what was now Paige's room. It was the same room she used to share with Julia.

But no light escaped from beneath Paige's door. Julia glanced at her phone, confirming it was only 6:45 – far too early for Paige to be asleep. So she tiptoed downstairs again and quietly poked her head into Robert's room, just long enough to see William tucking Robert under the covers, and to confirm that Paige wasn't downstairs, either.

Increasingly alarmed, Julia slid open the patio door and searched the backyard. Still no Paige.

Closing her eyes, fending off panic with several slow breaths, Julia considered. Surely Paige wouldn't be in Julia's bedroom, would she?

Then Julia remembered that she hadn't actually checked inside of Paige's bedroom. Heading upstairs again as quietly as possible, she opened Paige's door and flipped on the light.

Julia wasn't sure if the screams came from herself or Paige. Maybe they both screamed at the same time.

Or maybe they came from Xavier, lying in bed with Paige. Except they weren't just *lying* in bed.

The next thing Julia knew, Xavier was out of the bed on his own power. Xavier was by no means a small boy, but after landing in the corner of Paige's room, he cowered in a fetal position and smacked his hands over his ears.

Then Paige was on her feet, shouting words that Julia's brain couldn't decipher.

Suddenly William filled the doorway, reeling in shock at the scene before him. He quickly turned away when his eyes landed on Paige.

From somewhere in the house, Robert's cries were getting closer. William ran to head him off before he could see anything.

Finally, Julia 's brain cobbled together enough sense to notice that Paige and Xavier were still in their underwear. Xavier rocked side-to-side, his knees drawn up to his chest, his forehead resting against them. His hands still covering his ears.

Julia seized her daughter by the shoulders, scanning for any signs of trauma. "What happened?" she demanded, trying very hard not to freak out.

"Nothing!" shouted Paige, self-consciously wrapping her arms around herself.

Julia could hear William somewhere in the house, trying to settle Robert. *Somebody* needed to tend to Robert, because Julia was not going to turn her back on this situation. Not even for a second.

Julia struggled to control her shaking hand as she jerked her pointer finger across the hall at the bathroom. "In there," she ordered Paige, her voice quavering.

"Mom, I'm sorry, just... please don't call the cops on Xavier," pleaded Paige. "That's the worst thing you could do."

Julia blinked at her several times.

"He's a black boy with Asperger's," Paige whispered, her eyes pleading with Julia to understand. "How do you think *that* will go over?"

Julia finally snapped out of her panic-induced fog. She nodded slowly as understanding unfolded in layers. "I wasn't planning to," she hedged. The truth was, Julia hadn't even gotten that far in her thought process. "Just wait for me in the bathroom, please."

Paige heaved a sob of relief. Turning to Xavier, she said through her tears, "I'm sorry, Xave. I'm so sorry." Then, without meeting Julia's eyes, she brushed past into the bathroom.

"Xavier," Julia said, moving toward him, only to freeze when he flinched. "Xavier," she repeated, gentling her voice as much as possible. It didn't matter that he and Paige had been fooling around – at least, not in *this* moment. Slowly, carefully, she gathered his clothes from the floor. "I'm putting your clothes here, right beside you. I'm leaving the room now so you can get dressed."

Xavier gave no sign he had heard. He continued rocking side-to-side with his hands over his ears, his body curved into itself. Julia's head snapped up when she found William standing behind her.

"Robert's watching *Alice in Wonderland*," he said calmly. "What happened?"

Julia stood slowly, her eyes still on Xavier. She couldn't look at William. "They were... they were in bed, and..."

William pressed his lips together and took a moment to process. "I'll take care of Xavier. Go take care of Paige."

"Kelly?" prompted Julia, still not meeting William's eyes.

"Texted her. She's on the way. I unlocked the front door so she could let herself in."

There was nothing left to say. Julia gathered Paige's clothes from the floor and crossed the hall to the bathroom, where she knocked lightly on the door. "It's Mom. I have your clothes."

No reply came, so after a moment's hesitation, Julia opened the door a crack. Paige sat on the toilet lid, her knees pulled up to her chest, her arms wrapped around her legs. Lowering her eyes, Julia tossed Paige's clothes onto the bathroom floor. "Paige? Go ahead and get dressed, please."

Julia closed the door again and turned just in time to find William standing in Paige's doorway. His hand was on the doorknob.

"I'm going to close the door and sit here with Xavier for a while," he whispered. His eyes landed on hers, but the look he gave her was unreadable.

Julia's heart twisted itself into knots, and every knot represented another regret over how the night had turned out. But she nodded her understanding.

When Julia had gotten her breathing under control, she lightly rapped on the bathroom door. Paige let her in, then resumed her seat on the toilet lid. Julia, meanwhile, settled on the edge of the tub.

Paige stared ahead at the wall, but to Julia's surprise, her expression betrayed no anger or resentment. If anything, she seemed to be in shock.

"Paige, honey, I'm going to ask you some questions about what happened."

Paige merely nodded, still staring straight ahead.

"Just to make sure... was he hurting you?"

Paige shook her head.

"Was it... was he making you do anything you didn't want to do?"

Again, Paige shook her head. Slowly, Paige unfolded her legs and set her feet flat on the tile floor.

"Have you and Xavier had sex?" Steeling her stomach and plastering on as neutral of an expression as possible, Julia clarified, "Vaginal intercourse?"

Paige winced, but she shook her head.

"What about oral sex?"

Paige sat frozen, her gaze trained forward.

Julia's guts churned. "Did you use protection?"

After a moment's hesitation, Paige said simply, "We're both virgins."

Julia sighed. "Paige... how have things progressed this far between you two? You don't have a phone."

Paige blinked, and a solitary tear slid down her cheek. "We see each other at school every day."

Julia gulped past the lump of shock in her throat. "The oral sex is happening at school?"

Paige shook her head vehemently. "He came over here once in the middle of the night. I disabled the alarm and let him in."

"When?"

"The Monday after the housewarming party," she admitted.

"Have there been other times?"

"Just once. We arranged it at school." Paige swiped at a tear. They had been slipping down Paige's cheeks from time to time, but it was clear they were tears of sadness, not anger. It was almost as if Paige was resigned to her fate.

"Paige," Julia began gently, "just to be clear, I still don't believe there's anything bad about sex. I do wish you'd wait until you're much older, and I'm disappointed that you lied and sneaked around. There will be new boundaries after this, but I'm not naïve, and the most important thing is your health and safety. So if there's any chance you'll be having sex, you need to be on the pill."

Paige dug her toe underneath the bathmat on the floor in front of her. "We, um... we have condoms."

"Condoms are great for preventing STIs; and they're better than nothing for birth control. But they're not quite reliable enough."

Paige drew her feet up on the toilet seat lid again and started picking at a toenail. "We weren't planning to go as far as we did."

"That's often how it goes. It's a powerful instinct. Best-laid plans get scrapped in the heat of the moment. Even though I'd rather you didn't start having sex when you're still this young, it's even more important that you not get pregnant. So let's get you some better protection, just in case."

Downstairs, the front door slammed shut. Since Kelly's house was a carbon-copy of Julia's, Kelly's footsteps found their way to Paige's room with no trouble. A moment later, Julia heard her knock on Paige's door.

William and Kelly's hushed voices reached Julia through the bathroom door, but she couldn't make out what they said. Then, though Kelly's tone was gentle, it rose in pitch as she addressed Xavier.

A rhythmic sound started up, coming from Paige's room.

"He's stimming," Paige choked out, fresh tears streaming down her face. "He hits his head with his hands when he's upset."

A moment later came a sharp rebuke in Xavier's voice. Paige's door snicked shut again, and then they heard a rhythmic thump.

"He's banging his head on the floor," Paige practically wailed.

Julia stood and opened the door a crack to find Kelly in the hallway. She had braced herself against the wall with one hand, her head hanging between her shoulders.

Julia stepped into the hallway and closed the bathroom door behind her. "Is there anything I can do?" she whispered.

Kelly shook her still-bowed head. "It sounds bad, but the stimming actually helps."

"I understand," Julia murmured, thinking of the countless fuzzballs Paige had constructed from the myriad blankets she had decimated. Not to mention the way she chewed and picked at her nails until they bled. At least that was preferable to the cutting she used to do on her wrists and arms.

"Will's in there, in case Xavier truly starts hurting himself; but otherwise, we just have to wait it out." Then Kelly lifted her head, pinning Julia with anguished eyes. "I'm so sorry, Julia," she whispered. "When I left the house for trick-or-treating, Xavier was still in his room.

Pilar assumed he was still in there. He's never sneaked out – never done anything like this before."

Glancing back at the bathroom door, Julia silently beckoned Kelly to follow her. When they reached the living room, Julia still spoke in a low voice. "First, you don't owe me an apology, so you can let that go. But second, Paige just told me it *has* happened before."

When Kelly reeled back in shock, Julia explained. As she listened, Kelly steepled her hands together, pressing them to her lips, her eyes wide.

Julia draped a hand on Kelly's shoulder. "Yes, they're our kids, and there are things we should do to keep them safe. They'll need some clear new boundaries. But also, there's very little we can do to stop them if they're bound and determined, aside from chaining them to their beds."

Finally meeting Julia's eyes, Kelly deadpanned, "I wouldn't rule it out."

Julia gave in to some much-needed levity. Kelly dropped her hands from her mouth, but her answering smile was weak.

"I know you're right," Kelly said after a moment. "I just don't want to send the wrong message, either – like we're condoning it."

"That's why I think we should set some clear boundaries, moving forward. I just don't want those boundaries to do more harm than good, and I have no idea yet what that might look like."

Kelly nodded, growing pensive, so Julia excused herself to check on Paige. The thumping sound persisted from Paige's bedroom; and when Julia opened the bathroom door, she found Paige still on the toilet seat lid, still with her knees drawn up to her chest.

"This is all my fault," Paige choked out.

Julia went to sit on the edge of the tub and took Paige's hands in her own. "What do you mean?"

"*This.*" Paige gestured impatiently toward the bathroom door, which did nothing to block Xavier's stimming from reaching their ears. "If this is anybody's fault, it's mine, not his."

Julia sighed and squeezed Paige's hands. "It's nobody's fault, Paige. Besides, it takes two to tango – as long as this was consensual on both sides."

Shuddering, Paige withdrew her hands from Julia's grasp so she could wipe her eyes and cheeks with the heels of her palms.

"*Was* it consensual on both sides?" Julia verified again, anxiety thinning her voice to a near-whisper.

Paige immediately nodded. She resumed picking her toenail. "Are you going to keep us away from each other now?"

Julia straightened, shifting her weight on the edge of the tub. "Like I said earlier, there will be new boundaries. I'm not sure yet what those will look like, and I see a lot of conversations with Clio in our future. For now, though, no *unsupervised* time with Xavier."

Paige said nothing, but the two tears gliding down her cheeks spoke to her state of mind. Listening to Xavier's stimming did nobody any favors, so Julia gently prodded Paige downstairs to the den. There, Julia joined Paige and Robert in watching the rest of *Alice In Wonderland*. It felt appropriately surreal, under the circumstances.

LONG AFTER ALICE woke from her trippy dream – after Kelly had taken Xavier home, and Julia had soothed Robert and Paige to sleep – Julia still felt trapped in her own surreal reality. She didn't know how long she sat at the kitchen table, nursing a cup of chamomile tea, collecting her thoughts. She glanced at the clock on the wall: nearly one in the morning.

She supposed it was time to face William – her brand-new fiancé who, earlier that night, had blown off Julia's concerns about Paige and Xavier.

Still, she took her time washing, drying, and putting away her teacup, saucer, and the tea kettle. Finally, with nothing left to do, she took herself out of the kitchen and down the hallway to the bedroom she now shared with William.

Light escaped into the hallway through the gap beneath the door. She tapped lightly on the door, then opened it a crack when she got no response.

William sat on the edge of the bed, still in his pirate costume, minus the hat, wig, and belt with all its accoutrements. He hadn't even washed the black dye from his beard. It added to the evening's surrealism. He slumped forward, his hands clasped between his knees. When Julia swung the door wider, he barely lifted his head, just enough to peer at her from underneath his lashes. His forehead creased, and not just because he was looking up at her: the eyes that met hers were anguished.

Julia's pulse swished in her ears, her emotions a riot of disappointment, sadness, compassion, and even guilt. She came in, shut the door, and sat beside him on the edge of the bed. She, too, was still in her Gráinne O'Malley costume. She stared at the opposite wall, where she could watch their reflections in the dresser mirror.

"I'm sorry," William murmured after a moment, his voice thin and strained. "I'm sorry I doubted you. I know it's not an excuse, but... I've only been a parent for six months. You've had a lot longer to sharpen your parenting instincts."

"I appreciate your apology, I really do," Julia began. "I'm not saying I need you to agree with me on every single thing, but it felt like you weren't even open to the *possibility* that I might be right. I felt like you just dismissed my gut instinct out of hand."

In the dresser mirror's reflection, she saw him nodding. "You're right. I'm not going to sit here and tell you that's not exactly what I did. And I'm just so sorry."

Julia couldn't suppress the tiny furrow that appeared between her brows. "Is it because of what happened last time?"

In the mirror, William's head tilted. "Last time?"

Julia's eyes stung ominously. "In 2006," she whispered. "When my judgment was so poor. Do you still not trust me because of that?"

His features warping with anguish, William turned his whole body to face her. After a moment's hesitation, she also turned to meet his tortured gaze.

"Julie," he began, "I can honestly say I've put all of that behind me. I know what happened then, and I know we've both grown since then. No; what happened is that I had a blind spot, where Xavier is concerned. I forgot that he's a teenager, and a clever one, at that."

Julia nodded slowly, but her head was a cacophony of thoughts and emotions, broken only when William tentatively took hold of her hand. She looked up, meeting his earnest eyes with hers. He slid his other hand on top of hers and touched the engagement ring he had given her only yesterday.

"I'm sorry, sweetheart," he repeated, his voice tight with emotion. "I'll never trivialize your concerns again. I never should have in the first place."

The familiar warmth flooded Julia's chest. She picked up his hand and held it against her cheek, leaning into it and closing her eyes against its warmth. "Of course I forgive you, Will."

A sound poured from him, as if all the breath evacuated his lungs. Her eyes flew open again to find tears swimming in his. "You have no idea how worried I've been the past few hours," he confessed, his voice thin and strained.

"About what?"

"*Us.*"

"I love you, Will. It's going to take a lot more than this one little hiccup to get rid of me." He gave a ragged laugh, and she added, "Now go scrub that black dye out of your beard so I can kiss you."

Humming, he pointed out, "It didn't stop you from kissing me before." But with a grin, he took himself to the bathroom to do her bidding. And when he returned, he locked the bedroom door, undressed them both, and turned off the lights.

Later, sex-sated against his side, her voice thick with fatigue, Julia confessed, "I have no idea what we're going to do about this."

"Hmm?" murmured William, already half-asleep.

"Paige and Xavier."

The reminder of what had happened fully woke him. "I don't know yet, either, but I'm sure it can wait for tomorrow."

She poked him lightly in the ribs, causing him to squirm. "What's going to happen when they're no longer infatuated with each other, but they're still step-cousins?"

William shuddered.

"Exactly," Julia replied drily. "They'll still see each other at every family function."

After a moment's consideration, William deadpanned, "We're *all* going to need therapy for that."

Long after William's breathing had evened out, Julia muttered to herself, "Thank God for Clio."

THURSDAY, NOVEMBER 1, 2012 – MONDAY, NOVEMBER 12, 2012

Julia could not have anticipated just how prophetic her late-night gratitude for Clio would become.

There were tense sessions between Julia, Kevin, and William, explaining how the incident between Paige and Xavier came about, then settling on the consequences for Paige. Not to mention breaking the news to Kevin of Julia and William's engagement.

There were tearful, angry sessions between Julia, Kevin, and Paige in Clio's office, setting new boundaries or reimplementing old ones with Paige, and managing the predictable pushback.

But one of the things Clio, Julia, and Kevin discussed, when it was just the three of them, was that maybe the previous rules had been *too* restrictive, sowing the seeds for Paige's clandestine maneuverings.

So, they decided Paige would have to be chauffeured to and from school again – no more taking the bus. But as a consolation, Pilar, who was still on maternity leave, agreed to shuttle both her and Xavier to and from school, at the same time.

Paige would lose her job as Julia's social media manager – but in exchange, Julia granted her a lateral transfer to a new job as graphic designer, which wouldn't require as much internet access.

Paige still wouldn't be allowed a smart phone, but Julia and Kevin decided to give her a basic flip phone with no internet access and no way to exchange photos and videos. That way, Paige could at least make emergency calls, and maybe text certain approved contacts.

Finally, Julia and William installed a new security system at home – one that would alert them to any future sneaking around. At the same time, Julia and Kelly allowed Paige and Xavier to spend pre-arranged time at each other's houses – with doors open, of course, and adults present.

It made for a stressful two weeks, but Paige begrudgingly accepted that the new boundaries weren't going away, and that all of her various parental units stood in solidarity with each other.

Meanwhile, Julia and William started planning their wedding, with the enthusiastic assistance of their mothers. Ann, whose family had deep historical connections to the Fisherman's Chapel, pulled strings and scored the second Sunday of December for the wedding date. The chapel sat across from Cardone's and the former Dunphy's – soon to be Zeneize at Fisherman's Wharf. In an ironic twist, Marisa Zunino insisted on hosting Julia and William's reception there.

"It should serve as a great trial-run before opening night," Marisa argued when Julia initially balked. Marisa had proposed it during one of Julia's aquarium servicing visits to the restaurant. "Besides, in all honesty, it was Stephen's idea. He wants to give this to you guys as a wedding gift."

So after talking it over with William, then discussing it together with both Marisa and Stephen, Julia and William finally acquiesced.

"But only under one condition," William stipulated to Marisa over speakerphone. "No filming for the TV show."

"Aw, why not? It would make an epic wedding souvenir. Not to mention great advertising for Julia's business."

Julia pinned William with a resolute look and shook her head firmly. Leaning closer to his phone's mouthpiece, she said, "Thanks to you, Marisa, I don't need any more business. And we want to keep our reception very low-key and intimate."

So, with the date and venues settled, Julia and William turned to honeymoon planning. With their work schedules, and on such short notice, it wasn't like they could escape for long. But they were both eager to return to their "Eden."

The weekend after the wedding was technically Julia's weekend with the kids, so she called Kevin to ask if he would take them that Sunday and Monday. The pause that followed lasted so long that Julia finally said, "Hello?"

"I'm here," Kevin answered. "Just... I'm sorry, but I'll be in Hawaii those days."

"Hawaii," Julia echoed, unable to conceal either her disappointment or her surprise. "I thought you didn't like Hawaii that much."

He gave a noncommittal hum. "Well, if nothing else, it's paradise for marine biologists."

Julia's stomach bottomed out as a new thought occurred to her. "Kevin. Are you going there for a job interview?"

After a moment's hesitation, he admitted, "It's just an interview for an adjunct position at the University of Hawaii."

"Kevin, I thought the whole point of you moving back to San Francisco was to be closer to the kids."

"It was." Quickly, he corrected himself, "It *is*. I almost certainly won't take it. If nothing else, it's good interview practice."

"Okay," Julia said slowly, "so when do you get back from Hawaii?"

Another two beat rest. "Not until after Christmas."

Julia huffed in frustration. "You were supposed to take the kids on Christmas Eve."

Kevin stammered, "I – I was going to tell you."

And then, a second bombshell struck her. "Kevin... are you going to Hawaii with someone else?"

Once again, he heaved a sigh of resignation. "I was going to tell you about that, too. Very soon."

Finally, the last puzzle piece snapped in place. A petite, twenty-three-year-old puzzle piece with delicate features and lustrous black hair.

"I have a degree in marine biology from the University of Hawaii."

"Izumi," Julia said simply.

Breathless, Kevin demanded, "How did you know?"

Julia wasn't about to admit that William had gossiped about Kevin and Izumi leaving work together. "Paige and Robert told me she's a friend of yours who comes over sometimes. A friend whose apartment they visited with you."

Chastened, Kevin said, "I swear, I was getting ready to tell you in our next session with Clio."

"How long have you been seeing her?"

After a beat or two, Kevin admitted, "Pretty much since the day we met, four months ago. But I haven't told the kids she's my girlfriend."

"And yet you're going on a job interview in her home state." Bombshell Number Two Thousand struck at that moment. "Wait – are you meeting her family, too?"

Kevin's sigh was exasperated. "Look, I'm not taking the job in Hawaii; but even if I did, I could easily fly the kids back and forth."

"Not every other week, you couldn't," Julia balked. "They have school."

"That's why I won't take the job, okay?" he practically shouted.

Julia closed her eyes and slowed the pace of her breathing. From his silence on the other end of the line, Julia hoped he was doing the same.

Finally, after a minute, Kevin continued calmly. "I'm sorry. I know I should have told you and the kids by now, and I was going to, after our appointment with Clio this Thursday. It's just... been a whirlwind."

"So it's serious, then?"

"It is now," he confirmed quietly. "The kids like her, and she's very good with them. I just don't know how to explain to my daughter that I'm marrying a woman who's only ten years older than she is."

"*Marrying?*" echoed Julia, louder than intended.

Quietly, he admitted, "I'm going to propose in Hawaii."

"Jesus." But Julia supposed she was in no position to judge Kevin and Izumi's whirlwind courtship. "Have your parents met her?"

"Fuck no." Kevin's vehemence triggered a guffaw from Julia; and he followed that up with, "They'll shit a golden brick when I tell them I'm marrying a twenty-three-year-old who's not a member of their social set."

"Why do you still care what your parents think, though?"

"I don't, really," Kevin replied after a moment. "I just don't want to deal with their drama."

Julia hummed. "May I offer some unsolicited advice, while fully acknowledging that you can either take it or leave it, and that I'm probably the last person you want advice from?"

His answering chuckle lacked genuine humor, but he gamely agreed.

"For the sake of our kids and their future stepmom... if you value those relationships, you need to decide whose feelings to prioritize – theirs, or your parents'."

For a long time, Kevin said nothing, and Julia feared she had overstepped. She was about to check her phone to make sure the call hadn't dropped when he finally said, in a tone of resignation, "I'll tell everyone this weekend. That should give them enough time to process the news before Thanksgiving."

Julia nodded, even though he couldn't see her. It was an oddly poignant feeling, knowing they were both moving on with their lives. She certainly wasn't sad or jealous, and she definitely harbored no regrets. Still, it was somehow poignant.

Her voice nearly a whisper, she offered with complete sincerity, "Good luck."

SUNDAY, DECEMBER 9, 2012

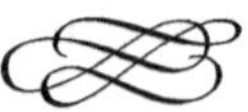

The second Sunday of December dawned clear and cold, at least by San Francisco standards. It was a good thing, then, that Julia had found a floor-length, crocheted-silk wedding dress with long sleeves. She didn't have time to make her own.

Of course, its flirty, low-slung back – a detail Julia had searched for, especially for William's enjoyment – canceled out any warmth the dress otherwise afforded.

Marisa had allowed the bridal party to use Zeneize at Fisherman's Wharf as a staging area, and that's where Julia styled her hair and applied her makeup. The men were relegated to the facilities at Cardone's, along with Kelly, who insisted William go right ahead and call her his Best Man.

"I just hope your groom doesn't smell like fish the entire wedding," Julia's mother joked.

Groom. All morning long, Julia's heart performed aerial maneuvers inside her chest, soaring in elation before barrel-rolling along with her nerves. She could hardly believe that after nineteen years and so many false starts, she was finally marrying William Quinn, the love of her life.

"Aw, look at her blush!" Alison teased, squatting a bit to press her cheek against Julia's and preen at their reflections in the mirror.

"Hey, don't mess up my makeup!" Julia chastised good-naturedly.

"Oh, so it's a proper Bridezilla then, is it?"

Julia tried to swat her sister's arm, but Alison dodged her. Alison was beaming and laughing, and she looked so radiant and voluptuous in her cranberry-red Maid of Honor dress that Julia was afraid she would steal her thunder. "Just make sure you and Mike get home before you let him maul you."

"Yes," their mother seconded after blotting her lipstick, "please respect the decorum of this sacred space."

Alison craned her neck every which way, examining her surroundings with feigned shock. "Dunphy's is a church now?"

"You know what I mean," their mother chided over Paige's snorts of laughter.

Speaking of Paige, Julia couldn't help marveling over her pretty and increasingly grown-up-looking daughter. She wore a cranberry-red bridesmaid dress of her own, and she had allowed Julia to pin a hairpiece of eucalyptus leaves into her coronet of chocolate-brown braids. She had also allowed her Aunt Alison to do her makeup, and the result was both age- and wedding-appropriate, while still paying homage to Paige's own emo / scene-kid aesthetic.

"I just hope Paige doesn't make Xavier trip and fall while he's escorting her down the aisle," remarked Julia's cousin, Holly, in her usual deadpan way.

Paige blushed at Holly's compliment before returning it, and Paige certainly didn't tell any white lies. Since handing over the reins of her legal nonprofit and accepting a job teaching law at Boston University, Holly had finally stopped straightening her glorious chestnut-brown mane of curls. She had also ditched the contact lenses in favor of a stylishly-oversized pair of glasses with teal tortoiseshell frames.

"I'm digging the whole vintage-Holly, sexy-librarian vibe," Julia remarked, gesturing up and down the length of Holly's hourglass figure, wrapped in its own cranberry-red dress. "By the way, how did you apply that lip color so precisely?"

"Let me show you." Holly fished the tube of wine-red lip stain from her purse and settled into the chair beside Julia to work her magic.

"I'm so glad you could make it," Julia murmured to her cousin in between coats. When Julia asked Holly to be her third bridesmaid, Holly dropped everything to fly in from Boston. Julia and Holly were best friends throughout high school at Holy Cross Prep; and when Kevin pulled his disappearing act in 2006, Julia had started her paralegal career in Holly's office.

"Me too, cuz," Holly replied as affectionately as she ever would. Sometimes her resemblance to Lilith Stern on *Cheers* was downright uncanny. "I'm just sorry I have to leave tomorrow. Your timing was dreadful."

"I know, I know – right in the middle of finals," Julia said, before sing-songing, *"But I know something you don't know."*

Holly drew back the lip stain applicator just before it touched Julia's lips. "What?"

"A certain someone will be in attendance today."

Holly quirked an eyebrow in her familiar *we are not amused* gesture. "Since I have no certain someones, I can't imagine who you mean."

"Niall Costello," Julia stage-whispered so everyone could hear.

While Alison snickered knowingly, Julia's mother and Paige traded confused frowns. Meanwhile, Holly leaned back in her seat and screwed the applicator into the tube of lip stain with a flourish, as if readying for battle.

"Have you no shame, Jules?" she said mildly, a smile playing at her lips. "The man is married."

"Not any-*mo*-ooore," Julia sing-songed again, and reveled in the spark of interest that flashed through Holly's brown eyes. "Niall and his wife divorced two years ago."

Holly and Niall, the Irish drummer in William's former band, had enjoyed a torrid fling six years ago. They met at MacGowan's Pub around the same time that Kevin ran away to Brazil and Julia and William rekindled their relationship. But Holly's distrust of men and aversion to commitment had sent her fleeing all the way across the country to Boston. *Permanently.* And in the six years since, Niall had married and divorced.

Blowing a dismissive raspberry, Holly said, "You know I don't date men with kids."

"You don't date, period," Julia pointed out.

Holly jabbed a finger at Julia. "Hence, I don't date men with kids."

"Fine. Then you'll be glad to know Niall and his ex never had kids." Julia in with a cheeky grin. "He's blessedly childless."

At Holly's deer-in-the-headlights look, Alison cried, "Aaaaand scene!"

While the rest of them laughed at her expense, Holly suppressed a smirk and casually unscrewed the lip stain applicator again. Waving it at Julia, she said, "Just remember who wields the real power here. It would be a shame if I suddenly got shaky hands."

"Shaky hands or no, you girls need to get a move on," Julia's mother admonished, prompting them to check the time.

"Oh my God," Julia gasped, anxious adrenaline dumping into her veins. "We only have fifteen minutes!"

Alison came around to massage Julia's shoulders and murmur words of reassurance, and then Holly finished applying Julia's lip stain. After that, Julia stood to allow her mother to pin her own eucalyptus hairpiece into her half-updo. Then, her mother simply held her by the shoulders and surveyed her for a minute, her eyes shimmering with unshed tears, her lips trembling through a smile.

"I've never seen a more beautiful bride," she said finally, her voice breaking, "and I've never seen a man more in love than William is with you. You're a very lucky woman, Julia, and you'll have a very happy life."

Julia's field of vision swam as she flapped her hands in front of her eyes. "You're going to make my mascara run," she choked out through a shaky laugh.

"Waterproof," Alison piped up, waving the mascara tube in Julia's face; and like always, Julia was grateful for her sister's comedic timing.

MINUTES LATER, Alison received Kelly's text signaling that it was time, and they were crossing the pier to the little brown wood-framed building she had known all her life: the Fisherman's Chapel. Standing ramrod-straight, Julia's father waited just outside the entrance with his hands clasped before him. He watched Julia's approach in his usual stoic manner; but when she finally reached him, a tiny hint of a smile tugged at the corners of his mouth as pride glinted in his eyes.

He bent to kiss her cheek, murmuring, "You look lovely." Positively effusive, for him.

"Thank you. So do you," she replied breathlessly. "Handsome, I mean."

As arranged, William's friend Niall popped his head out to confirm they were ready before signaling Aaron – their officiant. Niall's eyes snagged conspicuously on Holly for several awkward seconds before he retreated inside.

"Subtle," Holly muttered, eliciting laughter from Julia and Alison; but Holly's face flared red. Clearly, the encounter had flustered her, more than Julia would have expected from a mere summer fling six years ago.

But Julia didn't have time to contemplate that. Pilar's brother Rafael was quite the accomplished cellist, so Julia and William had engaged him to provide the music. Now, refrains of Bach's *Prelude from Cello Suite #1* floated out to summon them, and everyone but Julia and her father filed into the chapel.

Inside, William's Uncle Frank would be escorting Ann and Julia's mother to their seats in the front row. Then, Mike would escort Alison, followed by Xavier and Paige, then Kelly and Holly. Finally, Robert would process down the aisle as the flower boy, leading Diego on a leash as the ring bearer. Kelly had sealed the rings inside a tiny velvet pouch before attaching it securely to Diego's collar. Julia knew it was almost her turn when she heard the guests' laughter.

And then, through the pounding of her heart, she heard her father's steady voice beside her: "Are you ready?"

Adrenaline thrummed through her veins and electrified her skin. She peered up at him, and the corners of his mouth lifted again as he presented his arm. Smiling, she looped her arm through his, clasping her bouquet of succulents and eucalyptus in her left hand.

And then the chapel doors swung open.

From previous visits, Julia knew that a stained-glass window bearing the image of a nautical steering wheel filtered light into the chapel. She knew plaques lined the walls, bearing the names of fishermen lost at sea, including Cardones – William's own family. She knew that behind the simple, green-draped altar with its plain white taper candles, a picture window looked out over the bay. Underneath a peaked, wood beam ceiling, pews flanked a center aisle, and Julia knew those pews contained people who were standing and turning to face her.

But Julia saw none of that. The only thing she saw in that moment waited at the head of the aisle in an impeccably tailored dark gray suit, a cranberry-red tie, and a small green succulent in his lapel. William waited expectantly and a bit nervously, with his hands clasped before him.

But when Julia and her father stepped forward and William caught his first glimpse of her, his knees nearly buckled. Kelly and Mike tensed, preparing to catch him; but when he didn't collapse, they stepped back again with knowing grins.

Still, Julia saw nothing and nobody but William, who flushed as he watched her draw nearer. His breathing grew ragged, and two fat tears rolled down his cheeks – but he was smiling.

No, he wasn't smiling – he was glowing. Radiating pure, unadulterated joy.

Julia willed her own tears to remain at bay and riveted her eyes to William's so she wouldn't miss a single reaction. Kelly retrieved a handkerchief from her pocket, and William accepted it only long enough to dab his eyes and get himself under control. But his eyes still shimmered when Julia finally stood before him, and his chin and lips wobbled as she passed her bouquet to Alison.

She beamed up at William encouragingly as he took her hands in his. The slightly self-conscious twist of his mouth and the color on his cheeks spoke to his state of mind as he gazed down at her in front of his family and friends. But the corners of his eyes crinkled up as they always did when he smiled so lovingly.

"You're so beautiful," he whispered.

"So are you," she whispered in return.

William's eyes made a complete circuit of Julia's face, hair, and makeup. They skimmed the neckline of her white, hand-crocheted wedding dress. They traced the slightly bell-shaped sleeves down her arms and back up again until they landed on her mouth. She studied him just as intently – the swirl of his aqua irises. His straight nose and full mouth. The slight cleft of his chin, barely visible beneath the not-too-neatly-trimmed scruff of his beard – just the way she liked it.

Only then did they notice Aaron standing before them, and only because he conspicuously cleared his throat. Their guests chuckled knowingly, and Julia's surroundings finally came into focus. She registered the smiling faces of her daughter and son, her sister and cousin, and each of William's attendants. She registered their joyfully tearful mothers in the front row, and the rest of their family and friends filling the pews behind them.

But as Aaron began the ceremony, all of that once again faded away, until it was only Julia and William, peering into each other's eyes with pure adoration and devotion. And when it was time to say their vows, Julia and William's obliviousness to everything but each other only compounded their guests' amusement.

William, still clasping Julia's hands, gazed down at his bride with pure tenderness. "This first poem is by one of my all-time favorites, Pablo Neruda. It's called *I Love You Without Knowing How*, and I've been waiting to recite it to you at our wedding since we were eighteen."

It was hopeless – Julia's tears breached the dam. Somewhere in the distant recesses of her consciousness, she registered sniffles coming from the pews. But though Julia shuddered through a sob, and William's face swam in her field of vision, she was still beaming.

The quaver in William's voice was the only clue to his state of mind as he recited from memory.

I don't love you as if you were a rose of salt, topaz,
or arrow of carnations that propagate fire:
I love you as one loves certain obscure things,
secretly, between the shadow and the soul.

I love you as the plant that doesn't bloom but carries
the light of those flowers, hidden, within itself,
and thanks to your love the tight aroma that arose
from the earth lives dimly in my body.

I love you without knowing how, or when, or from where,
I love you directly without problems or pride:
I love you like this because I don't know any other way
to love,
except in this form in which I am not nor are you,
so close that your hand upon my chest is mine,
so close that your eyes close with my dreams.

Julia's tears were officially destroying her makeup. She accepted a tissue from Alison and tried to salvage as much of it as possible before taking William's hands in her own.

She could only pray that the look she pinned on him conveyed at least a fraction of the love she felt. "This poem is called Heart to Heart, by Rita Dove," she managed to warble out, and from the intrigued sparkle in his eyes, she knew he had never heard it.

It's neither red
nor sweet.
It doesn't melt
or turn over,
break or harden,
so it can't feel
pain,
yearning,
regret.

It doesn't have
a tip to spin on,
it isn't even
shapely—
just a thick clutch
of muscle,
lopsided,
mute. Still,
I feel it inside
its cage sounding

a dull tattoo:
I want, I want—

but I can't open it:
there's no key.
I can't wear it
on my sleeve,
or tell you from
the bottom of it
how I feel. Here,
it's all yours, now—
but you'll have
to take me,
too.

William laughed gamely, and their guests chuckled along, too. Then, hand in hand, they each lit a single candle on the altar.

Back in their spots, William took her hands again and recited another poem, this one by Rumi; and their guests' soft sighs echoed the ones whispering through Julia's spirit. Blinking back more tears, she squeezed his hands once, then recited from Maya Angelou.

With that, they each lit another candle on the altar.

Finally, it was time for Kelly to retrieve the rings from Diego's collar and pass Julia's to William. Capturing Julia's eyes with his, his lips trembling through a smile, William turned the Claddagh ring so the heart faced inwards. Now it was a wedding ring, and he slid it onto her left ring finger. His hands never left hers as he recited the words of Hafiz.

Let us be like
Two falling stars in the day sky.
Let no one know of our sublime beauty
As we hold hands with God
And burn

Into a sacred existence that defies—
That surpasses

Every description of ecstasy
And love.

Still beaming, Julia squeezed William's hands again before turning to accept his ring from Kelly. Like her own, it was a Claddagh ring, but made of titanium. Besides the iconic Claddagh heart, hands, and crown, the Irish phrase *A chéadsearc* – "my first love" – encircled the band in Ogham script.

William admired it for the first time when she slid it onto his finger, and then his eyes lifted to hers in anticipation.

"The final stanza of *At Last*, by Elizabeth Akers Allen," she announced simply.

I count no more my wasted tears;
They left no echo of their fall;
I mourn no more my lonesome years;
This blessed hour atones for all.
I fear not all that Time or Fate
May bring to burden heart or brow,—
Strong in the love that came so late,
Our souls shall keep it always now!

Julia's heart flipped somersaults as tears welled again in William's eyes. He used the heel of one palm to wipe them away before blinking tenderly down at Julia. As her own tears spilled over, Julia turned with a wobbly smile to beckon her children forward. The four of them – Julia, Willliam, Paige, and Robert – each took a single, lit candle from the altar. With Alison assisting Robert, their individual flames converged at the wick of the Unity candle.

With that, Aaron pronounced Julia and William husband and wife, and without a moment's hesitation, William pulled Julia closer.

Clasping her cheek in the palm of his hand, he whispered, "I've been waiting for this since I first laid eyes on you." And before he pressed his lips to hers – before the chapel rang out with their guests' cheers – Julia wondered if he meant the first time he laid eyes on her *today*, or *ever*.

~

AFTER EXITING the chapel hand in hand to the serenades of Rafael's cello, Julia and William crossed the pier to enjoy a few precious minutes alone in the restaurant before the wedding photos.

Pausing in front of Julia's massive aquarium with its swirling tropical palette, William pulled her against him. They indulged in kisses for a minute or two, then William's eyes devoured Julia in several lingering courses.

He sounded almost pained as he echoed his earlier words: "You're so beautiful."

"So are you," she murmured, blinking back the tears that threatened to fall, yet again.

Pulling her close again, he touched his forehead to hers and smiled down at her. "This is the happiest day of my life, Julie."

Her heart flooded with a familiar warmth. "So many of the happiest days of my life have been with you."

"And more to come." He held her left hand in both of his and touched her ring. "I can't believe you're really, finally my wife."

"I can. As Dad would say, it's about freaking time."

He laughed almost giddily. "I believe he used stronger language."

Her adoring eyes scanned his, back and forth. He dipped his head and kissed her deeply, then rested his forehead against hers and bit his bottom lip, savoring.

"Jesus, I wish we could be alone right now," he said finally.

"You're the one who wanted a wedding and a reception," she teased him.

"I let my pride and ego get the better of me," he admitted. "I wanted to show you off in front of everyone. I mean, who could blame me, with such a smoking-hot wife?"

"Would you guys cut it out with the derpy heart eyes? I'm throwing up in my mouth a little."

Julia and William hadn't even registered Alison's presence – and that was saying something, since Alison never made a quiet entrance. They reluctantly disentangled themselves, but Alison's grin belied her professions of disgust. Snickering, Julia allowed her sister to drag her into the ladies' room to fix her hair and makeup.

After the wedding photos, the newlyweds and their mothers worked the dining room, welcoming family and friends, accepting their compliments and congratulations, and thanking them for coming. Julia and William barely had time to take in the restaurant's coastal-chic-meets-urban-industrial remodel, nor all the simple but elegant decorations their mothers and sisters had festooned it with. They had even less time to savor the incredible spread of Genoese Christmas-season classics Marisa and Stephen had catered for them.

Food was eaten, toasts were made, and Alison's cake was cut and enjoyed. All too soon, Julia and William were fleeing the restaurant through a shower of birdseed and escaping in William's Jeep. *Someone* – Julia placed bets on Alison and Mike – had painted *Just Married* on every window in white shoe polish. But Julia and William didn't notice the shoes and cans they had tied to William's bumper until the racket finally betrayed them.

William pulled over at the nearest gas station to untie the noise-makers and squeegee the shoe polish so he wouldn't kill his new bride in a wreck. The scene drew an audience of fellow customers and even the station clerk, who either stared, laughed, or congratulated them. After that, they were on a mission to get home as quickly as possible. An empty house awaited, thanks to Kelly and Pilar agreeing to keep Robert overnight, and Alison keeping Paige.

"There's something that needs to happen," William declared after unlocking their front door.

Julia yelped as he scooped her up and carried her, laughing, across the threshold. With her free arm, she clumsily helped close and lock the door, and then he carried her upstairs to the bedroom, where he finally set her down on her feet.

Between spurts of laughter, she awaited his next move. Smiling warmly down at her, his eyes crinkling at the corners, he unpinned her eucalyptus hairpiece and set it on the dresser. Then he loosened the sections of hair that she had pinned, allowing them to tumble over her ears.

"You chose this dress just to torture me, didn't you?" he murmured, his breath warm against the shell of her ear. By way of explanation, he pressed his fingertips lightly against the bare skin of her back.

Goosebumps erupted over every square inch of her skin. "Smart man," she quipped, his touch making her words mushy.

His hand swept over her hair, tucking locks of it behind her ear. She unpinned her earrings and set them on the bedside table. Smiling impishly at him, she started loosening his tie, then laughed when he ripped it the rest of the way off and flung it to the floor. Smirking, he peeled off his suit jacket and tossed that aside as well. Then he tapped her shoulder and spun his finger in the air, signaling her to turn around. After undoing the tie below her neck that held everything together, he peeled the wedding dress from her shoulders, down her arms, and all the way to the floor. And he did it with such agonizing slowness that Julia decided it must be payback for the torture she had inflicted on him.

From where he knelt on the floor, his palms and lips traveled a slow, winding route up her calves. As they smoothed their way up the backs of her thighs, Julia closed her eyes, her lips falling open slightly, her head tipping back. She savored his wide, rough palms and warm, full lips as they lavished attention on the round curves of her bare bottom.

"Correction: you wear *these* to torture me, don't you?" he rumbled. His fingertip traced the string of her thong to where it vanished into the cleft of her backside and beyond.

"Absolutely," she gasped, shuddering in anticipation. "And if this is what you call revenge, I'll keep torturing you."

His fingertip froze on its journey through her cleft, then suddenly, he pulled away. "We can't have that, now, can we?" he rasped out, his breath hot against her skin.

She whined as he started to stand, but her whines turned to moans when his tongue traced the groove of her back – slowly. Always so slowly. Inch by inch, up her spine, through the valley between her shoulder blades, until his warm, wet mouth latched onto the curve where her neck met her shoulders. She exhaled a long, ragged breath as he suckled the skin there – as his palms simultaneously traveled up her ribcage.

"I wondered how you were wearing a bra with that backless dress," he murmured against her neck when he found her self-adhesive silicone bra cups. "I was kind of hoping to find nothing, like that time in Eden."

"Oh, so *that's* what you were thinking about while we were exchanging our vows," she teased, her voice thin and quavering, like a violin strung too taut.

"And also during the reception."

She laughed out loud, then winced as she peeled away the bra cups.

"Ouch," he sympathized.

"I know; it's probably not very sexy," she replied.

"You could do, say, or wear *anything* right now, and I would find it sexy," he murmured, turning her to face him again. And then his tongue delved into her mouth, tangling with hers, and the hand on her backside pushed her hips into his. She loosened his suit trousers, allowing them to fall around his ankles.

"Already at full mast, I see," she purred as her hand dove into his boxers, and he answered with an erotic, starved kiss.

A minute later they lay in bed, naked, their bodies and lips and hands sliding over and around each other. Taking their time, not in any special hurry; yet keenly attuned to each other, to the exclusion of all else.

"Jesus, I'm so fucking turned on right now," he ground out, his voice raw and gravelly.

She rose over him and shifted forward to straddle his lap, one knee on either side of his hips. His eyes, dark azure with lust, pored greedily over every inch of her, down and back up again. He rested his hands in the curves of her waist, then did a little sit-up to lavish attention on her breasts, each in turn. Grasping them in his warm palms, he gently pulled her nipples between his lips.

"Will," she breathed, stroking the soft hair on the crown of his head. Watching him languidly worship her, his eyes closed in pleasure.

She slowly lowered herself right down onto him, and they both gasped at how effortlessly he sank in, so deep.

He growled softly into her ear, then pulled back just enough to capture her eyes with his. His forehead creased, and the blue of his irises swirled with the most aching sort of need.

Immediately she bobbed up and down on him, and he stared

unabashedly at her breasts as they bounced along with her. He reached for them again, kneading with his hands. Cupping the back of her head in his palm; pulling her down to him. Tonguing her wide-open mouth.

He stiffened and lengthened even more, and she moaned with the sharp pleasure of it. He reached between their bodies, finding the most sensitive part of her with his thumb and starting to circle.

"Oh God–" She seized his shoulders and dropped her head back, moaning even louder. Bucking wildly on him in sheer elation.

Suddenly his fingers stopped, and she whimpered in dismay. In one fluid movement, he did another sit up, grabbed her waist, and lifted her right out of bed, setting her feet on the floor.

"I want you to see every single thing I'm doing to you," he explained, his voice thick with need as he climbed out of bed. He took her hand and led her right to the full-length mirror hanging on the inside surface of the bedroom door.

He positioned her in front of it so she could see all of herself in its reflection. Standing behind her, he wrapped his left arm around her waist, while his other hand snaked its way up her torso to cup and squeeze her breast. The entire time, he watched her reaction in the mirror with wolfish blue eyes.

Teasing her earlobe with his teeth, he whispered, "Jesus Christ, Julie – look how beautiful you are. I still can't believe I'm the one who gets to do this with you."

Overpowered with emotion and sensation, Julia could only close her eyes and release a long, shuddering sigh. With his right hand he touched her chin, turning her face and meeting her open mouth with his tongue. She whimpered in surrender, and he responded by trailing his right hand down her neck, over her breast, down her belly.

And then his fingertips were separating her, circling – slowly at first, then faster. At the same time, his tongue tasted hers; and with his left hand he caressed her breast and brushed his thumb back and forth over the stiff peak of her nipple, occasionally pinching it between his thumb and forefinger. With every exponential crescendo of pleasure, her moans increased in pitch; and with every increase in pitch, he groaned with frustrated lust. And all the while, he keenly watched her every move-ment and facial expression in the mirror, and she watched his; and then her skin was pink and glowing, and her eyelids grew heavy, and her mouth slackened, and she cried out – a long, raw, uninhibited gust. With the arm encircling her waist, he squeezed her against him for support, whispering words of praise into her ear while she exploded against his fingers.

She wasn't even finished pulsating before he said tightly, "I'm sorry, Julie, but I need inside of you right now before I come all over your back."

Her orgasm had mostly carried away her powers of speech, but she managed to croak out a strangled, "No." He froze, his wide eyes catching hers in the mirror, until she clarified, "I have a better idea."

Before he could respond, she spun around and fell to her knees before him. She dragged her palms along, sweeping them down his perfect chest, his taut stomach, his lean waist, until they rested on his hips. They locked eyes as her hands closed in on the part of him that was hard as steel and pointing right at its target. She kept her eyes glued on his as she flicked his tip with her tongue, sucking the sweet little drops that collected there like honeydew – as she took all of him, all the way into her mouth and down her throat.

He sucked in air through clenched teeth, scraped his fingers through her hair, and rewarded her with a truly legendary streak of dirty words.

Each time her eyes flitted up to his, he was either staring down at her with an open mouth and a heated expression; or he was watching their reflection in the mirror behind her.

"Julie... God, Julie, your body..." He sucked in another gasp through his teeth, and she moaned low in her throat as he jerked and lengthened. "*Fuck*, your mouth is perfect."

When she lifted her eyes, he was watching her in the mirror again. He moaned so eagerly as she dropped one hand just beneath the solid straining length of him and squeezed – careful but firm. He was already drawn up tight into his body – so close. His eyes rolled shut and he exhaled sharply, gripping her head between his hands; and she watched his face contort.

"Oh God – I'm gonna come–"

A series of vocal gasps reached a crescendo, and he groaned hoarsely as he careened over the precipice, jetting against the back of her throat.

He was shouting her name, and God's name; and groaning that he was coming hard for her; he was coming so hard.

Her mouth continued its steady drive along him, until his groans and gasps subsided to heavy panting. He still held her head between his hands, and when his eyes gradually rolled open again, they were tinged with awe. Her lips, still wrapped around him, curved into a smile, and as he began to soften, she gave him a couple of parting kisses.

Then he took her hand, helped her to her feet, and tucked her sweetly against him. He curled his long arms around her until one palm rested on her shoulder and the other on her ribcage. She pressed her ear to his chest and listened to his heartbeat, still flapping wildly against his sternum. His breathing gradually returned to normal.

Eventually he pulled back from her, but only enough to tenderly clasp her face in his hands. His breathtaking eyes flickered back and forth between hers, roaming the length and breadth of her face.

Her heart was a balloon in her chest, heat expanding it into the most sublime ache. The warm ache spread to her face, down her limbs, and all the way to the fingertips that traced his lips. He licked those perfect lips, and the ache plunged down her torso, pooling between her thighs like warm honey.

"I don't understand how you do this," she whispered.

"Do what?"

"Make me need more. Already."

His eyes were a study in pure devotion, rolling shut just long enough for him to press a soft, lingering kiss on her lips. Then, without another word, he took her hand and led her back to bed.

"WELL, we didn't waste any time, did we?" Julia laughed after Round Two. She had collapsed on top of William, her forehead pressed into the same pillow that cradled his head. He wrapped his arms around her torso, squeezing so as much of their skin made contact as possible.

"No time like the present," he replied; and they laughed deliriously, stupidly, their hilarity entirely out of proportion to the joke. Kissing each other again, and again.

Eventually she flopped onto her back, and he rolled onto his side, facing her. He traced her sweaty torso with his fingertips, up and down – between her breasts, to her navel and beyond, and back up again.

"Isn't this where we're supposed to light a cigarette or something?" she quipped.

He propped his head up on his fist, his elbow on the mattress. "I thought you said you were allergic to cigarette smoke."

"When did I say that?"

"On the beach, at the bonfire." When she still looked confused, he clarified, "The day before we went whale watching the first time."

"You mean when we were seventeen? I was lying, you goofball! I was using it as an excuse because I was too scared to try marijuana."

He flopped onto his back laughing now, and this time she was the one who rolled onto her side to face him. She smiled tenderly, her fingertips tracing circles through the hair on his chest; and as always, she marveled at the beauty of his face as he submitted wholeheartedly to joy.

"How do you think I survived working at Dunphy's all those years, before the indoor smoking ban?" she persisted. "Or at your house with your family, for that matter? Didn't that tip you off?"

"I think I was ready to believe anything you said back then," he admitted. "I was desperately, hopelessly in love with you."

"Well, it's nice to know how you felt *back then*," she teased.

"I still do," he protested, poking her in the shoulder. "In case the fact that I literally just married you isn't proof enough."

"No, you literally just screwed me stupid. And by the way – despite its tepid reputation, it looks like married sex will be *at least* as hot as living-in-sin sex."

Laughing again, he rolled onto his side and pulled her in close; and it gave her so much happiness to know that she could give him so much happiness. For the longest time, they kissed relentlessly while savoring the pleasure of their bodies pressed together.

But finally, William said, "If we're going to make it to Eden before dark, we'd better get moving."

So they reluctantly dragged themselves out of bed and put on their everyday, non-wedding clothes. Loading their already-packed suitcases and groceries into William's Jeep, they set out shortly afterward and made it to Eden just before sunset.

"Oh, look!" Julia cried as they pulled up to the farmhouse. Aaron's daughter, Rina, had decorated the farmhouse and many of the surrounding cypresses with Christmas lights. And she had decked the front porch and some of the windows with evergreen garlands, wreaths, and red bows.

After unloading the car, they discovered that Rina had also left them a note of congratulations on the dining table, along with a bottle of sparkling grape juice in an ice bucket and two champagne flutes. They gladly partook, along with the light supper of antipasti they had packed. Then, after stargazing a while, they collapsed into bed and immediately dropped off to sleep, too exhausted for any more wedding night shenanigans.

The next morning, when Julia's eyes finally opened, she found William already awake and gazing at her.

"Good morning, wife," he greeted her.

She reached between his legs. "Good morning, wood."

After making up for last night's missed shenanigans, they brought their coffee and breakfast to the front porch, where they could look out over the dormant winter vineyards. They wrapped themselves in blankets and ate the eggs William had scrambled.

After a long silence, Julia declared, rather optimistically, "I could see myself chucking it all and buying a place like this."

William's eyebrows lifted. "Et tu, Brute?"

She gave his arm a playful shove. "What do you mean, 'et tu,' and who's this Brute guy?"

"It just seems like everyone and their dog is going off the grid or taking up urban farming."

"Says the man who took over my mom's garden and won't let me set foot in it. Maybe Alison's 'Farmer William' comment was on point, after all."

"Farmer William?"

"Yeah, remember? The first time you came to dinner, in May, you and Mom geeked out over organic gardening. Alison dubbed you Farmer William."

"Oh, yes," he groaned. "How could I forget?"

"So how about it, then? Is farm livin' the life for you? Could you picture yourself geeking out on our very own private *Green Acres?*"

"Mrs. Quinn, I can picture myself geeking out in Timbuktu, as long as it's where you are."

Her heart fluttered, and she couldn't suppress her giddy smile. He leaned across the table to plant a soft kiss on her lips. "But just for practice, why don't you try cleaning out the chicken coops today?"

Julia considered this proposal for roughly two seconds. "On second thought, I think I'm Eva Gabor in this *Green Acres* reboot: '*I get allergic smelling hay,*'" she added in the speak-sing of the theme song.

"I don't believe you. You said the same thing about cigarette smoke."

Julia clapped her hands together and laughed so hard that she nearly fell out of her chair. He just sat there and watched her, a satisfied smile playing at his lips as he sipped his coffee.

"You know, there's something I've been saving for the right moment," he murmured when she finally got a grip on herself.

"Oh?" Curiosity piqued, Julia sat up straighter. "I already have your love, your son, your mermaid necklace, and your ring. What more could I ask for?"

His smirk hinted not-so-subtly at what more she could ask for.

"Good point," she deadpanned.

"But first, something a little more intangible." He unwrapped himself from the blanket and retrieved his cell phone from the back pocket of his jeans. After unlocking it and tapping his phone screen, he surprised Julia by coming around to her side of the table. He knelt before her, as if he were about to propose again.

"Um... did you forget the part where I already have your ring?" teased Julia, stretching her left hand out for emphasis.

"Hey, sweetheart?"

"Yeah?"

With the most tender of smiles, he took her left hand in his right one. "Shut up, please."

Julia stifled a snort of laughter. "Aye aye, captain."

With his free hand, he lifted his phone and fixed her with his earnest blue eyes. "I considered reading this at our wedding, but I decided to save it for the two of us. It's called *Home*. I'll leave the poet's identity to your imagination."

Anticipation quickened Julia's pulse, and deep love for her new husband flooded her cheeks with heat. He saw it happening and answered with a tiny smile – the kind she loved most on him. The shy kind that barely lifted the corners of his mouth. The kind that crinkled the corners of his eyes as they lingered a moment, then flitted to his phone screen.

In silence between breaths
There, in copper sanctuary
Seek asylum
Pure, strong, pliant
No alloy, you

In the shape of light
Yours
Ineffable radiance
Refuge with no quarter for shadow

I've charted the labyrinth outside
(Or tried)
A puzzle with no solution but one:
A river
Another labyrinth

Til then,
You
Fellow wayfarer
True north
Compass rose

THE END

Please leave a review! https://Linktr.ee/JennaMalabyReviews, or scan the QR code below.

Want a FREE bonus epilogue to The Hold? Subscribe to my monthly email newsletter, and I'll send you *Santa's Baby: A Catch & Hold Holiday Story*, as a thank you gift! To subscribe, go to www.jenna malabyauthor.com/subscribe, or scan the QR code below, and own it forever!

Or read it on Kindle Unlimited; go to Books2Read.com/SantasBabyBy JennaMalaby, or scan the QR code below:

If you enjoyed The Hold and want to read more from me, know that nothing helps indie authors more than reviews. So please, **leave a review** on your platform of choice by going to https://linktr.ee/ jennamalabyreviews or scan the QR code below:

Want more of Julia and William? Read *The Compass*, a "midquel" of sorts to *The Catch* and *The Hold*, from William's POV! Go to Book s2Read.com/TheCompass, or scan the QR code below:

Let's keep in touch! Subscribe to my monthly email newsletter for freebies and first looks. www.JennaMalabyAuthor.com/subscribe, or scan the QR code below:

Thank you *so* much for reading (and reviewing!) my books!

Jenna Malaby (formerly Jenna Miles)

ACKNOWLEDGMENTS

I have so many people to thank for their incredibly generous time and talent in helping me to sound like I know what I'm talking about.

Adison Landon of Fish Perfect, LLC, for her insights into the aquarium servicing business, particularly as a woman aquarist.

Diana Pinacho, for her invaluable insights into Afromexicano culture.

Terri Fennelly, LCSW for research questions related to child and family therapy.

Amanda Gordon of Gordon Family Law, and **Alan Silverman, PhD,** of Silverman Family Law, for insight into various family law questions.

And of course, all of my beta and ARC readers, and everyone who reads my books!

ALSO BY JENNA MALABY*

See where Julia and William's love story began with *The Catch!*

Poignant and powerful, *The Catch* is a retro Gen X second chance romance with an angsty love triangle. Told in nonlinear fashion between 1993, 2006, and 2012, it captures the nostalgia of young love, along with the relatable trials of motherhood and responsibility.

Julia Dunphy's husband just left her for the second time, her thirteen-year-old won't stop swearing in public, and to top it all off, her four-year-old just asked to buy condoms. Needless to say, this isn't how she expected her life to pan out.

As a teen in the nineties, Julia had bold plans to study marine biology far from home. Not even William Quinn, the working class boy-next-door, could derail her dreams. Not with his blue eyes. Not with his quiet brilliance. Not even with his loyal heart.

Still, despite time, distance, and marriage to another man, Julia's most tender memories revolved around William. Then, after eleven years and countless broken dreams, Julia and William got an unexpected second chance when they imagined a whale-watching business together – until that, too, ended in a rupture too big to heal.

Now, amid the wreckage of her marriage, and despite a fresh start in her own aquarium shop, Julia knows a third chance with her first love is wishful thinking. But when she uses her training as a paralegal to save William's whale-watching business, and he shows up to thank her, she dares to wonder - are third chances possible, after all?

Equal parts witty, heartwarming, and gut-wrenching, *The Catch* is perfect for fans of Colleen Hoover and Christina Lauren, and reminiscent of classics like Jane Austen's *Persuasion*. It offers a guaranteed Happy For Now ending, with a Happily Ever After in its sequel.

Get THE CATCH at https://Books2Read.com/TheCatchByJennaMalaby, or scan the QR code below:

~

Follow William's story in *The Compass,* a "midquel" to *The Catch.*

From the author of *The Catch* comes THE COMPASS, Part One of its stand-alone "midquel." With brand-new material as well as flashbacks

to *The Catch*, all told from William's point of view, *The Compass* is equal parts hilarious, harrowing, heartwarming, and hopeful.

It's 1995, and twenty-year-old William Quinn's quest for reprieve after a breakup reunites him with Serafima "Haze" Temkina, a mysterious older woman who's twice played a pivotal role in his life. Although their friendship and blooming intimacy promise a foothold, old memories and new temptations threaten to bury him beneath their weight. Soon, William is losing his already-tenuous grip on himself, his mental health, and everything he values. But after his downward spiral costs him nearly everything, will his oldest friend still be there when he finally digs himself out from beneath the layers of his past?

Told in a non-linear fashion, *The Compass* alternates between William's present and past. Equally enjoyable as a stand-alone novel, it offers an intriguing look at how William got his albatross and compass tattoos.

Get The Compass at https://Books2Read.com/TheCompass, or scan the QR code below:

~

Read the holiday-themed bonus epilogue to The Hold!

Subscribe to my email newsletter and own *Santa's Baby: A Catch & Hold Holiday Story* forever; go to https://www.jennamalabyauthor.com/subscribe, or scan the QR code below:

Or read it on Kindle Unlimited; go to https://Books2Read.com/SantasBabyByJennaMalaby, or scan the QR code below: